# HONOR BOUND

LIGHT *in the* EMPIRE

# HONOR BOUND

## CAROL ASHBY

CERRILLO PRESS

But I do not want you to be ignorant, brethren, concerning those who have fallen asleep, lest you sorrow as others who have no hope. For if we believe that Jesus died and rose again, even so God will bring with Him those who sleep in Jesus.

1 Thessalonians 4:13-14 (NKJV)

For His anger is but for a moment,
His favor is for life;
Weeping may endure for a night,
But joy comes in the morning.

Psalm 30:5 (NKJV)

And we know that for those who love God all things work together for good, for those who are called according to his purpose.

Romans 8:28 (ESV)

*To my children, Paul and Lydia,*
*for their love, support, and encouragement.*
*And especially to my husband, Jim,*
*who blesses me with his love every day.*

*And most of all, to Jesus.*

*Soli Deo gloria.*

# A Note from the Author

The wrenching pain of loss. It comes to us all. Whether from the death of someone we love or someone moving away so we'll never be together again, goodbyes hurt.

It's human nature to want to find something or someone to blame when we're hurting. Sometimes we blame a person. We might focus on something they did, or at least we thought they did, and the more we think about it, the more we want them to pay for causing our loss.

But that's not how God wants us to respond. He requires two things of us: love Him with all our heart, mind, soul, and strength and love others like we love ourselves.

The love God calls us to isn't a feeling. It's a decision we make followed by what we do. It's wanting what's best for another person, even when that costs us something. It's doing what we can to help when it's needed, even if we'd rather not. It doesn't depend on what they do or how we feel about them.

Part of that love is forgiving the people we want to blame, even if they truly are responsible. Jesus made it very clear that we have to forgive because we've been forgiven. It isn't something we can do on our own, but God's Spirit within us gives us the power to do superhuman things.

Although we often can't see it while we're battling fresh grief, God can lead us through to a better place than we could have imagined. He can work all things together for good for those of us who love Him. Even before the end of pain and grief is in sight, we can trust Him for the good we can't yet see.

But for those who don't follow Jesus and don't accept his command to love and forgive those we believe are responsible for our pain, how can they get past the grief without anger and hatred? What if they blame God or his followers for their suffering? How can we help them past that to find hope and peace?

There is deep truth in Paul's statement in his first letter to the Thessalonians (4:13) that we don't need to grieve as the unbelievers do, at least not when the person who's gone belongs to Jesus. I've known deep sadness over being separated by death from someone I love dearly, but I also know it's like them living where there's no cell service or internet. We can't talk now, but we'll be together again someday, joyful in the company of all the faithful believers who've ever lived.

I hope you enjoy the story of Licinia, Brutus, and Africanus as they move past grief to the joy that only God can give. May we always remember, as David proclaimed in Psalm 30:5, that God's favor is for life. Weeping may endure for a night, but joy comes in the morning.

# *Characters*

Antonius Brutus family and slaves

Marcus Antonius Brutus (39): wealthy equestrian owner of gladiator school, Ludus Bruti.

Africanus (37): Brutus's favorite gladiator as bodyguard, sparring partner, and best friend

Rufus (20s): another of Brutus's favorites as bodyguard

Camilla (30): Brutus's wife who died in childbirth,

Vera (25): Camilla's handmaid, then nanny to baby Marcus

Marcus Antonius Brutus (baby): Brutus's only child

Dorcas: Africanus's wife

Cellarius: Brutus's steward in Rome

Bernhard: Brutus's steward at Lousonna estate

Lanista Felix: head trainer over the Ludus Bruti

Fortis: gladiator used as second-level trainer of young men

Pugnus: gladiator used as beginning level trainer

Nutrixia: wetnurse for baby Marcus

Burdonarius: Brutus's carriage driver

Licinius Crassus family and slaves

Licinia Crassa (27): senatorial daughter who follows Jesus (alias Calvia Lucilla)

Sextus Licinius Crassus (39): *paterfamilias* and brother of Licinia

Octavia Laena (35): Sextus's wife

Primula (22): Licinia's Christian lady's maid

Damalio (32): Licinia's protector and overseer of Licinia's slaves, a Christian slave

Fidus, Sollus, and Robustus: Christian slaves serving Licinia

Priscus: Sextus's steward in Rome

Vicarius: Sextus's secretary

Custos: assistant to Sextus's secretary

Antistes: Sextus's steward at Octodurus estate

Gaius Licinius Crassus (deceased): Licinia's uncle who led her to Christ

Galen (Gaius Licinius Crassus) (21): Christian son of Gaius, impressed Brutus in *Faithful*

# Cities and Towns

Alpes: the Alps, mountains between Italy, Germany, France, and Switzerland

Alpes Poeninae: Roman province, capital Octodurus, present day Switzerland

Augusta Praetoria (14): Present day Aosta

Arausio: present day Orange

Arelate (4): present day Arles

Avenio: present day Avignon

Colonia Iulia Equestris: also Noviodunum, present-day Nyon

Etanna (7): town north of road fork for Pasa Alpis Graia and Pasa Alpis Poenina

Florentia (16): location of one of Brutus's ludi, present-day Florence

Fossa Mariana: a canal made B.C. 102, by Marius, from the Rhône to the Gulf of Stomalimne,

Genava (8): town where Rhone River exits Lake Geneva, present-day Geneva

Genua (3): present-day Genoa

Lacus Lemannus: present day Lake Geneva/Lac Leman

Lousonna (9): present-day Lausanne

Liternum: coastal town near Neapolis (present-day Naples); near Brutus's best vineyards

Lugdunum (6): present-day Lyon

Noviodunum: present-day Nyon

Octodurus (12): provincial capital of Alpes Graiae et Poeninae; present-day Martigny

Pasa Alpis Graia: Little St. Bernard Pass

Pasa Alpis Poenina (13): Great St. Bernard Pass

Penne Locos (11): town at east end of Lake Geneva

Ostia (2): older port city for Rome on Tiber River

Portus (2): port city for Rome on Tiber River

Puteoli: major port city for Egyptian grain and other goods; present-day Pozzuoli

Rhenus: Rhine River

Rhodanus: Rhone River

Roma (1): capital of the Empire

Stomalimne (Bay/Gulf of): Bay near Arelate; Canal to Rhone River
    starts here
Ticinum (15): present-day Pavia
Vienna (5): present-day Vienne, France
Valentina: present-day Valence, France
Vivisco (10): present day Vevey

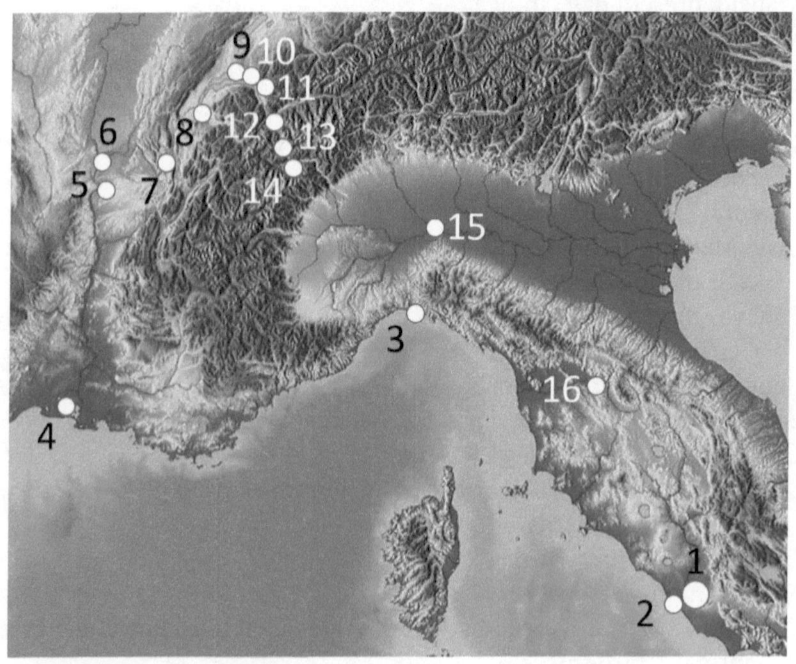

# Chapter 1

## Goodbyes



*Roma, Fall of AD 122, Day 1*

The ring of steel on steel echoed across the practice arena of the *Ludus Bruti*, Marcus Brutus's gladiator school in central Roma.

When Brutus lowered his gladius and backed away from his favorite sparring partner, he wiped some sweat from his forehead with his forearm. "A good match, Africanus, but were you holding back more today?"

The muscled, curly haired Nubian who was four inches taller than Brutus raised his eyebrows. "Holding back?" He pressed his lips together to stop a guilty smile. "Don't you always want our best efforts, practice or combat?"

"So, the answer is yes."

Africanus shrugged. "You seemed tired today."

"I couldn't get to sleep, so I read most of the night." He fingered the edge of the blade. "Camilla's time draws near."

"I found waiting for my first child hard. By the third, it becomes easier."

"Your wife is strong and healthy. Camilla..." He chewed his lip. "The third try almost killed her."

"But all has gone well this time. Not like the others."

Brutus pulled a deep breath and blew it out through pursed lips. "True, but I'll have no peace until she hands me the baby and calls me 'Father.' I'll relax then, not before."

The rapid slaps of sandals drew Brutus's eyes to the hallway beside the armor room. His jaw clenched when one of the slaves from his villa trotted onto the arena sand.

"Stabularius. Why are you here?" His whole body tensed, fearing the answer.

"The mistress's labor started a few hours ago, master."

"A few hours? Why didn't someone come for me immediately?"

"Mistress Camilla said you'd be home soon enough anyway, but then the physician decided you should come as soon as possible...because of the mistress's problems in the past."

Brutus handed his *gladius* to Africanus. "Bring my stallion back to the villa."

He trotted down the hall to his office to snatch his tunic and belt. He pulled the tunic over his head as he strode toward the stableyard. He was still fastening his belt when he entered it.

The horse Stabularius had ridden from the villa lifted its head from the trough, water dripping from its muzzle. Brutus scooped up the reins, grabbed a handful of mane, and hurled himself onto its back.

"Open the gate."

The stable slave scurried to obey and held it open as Brutus rode through.

Labor took many hours, and the first baby was the slowest to come. But the physician had said as soon as possible, and fear gnawed at him. What if as soon as possible wasn't soon enough?

◆

Africanus sucked air between his teeth as Brutus trotted down the hallway. Then his gaze shifted to Stabularius.

"Is the physician overcautious, or is something wrong?"

The villa stable slave shrugged. "I don't know. They only told me to get here quickly."

"Go saddle Master Brutus's stallion and my horse as well. I'll ride back with you."

Stabularius nodded and disappeared into the hallway.

Africanus turned toward the red-haired gladiator who'd been wielding a wooden practice sword against one of the heavy wooden stakes around the edge of the arena.

"Rufus."

Rufus turned, eyebrows raised.

"Go tell my wife I'm going out to the villa. I doubt I'll be home for dinner."

Rufus nodded. "Fortuna smiled on you, giving you such a good cook for a wife."

Any other time, Rufus's comment would have drawn a smile. "Tell her I want you to eat what she's prepared for me."

Africanus carried the steel *gladii* into the armor room and placed them in the rack. Then he selected two wooden ones that were used for practice by the gladiator slaves. Brutus would want to spar to relieve the tension as he waited.

They usually sparred with metal swords, but he'd rather not fight the master, even with dull-edged steel, when Brutus was distracted. He ran his hand down the weighted wooden blade. Wooden swords should be safe enough.

If the mistress did not survive the delivery and Brutus needed to fight in anger and grief, he'd rather not die as well.

It had been several hours. Brutus paced in the peristyle, staring often at her closed door on the balcony above. Africanus sat on a chair, tipped on its back legs, with the wooden swords across his lap.

Her every cry cut like a sharpened sword nicking him when his timing was off while sparring.

Then her scream blended with another sound, higher pitched and angry. A piercing, lusty wail.

Their child.

He slapped Africanus's shoulder as a grin split his face. Two steps at a time, he bounded up the stairs and trotted down the balcony to her door.

His palm pushed against it...and it didn't budge.

Why latched?

He knocked softly, but it didn't open. Several harder raps with his knuckles, but still it remained closed.

His fist pounded on the carved door panel. "Open this door. Now!"

A slow, scratching sound as the bolt was drawn back, then Camilla's maid, Vera, opened the door and stepped behind it.

Brutus stood in the doorway, taking in the vision of Camilla cuddling a tiny bundle at her breast. Her hair was soaked with sweat, and she seemed pale, but he'd never seen her more beautiful.

She tipped the baby to turn its face toward him. "See your father, Marcus?" Her lips brushed the baby's cheek.

Brutus strode across the room and sat on the bed beside her, grinning like a fool.

"Reach out your arms. Hold our son."

He took the tiny bundle and gazed into their baby's eyes.

Camilla lifted her hand to stroke his tiny cheek. "He has your eyes. Raise him to have your honor and courage, and he'll be the finest man."

He grinned at her. "We'll raise him to have your wisdom and humor, too."

Her eyes locked on his, and something changed. Their expression shifted from joyful to...wistful?

She shifted in the bed. "Vera, take our son. Everyone, leave us."

Her maid stood before him, arms outstretched, and he transferred the precious bundle to her.

Physician, maid, and two other slaves filed out of the room and closed the door.

Brutus's gut twisted. "Why did you do that?"

"I have some things to tell you that only you should hear."

He shifted on the bed to face her, resting his knee against her side and taking her hand in his. "What?"

"The bleeding isn't going to stop."

"You don't know that. It stopped last time. Why not—"

Her fingers rested on his lips, silencing him.

"I just know. I want you to promise to bury me by the olive grove where we watch the sunset. Don't cremate me, and don't have the usual Roman funeral rites." She drew a deep breath. "I'm a Christian, and I want to be buried like one."

He stared at her as his whole world crumbled. A Christian? It couldn't be. That would bar her forever from the Plain of Asphodel, the place of reunion in the afterlife, reserved for the good and pious. To lose her now would rip his heart out, but to never see her again?

Her fingers shifted from his lips to his cheek. "You haven't promised."

He forced his voice to sound calm, pushing down the surging anger. "I promise. But who convinced you to become one?"

"I won't tell you her name." She stroked his jaw. "You'll try to find her, and I don't want her hurt."

"But what could she have said to turn you from the gods? I was the one who questioned whether they were real, not you."

"It didn't start with what she said. It's what she did. I told her I wanted to give you a son more than anything, but after losing three babies, I knew the gods were against me. Just before you went to the

Liternum estate, she prayed to her God for me to conceive. Before the last words of that prayer, I knew something was different inside me. When I begged you to lie with me the night before you left and you gave in, I knew we would have a son."

"But that doesn't mean her prayer did anything. You conceived three times before."

"That was only the start. I wanted to know the God who has real power. She told me how much God loves me, that He came as Jesus to let me become His child if I just believed, that I would feel that love when I did. And she was right. God gave me love and peace and joy. I used to fear death, but not now. I'll be with Jesus when I die."

Her thumb stroked his cheekbone. "God truly blessed me because He gave me the son I always wanted for you. My only regret is I won't be with you to raise him."

Married for fifteen years, and he'd thought they kept no secrets from each other. How could she hide this?

"Why didn't you tell me before?"

"I wanted to. I almost did, several times. But then you'd mock the Christians who died for their faith in the arena, and I knew it wasn't the right time. But time has run out."

Her fingers stroked his hair. "I wish I'd told you. Then you'd know how wonderful it is, and we'd be together for eternity. I'll keep praying for you to come to Jesus, too."

He tried to hide the emotions from her as he oscillated between pain and anger. Come to Jesus? He would never worship the god who took her from him.

Again and again he'd told her he didn't need her to give him a son. He could adopt one, and he knew several men willing to give him one of theirs. Nothing was worth losing her in childbirth. Why had some Christian convinced her it would be safe to try again?

Her fingertips drifted down his cheek to his lips. "I don't want you to grieve too deeply or too long. Promise me."

His jaw clenched. His nod drew her smile. "I'll try." *But the best part of me dies with you. How can I not grieve until death swallows the rest?*

A wave of shivers swept over Camilla. "I feel so cold."

Brutus lay down beside her and drew her trembling body against his own. "Better?"

"Much." She turned her head enough for their eyes to meet. "God has truly blessed me with you."

He kissed her forehead and wrapped her tighter in his arms. As he willed the warmth of life to flow from him to her, her contented sigh was a sword impaling his heart.

Her breaths grew shallower...and stopped.

He held her closer. Her body still warm and soft—like when he wrapped an arm across her and drew her close as she slept. But it was only an empty shell now, and by morning it would lie there cold and stiff. And when he looked at her then, his heart would wail in silent agony.

When he finally stood, he stared at the red patches where blood had soaked into his tunic. Her blood, but he would have given anything, everything to have it be his instead. It might as well be his. Her final sigh had sliced into him like a dagger opening an artery to drop a defeated gladiator face-down on the sand.

He strode from her chamber.

Africanus stood, grim-faced, in the peristyle below, his arms hanging, each hand holding a wooden gladius. Brutus charged down the stairs. His slave yet closest friend held one out as he neared.

Brutus's knuckles whitened as his grip tightened on the hilt.

The clack of wooden sword on sword echoed through the house until sweat soaked Brutus's hair and his arm was too leaden to raise the sword one more time.

And with every strike, he cursed the Christian woman who'd taken his beloved from him...in this life and the next.

*Portus, seaport of Rome, that evening*

Licinia's fingers gripped the ship's rail. The sun had vanished below the edge of the sea an hour earlier, but the wharves of Portus still swarmed with slaves unloading and loading cargo by torchlight. None of them wanted to be there, and neither did she.

A deep sigh drained her lungs. "I know you only want to protect me, Sextus, but to leave with only one day's warning? To be parted from everyone I care about like this?" She bit her lip. "I didn't even get to tell Camilla goodbye."

Her brother's brow furrowed. "It's too dangerous to delay."

She blinked hard to force back the tears she was determined not to shed where her brother could see. "You and Father have kept my secret for fifteen years. I still don't think his death has to change everything."

Sextus rested his hand on hers and squeezed. "I wish it didn't, but it does. Father let everyone think he couldn't bear to give you in marriage because you were so much like Mother. Some thought that foolish, but no one questioned his right to do it. But I've been *paterfamilias* for two months now, and I can't use that excuse. Eyebrows are already raised because I haven't arranged a marriage for you yet."

He withdrew his hand. "You're twenty-seven, and most women have half-grown children by your age. Many think marriage to a Licinius Crassus has great political value...and they're right. I've already had several inquiries about you."

"I could keep my faith secret from a husband. Camilla has."

Sextus's head drew back. "No, you couldn't. What would you do the first time he asked you to offer a libation to his household gods? Or go with him to one of the temple ceremonies? Or host a dinner with male and female slaves to entertain his guests?" A frown accompanied the shake of his head. "You'd never go against what your god commands just to make a husband happy."

He rubbed the back of his neck. "Gnaeus overheard one of Manius Sabinus's allies asking a few of my clients why I didn't want you to marry...what was wrong with you. One of those clients was fishing for information about you when he came to the salutation yesterday." His mouth turned down. "For enough money, Certus will betray us.

"No one important is asking me dangerous questions...yet, but what can I say when they do? I'm not a good liar. Sabinus is looking for any way to undermine me. Even if that means getting you killed."

His eyes turned away from her. "As *praetor*, it's my job to judge and condemn the Christians brought before me. Imagine the scandal if it comes out that my own sister has been one for years." His jaw clenched. "Nothing would give that reptile greater pleasure than exposing you to hurt me. Emperor Hadrian wouldn't care about your religion if you were a slave or some shopkeeper's wife, but a daughter of one of the noblest families, the sister of one of his magistrates...he'll demand action against you."

Licinia's lips tightened. "And that would keep you from ever becoming a provincial governor."

The pain in his eyes at her words made her wish she'd never uttered them. She reached for his hand and squeezed. "I'm sorry I said that. I know that's not why you're sending me to the Octodurus estate."

His eyes clouded, but the pain was gone. "Uncle Gaius barely escaped his estate with Priscilla and his children before the soldiers came to arrest him. He was no more threat to Rome than you are, but that doesn't seem to matter to the ones who want you Christians converted back to worshiping the Roman gods...or dead." His eyes closed as his lips tightened. Sadness darkened them when he fixed them on her again. "I hate condemning them just because some Christians won't make a meaningless sacrifice to the genius of the emperor and the Roman gods, but I have no choice when that's the law."

She drew a deep breath, then let it out slowly. No more sighs...she didn't want to make sending her away harder for her brother than it already was.

"I only wish I could stay in Rome until Camilla's son is born. For years, it's been her deepest desire to give Brutus an heir."

A skeptical smile accompanied the shake of Sextus's head. "What if she has a girl?"

"She won't. When I prayed for her to conceive, God told me it would be a son."

His laughing snort was exactly what she expected.

"Laugh if you want, Sextus, but I know I'm right." She raised her chin as she smiled. "You'll hear when the newest Marcus Antonius Brutus is born. When he is, I want you to deliver the special blanket I wove for him to Camilla. I promised her I'd be there for the delivery. I was going to give it to her then, but now..." A tear tried to escape again.

"I will, but it will have to be an anonymous gift. I don't want to draw Brutus's anger if he discovers you've corrupted his wife by convincing her to become a Christian, too."

"It's not corruption. It's liberation from silly superstitions to freedom and joy in the presence of the only true God."

Sextus rolled his eyes. "So you've told me for years, but that's not how Brutus will see it. He's an honorable man, so I don't expect him to openly support Sabinus. But if he suspects you, he might refuse to support me. Brutus is only an equestrian, but his wealth and network of connections make him a political force. I don't want him as an enemy."

He rested his hand on her cheek. "Time to bid you farewell, little sister. I don't want anyone to know which ship you're on, so I'd better leave before someone recognizes us. Stay in the cabin out of sight until you're out to sea." His thumb caressed her cheekbone. "I'll miss you. Don't forget to write to me as freedman Sextus Licinius Gratus. I can't be certain your letters won't be intercepted by one of Sabinus's agents, and he must not discover where I've sent you."

She shook the sleeve of the plain white tunic he'd borrowed from their steward. "You may think the famous Senator Crassus is recognized everywhere, but I think you can pass incognito without your purple stripes."

Her teasing relaxed the grim lines around his mouth, just as it always had.

"I'll write as soon as we reach the estate." She took his other hand between both of hers. "And I'll pray for you every day."

The corner of his mouth pulled up. "You can pray for my health and success, but I want you to promise you will not be praying for my conversion."

She stood on tiptoes to kiss him on the cheek. "That's one promise I will never make."

Their hands slipped apart as Sextus stepped back. Then he strode down the gangplank and wove his way through the cargo on the wharf. His pace quickened as he climbed the ramp to the road. He paused in a circle of light beneath one of the torches and raised his hand. Then his figure was swallowed by darkness.

Licinia clenched her teeth, but some tears escaped anyway. Was this the last time she would she ever see the brother who'd teased and taught and defended her? *Please, God, protect him until you claim him as your own.*

She swept the teardrops from her cheeks and squared her shoulders. Father was dead, and life in Rome was over.

She glanced at the cabin door. Primula, her maid and sister in Christ, awaited her in the cabin, and the four male slaves traveling with them were brothers as well. The life she'd known was gone, but she wasn't completely alone.

She belonged to Jesus, and even though she couldn't see it now, maybe this was God's plan after all.

# Chapter 2

## His Mother's Eyes

*The Ludus Bruti, Day 8*

When Africanus entered the office, Brutus sat in his chair, arms on the desk, face on his arms. The gladiator settled into the chair across the desk from his grieving friend.

Brutus raised his head and leaned back in his chair. "What do you want?"

"I want to speak freely, but it's something you won't want to hear."

With one eyebrow raised, Brutus crossed his arms. "Speak."

Africanus rubbed his mouth. "The last time you were at the villa was the mistress's burial. How long before you go back and see your son?"

"It doesn't matter when I go." Brutus ran his hand through his hair. "Nothing I do matters now."

"What a man does always matters." Africanus leaned forward in his chair and frowned. "You haven't looked at your child even once since Vera took charge of him. Mistress Camilla expected you to be the best of fathers to her son. She died giving the baby life because she wanted you to be a father. It's time to be the one she knew you could be. The sooner you start looking at the boy as her final gift instead of what killed her, the sooner the pain will fade."

The master's scathing look raked him. "You think this pain will fade? Only someone who's lost a wife like her could understand how ridiculous that sounds."

Africanus snorted. "I know about loss. I lost everyone when I was fourteen, but a man must decide to go on with what life has forced upon him."

Brutus put his elbow on the desk and rested his forehead in his palm. Eyes closed, he sat in silence. Arms crossed, Africanus watched the emotions flicker across his master's face.

Finally, Brutus released a deep sigh. When he fixed his gaze on Africanus, resignation pushed defeat from his eyes. "Have both our horses saddled. It's time to go home." His mouth twitched at that last word.

Africanus dipped his head once and rose. As he stepped through the door, Brutus called after him. "Get two wooden swords to leave there." Another deep sigh. "We're going to need them."

*The Brutus villa*

When Africanus and Brutus rode into the stableyard, Stabularius trotted over to take their horses. "Welcome home, master."

Africanus raised his hand and shook his head. It was unwise to say too much to a master who didn't want to be there. Stabularius tipped his face down and took the reins without looking up at Brutus.

Brutus swung his leg over his stallion's neck and slid off. Three steps, then he looked over his shoulder at Stabularius. "Rub them down and stable them. I'll return to the ludus in the morning." He strode toward the peristyle entrance.

"Yes, master." Stabularius raised his eyebrows at Africanus.

Africanus handed him the swords and slapped his shoulder. "Put these in my room. I'll spend the night and leave early with the master."

He lengthened his stride to catch up with Brutus. When a fighter had been mauled in one battle, he needed a friend at his side when he faced the next.

When they entered the peristyle, Cellarius, Brutus's steward, stood in conversation with a housemaid. He glanced at them, then locked his full attention on Brutus. "Master. We didn't expect you for dinner." He snapped his fingers, and the girl straightened. "Tell Coquula the master and Africanus are here. Will it be full dinner tonight, master?"

Brutus nodded, and the girl scurried from the room.

He cleared his throat. "Where is the baby?"

"Vera is caring for him mostly. One of the housemaids has a new daughter, and she's nursing him as well."

The muscle in Brutus's jaw twitched. "That wasn't my question. Where is he?"

Cellarius blanched, and his eyes bounced from Brutus to Africanus and back.

"She has him in the room next to Mistress Camilla's. It was already prepared as a nursery."

Brutus's gaze settled on the door to her bedroom. His jaw clenched, and he closed his eyes.

When they opened, Africanus's breath caught. Brutus's face had hardened into his battle mask.

As Brutus went up the stairs two at a time, Africanus was right behind him. At Camilla's door, Brutus made a fist, as if to pound on it. But as it neared the door, it slowed until it rested on the wooden panel without making a sound.

Africanus lowered his voice so none but the master would hear. "The future lies through the next door. Live it like she would want you to."

◆

Brutus's hand dropped to his side. A baby's cry started softly in the next room and grew louder until it bounced off the marble columns Camilla had loved.

He'd watched his men march onto the sand and take their battle stances more times than he could count. Their stamina and courage facing death made him proud of them, win or lose. Would he have that same courage and stamina facing life without his beloved? Could he ever be the father Camilla would be proud of for the baby whose birth had killed her?

"He knows you're here."

At Africanus's quiet words, Brutus's gaze shifted from her door toward the cries.

"Dorcas says my children always know. She says nothing stops them crying faster than being in my arms."

Africanus took a step past him toward the nursery door, then waited.

Brutus squared his shoulders and strode forward to face the future he never wanted.

When he entered the room, Vera was pacing the floor, murmuring to the small bundle in her arms. Her head jerked up, and her eyes widened like a deer startled during the hunt.

He held out his arms. "Give him to me."

She hesitated, her eyes searching his face as she held the baby closer to her breast.

"I won't hurt him."

With her eyes focused on the baby's face, she crossed the room and placed the squalling infant in his arms.

Silence fell, and a tiny hand reached toward him. Brutus shifted his grip to put a thumb in range, and the little fingers grasped it.

And as he stared into the eyes of his son, a sigh drained his lungs. Camilla was wrong. Their son didn't have his eyes. He had hers.

# Chapter 3

## A Wise and Careful Man

*Arelate, Narbonensis, Day 8*

Licinia leaned on the ship's rail, Primula beside her, as they sailed up the final stretch of the Rhodanus River south of Arelate. Sextus had booked her passage as Calvia Lucilla, wife of an equestrian businessman traveling with her maid and four male slaves to meet him in Arelate.

He'd said she looked too old to be a never-married woman, and that might make the wrong people too curious. So, she'd packed several of Mother's old *stolae*, and she slipped one over her tunic before leaving the carriage a few blocks from the piers. But it felt dishonest to wear the garment that only married women wore, even if Sextus thought it necessary.

Dishonest, but probably wise. The Greek businessman had been too attentive at their first breakfast until the equestrian inquired about her husband's name. Then they both lost interest, but to avoid further inquiries, Licinia had Primula bring her meals to their room for the rest of the trip.

She fingered one of the ornate brass clips that held the stola at her shoulder. A Christian woman should only marry a Christian man, and the daughter of a senator could only marry a freeborn Roman citizen. Not even one man of her acquaintance was both. She'd take the stola off as soon as the *raeda* left Arelate and never wear one again.

"Are you all right, mistress?"

"Yes." Licinia hadn't meant to sigh so Primula would hear.

The rocking of the *corbita* on the open sea and the rhythmic slap of the waves against its side had created an aura of predictability even as they sailed away from Rome and all she knew. When the captain steered the ship first into the quiet waters of the Bay of Stomalimne and then into the Fossa Mariana to reach the river, she missed the gentle motion.

Sixteen miles of canal dug by the legionaries of Marius more than two hundred years earlier had made a reliable entrance to the river she would follow to her future. The enormity of what they'd done, one shovelful at a time...the canal was fitting testimony to what determined men could do to bend the physical world to their will.

If only she could change her future as easily as they'd changed a river's path. The canal ran straight as a stretched string from start to end, but only God knew what twists and turns would define her way.

The sea had soothed her; she felt anything but calm now. She closed her eyes and drew three deep breaths. *God, I know your plan is best, even when I don't understand it, but I wish I could at least see past the first bend in the river.*

A short distance ahead on the right bank, the roar of a crowd burst forth as a chariot race ended. As they drew closer to the circus, the man Sextus had placed in charge of all arrangements during the trip and made overseer of the other male slaves joined her at the rail. Despite his Latin name, Damalio was Germanic, tall with blond hair, steady blue eyes, and a smile that started slowly but stayed once it came.

"I expect one, maybe two nights in Arelate, mistress. I want to buy what we need for the rest of the trip and find the right caravan to join."

"Caravan?"

"Yes. It's safer to travel with armed guards. We'll be armed as well, but none of us are trained fighters." A wry smile started, but he turned it off.

"Well, let's pray there won't be any need for fighting." She glanced downriver. "The first part of the trip has been easy enough, but what lies ahead of us..." Her own smile felt a little shaky. "I have some concerns."

His smile tried to escape again, but he stopped it. "Fidus might not agree. His stomach has been unsettled since we left Portus."

"You should have told me. When I traveled by ship with Father, I learned that sucking on a ginger root would help. We could have purchased one for him when we landed at Cosa to change cargo. Next time, tell me when there's a problem, no matter how small. Even if I don't know what to do, I can always pray."

Damalio's eyes crinkled as a smile formed. "The last time a master told me that was Master Gaius before the soldiers came to arrest him. I was sixteen then. Your brother is a good master, reasonable and fair, but it's not the same as belonging to a brother."

His mouth opened as if to speak but no sound came before he shut it. His brow furrowed; then his whole face relaxed. "My faith...it's why Master Sextus chose me to lead this trip. It's why he let me pick three more brothers to go with us." His eyes swept the deck around them, and he lowered his voice. "He's counting on us to serve as unto the Lord, even though he doesn't believe in the Lord we serve."

They had drawn abreast of the circus. Some horses grazed in the field between the river and the gray stone walls of the hippodrome.

Licinia leaned on the rail again. "I always enjoyed watching the chariot races with my cousin's wife before he died. He loved his racehorses, but his son sold them." She sighed. "So many things change when the paterfamilias dies, and sometimes his death brings great loss."

"I liked watching them race in the fields when I belonged to an estate where they bred and trained them."

"Whose?"

"Gaius Licinius Crassus before he fled, then his cousin, also Gaius."

She straightened. "It was his wife Messalina that I used to go with."

Damalio's slow smile reappeared. "I know. Your brother bought me from him three years ago."

"Three years? Why haven't I seen you before this trip?"

"He bought me to be understeward over shipping produce to market from the estate south of Rome. Master Sextus often puts Christian slaves in charge of others. We work hard and don't cheat him. When he chose me for your escort, I asked him to buy Fidus, Sollus, and Robustus. They're all men I know I can trust."

He slid his hand back and forth on the rail. "Life on Master Gaius's estate wasn't as good with the old master's son. God's hand was upon them when He opened the way to serve with me again."

They had passed the circus, but Licinia's gaze lingered on the horses. "I've seen God's hand on His people often, but right now, I can't see why He's taking me from all I know and everyone I love." She shrugged. "I expect I'll know someday, but waiting for that...it's hard."

Damalio's tightened lips and silent nod said more than words could.

As they passed the city wall where it reached the river, the theater lay ahead and just past it, the amphitheater. It was a beautiful building of white stone with two stories of graceful arches.

Beautiful until one thought about what happened there. Sextus loved the games, and that grieved her heart. How could a kind, gentle man like her brother take delight in the suffering and death of other men? What kind of men made money off the misery of others and were proud of it? The wealthy equestrians who owned the gladiators—such men could never command her respect.

When they reached the stretch of piers, two ropes were connected to a rowboat with six men at the oars, and the sails were lowered. As the oarsmen started pulling the ship toward the shore, Damalio pointed toward the rear of the ship, and they moved back near the cabin so they wouldn't be in the way of the crew's preparations to dock. More ropes were tossed to men on the pier, and the ship was pulled against large cushions that protected the ship's planking from rubbing against the wharf.

Damalio's three men joined them at the rail, and Licinia's stomach knotted. Only the six of them against who knew what dangers that lay ahead.

"Fidus, Sollus. You two oversee getting the mistress's two trunks from the cabin and watch for the third as the cargo is unloaded. I'll rent a cart and send it down to get them." Damalio's calm voice left no doubt he was in control and expected no problems. "I'll speak with the harbor master about where to find a reputable inn for a night or two while I buy what we need for the rest of the trip. Robustus, you'll stay close to the mistress and her maid."

The sound of fist on flesh followed by passionate swearing drew Licinia's gaze to a cluster of rough-looking men near the dock. "Perhaps it would be a better idea if the three of us came with you. Surely that would be safer than staying near those." She tipped her head toward the drunken men just as one pointed at her.

Damalio pulled air between his teeth. "If you insist, mistress, but I'd advise against it. I've been to Portus and Ostia many times. Areas near the docks can be more dangerous than the docks themselves."

Raucous laughter struck Licinia as a second ruffian fixed his eyes upon Primula and leered. "On second thought, the five of us will wait with the trunks until you return with a wagon."

His eyes crinkled as he nodded. "A wiser choice, mistress."

As Damalio walked down the gangplank, Licinia relaxed...a little. Sextus had chosen a wise and careful man to take her to Octodurus. But it was still two weeks before they'd get there, and in fourteen days, many things could go wrong.

# Chapter 4

## Finding the Weak Point

*The Sabinus villa outside Rome, Day 8*

Quintus Flavius Sabinus snapped his fingers, and the slave refilled his goblet with Falernian wine. He took a sip and, with a nod, dismissed the slave to stand once more by the wall.

"Good enough Falernian."

His second son, Manius, inhaled the fruity aroma. "It's premium Faustian."

"Yes, but I want some of Antonius Brutus's special vintage that my nephew Titianus told me about." He took another sip and swished it around with his tongue before swallowing. "I still can't find any wine dealer who can sell it to me."

"I asked him to help me get some of it for you." Manius swirled the amber liquid in his gold-lined silver goblet. "Titus said Brutus is very selective about selling it only to men of honor and perhaps I wasn't on his list of such men." His nostrils twitched. "When I asked him who could buy it and then sell it to me, he laughed. Then he said he couldn't name a single man on that list who wouldn't know why we couldn't buy directly from Brutus, and the kind of men who can buy it wouldn't sell it to us."

After a small sip, his lip curled. "Titus prides himself on being a principled man. But he's a fool choosing to do what is proper instead of profitable. Tribune of the Urban Cohort should have been the perfect place for him to replenish his family's fortune. He's been tribune there five years. You would think he'd have relaxed his standards some after seeing the possibilities presented by his position." His finger traced the

18

rim of the goblet. "So many opportunities for gain...if he'll just take advantage of them."

Sabinus lifted a star-shaped pastry and popped it into his mouth. "Titianus hasn't accepted the fact that rapid advancement almost never depends on doing the honorable thing. But even honorable men can be manipulated to do a dishonorable thing if you know how to pull their strings without them knowing you're doing it. You can often maneuver them into corners where they have to give up their honor to survive."

Manius selected a pastry from the same tray. "Sextus Licinius Crassus—there's another one who's too honorable. He almost caused me a problem, but I resolved it before it got out of hand."

A second pastry followed the first between Sabinus's teeth. "What was the problem?"

"Someone filed a case in his court accusing me of taking a bribe to rule for the opposition." He bit the pastry before a crooked smile grew. "But it was withdrawn."

A single clap, and Sabinus's slaves all looked at him. "Everyone, leave. I'll summon you if I need you again tonight."

As the slaves filed out, the wine slave moved the decanter of Falernian to the table beside Sabinus before joining them.

Sabinus tipped his head toward the door, and Manius sauntered to the entrance and scanned the hallway. "They're gone."

Sabinus's brow furrowed. "How did you manage that?"

"A family member disappeared, and the accusation was withdrawn." One corner of Manius's mouth lifted. "Then the missing person resurfaced but refused to tell anyone where they'd been. Crassus suspected my involvement and tried to make inquiries into the matter, but I kept the key people beyond his reach."

Sabinus rubbed his chin. "What is Crassus's weak point? We need to make him unwilling to challenge us before another problem arises. Look for something to use as leverage to get him to look the other way when we want him to."

"I've already started on that." Manius's full smile appeared. "There's something strange going on with his sister since their father died. His father rejected every inquiry about marrying her, claiming she was so much like his dead wife he couldn't part with her." He shrugged. "No woman is so special she can't be replaced, but a paterfamilias can do what he wants. Expectations were that she would be betrothed within two months of his death. But Crassus says her deep grief makes it too soon." His nostrils flared." But I've seen her in public. She doesn't look devastated by grief."

He lifted an almond from the nut bowl and rolled it between his fingers. "I found one of Crassus's freedman clients with a large loan coming due. I bought the debt, and he's paying it off slowly with information about Crassus."

He tossed the nut into the air and caught it with his mouth. "Sextus Licinius Certus. Ironic that a man named 'trustworthy' is a traitor. But he's not the best spy. Right after I had him ask Crassus about the sister, she seems to have disappeared."

"A promising plan of attack." Sabinus lifted his goblet in salute. "Find her, find out what's wrong with her, and use it against him. If he cares for his sister half as much as his father did, he'll lose interest in our affairs to protect her."

He rose. "I have something pleasing to share with you. The new kitchen slave is a feast herself. I have some business to finish in the library, so you can have her first."

As they walked past the library, Sabinus turned in. "When you're through, join me for a game or two."

Manius raised his eyebrows. "*Tabula?*"

Sabinus stepped into the library and grinned over his shoulder. "I prefer battle tactics tonight. *Latrunculi.*"

# Chapter 5



## Protected by God

*Arelate, Day 9*

Licinia rolled the papyrus with the address of Sextus's villa on the outside and sealed it with wax. Then she carried it onto the inn's balcony, where Damalio was waiting.

"I want to get this to Sextus as soon as possible. Camilla is due to have her baby in a week or two, but sometimes babies come early. I want him to include my note with the blanket I made for her son."

Damalio took the rolled papyrus. "Horse-relay messengers travel the coastal highway. From here to Rome, it should take them four, maybe five days."

Licinia fingered her stola. "Now we're off the ship, it will be good to be Licinia again instead of Calvia."

"About that..." Damalio cleared his throat. "It would be wiser to continue the pretense while we're still traveling. An older married woman draws less attention than a pretty maiden."

She raised an eyebrow. She was twenty-seven, but the face she saw in the mirror was still young enough to draw men's eyes.

Damalio's ears reddened. "I beg pardon, mistress. I didn't mean to imply...anything. A married woman of any age has less appeal."

She tilted her head and tightened her lips to hide the smile his embarrassment triggered. "I see."

His usual business-like demeanor returned, even as his ears remained red. "Robustus will stay with you. He'll be outside your door if you need him. The others are coming with me to find what we'll need. From here to Octodurus is about two weeks. One wagon and a raeda will carry everything. Fidus and I have both handled mules. Sollus and Robustus will learn fast enough."

"As will I."

His eyebrows shot up under the rough-cut fringe of blond hair that hid most of his forehead, and that drew her smile. "That's the reaction I'd expect from Sextus. I know a proper Roman noblewoman doesn't drive a mule team. But this isn't Rome, and I'm years past being a delicate Roman maiden. One never knows when that skill might be life-saving."

His tightened lips with a smile trying to escape and his quick nod were exactly the response she expected. "As you wish, mistress. I'll teach you and Primula as well, if that's what you want. Now, if you'll excuse me, I'll arrange everything so we can leave tomorrow."

He dipped his head before heading down the stairs.

When Primula joined her at the rail, Licinia closed her eyes and squeezed the back of her neck. "The ship felt safe, but traveling so far through lands none of us has seen before...that doesn't feel safe at all."

"I know." Primula bit her lip. "But surely God will protect us."

Licinia tipped her head back and fixed her eyes on the blue sky above. "He has so far, and He's promised to be with us always." Her gaze returned to Primula. "And if I seem to be doubting that, I want you to remind me we serve the God who loves us and holds us in the palm of His hand."

"Always, mistress."

Licinia closed her eyes and relaxed as God's presence warmed her. Who could feel unprotected when surrounded by His love?

It was late afternoon, and Licinia sat with Primula at a plain wooden table in the courtyard of the inn. Robustus stood at the wall behind them, arms crossed while he watched all the comings and goings around them.

Licinia leaned her elbow on the table and rested her chin in her hand. "When I traveled with Father, we always stayed at the home of a friend or relative. There were gardens to explore, libraries with history and philosophy to read, sometimes musicians for background music. Just sitting for hours like this is quite boring."

Primula picked up the bowl of dried dates and offered it to her. "I'm sure Damalio will get everything arranged so we can leave tomorrow."

"Quite likely. With so little time to prepare, Sextus chose the person to lead our party well." She straightened. "And there he is."

Damalio paused in the archway as his gaze swept the courtyard, then strode toward her.

He dipped his chin, then met her gaze straight on. "Good news, mistress. The raeda and wagon I found are both well built, and the mules are well trained and fit for the journey. They're in the stableyard now, ready to load in the morning. But best of all..." The corners of his mouth turned up. "I found the perfect caravan for us to join."

"Perfect?" She raised her eyebrows at Primula, who tipped her face to hide her smile.

"For safety's sake, yes. I met a merchant from Lugdunum who was getting a new wheel before heading north. He has twelve wagons of goods and brought his own squad of guards for armed escort. He's willing to let us join his party as far as Vienna. That's six to seven days north along the Rhodanus and halfway to Octodurus."

"That does sound close to perfect, and hopefully he knows the pleasantest inns along the route."

Damalio's mouth straightened. "I also bought two tents and some cots and bedding. He doesn't always stop in a town at night." He cleared his throat. "Perhaps perfect was too strong a word. But your brother charged me with your safety more than your comfort."

"And I agree with him." She laced her fingers and rested her hands on the table. "I was just telling Primula how boring I've found it to sit in this courtyard all day. Camping in tents like Sextus did as a tribune...I'll be able to trade stories with him someday."

His smile returned. "We're to meet his party by the bridge an hour after dawn. I'll have everything ready for us to leave here half an hour earlier."

"Very good. A decent meal, a good night's sleep, and then off on the next step of our adventure."

"Yes, mistress. Now, if you'll excuse me..."

A single nod from Licinia, and Damalio retraced his steps to disappear into the stableyard.

Licinia's gaze lingered on the doorway. Sextus had done the best he could, but God was her true protector. It was His hand that had guided Sextus to choose the right brother in Christ to keep them all safe.

*Day 10*

When Licinia and Primula entered the stableyard, Fidus and Robustus sat in the wagon, and Sollus was on the raeda seat. Damalio helped them in before climbing up to take the reins.

From the driver's seat, he leaned around the side until his face appeared in the doorway. He waited until Licinia settled into the padded seat with a fluffy cushion at her back. "Ready, mistress?"

"As much as I can be."

He withdrew, and a snap of the reins started them forward. With a window on one side and the large open doorway on the other, Licinia looked first one way, then the other, capturing memories of things she could tell Sextus when she wrote as his freedman. He'd be bored to tears if all she wrote about were things that Camilla would have loved to hear.

She drew a deep breath and released a sigh. Another two weeks, and Camilla would be cradling the beautiful son she'd longed to give her husband. She would wrap her boy in the blanket Licinia had woven so carefully for him and kiss his tiny cheek. And Licinia would have held him and loved him, too.

If only she could have stayed long enough to be there for his birth.

She blinked to stop what could too easily become tears and squared her shoulders.

Sextus was probably right that it was too dangerous to stay. At least Camilla would receive the blanket and note she'd sent home by horse relay. And maybe someday, if—no, when Sabinus was no longer her brother's enemy, they could be together again.

She shoved aside those thoughts and focused on watching the ships on the river. One had lowered its sails, and a rowboat was pulling it toward an open drawbridge. On each side of the river stood a six-arch section of a stone bridge, each ending in a drawbridge. Most of the river was spanned by a wooden roadway supported on more than a dozen boats.

Licinia tapped on the roof, and Damalio's head appeared near the top of the doorway. "Did you need something, mistress?"

She pointed. "That bridge is made of boats. How strange."

"I asked about it. Each boat is anchored in place, and there are two columns upriver that they're tied to as well. The drawbridges were used to make it easy to stop an enemy army at the river before Gallia became fully Roman."

"We're not going over it, are we?" Primula's blinks came faster.

Damalio didn't let the smile in his eyes reach his lips. "No. We meet Ambarrius and his wagons this side of the bridge and head north on the Via Antonina. We'll stay on this side of the Rhodanus most of the way to Genava."

Primula's brow furrowed. "Most of the way?"

"Romans build good bridges. I wouldn't worry."

A sudden jostle of the carriage, and Damalio smacked his head on the doorframe. "Anything else, mistress?"

"No. I hope that doesn't bruise."

A quick tip of his head, and his face withdrew.

Primula raised an eyebrow, then kept her voice low. "I'm not sure anything worries him."

Licinia matched Primula's volume. "I'm sure he considers everything before he decides what to do and only then does he tell us. I'm equally sure part of that considering is praying. I trust his choices."

She wiggled her shoulders to make the pillow more comfortable. Six or seven days with the Ambarrius caravan, then...what? Another seven days to the Octodurus estate, but what difficulties and dangers awaited them as they moved into the wilder country to the north?

She drew one deep breath and held it before blowing it out. God had provided a guide who would ask Him for guidance before problems even arose. When faced with trouble, he'd choose the safest path he could see. But surely the Apostle Paul had asked God's guidance and protection before every trip, and he had many problems. God always brought good out of those, but still...

With a mental shake, she set that trail of thought aside. Too many questions could be worse than no questions at all. It was time to simply trust God to protect them and move on.

*The Brutus villa, Day 10*

Brutus fingered the short silver chain. The right size to hold a *bulla* on a baby boy. Marcus was nine days old, and the gold-coated lead globe would hang from his son's neck until he exchanged the toga of a boy for that of a man when he was fourteen.

He'd worn one himself. For protection, his mother had said. A good-luck charm to ensure the favor of the gods and their protection as he grew.

He blew his breath out through his nose. He didn't believe in the Roman gods or good-luck charms, but he followed the Roman way. If a noble son of Roma was supposed to wear a bulla, then Marcus would wear one.

As paterfamilias, it was his responsibility to drape the chain around his son's neck and speak the words of the rite that was supposed to earn the gods' favor. But while most made it a time of family celebration, he had nothing to celebrate. It would be a private act for his son.

He glanced at Africanus, who stood, arms crossed, waiting for him at the base of the stairs.

As they began the climb to the nursery together, Brutus stared at the golden amulet. "Did you have many come when you did this for your boys?"

Africanus's mouth pulled sideways into the half-smile that usually preceded a witty comment. Or at least signaled he was trying not to laugh.

"No. The Roman gods are not my gods. I haven't had a god I expected to protect me since the slavers took me at fourteen. I'm teaching my sons to expect the same."

Brutus wrapped the bulla in his hand and squeezed. "If Camilla were here, she'd probably say the Christian god wouldn't like me doing this. But he's no more real than the Roman ones. She'd still be with me if he was." His sigh was deep. "So, if we're going to play our parts in the divine farce, pretending to appease the gods of Roma is the better choice."

They had reached the door of the nursery, and Brutus pushed it open. Vera held his son, singing softly to him.

As he strode toward them, he knew the truth. The only protection Camilla's son could count on was what he could give him. That would have to be enough.

# Chapter 6

## WHEN NO ONE IS WATCHING

*Between Arelate and Arausio, Day 11*

As Licinia stood by the raeda, she arched her back and rolled her shoulders. Her first time sleeping on a cot had been less than restful. A sheet of canvas strung between two poles was a far cry from the soft mattress at home or even the firm ones of the ship and the inn. The small pillow scarcely deserved the name.

But it was better than the ground where Damalio and the men had slept, even if they were in a tent. And he had purchased a cot for Primula, even though she was a slave like they were.

Sollus had cooked up a tasty porridge last night and served it with many apologies that he had no time to make her something more suitable. Their breakfast of cheese, dried dates, and bread was eaten quickly since Ambarrius allowed no time for a leisurely one.

As Fidus packed the second rolled-up tent into the wagon, Damalio approached.

"If you still want to learn to drive, mistress, today is the day for that."

"I do, but why today? We have two weeks before we reach Octodurus."

"Yes, but it would be wiser for me to teach you when our travel companions are only Gauls. It would seem strange to Romans for a noblewoman to be learning to drive a mule team. People talk, and we don't want them talking about you."

Tightening her lips was barely enough to stop Licinia's chuckle.

"Why would any Roman man, especially in Gallia, care about what a Roman woman they'd never met before did?"

His eyes showed no sign he shared her amusement. "Too many take delight in causing problems for others. It's best not to give anyone reason to write home about Calvia Lucilla doing strange things. Letters can cause as much trouble as gossiping face to face."

Licinia's mouth twitched. For a man who'd spent his life as a farm slave, Damalio's insight was remarkable. She could name at least a dozen women who'd be scandalized by her desire to drive and would take great delight in sharing their shocked disapproval. "Won't it seem strange to Ambarrius?"

"He won't care what you do as long as we don't slow him down, and his slaves won't ever be talking to noble Romans. Only God knows who will be our travel companions for the second half of the trip."

He pulled a small stool from beneath the seat and placed it by the wheel. "Stool, hub, then footboard." He offered his hand to help her make the climb.

As she moved to the far side of the seat, he slipped the stool under it. Then he climbed up beside her.

As he unwrapped the reins from the post, she watched his profile. "That stool."

His eyebrows rose. "What about it?"

"Is there ever something for which you don't plan ahead?"

His mouth twitched before the smile grew. "No one can know everything God has in store for us. I do what I can, but it's really all in His hands. My three men expected to work until they died on the Gaius Crassus estate. I expected to oversee shipping from your brother's estate south of Rome. If the estate steward liked my work well enough, I hoped I might become overseer of the entire estate someday."

He handed her the reins. "I never expected the master himself to entrust his father's greatest treasure to my care for this trip and beyond."

It was too hard to keep from laughing. "I can't picture Sextus ever calling me a treasure."

Damalio shrugged, but his eyes warmed. "The word doesn't have to be spoken for one man to see what another treasures. I'd say your brother treasures you as much as your father did."

Her laughter faded into silence. "I know."

Their wagons were falling behind, and she slapped the reins. "And someday he might see how valuable I could be as a mule driver. Perhaps he'll even let me drive his chariot sometime...when no one who might tell is watching."

*The Sabinus villa, Day 12*

Sabinus popped a pastry into his mouth. A single clap, and all his slaves stood at attention. "Leave us."

As the slaves filed out, Sabinus tipped his head toward the door. Manius strolled over to watch until the last disappeared into the kitchen.

"We should soon have the leverage that will make Sextus Crassus receptive to whatever we want." Sabinus topped off Manius's goblet and then his own.

His son's head drew back. "Really? I've been looking for something he's done that he's tried to keep secret. The man's honor is unquestioned, and except for his sister disappearing, I've yet to find anything that might start those questions."

"In the privacy of his own home, no man is as honorable as the world thinks him. It's not hard to put a spy in place, but for him to build the kind of trust that gives access to useful secrets—that takes time." One corner of Sabinus's mouth rose. "But I've made a good start."

Manius settled back onto his couch and picked up the goblet. "What have you done?"

"There was an unfortunate accident, and Crassus's secretary lost his assistant."

"What a shame. A good one can take many months to train."

The second corner of Sabinus's mouth lifted to form the full smile. "Crassus is fortunate to have many friends with well-trained slaves, and one just made him a gift of a promising young man to thank Sextus for his support in getting a praetor position."

Sabinus sank his teeth into the last pastry and tore off the corner. With his tongue, he scooped out some of the blood-red berries. "But there was another person who provided far greater support than Crassus, and he supplied the perfect young man to be that gift."

His son's eyebrows rose. "You have a spy helping Crassus's secretary?"

A single nod accompanied Sabinus's grin. "Now we simply wait for him to discover the way to threaten Crassus's reputation for integrity.

It will take some time to prove himself trustworthy, but it shouldn't be long until no one is watching him."

Manius raised his goblet. "I salute you, Father. Once more you prove the old saying. A son is never too old for his father to teach him something worthwhile."

# Chapter 7

## The Special Gift

*The Crassus townhouse, Day 14*

The slap of sandals scurrying across the mosaic floor drew Sextus's gaze from his new scroll to the library door.

"Just delivered by horse relay, master." His door slave held out the tightly rolled papyrus.

He took it and waved the youth away. After settling into his chair once more, he broke the wax seal and unrolled it.

> Sextus Licinius Medicus to Sextus Licinius Crassus, my noble patron, greetings.
>
> I have made excellent progress toward completing the task assigned, and the tools you provided have proven exceptional. Please include the note below with the item to be delivered. May the most divine guard your safety.

A line divided the two sections.

> To Camilla, my dear friend, greetings.
>
> Circumstances have prevented me from presenting this in person, but know that this was made with my utmost love for you to share with the two you love most. I hope to see your son wrapped in this and in your arms someday.
>
> May the most divine guard your safety and that of your beloved son.

Sextus tossed the papyrus on the desktop as if it were on fire and ran his fingers through his hair. Licinia was supposed to wait until she reached Octodurus and include a letter among the papers sent by his steward every month. But at least she used a freedman alias, and no one but him had read it.

He rubbed both sides of his nose with his fingertips. No one had seen it, but it still posed a problem.

Thirteen days ago, word circulated that Marcus Brutus's wife had died in childbirth but his son had survived. Brutus, who was usually a daily patron at the Baths of Trajan, hadn't been seen there since. Gnaeus's son was training at the Ludus Bruti before his first tribune posting. During dinner at Gnaeus's house, his son mentioned how Brutus usually stopped in to watch the training, but none of the trainees had more than a glimpse of him since his wife died.

Sextus glanced at the array of cubicles that held his scrolls. In an empty one sat the baby blanket Licinia had made for Brutus's wife. He'd planned to leave it there. The woman she made it for was dead, and Brutus's baby would have plenty of blankets without it.

He picked up the letter. The only reason she'd sent it by horse relay was so her friend would know she couldn't keep her promise to be at the birth. If it mattered that much to his sister, he'd have to deliver both letter and blanket. Nothing in the letter revealed who sent it.

She'd be asking about Camilla and her child someday. It was bad enough he had to report her friend's death. To confess he'd kept the blanket from her baby when he'd promised to deliver it? Licinia wouldn't say anything, but he'd see the pain of betrayal in her eyes.

Honor bound him to make that delivery, but it didn't require him to reveal himself while doing it.

With a knife from the desk drawer, he sliced off the portion intended for Camilla. He spread the blanket on the desktop, placed the fragment of papyrus in the middle, and refolded it. Blanket in hand, he headed toward Vicarius's office. His secretary could send a slave no one would recognize to deliver the gift and leave immediately. A promise kept in secret was still a promise kept.

*The Brutus villa, that evening*

When Brutus rode into the villa stableyard, Stabularius hurried over to take his reins. Then he leaned sideways, craning his neck to look through the archway to the road.

Brutus slipped from his stallion. "Africanus is with his family tonight. It's been two weeks..."

Stabularius lowered his face and nodded.

Brutus entered the peristyle and headed upstairs to Marcus's room. Vera sat by the window, her hand resting on the railing of Marcus's wooden bed and gently rocking it.

"Is he asleep yet?"

She shook her head, then glanced down at the baby, smiling.

Brutus scooped him out of the crib and cradled him close. A hand reached for his face, and Brutus bent his neck so the tiny fingers could touch his nose.

Vera picked up a stack of folded cloths from her bed and put them in the trunk that held Marcus's clothing.

As he let his son finger the stubble on his cheek, something seemed different. The blanket wrapping Marcus had bands of several colors, ordered like a rainbow. It was beautiful, soft, and one he'd never seen before.

"This is pretty. Where did it come from?"

Vera straightened as her eyes focused first on Marcus, then on Brutus's feet. "It was delivered without the name of the giver."

By her bed was a small table for an oil lamp. A strip of papyrus lay next to the lamp. Still cradling Marcus with his left arm, he picked it up with his right hand.

As he read it, his eyebrows lowered. "This note. Where did you get it?"

"It was inside the folded blanket, master."

"Who is it from?"

"It doesn't say."

"But you know anyway. 'May the most divine guard your safety.' No worshiper of the Roman gods would use that to close a letter." He shook it at her. "It's from that Christian who corrupted Camilla. Who is she?"

Vera's cheeks reddened before her whole face blanched. Her eyes stayed locked on his feet. "I can't tell you, master." She swallowed hard. "I promised Mistress Camilla I wouldn't. I swore I'd never reveal anything about her faith or those who shared it to anyone." Her gaze flipped up to his face, then dropped immediately to his feet. "Not even to you." Her jaw clenched, then relaxed. "Not even under torture." Tears threatened to escape. "Please don't make me break that vow."

Her eyes closed, and teardrops clung to her eyelashes.

He dropped the letter on the bed and rubbed his forehead. Camilla had been fond of Vera. It would grieve her if she knew he deliberately hurt the girl.

"I have no intention of torturing you, but I will take Marcus from your care and sell you if you don't tell me right now."

Her eyes popped open, and the tears that had pooled in them trickled onto her cheeks. "Please don't do that, master. I loved Mistress Camilla, too. It was giving you a son that she wanted most in life, even if it killed her. Please let me love and care for her boy like she would have. Please let me stay and tell him stories about her when he's old enough to understand so he can feel he knows his mother."

She swept the teardrops away, but more rolled down to wet the front of her tunic. "I know you can sell me and buy another dry nurse, but you can never buy someone who would love Marcus for his mother's sake like I do."

Marcus whimpered, and Brutus looked into his eyes. Camilla looked back at him. His son reached for his face, just like she used to. He turned his gaze back on Vera, who still wept silently, eyes pleading him to let her stay.

"The stories you tell had better have nothing to do with her faith. I will not lose another person I love to the Christian god."

Vera wiped her face and offered him a teary smile. "Yes, master."

He fingered the blanket. The woman who corrupted his beloved was somewhere in Roma. To confront her, to make her sorry for what she'd done—he longed for that. He would figure out who she was and then...

A sigh drained his lungs. Camilla had made him promise not to hurt her. But for his own peace, he needed to know who she was, to confront her with what she'd done. He would leave it at that. His word to a dead man was as binding as his word to a live one. And his word to Camilla was the most sacred of all.

# Chapter 8

## The Best Kind of Escort

*Vienna, south of Lugdunum, Day 17*

Fields and vineyards still lined the road when Licinia caught the first glimpse of a Roman temple atop the hill to the east. The late morning sun made it gleam against the green trees behind it. Beautiful on the outside, but inside the people made offerings to the work of some dead craftsman's hands, not the only true and living God.

She tapped on the roof, and the raeda stopped. Damalio jumped down and climbed inside. He slapped the wall outside, and Sollus snapped the reins.

"What is it, mistress?"

"Is this Vienna?"

The carriage jerked as the mules resumed pulling, and he gripped the doorframe. "It is."

"What do we do next?"

"We keep going to Octodurus. I'll figure out the details for the next leg of our journey when we reach the city."

Licinia pressed steepled fingers to her lips. "I'd rather know sooner than later."

"So would I, but sometimes God makes the right path clear only when you take the next step."

"I've never traveled when we didn't stay with Father's relatives or friends." She squeezed the back of her neck. "How will you find a safe inn and then the second caravan for us to join?"

"I'll ask Ambarrius where we should stay, but it's close enough to his home city he might never spend the night here. Your brother said to go to the garrisons or government offices and ask for a recommendation. I'll do that if Ambarrius has no suggestions." His mouth twitched. "But your brother doesn't know how God looks after His people when we pray." As one corner of his mouth lifted, he shrugged.

She took a deep breath and released it. "You're right, and I have been praying."

"As have we all."

The carriage stopped, and Sollus's voice reached them. "Ambarrius is riding toward us."

"I must thank him for letting us join him and ask him a few more questions about Vienna before his wagons leave us. If you'll excuse me, mistress."

She nodded, and his large frame filled the door as he stepped out. She called after him. "Do tell him how much I appreciate being under his protection."

He raised his hand but didn't slow his steps toward the mounted merchant.

Licinia settled back against the cushion. The smile she gave Primula was meant to hide her own nervousness, but the concern in her maid's eyes showed she'd failed. "One week on the ship, one week to here. One more week, and we'll reach Octodurus. God has protected us well for the first two; He'll do the same for the third."

"Yes, mistress. He has, and He will." Concern shifted toward confidence in Primula's eyes.

Licinia turned her gaze back on Damalio where he stood with arms crossed, nodding as he listened to Ambarrius.

*God, make the right path clear for all of us to Octodurus and beyond.*

Damalio guided his mules toward the center of the travelers' campground. He raised his hand so Fidus could see it and signaled for him to bring the wagon forward to park beside the raeda. Then he jumped down and leaned into the carriage.

"Ambarrius said it should be safe to wait here while I find a decent inn. The men will stay with you and the wagons while I go to the garrison."

Mistress Licinia laced her fingers and rested her hands in her lap. "How long will we be here?"

"I'm planning on two nights. That will give the mules a full day of rest before we head into the mountains. We'll take the trunks into your room, which one of us will guard. Once the mules are unhitched, the empty wagons might be safe enough to leave unwatched for a while during the day. One of us will guard them at night."

"Surely a night guard isn't needed. This isn't Rome."

"Dishonest men live everywhere. When shipping the estate's produce, I took steps to prevent theft. You're more valuable to your brother than wine or melons."

His gaze swept the distant mountains. "Winter is coming. We can't afford a delay while we replace a wagon or carriage."

She tipped her head. "As always, I defer to your greater experience. A day not traveling...I must say that sounds inviting. While we're here, I want all the men to enjoy a hot bath and some hot meals. They need to rest as well."

His smile grew at her kind suggestion. "On their behalf, I thank you. Sollus needs to restock the food supply. More important, we need to buy clothes."

Mistress Licinia's brow furrowed. "Clothes? I packed plenty for myself and Primula."

"It will get colder as we climb. My father told me about water turning hard so you could walk on it in Germania Superior, where he was a child. A winter night in Rome is warmer than the heat of the day where we're going. We'll need warm cloaks, socks, solid shoes instead of sandals, long-sleeved tunics, trousers for the men. I can find everything here."

She glanced at Primula, and the two women exchanged smiles. "Shopping in a strange city... that should prove entertaining."

His mouth twitched as he held in the frown. Taking two women shopping wasn't his idea of entertainment.

"But first I must find an inn and armed escort for the rest of the trip. If you'll excuse me..."

With a flick of her fingers, she dismissed him. As he walked away, her voice came from inside the raeda. "We'll be praying God will guide you in your choice of both."

He raised his hand in response but kept walking. He'd be praying for God's guidance, too.

As Damalio headed down the street where Ambarrius said he'd find the Roman garrison, he rubbed the back of his neck. But that didn't stop the feeling that something was crawling on it.

Sandals and shoes of the sort they'd need were spread out on a counter, and he turned to examine them. A pair of men fifty paces back also stopped, but why would they be so interested in a display of cookpots and kitchen knives?

He walked on, pausing at a weaver's stall to ask about winter cloaks. The same men turned to look at the shoes he'd just been handling.

He moved another hundred paces down the street and spun to scan the route he'd just taken.

No sign of the pair. His mouth pulled into a smile as he silently laughed at his suspicions. The garrison was just ahead, and no one would be foolish enough to try anything so close to Roman power.

As he approached the guard on the door, an *optio* came out with a cavalry officer beside him. The *decurion* placed his crested helmet on his head and strode away, leaving the optio staring after him.

Damalio cleared his throat, and the officer shifted his attention to Damalio.

"I serve an equestrian matron. We've just arrived from Arelate, and we're unfamiliar with your city. We need to find a respectable inn and a caravan going to Octodurus that we can join."

"The inn is no problem. End of this street, turn right, and you'll reach the inn of Gaius Corvus. Tell him Regillus sent you. The caravan—you should go down to the warehouses on the river and ask there."

"Thank you."

The optio's reply was one quick nod as he turned and reentered the garrison.

As Damalio turned to go to the inn, the movement of two men caught his eye. The ones who'd trailed him down the street of shops hurried away toward the river.

He stroked the beard that had grown since Arelate.

*God, deliver us from the plans of evil men.*

At the river's edge, wagons lined up to receive the goods brought up the Rhodanus, and Damalio approached the blond-haired man directing the loading of a string of them.

"I'm looking for a caravan to join going to Octodurus."

With middle finger and thumb, the wagon master smoothed the mustache that framed his mouth. "I'm sending some wagons up that road toward the Pasa Alpis Graia, but they will continue east to Darantasia and Berginnum, not north to Genava."

"Do you know anyone who is taking the Genava road?"

The man pointed toward a shipping office. "Ask in there. Scaurus might know."

Damalio took one step, then froze. Leaning against the wall by its door were the two men who'd followed him. As he started up the steps, the shorter one stepped into his path. "We're going to Lousonna. We'll be passing through Genava. I couldn't help overhearing you're going the same way. We've hired gladiator guards, but we're looking for someone to share the cost."

The man smiled, but in the lines beside his mouth and eyes, Damalio saw the lie.

His companion moved behind Damalio, and he shifted to get both in view again.

"How many guards and how much?"

"Four guards, twenty denarii. Your share would be ten, but it might be only half that if we can find two more travelers to join us."

One started to flank him again, and he stepped back against the wall. "Where did you hire the gladiators? I didn't see an amphitheater."

The mouth of the taller one twitched. "They stage occasional fights in the theater. The ludus here rents out their fighters as guards most of the time."

A web of lies from a pair of spiders, but how could he extract himself from it and not lead them back to the mistress?

*God, please make these two leave and not return when we're on the road.*

The door swung open, and the decurion who'd been talking with the optio stepped out, helmet under his arm. He strode past them, but when he was behind the spiders, he turned and placed his helmet on his head. His gaze settled on the pair as he stood, arms crossed.

Damalio cleared his throat. "I'm going to Octodurus. I'll join someone going all the way."

The shorter one moved closer. "We might continue on to there. Or maybe you'd like to pay the guards full price for the last part of your journey."

"I don't want to take you out of your way. I'll find someone else."

The taller placed his hand against the wall beside Damalio and leaned on it. "You won't find anything better than going with us."

"I'm going to Octodurus." The decurion's voice was like cold water dumped on the pair. "Who is in your party, and how are you traveling?"

Damalio shoved past the two men, bumping one aside with his shoulder. "A Roman matron and her maid in a raeda and a wagon, both with good mule teams. We have tents and can stop for the night whenever and wherever you want."

"My troop is escorting the young sons of the proconsul to join their father. They also have a raeda and a wagon. You are welcome to join us."

One raised eyebrow and a scowl from the decurion, and the would-be robbers slipped away.

"Thank you, decurion." Damalio's mouth curved into a smile. "I think they were planning to rob us if we went with them. They might have lain in wait for us even if we didn't."

"That won't be a problem now. I have a *turma* of 30 men with me. Bring your party to the garrison by half an hour past dawn. It's an eight-day trip. What's the name of your mistress and where is she from?"

"My mistress is Calvia Lucilla. We left Rome two weeks ago."

"It's a good thing you didn't start later. Winter is coming, and if it comes early, traveling with a wagon can become impossible in the hill country. I'll be returning to Lugdunum as soon as I hand off my charges."

"Thank you for letting us join you. I'll have my party here and ready to go."

"I'll speak to the garrison commander about those two." The decurion tucked his helmet under his arm again. "Until tomorrow."

As the decurion walked away, Damalio's smile turned into a grin. When His people needed help, God knew how to provide.

Licinia paced beside the raeda. Damalio had been gone too long.

"Mistress." Sollus stretched his neck for a better view from the raeda seat. "He's back."

Relief flooded her as Damalio approached with lips curved in a satisfied smile.

"Success, mistress. I've arranged two rooms at a good inn, and God provided the best kind of escort. Some suspicious men were too interested in traveling with us, but we'll be with thirty cavalrymen instead."

Her eyebrows rose. "God certainly did provide."

"But we have to leave tomorrow at dawn."

She blew out a breath. "I thought we'd have a day to rest. Can we do everything we need to leave then?"

"You'll have to shop quickly, but we can."

"As our shopping escort, I'm sure you like the new plan."

His sheepish smile confirmed her words.

Licinia squared her shoulders. "Let's get settled at the inn and shop. Then everyone should refresh themselves before we dine."

Damalio's smile broadened. "There's a bath across the street."

"Excellent. A bath, a good dinner, a comfortable night's sleep... that's all I need before we start the trek north."

As Damalio offered his hand to help her into the raeda, she put on a smile. They would be safe on the last stretch of the journey, but what waited for them at journey's end?

# Chapter 9



*The Ludus Bruti, Roma, Day 17*

Brutus stepped back and saluted Africanus with his gladius. "Another good match." He snatched a towel from the stack and dried his face. Still draped across his hands, he stared at it.

"Since that blanket came, I've given some thought to how we can find out who sent it. It's time to start the hunt."

"Hunt? That says you want to hurt her." Africanus wiped his face and chest and tossed his towel in the basket.

"I do, but I promised Camilla I wouldn't. So we'll start the search, if that's what you'd rather call it."

"A better word as long that's all we do, and what we find we should keep to ourselves. Mistress Camilla wouldn't want the woman exposed. It could lead to her death."

Brutus's lips tightened. "I'm not planning to reveal the woman's faith, even if she does deserve what that might bring. But I am going to warn her to stop trying to spread it. She might be leading other women astray, endangering them should the emperor decide to make a general policy of killing citizens who abandon the Roman gods. The provincial governors deal with the peregrines however they wish, and some kill them."

"You don't know if her friend is a citizen."

"No, but it had to be someone she spent a lot of time with, and that's mostly equestrian and a few senatorial women. We'll start the hu—search there. And we'll start with Vera."

*The Brutus villa*

Brutus sat at his desk, drumming on a tablet with a stylus, when Vera entered his office. Africanus leaned against the wall, arms crossed.

"Cellarius said you wanted me, master."

"You know all Camilla's good friends. I'd like their names."

She blanched. "But I promised Mistress."

"And I'm not asking you to break that promise. You don't have to tell me which one is the Christian."

"But if I tell you all, she'll still be one of them, and what's to keep you from narrowing it down to just her?"

Nothing would. That was why he asked her. "Then only tell me the ten closest who aren't Christian."

Vera chewed her lip. "But when you see who's left out, you'll know."

Brutus rested his forearms on his desk and leaned forward. "I'm not going to hurt her. I only want to know who sent that blanket."

Her eyes darted to Africanus, then back to him. "If I say any names at all, you'll figure out who she is. I can't do it."

Africanus straightened and stepped away from the wall. "We'll find out without your help. You might as well make it easy for your master...and yourself."

Tears glistened at the corner of her eyes. "Please, master. Don't make me betray the mistress." Her voice quavered.

Brutus opened his mouth, then clamped it shut. Open defiance was not something he tolerated, but when it was born out of deep loyalty...

"Go back to Marcus." He waved toward the door.

As she hurried out, Africanus stared at him.

"What? I never break my word. It wouldn't be right to force her to break hers."

"Then how will you find out?"

Brutus ran his fingers through his hair. "Not from Camilla's litter slaves. Cellarius already sold them. The buyer doesn't live in Rome, or I'd get the names of those she visited from them."

Brutus pointed at the second chair by the desk, and Africanus lowered himself into it. "Your steward will know everyone who came to the house to see her."

"But he can't tell me everyone she visited." His eyes narrowed. "The woman might not have been fool enough to talk about the Christian god anywhere but her own home."

He shoved the wax tablet toward Africanus. "Find Cellarius and have him write down everyone who came here often enough he'd consider her one of Camilla's friends."

With a nod, Africanus picked up the tablet and a stylus, then left the room.

Brutus filled his gold-lined silver goblet and slowly traced the rim with his index finger. A sip, then more circles around the rim. He'd only drunk half when Africanus returned.

Africanus settled in the chair, opened the tablet, and placed it on the desk. "Ten women, with the first five coming more than once a month."

Brutus scanned the list. He'd seen all of them at temple ceremonies in the last few months. His eyes settled on the wife of one of his friends. He'd seen her and Camilla in relaxed conversation every time they dined together. If any of them might know who Camilla visited, it was her.

He tapped the name, and Africanus leaned forward to read it.

"She should be home from the baths, so let's pay her a visit. I expect she'll know all Camilla's good friends who aren't on this list."

He rose and, tablet in hand, led Africanus toward the stable.

*Baths of Trajan, Day 18*

Brutus swam his last lap and rose from the cool water. It was good that Africanus had persuaded him to resume their daily trip to the baths. The words of condolence so many felt obligated to offer cut like a hundred nicks with a razor-sharp dagger, but by the third day, that was mostly over.

He closed his eyes and swept off the water still clinging to his face. When he opened them, one corner of his mouth rose. Across the natatorium was Sextus Licinius Crassus, senator, praetor, and the older brother and now paterfamilias of Licinia Crassa, one of three identified by his friend's wife.

He turned the wry smile on Africanus, who stood, dripping, next to him. "Not our quarry, but the quarry's brother." He slapped the Nubian's arm. "Let's go arrange a visit."

"*Salve*, Licinius Crassus." As he walked toward him, Brutus kept his voice friendly but not too familiar toward the man he'd not yet met. Crassus's sons were still too young to be his students.

Crassus turned. "Salve." A political smile curved his mouth.

Brutus moved closer, but not within the space senators reserved for family members, close friends, and their own slaves.

"Antonius Brutus. I believe your sister was a special friend of my wife Camilla, younger daughter of Furius Camillus."

Crassus's eyes veiled. "I think they might have been acquainted, but I'm not in a position to say how close they were. My condolences on the death of your wife, but my congratulations that the gods smiled upon you in giving you a fine son to remember her by."

Brutus tipped his head in thanks. The pleasure from one had not made up for the agony of losing the other. "I would like to call upon your sister."

Crassus cleared his throat. "That will not be possible for some time. She and my father were extremely close. She's been deeply distressed by his death, and I decided it would help her grief pass if she wasn't in the house they shared for so many years. She's traveling."

Brutus's jaw twitched. "I have heard that sometimes works. But perhaps she won't be gone long. I would like to see her when she returns."

Crassus's smile tightened into a mask. "She's often spoken her desire to see Ephesus and many different places in Greece. She had no set destination there, and I don't know when she'll come home."

"I'm certain I'll hear when she does." Suspicion confirmed, and Brutus's smiling frown returned for the first time since Camilla died. "The affairs of your family have been bright threads in the fabric of Roman society for generations."

Crassus's smile couldn't hide the unease in his eyes. "My family has always served Roma, and what's important to her is important to me."

"I won't detain you longer. I'm sure you have affairs of state to discuss with your colleagues." Brutus tipped his head toward a cluster of senators. He stepped back. "*Vale.*"

As he turned, Crassus's voice followed him. "Vale, Brutus."

The slightest tip of Africanus's head was enough to confirm Brutus's suspicions. He'd found the Christian woman, and her brother had sent her east to protect her.

Travel held many dangers, especially for a woman. It would only be justice if one of them claimed her life before she could return.

# Chapter 10

## The Wisest Choice



*Vienna, Day 18*

Licinia leaned on the windowsill of the raeda, watching the flurry of activity that accompanied a cavalry troop preparing to move out.

An officer rode toward them. His bronze body armor of overlapping scales below an embossed breastplate flashed rays of light as he rocked on the cantering horse. The crest-tube of his helmet held a plume of long red hair straight up before it draped down almost to his neck, so much like the water of her favorite fountain in Sextus's garden. Two rows of red leather straps, one short and one halfway to his knees, hung from his waist. More red straps protected both his shoulders.

Damalio stood by the heads of their mules, and the officer was reining in to speak with him—until his gaze settled on her. He veered and halted beside her window, lifting his helmet off when the horse stopped.

The aloof expression he'd worn near Damalio vanished as his eyes took her in. "Calvia Lucilla, it's a pleasure to meet you. I'm Titus Servilius Brocchus, decurion attached to the garrison in Lugdunum. I've offered you and your party escort to Octodurus."

Licinia tipped her head and offered a gracious smile. "So I've been informed by Damalio, and we are very grateful."

"Our meeting was well timed. I'm escorting the sons of the proconsul of Alpes Poeninae from Lugdunum, where they've been living with their *mater*. But boys of six and eight are ready to learn from men, not mothers."

"An escort of…" She scanned his men. "Thirty horsemen for two small boys? They must be quite lively." She graced him with her social smile.

Brocchus's mouth started to turn down, then flipped into a smile. "Nothing a turma of Roman cavalry can't handle. It's an opportunity for my men to get out of quarters and good for increasing the fitness of the horses." He nudged his horse closer. "This is turning into a promising expedition. It's giving me a chance to talk with someone from Rome whose beauty adds to the pleasure."

A slight tilt of her head and one more social smile was enough acknowledgment. She was long past being affected by flattery. "Perhaps you'll find me terribly boring, and watching the boys will entertain you better."

He glanced over his shoulder. "It appears my *duplicarius* has everything in order for leaving. As for this evening, the second-in-command of a turma can easily control two small boys accustomed to only their mother's discipline. My help won't be needed."

He placed his helmet on his head. "I'll join you to hear news of Rome when we stop for the night." With a single quick nod, he reined his horse away from her and kicked it into a trot.

Licinia glanced at Damalio; his slight frown matched her thoughts, if not the curve of her mouth. She watched Brocchus until he was out of earshot. "That's unfortunate. I'd hoped to pass unnoticed through these regions. I hope he doesn't ask anything too personal. I really haven't thought through the details of my fake life." She sighed. "All this pretending…I don't like it."

Damalio opened his mouth as if to speak, then closed it.

Licinia raised one eyebrow at him. "What were you going to say?"

He rubbed his lip. "Decurion Brocchus finds you attractive. I think we can expect him to want to talk with you often."

She wrinkled her nose. "Attractive? In Arelate, you said an older married woman like me wouldn't draw as much interest as a pretty maiden." She stopped her smile as his ears turned pink. "But perhaps a noble Roman in the provinces has to lower his standards."

"That's not what I meant, mistress. Most men would find you attractive."

"Most? So there are men who wouldn't."

The pink shifted toward red. "Not many, but most would know your rank puts you out of their reach. A wise man never lets his heart even start wanting what is impossible." He cleared his throat. "His men are mounting. Time to leave. If you'll excuse me…"

She tipped her head, and he climbed onto the driver's seat.

Primula's hand dropped away from her mouth, and the smile she'd hidden from Damalio lit her face. "You can tell he's used to talking mostly to men." Her voice was a whisper.

Licinia whispered back. "He'd make a fine husband for a Christian woman. If it's God's will for him to marry, perhaps I can find the right one for him after we get to Octodurus."

She turned her gaze out the window, but her eyes weren't focused on the scenery. Damalio was right. She was a senator's daughter. Only a freeborn Roman citizen qualified to marry her under Roman law. As a Licinius Crassus, she needed at least an equestrian, if not a senator. The chances of meeting such a man who both loved her Lord and was unmarried were small in Rome. Out here in the provinces, there was no chance at all.

Licinia stared out the window at fields and vineyards as they left Vienna behind. The straight road the decurion had chosen headed east while the river continued north to Lugdunum. But the river turned east there, then southeast, and near the curve where it turned northeast toward its headwaters in the Alpes, they would intercept and follow it the rest of the way home to Octodurus.

Home. Perhaps not the right word yet, but surely the estate would feel that way in time. In the distance, the mountains, dressed in green at their bases and frosted with snow at their peaks, squeezed their route into the narrow valley of the Rhodanus. It was beautiful country, but with an aura of barely concealed menace.

With a quick shake of her head, she tossed those thoughts aside. A more immediate danger lay before her: the curiosity of the too-friendly decurion.

She plucked at the stola that declared her a married woman. "This has started to feel natural, even though it's not. But when Brocchus interrogates me this evening, I can't let him discover that. I have served as *domina* for Father since I was fifteen. I directed his household like a married woman, but I didn't dine with his male friends. He was afraid someone would ask me something where my answer would betray my faith." She adjusted the stola folds where they draped across her chest.

"Father, Sextus, and I enjoyed many meals together, but I've never had to talk with a strange man who's interested in me. Sextus usually dined at our house. He didn't want me to spend time with his wife. It's a political marriage, and he never trusted her with the family secret. I wasn't sorry. She always looks for the worst in people and gloats over their misfortune. But that meant I never got to know my nephews well. I hope they turn out like Sextus, not Octavia."

"Master Sextus is a good man."

"I wish I could have married someone like him, except a brother in Christ." Licinia blinked hard as the memory of his final wave at the pier made her eyes burn.

"Maybe you'll meet one in Octodurus." Primula's dipping eyebrows made her words unconvincing.

Licinia's sigh was deeper than she intended. "I can't see how. I never met one in Rome. Aunt Priscilla and Uncle Gaius taught me about Jesus, and I chose to follow Him when I was twelve. After they barely escaped arrest, Father decided the only safe course was telling people he wanted me with him. He declined all betrothal requests before I even met the young men."

She tapped on the roof. "I'm more like a naïve girl than an experienced woman. But perhaps our guardian and guide can advise me."

The raeda stopped. Damalio jumped down and climbed in. Sollus snapped the reins, and the carriage started with a jerk.

"You wanted something, mistress?" He spread his feet and gripped the top of the doorway.

"The decurion—what will he ask about? What have you already told him? We need to keep our stories the same."

The raeda jostled, but Damalio's slightly bent knees kept his balance. "It's not information he seeks. It's time spent with a pretty noblewoman. He might not even care about the noble part, except it means he won't go beyond conversation without your clear invitation."

Her hand went to her throat. "I don't want to encourage that. Don't get too far away so I can signal you to come if I need to...distract him. What does he think he knows about me?"

"Very little. Your married name. That we came from Rome two weeks ago and are going to Octodurus. I only told what he needed for us to join him."

"So, I have to invent my whole story?"

"Yes, mistress."

She blew her breath out through pursed lips. "Very well, but you need to hear it before I tell him."

Damalio's slow smile leaked out. "I look forward to learning who I'm serving. Now, if you'll excuse me. He might be watching. We don't want him thinking I'm in here too long."

After she nodded, he slapped the outer carriage wall. Sollus paused long enough for him to climb back to the seat and resume driving.

Licinia looked at Primula and rolled her eyes. "Calvia Lucilla, wife of... Gaius Aelius Valerius, equestrian great-grandson of an imperial freedman?" Primula nodded her approval. "Born and raised in Rome—but exactly where? What if Brocchus knows Rome too well?"

Primula rested her palm on her cheek. "Maybe a smaller town near Rome is better?"

"Probably safer." She rubbed her neck as she watched the passing fields. "Father and I visited Sextus's estate where Damalio worked. I'll use that." A deep sigh drained her lungs. "I hate not simply being me."

She turned her eyes back on the vineyards outside the window. Was being Licinia Crassa as dangerous as Sextus thought? And if she were found out, would that put her traveling companions in danger as well?

*Between Bergusium and Augusta, evening of Day 18*

Licinia and Primula strolled over to the stream by the edge of the campsite. It gurgled across the rocks, carrying away the tension that had plagued her as their time for stopping approached. As they had during the trip from Arelate, Sollus started the cooking fire while Fidus and Robustus pitched the tents. Damalio hobbled the mules so they could graze.

At the water's edge, Licinia settled onto a rock, dipped her fingers in the water, and let it flow past them. "Seven more days—that's all until we reach the estate. I'm tired of traveling, but I'm unsure about what awaits us."

Primula tipped her head toward Brocchus. "The decurion is coming. Maybe he can tell you something."

Licinia's nose twitched. "I'd rather remain ignorant than ask him."

Brocchus's gaze swept Primula before he ignored her. He offered a quick, shallow bow to Licinia. "Calvia Lucilla. You look as fresh as if you'd only spent an hour at the theater instead of a day on the road."

The corner of Licinia's mouth turned up. "This stream makes a poor mirror, but if it was as smooth as a lake at dawn, it would contradict you. It's been a long day, and I'm sure it shows. But we'll be ready as early as you wish tomorrow."

Brocchus's lips had tightened when she challenged the compliment, then relaxed into a teasing smile. "Too many from Rome need their vanity fed. I apologize for thinking you one of them."

Licinia tipped her head with a gracious smile. "Simple truth is always better than false praise."

"I agree." His gaze shifted from her eyes to something past her shoulder. "Your cook is signaling your maid that your dinner is ready, and your man is coming to tell you. Until later..." He walked away with shoulders squared.

Damalio stopped beside her without speaking.

Her brow furrowed. "I tried to discourage him."

"You didn't succeed. Whatever you said, you intrigued him more."

Licinia stared at him. "Why do you say that?"

His eyebrow rose. "Have you spent much time with officers?"

"Father had many to dinner, but I seldom joined them. Sextus served in Germania, so he didn't bring his tribune friends home."

"Some men like a challenge, and he's one of them."

"What will discourage him? Acting the silly young woman impressed by his shiny armor and handsome face?"

"He wouldn't believe it now. Be careful to stay Calvia Lucilla with him."

She pushed an errant tendril of hair behind her ear. "I'll try. It's only seven more days, but it will be good to be Licinia again."

"But safer to be Calvia. Your brother was wise to make that change."

"And you were right about me remaining Calvia while we travel." Her smile drew a fleeting one from him in return.

"I'll always advise what will keep you safer, mistress, even when it's harder. Sollus is waiting to serve the men until he serves you." He offered his hand to help her rise. As soon as she was on her feet, he stepped back. "After you, mistress."

As Licinia led him and Primula to dinner, the corner of her mouth curved. Sextus's wisest choice wasn't making her Calvia Lucilla. It was putting Damalio in charge of them all.

# Chapter 11

## The Decurion

Dinner was over, and Licinia leaned against the side of the raeda as she gazed at the mountains to the northeast. Foothills clothed in forest green stood between her and the jagged rocks at the mountain summits. They'd traveled many miles that day. Somehow the mountains seemed bigger, yet no closer than the night before.

Primula hummed to herself as she prepared their beds inside the tent. Her head popped out. "All is ready, mistress."

Licinia straighten, then froze. As promised, the decurion was coming for more conversation.

She had too little experience talking with strange men, but Camilla had often entertained Brutus's friends. Her dear friend claimed most men would think a woman unusually intelligent if she listened intently to all he said and asked questions as if he were brilliant. Then she'd laugh and say that didn't work with her Brutus, who didn't like anyone to pretend he was more than he was and always wanted the truth.

She pasted on a smile as Brocchus reached her. Like Camilla's Brutus, she didn't like pretending she was something she wasn't. But Damalio thought it important for the safety of them all, and he was much wiser in the ways of the world than she was.

"Good evening, decurion." She swept her hand toward the mountains. "The sunset on the bare rock is painting such pretty colors. We don't see that back in Rome." Her smile turned more natural. "But you're probably used to it. How long have you been stationed in this part of Gallia?"

"It's been five years, but I still see the beauty. If anything, I appreciate it more now than when I came."

"Where would you like to be stationed next?"

His brow furrowed, and Licinia kicked herself for a question he considered odd or impertinent. But perhaps it was a good thing if it doused his interest.

Then his face relaxed into a smile. "I have no plans to join a different auxilia. There are many opportunities to serve Rome here." He lifted his eyebrows. "And you...are you joining your husband in Octodurus?"

How best to answer that question? If she said yes, would Brocchus insist on escorting her to an estate she'd never seen before to meet her imaginary husband?

Licinia offered a faint smile. "No. Joining him again...I'm afraid that's impossible."

Sympathy softened his eyes as he responded with a tight-lipped smile.

Had she just made a strategic error? She hadn't meant to imply that she was not still married.

His normal smile returned. "Are you planning to remain in Octodurus for a while?"

"I hope so. I'm tired of traveling. One wouldn't expect to get so fatigued simply sitting in a carriage all day, but that's been more tiring than overseeing a household."

The corner of her mouth lifted. "I want nothing more than to retire for the night. Perhaps your second-in-command would also like to retire after entertaining two energetic boys."

She moved toward the tent. "Good evening, decurion."

"Until tomorrow, Calvia Lucilla."

She stepped into her tent and let the flaps fall. Then she peeked through the crack between them to watch Brocchus walk away.

*South of Etanna, evening of Day 19*

Licinia lounged in her folding chair by the embers of the cookfire. She would never have thought to get the chair in Arelate, but Damalio had planned well for her comfort on the trip. He'd even bought folding stools for the rest of her party in case they camped where the ground was too damp for sitting. Sollus had prepared another satisfying stew and served dried fruit as a final course. The river was calm here, and its soft murmur was like music in the background. It was a pleasant ending to a good day.

Her eyes were drawn from the glowing coals when Damalio, who sat nearby on a stool, cleared his throat. A quick glance, and she had to command her shoulders not to slump. Decurion Brocchus was striding toward her, a broad smile on his lips. He scooped up an unoccupied stool as he advanced.

As he was about to sit, she rose. "Decurion, perhaps you would care to join me at the river's edge for a few moments before I must retire."

Primula moved behind her, ready to accompany Licinia wherever she went.

Licinia donned her social smile. "I find it soothing to watch the flowing water."

Brocchus set the stool down and moved to her side. "As do I." He swept his hand toward the river, and she began the stroll that should keep him from staying too long.

At the river's edge, a pile of rocks provided perfect seating to defeat her purpose. She kept her lips from curving down.

He offered her the closest boulder. "Perhaps you'd care to sit as we watch."

"They look a little too dirty. I'm content to stand."

She moved closer to the bank, and he followed to stand within an arm's length of her.

She wanted no questions, but Father had always said the best defense is often a good offense. If he was a man who liked to talk about himself...

"I believe Damalio said you're stationed in Lugdunum. I've never been there. Is it a pleasant place to live?"

"The city itself is pleasing, but pleasant is not the first word that comes to mind for any garrison. I stay in the officer barracks. For an unmarried man, it's simpler that way. My family has a good estate north of Rome, but during the years I've served here, I've come to love this country. I'm using my wages to buy a second estate near Lugdunum for when I retire from the cavalry. It's north of the town, close to the Sauconna."

That thought lit his eyes. "Vineyards and pastures to feed Lugdunum. Maybe wine to ship farther south. Down the Rhodanus is the route to the sea, but the Sauconna is almost as large where the two rivers meet. I can ship everything to market by boat."

Licinia nodded while trying not to seem too interested. "I do like the mountains being so close. Snow-capped peaks in the distance are lovely. While I never found my family's home near Rome to be boring while I lived there, I can see how living in wilder country could make life in Italia seem too tame for a man."

His approval of her comment warmed his eyes and broadened his smile. Not what she intended. "A woman who would undertake a cross-country journey like you have is much better suited to the wilder lands than the quiet life nearer Rome." He moved a little closer.

Her hand went to her throat. "But living on the wilder side tires out a person not used to that life. I'm not as adventurous as you think. Today has fatigued me. It's time for me to retire so my party will be ready to go at dawn when you summon us."

Disappointment flickered across Brocchus's face, but it vanished almost as quickly as it appeared. "I look forward to continuing our conversation tomorrow evening."

She started walking toward the dying fire. "Yes, well, the beauties of the new country should inspire some worthwhile conversation even between passing acquaintances such as ourselves."

"It's easy to grow from acquaintances into friends when two people spend enough time talking."

"That's true." They had reached the tents by her raeda. She clasped her hands at her waist. "I bid you a good night, decurion."

"May you have the same." With a friendly smile and a quick dip of his head, he turned and headed toward his own tent.

Licinia took a step back to stand beside Primula. "Your thoughts?"

Primula drew her breath between her teeth. "He seemed more eager to be with you when he left than when he arrived, even though you did nothing to encourage that."

"I don't understand why he's acting that way, but perhaps I don't need to. Six nights of very little conversation are hardly enough for anyone to go from passing acquaintance to good friend."

"I wouldn't think so, mistress." She pulled back the tent flap. "I'll have everything ready for you to retire in a moment."

Primula disappeared into the tent, and Licinia let her gaze drift over their encampment. Damalio stood by the fire, his gaze fixed on the retreating decurion. As Sollus spread the coals of their fire to cool, he spoke quiet words that drew Damalio's gaze. A quick shake of his head was Damalio's only answer before his eyes returned to Brocchus.

She'd been careful what she said, getting Brocchus to talk about himself instead of asking questions about her. She'd kept her fake identity securely in place.

So why was Damalio rubbing his lip as he watched Brocchus walk away?

*Genava, evening of Day 21*

As the buildings of Genava rose before them in the late afternoon, Licinia breathed a sigh of relief. Traveling with Ambarrius had been a leisurely affair with frequent stops to rest his mules. She'd enjoyed those breaks. It felt good to leave the close confines of the carriage and stretch her legs as she surveyed the changing views. The decurion kept the whole troop moving, occasionally pausing at a stream for the horses and mules to drink, but never long enough for her to go more than a few paces from the carriage.

But Brocchus had told her they would be spending the night in Genava. As hard as Damalio had tried to provide for her material comfort, sleeping on a cot in a tent was a poor substitute for a soft bed in a villa. They were four days from Sextus's estate, and an evening at an inn would be most welcome.

The thuds of trotting hooves announced the arrival of the decurion before he appeared beside her window. "Genava lies ahead, and it presents an opportunity. The boys will be staying at the garrison, but I know of a respectable inn on the shore of Lacus Lemmanus. Their chef is skillful, and they have a private bath for women. You should find it a refreshing change."

The prospect drew her smile. "I'm sure I will. But can they accommodate my men and our wagons? I'll want at least one of them near me for protection."

"Of course. After I take you there, I'll get the boys settled at the garrison. Then, if you wish, I'll join you for a full dinner like those in Rome."

Licinia's breath caught. The last thing she wished was a leisurely three-course meal with Brocchus. But how could she decline? He was their escort, and she had no reason to think he was not an honorable man.

"To dine alone with you would be...inappropriate." She looked away.

His silence pulled her eyes back in his direction. His mouth had straightened; then his smile slowly returned. "Then we won't dine alone. Damalio will joins us."

"Then I look forward to it."

His smile broadened. "Good." He reined his horse away from her and trotted back to the head of the column.

She knocked on the roof, and Damalio leaned down to look through the door. "Yes, mistress?"

"I hope you don't mind eating with us. I couldn't see any way out of it."

"A good meal while watching over you and Brocchus...I can think of worse ways to spend an evening."

His face disappeared, and Licinia settled back against the cushion. An evening asking the decurion questions should pose no problem as long as Damalio was there, too.

# Chapter 12

TO EARN HER RESPECT

*Day 22*

When Brocchus came shortly after dawn to fetch her party from the inn, Licinia and Primula were already in the raeda and prepared for another long day of sitting. For several hours, the road had followed the shore of Lacus Lemannus, occasionally crossing streams that fed into the enormous lake. A strip of fields and vineyards lined its shore, but on either side of the lake, steep slopes covered with forests rose to become naked stone crags with a frosting of snow.

Father had Alpine murals on the walls of his office. She'd loved them as a child, but they hadn't captured the overwhelming splendor of the real thing.

She pointed at the highest peak. "Who wouldn't want to live amidst such beauty? I can see why Decurion Brocchus doesn't want to return to Italia. Last night, he said he likes the wild country much better."

Primula leaned over to look out the window. "I like the wildness, too."

"I'm glad God provided him as our escort. Dinner was more enjoyable than I expected. The food was good, but the conversation was better. He shares my interest in history. We both admire Tacitus, especially his writings about Germania and Agricola in Britannia. I wouldn't have expected a career soldier to agree so heartily with Tacitus's conclusion. 'To ravage, to slaughter, to usurp under false titles, they call empire; and where they make a desert, they call it peace.'"

Her lips twitched with the start of a smile. "When I quoted it, you should have seen how far his eyebrows rose."

Primula grinned. "Your knowledge would surprise any man, mistress."

"It was almost like talking with Sextus. He didn't ask me any personal questions that might make our wise guardian worry. He's a nice man, and it was an enjoyable evening. I'm glad I agreed to dine with him after he suggested Damalio join us."

As they entered Noviodunum, their caravan moved past dwellings ranging from small cottages to large houses built in the Roman style. Licinia leaned out the window. Ahead lay the stone and concrete public buildings surrounding the forum of Colonia Iulia Equestris: basilica, curia, and temple.

"On a smaller scale, it's almost like home."

Primula leaned over to see. "Will Octodurus be like this?"

"Perhaps. It's the provincial capital. Sextus says wherever Rome rules, she brings order and peace and civilization."

They drew abreast of the amphitheater, which lay between the road and the lake.

"But she also brings that." Licinia's lips tightened. "It looks big enough to seat several thousand, maybe all the men of this town. We've seen too many of these. Luna, Arelate, here. There are three in Rome and at least six more within half a day from the Forum, but I never realized how Rome has infected the whole Empire with its love of men dying for entertainment while calling it sport.

"When I asked Father and Sextus what they could possibly enjoy about one man killing another just to entertain the screaming crowds, they said only a man could understand. It wasn't the bloody deaths; it was the courage of the gladiators that inspired the men who watched the fights."

"More than gladiators die there." She wiped the corner of her eye. "The provincial capitals all have them. I shudder to think how many of our brothers and sisters have been executed in them. Uncle Gaius and Aunt Priscilla took Galen and Rhoda and fled so they wouldn't be among them."

"Are they killing Christians in Octodurus?" Unease colored Primula's voice.

"I don't think so. Sextus expects us to be safe there."

Sextus was sending her to Octodurus so Sabinus wouldn't get her killed, but was living in Octodurus or the capital of any province safer than being in Rome when the next governor might decide to kill Christians? Primula, Damalio, and the rest of her men might die horrible deaths. As a citizen, she'd be shipped back to Rome where Sextus or one of his friends might be able to help her, but no one could protect her slaves.

*Lousonna on Lacus Lemmanus, Day 23*

When the sun peeked through openings in the clouds as they approached Lousonna, the wind-driven waves made its rays dance on the lake's surface. Licinia was torn between gazing through the window at the distant mountains across the blue expanse and looking out the door at the terraced vineyards that stair-stepped up the steep slopes that came almost to the shoreline. White-walled villas perched a short distance up the hillsides, each with a magnificent view of the shimmering lake, verdant forests, and naked-rock peaks. Naked except for the fresh coats of snow on the pinnacles.

She drew the warm woolen cloak around her as a gust off the lake passed from window to door and out again. She shivered and moved closer to Primula, who smiled as they shared their warmth. Once more, Damalio had foreseen the need for something beyond what she'd had in Rome. The men were exposed to the weather on the driver seats of their wagons, but he'd purchased fleece-lined coats and gloves and socks and trousers and felt boots and scarves and all manner of items that should keep them from getting too cold. It was only two more days before they'd be sleeping in warm rooms instead of cold tents.

That couldn't come too soon for her.

They were passing the town's forum when the raeda stopped. The row of shops between them and the lake blocked the wind. The thud of four feet hitting the ground told her Damalio and Sollus were taking a break while the mules rested.

Damalio's face appeared in the doorway. "Decurion Brocchus said he'd be getting fresh bread for his men and for us at the bakery here. It shouldn't be more than a few minutes." He stretched his arms out sideway. After dropping them to his sides, he rotated his shoulders.

She moved to the door and held her hand out. "If you'll help us down, we can stretch a little, too."

He extracted the step stool from beneath the driver's seat and held first Licinia's hand and then Primula's as they climbed down.

"How big is this town? The whole area is delightful."

"Brocchus said maybe two thousand live here and nearby. There are good piers on the lake for shipping produce down river."

"It is refreshing to be in a town where the largest building isn't dedicated to killing people."

"There is a theater."

"I like musical performances and some plays."

"Yes..." He cleared his throat, and Licinia turned her eyes on him."

"Yes what?"

"Towns with no amphitheater often stage the gladiator fights in their theaters."

The corners of her mouth turned down. "I wish you'd never told me that. I'll never be able to watch a play again without looking for traces of blood-soaked sand."

"I'm sorry to be the one to tell you, mistress." He glanced toward the theater, then back at her. "But a painful truth deliberately avoided is still true. As long as there are men who will pay money to watch other men die, there will be men who buy and train the fighters who will kill or be killed."

"Well, I would never be able to respect a man who would send other men to be slaughtered like cattle just to make money. No woman who follows Jesus ever could."

Damalio opened his mouth, then closed it without speaking.

Sollus came toward them, several loaves of bread in his arms. "Decurion Brocchus sends this to you with his compliments, mistress. He's almost ready to leave."

As Damalio handed her back into the carriage, her eyes scanned the hillside villas. It was a lovely town. It wasn't that far to Noviodunum, and anyone who wanted a bloody spectacle could go to the amphitheater there. Maybe the theater here was only that...a theater.

But as they drove by the theater's stone columns on their way out of town, she knew that wasn't true.

*Camp between Penne Locos and Octodurus, evening of Day 23*

The clouds had cleared, and the wind had died. Licinia sat by the fire, watching the coals near the edge fade from yellow to red to black while flames still danced at the center.

"A lovely evening, Calvia." She startled. Brocchus's voice was right behind her.

He placed a stool across the fire from her and sat. "Today was a taste of November weather here. It's been unusually mild until today."

"This whole trip has been more pleasant than I expected." She lowered her gaze from his face to the fire, then raised it to his eyes again. "We have you to thank for part of that."

Her words triggered the smile she expected.

Brocchus rested his arms on his knees and leaned closer to the fire. "I especially enjoyed our dinner and discussion in Genava."

"As did I." The fire popped, and an ember flew toward her feet. She flinched, but it fell short of the toe of her felt boot. She picked up the stick Damalio had left for repositioning the logs and flicked it back into the fire.

"It's not often I find someone who wants to discuss history with me...or who even can." Brocchus cleared his throat. "I supposed you'll have your family for such conversations in Octodurus."

"No. I'll be staying at the estate of a friend."

The corner of his mouth started to rise. "Your friend...is he also an admirer of Tacitus?"

"He is, but he won't be there for any discussions. The estate belongs to the brother of a woman from Rome whom I know as well as I know myself. Her brother is almost never there, but I hope she will be soon."

His mouth curved into a full smile. "So, you're free to do what you wish?"

"Are any of us truly free to do that? I'm freer than some, less free than others. But in Octodurus, I'll mostly have the power to choose."

"I'm glad to hear it." His smile lingered as his gaze returned to the fire, and silence descended between them. She watched the flames die down, but several times when she raised her eyes to glance at him, she caught him watching her, too.

Damalio entered the circle of light around the fire and picked up two stools. After carrying them to the wagon, he folded them and slipped them under the tarp. When he returned and picked up another, Brocchus rose and handed his to Damalio.

"I see it's time to retire. Until tomorrow, Calvia." With a tip of his head, he turned and walked away.

Licinia couldn't keep the smile from playing on her lips. She didn't like outright lies, but it was rather fun to play with words with the decurion, speaking the truth but in a way that he would misinterpret what she said.

"May I speak, mistress?" Damalio's voice drew her eyes from the few remaining flames.

"Of course. You don't need to ask."

"I couldn't help overhearing your conversation. The woman you know as well as yourself, her brother owning the estate...was it wise to reveal so much that's true about you? Brocchus will remember what you said. There's probably no danger because he won't be staying here, but you need to be more careful what you say to local people who might remember your words and suddenly grasp their true meaning."

What she'd said...it felt better to tell the truth even if the person listening chose to misunderstand it. So far from Rome, who would care, anyway?

"I was careful. I have been ever since my cousins had to flee, even if Father and Sextus used to worry that I might not be. You're sounding just like my brother."

The brother who loved her so much he'd sent her away, perhaps forever, to keep her safe. She wiped the corner of her eye.

"I take that as a compliment, mistress. Your brother only wants to keep you safe. Master Sextus passed that responsibility to me, and I intend to fulfill the duties he gave me."

"I know you're only trying to protect me, to protect us all." A deep breath, then a sigh before she straightened her shoulders. "I'll be more careful in Octodurus, but I'm not worried about Brocchus. He's a good man. He treated me with respect and earned mine in return. He wouldn't try to hurt any of us."

"I agree, mistress. The decurion is a very good man."

She stood and moved away from the fire. "I'm going to retire now."

As she walked toward her tent, he folded her chair and returned it to the wagon.

She opened the tent flap, but before she stepped through, her gaze drifted to the tents of the cavalrymen.

Brocchus was a good man. If he were a Christian, she'd be sorry he was going back where she'd never see him again. But since he wasn't, it was better if he did.

## *Chapter 13*

RAISING A SON PROPERLY

*The Sabinus villa, evening of Day 23*

Quintus Sabinus wiped the corner of his mouth and tossed the napkin aside. "The new pastry chef I acquired from Lucius Juncus has proven quite satisfactory."

Manius slipped the last fruit-filled treat between his teeth. "Satisfactory doesn't describe this. I want to borrow him for my next banquet. What did he cost?"

The corner of Sabinus's mouth lifted. "Nothing. Or more precisely, the promise of support when he needs it. Juncus is equestrian, and senatorial assistance is worth much more to him than a skilled slave."

Sabinus ran his finger around the lip of his goblet before taking a sip. "Speaking of skilled slaves, I'm starting to get information from the one I planted with Crassus's secretary. He gives his secretary more authority than I give mine. The secretary sorts who speaks with Crassus and in what order, but he also deals with many minor things without consulting Crassus. Even with an hour more than I allow for salutation, there are too many for Crassus to deal with them all. Our man stands right behind the secretary now, taking notes as required."

"Anything useful yet?" Manius topped off his goblet and settled back on the couch.

"No. Crassus runs his affairs with precision and honor. But in time we might identify a client with a problem that Crassus doesn't help solve, a man who could be persuaded by money or other means to maneuver Crassus into the appearance of wrongdoing."

He took another sip. "I have him watching for anything out of the ordinary. Nothing useful yet, but there was one thing odd. Right after our man got there, Crassus sent a baby blanket to Antonius Brutus."

Manius snorted. "How could an inexpensive gift from one honorable man to another equally honorable be useful to us?"

"It's not the reality, son. It's the way we can twist the perception that counts. Use your imagination on this."

"My imagination?" Manius swirled the golden liquid before taking another drink. "I see why you might think it odd. There's no frequent connection between them. Brutus is on friendly terms with half the senatorial families from training their sons, so his support has political value. More to the point, his open criticism could influence those who have not yet taken a side. But Crassus's first son isn't quite old enough for Brutus to train, and he's not known to visit the ludus to spar himself."

"All true. I haven't quite figured it out myself. Perhaps it was a condolence gift. Brutus's wife died, but she did give him a son. Brutus shutting himself away over her death was discussed at the baths for a few days. No man should grieve the loss of a wife as much as he has. His son survived, and that's what matters. When Augusta miscarried and died, I got over it quickly enough. That baby was a girl, so not much was lost. Julia proved a suitable replacement to give me another son."

Sabinus leaned over to slap Manius's upper arm. "The proper raising of his son is what Brutus should concern himself with now, as I did with you and your brothers."

Some wine sloshed out of Manius's goblet onto the sheet draping his couch. "No one would dare accuse you of failing to teach us well."

Sabinus smiled as his second-born drained his goblet and set it down to refill. Manius was a son to be proud of.

*The Brutus villa, Day 23*

Brutus and Africanus entered the peristyle from the stableyard and settled into the chairs near the spouting dolphin.

Vera entered from the atrium, Marcus wrapped in her arms. "Welcome home, master." She blew softly on the baby's cheek, and the hand he raised in response received a kiss. "He's been waiting for you."

Brutus held out his arms to receive him. She transferred the precious bundle and brushed his forehead with her lips before stepping back.

"I'll keep him a while. You can go do…whatever."

He leaned back in the chair as she left the room. The smile triggered by the first sight of Marcus turned sad.

Africanus leaned forward. "He's doing well."

"He's growing fast, but…" Brutus shook his head. "Camilla told me to raise him to have my honor and courage. But how does a man do that? When does he start? Babies can't learn anything. They eat and sleep." He lifted his hand away from Marcus's bottom and looked at it. His nose wrinkled before he put it back. "And need cleaning."

Africanus's smile headed toward a grin. "True, but Dorcas says they know when the one holding them cares. She thinks they know what you say long before they talk themselves. She might be right. He looks at you like he knows."

"I wanted Camilla to raise him to have her wisdom and humor. I can teach him the things he needs to know, but how can I raise him to joke and laugh when I can't do either myself?"

Africanus settled back in his chair. "I had no laughter in me when I was taken and sold into the arena. After I started traveling with you, I found humor in life again." A smile grew. "My children make me laugh. He'll do the same for you."

Brutus turned his head toward the door through which Camilla's maid had vanished. "Vera!"

She scurried into the peristyle carrying a stack of clean cloths. Brutus held his open hand toward her. "He's wet again."

She set the stack on a bench and brought him one. He handed her Marcus and wiped his hand as she carried him away.

Brutus's mouth drooped as he turned back to Africanus. "I hope you're right."

He tossed the cloth aside. "I'm going to take Marcus with me when we go to the Lousonna estate in the spring."

Africanus's eyebrow rose. "Babies are not very sturdy. A six-year-old I would gladly take along. A six-month-old…" He shook his head.

"I'm not going to leave Camilla's son behind with people who couldn't possibly care about his welfare as much as I do. It's a good legionary highway across the pass. We've seen many raedae on our trips between Roma and the Lousonna estate. We'll take a ship as far as Genua. That cuts the travel time by ten days. I'll buy the best carriage and mules I can find there. Top quality horses, too, that I can use for breeding stock in Lousonna. Vera and a wet nurse can care for Marcus just as easily on the road as at home for two and a half weeks."

Vera's approaching footsteps drew his gaze. As she passed through the doorway with a clean, dry Marcus, he held out his arms. Once he held the precious bundle, he cuddled the infant against his chest. "We'll come home through Arelate. That only takes about three weeks. Then we'll know which is the better route for the next time."

The baby reached up to grab his nose. Brutus intercepted and blew against the tiny hand. Then the corners of Brutus's mouth curved up as he gazed upon his son.

And Marcus looked back with Camilla's eyes.

# Chapter 14

The End of the Journey

*Octodurus, Day 24*

It was midafternoon when their caravan rolled into Octodurus, and Licinia's stomach fluttered. Only a few miles up the road to the pass was the Crassus estate that would be her new home. After two weeks traveling with tents and campfires, it would seem luxurious to sleep in a soft bed and recline at dinner. So why were tendrils of unease wrapping around her mind?

A large building, two stories tall and made of light gray stone and concrete, lay less than half a mile ahead of them. The provincial government offices would be there, and the officer who had become her friend would be leaving them.

Her jaw clenched. Why did the thought of saying goodbye to a man she'd known such a short time hurt? Perhaps it was only because there had been too many goodbyes already.

As they approached the amphitheater, she shuddered as the cheers of a few thousand men washed over her. How many would die that day?

The roar of the crowd was replaced by silence. Licinia glanced at Primula. The sadness in her maid's eyes mirrored her own as the stillness that announced a fighter's death surrounded them.

When they reached the forum, the raeda stopped. Hoofbeats announced Brocchus's approach. When he reached her window, she looked up at him, clothed in his armor of red leather and bronze freshly polished to reflect the sun.

He dismounted beside her window, putting their eyes at the same level. He removed his helmet and tucked it under his arm. "I need to drop the boys off at the governor's house, but then I'll be able to escort you to your friend's estate, if you wish."

She did wish it, but it wouldn't be best for either of them.

"Thank you, but that won't be necessary. It's only a short distance up the road toward the pass, and Damalio knows the way. It's only midafternoon, so it should be perfectly safe without a military escort. I don't want to keep you from spending some time with the governor when you deliver the boys. That could prove beneficial to your career."

"I'm willing to forgo that if you need my help with anything." He turned his eyes down as he fingered his reins. "I would like our acquaintance to become friendship." His gaze shifted to her eyes. "And maybe more."

Licinia's breath caught as his eyes lit with hope. Father had kept her from spending much time with young men. She wasn't skilled in reading a man's mind, like so many of her friends were. But no one would expect discussing history over dinner, a handful of short strolls, and a few fireside chats to inspire romantic feelings.

"I'm honored by your regard, but the man I dearly loved recently died, and there's not a man alive who can take his place in my heart."

She spoke the truth, but the decurion would never guess she meant her father, not her imaginary husband.

"I understand. I lost my wife three years ago. Our marriage was much more than a political alliance. But we had no children, and the passage of time has made me willing to marry again."

He summoned a smile. "I wish I was stationed in Octodurus, but I must return to Lugdunum as soon as I deposit my charges with their father. But I sometimes come here on Imperial business, and I would like to visit you...to see if anything has changed. At which estate might I find you?"

She fought the urge to bite her lip. She could make one up so he couldn't find her, but wouldn't that make him suspicious if he came looking? And part of her wanted to see him again, even if nothing could ever come of it.

"The Licinius Crassus estate."

He placed his helmet on his head. "I won't detain you any longer, so you'll reach your destination in time to refresh yourself before dinner. May Fortuna smile upon you. If she smiles on me as well, this won't be our final goodbye."

Her eyes stung, but the smile she gave him was the warmest yet. "May you have a safe trip home. Vale, Titus Servilius Brocchus."

He mounted and reined his horse away. But he looked back over his shoulder before he kicked its sides and trotted out of her life. When he could no longer hear her, she blew a breath out and raised her eyebrows at Primula. Her maid's eyebrows rose as she shrugged.

Damalio climbed down to check the raeda before they started for the estate. He'd done that every morning before they left camp and each time they stopped to rest. First the harness and wheels at the front, then the rear. He started past her window.

"Damalio."

He rested his hand on the windowsill. "Yes, mistress?"

"Did I just hear what I think I heard?"

"Brocchus saying you're a woman he might want as his wife after you get to know each other better?"

"Exactly that. Why would he do that? I gave him no encouragement to think I was even remotely interested in him that way. We share an interest in history and an appreciation of the wild beauty of the Alpes, but that's all."

"Perhaps that's what attracted him. Some men admire a strong, intelligent woman who isn't desperate to find a husband."

"Or maybe he's simply desperate to find a Roman equestrian to marry, and I'm the first to come along."

One corner of Damalio's mouth turned up. "He's not desperate. An equestrian officer with an estate of his own here and a family estate near Rome could find many fathers eager to give him their daughters. There'd be no shortage of mature women who'd want to marry him as well."

She drew a deep breath and blew it out. "Well, an officer of Rome would be most unsuitable for me. Sextus laughed when I said I could hide my faith from a husband like Camilla has, and rightly so. I hope Brocchus finds the right woman soon, and I wish him great success in his career...in Lugdunum."

"As do I, mistress." He stepped back from the window. "But it's time to drive the last few miles, so if you'll excuse me..."

Her nod sent him toward the rear of the raeda for his final inspection. She leaned back and offered a shaky smile to Primula. "This journey is almost behind us, but only God knows what lies before us."

"Yes, mistress, and He works all things together for our good."

Licinia smiled. She had taught Primula that herself and prayed with her maid to receive the Lord. "And if I ever seem to forget that, feel free to remind me."

The carriage tilted slightly as Damalio climbed aboard. One sharp slap of the reins, and the carriage jerked as the mules began to pull. Licinia settled back against the cushion. A few more miles, and their new life would begin.

*The Crassus estate south of Octodurus, late afternoon of Day 24*

Licinia watched for each milepost, counting down the three miles to where they would leave the stone-paved public road and drive a private road to the estate headquarters. Sextus had described the estate and its villa to her, but that hadn't helped much. Lengthy descriptions of vineyards, fields, pastures, and the buildings where grapes became wine were followed by "the villa's like most other rural villas. You'll need to take what you want for a library." When she asked for more details, he'd confessed he hadn't been there since he rode back from his tribune post in Germania...more than ten years ago.

The carriage stopped, and Damalio jumped down. He climbed inside, and the deep breath he took before his first word made her own breathing pause.

"I can see the estate buildings already, mistress. Before we reach them, we all need to know who you'll be here."

Her brow furrowed. "Who I'll be?"

"Yes. Licinia Crassa or Calvia Lucilla." He rubbed his lip. "I think you should remain Calvia, at least until we know whether anyone in this area would be a threat to Licinia. Master Sextus gave me a letter for Steward Antistes telling him to host us as long as you want to stay. He didn't use your name. 'This woman and her slaves' is what he wrote. He says you are to have authority like he would himself. I'm not sure how much the master trusts this steward. Beyond him, everyone is suspect until I know for certain they can be trusted. I'm supposed to burn the letter as soon as Antistes reads it."

"I see the wisdom of what you're advising." Raised eyebrows as she glanced at Primula were answered by confirming nods. "Very well." She plucked at her stola. "Wearing these will at least keep me warmer this winter."

"I'll tell the men." The smile in his eyes spoke his approval.

"Calvia Lucilla. I thought I could leave her behind when we got here." She sighed. "I don't like telling people I'm not who I really am. I've spent most of my life hiding my faith, but I didn't have to pretend I wasn't me."

"I understand, mistress, but the name someone calls me doesn't change who I am. Whenever one of us is sold, the new owner often changes our names. But we're still the same men on the inside. Using your real name might get you killed. It might kill the rest of us, too. Thank you for making it easier for me and my men to protect you."

Her nod started him toward the carriage door. Then he stopped. "No matter what happens next, the men and I consider it God's blessing to have been chosen to come with you. Now, if you'll excuse me, we'll proceed."

Her brow furrowed. "We'll proceed, but with caution. Sextus might trust Antistes, but I'm not sure that's wise. He's had total control here with Sextus living so far away and never checking on anything personally. Let him read the letter with both of us watching. Then he needs to give it back to me. I want proof in my hands that Sextus has given me authority over what goes on at the estate. If there's something happening that's not right, I might need to prove I have the power to order a change."

Damalio's lips twitched before his slow smile appeared. "A wise choice, domina."

She blew out a breath. "Take us home."

He stepped out and returned to the driver's seat. The carriage jerked, and they began the short drive to the villa.

Home. It wasn't that yet, but God could make it one in time.

The road ended in a large grassy area that separated two rows of buildings made from plaster and wood. The roofs were a mix of clay tiles on the larger and thatch on the smaller. At the far end stood the villa house. Through the open wooden gate to her left, Licinia could see fermentation vats in the courtyard of the nearest building.

When a man came out, Damalio stopped the carriage and climbed down. "Salve. We've come from Sextus Licinius Crassus, and I need to speak with your steward."

The man's brow furrowed. "Who?"

"Your steward."

"No. You come from who?" Latin words, but spoken like a two-year-old child.

"Sextus Licinius Crassus."

With eyes like those of a sleepy sheep, the man stood still, staring at Damalio.

"Sextus Crassus, the owner of this estate." Damalio spoke slower, carefully pronouncing each Latin word.

The man's mouth formed an O, but no sound came out. "Owner of estate? I get Steward Antistes." He had a heavy accent and the wrong endings on words, but at least his words were Latin. He lowered his head and watched his feet as he strolled toward the main house.

Damalio stepped back by the window. "I've never met a man who didn't know who owned the estate where he works."

"He didn't understand Latin well. Maybe he misunderstood the question."

"Perhaps." His eyes narrowed. "Or maybe the steward prefers that the slaves think of it as his."

"Do you know any of the local language?"

"Not much. My mother taught me some Germanic, but that's been more than twenty years." His smile began to leak out. "The words a mother speaks to her child...not too useful with people serving under you."

"It might be wise for you to learn more as soon as you can. I will, too. I want to know what's going on around us. What we don't know could be dangerous."

His mouth straightened. "A wise choice. I'll look for a tutor in Octodurus who can live here while we learn."

"With nothing else to do, we should learn quickly. If any of the slaves speak reasonable Latin, we can have them teach some to the others." She craned her neck to look past Damalio toward the house. "Do you think he found the steward yet?"

Damalio's smile started again, but he stopped it. "Will he remember to tell him we're out here even if he does?"

A tall man in his early forties emerged from the house. Dark blond hair brushed his shoulders, but the brown eyes and aquiline nose revealed some Roman parentage. Trousers tied at the ankles, tunic halfway down his thighs, a knee-length cloak clipped at his shoulder with a brass pin shaped like a boar's head—he looked more like a Germanic chieftain than the steward of a Roman estate. The hint of swagger in his walk added to the impression.

With thumb and middle finger, he smoothed the mustache that framed his mouth when he reached them. "Lepus said someone was looking for me."

Shoulders squared and head tipped back just enough to let him look down his nose, Antistes's bearing proclaimed master, not steward.

Licinia withdrew from the window before he saw her swallow hard, climbed out of the raeda, and joined Damalio as he faced the steward. An aura of calm surrounded her guardian, as it always seemed to, and her nerves quieted.

The steward's eyes turned on her for a moment, but quickly returned to Damalio.

"Are you steward Antistes?" Damalio's face relaxed into a friendly smile.

"I am. Your business here?"

"Our business is yours as well." Damalio reached into a leather pouch that hung from his shoulder. He withdrew the rolled papyrus that bore Sextus's seal and offered it to Antistes. "As you will certainly recognize, this bears the seal of Sextus Licinius Crassus, the master of us both. I've brought this to you from Rome on his behalf."

As Antistes inspected the seal, Damalio continued. "It's been a long trip, and we're glad to have reached our final destination."

"Hmph." Antistes slipped his finger beneath the seal and broke it. He scanned the letter, his expression first hardening, then relaxing. "Welcome. I'll instruct my housemaid to prepare guest accommodations for you. I hope you'll be able to finish your business in Octodurus quickly. Winter is coming, and you won't want to delay your return to Italia too long. Travel becomes difficult after the snows start."

He startled when Licinia pulled the letter from his hand and handed it back to Damalio. "But we won't be returning before winter. As the letter clearly states, Sextus has made me domina of the estate, not a guest, for as long as I choose to stay. But I trust Sextus has been wise in his choice of steward and that all is as it should be. I shouldn't have much to do."

Antistes's eyes narrowed as his smile turned wooden. "Master Crassus and his father have relied on me to run the estate well for more than ten years, and they never had any complaints."

"I'm glad to hear that." She graced him with a smile, and his face relaxed. "It's been a long journey, and we all appreciate the welcome you're giving us. All my men have skills that should be useful to the estate. As soon as they unload the wagon and take my trunks to my chamber, they can rest as well. You and Damalio can talk tomorrow to figure out what they can do here to help."

Antistes signaled Lepus, who had been standing under the house's portico. He scurried over. "Tell Ancilla to prepare a chamber for...?" His arched eyebrows completed the question.

"Calvia Lucilla." She directed a slight smile at Lepus. "Your new domina. Prepare something suitable for Damalio as well."

"Then help her men with the trunks."

Lepus's head dipped. "Yes, steward."

Antistes pointed to a long building with a corral past it. "Take your wagons over there."

He turned cold eyes and a cool smile on Licinia. "Follow me, Mistress Calvia, and we'll get you settled in your new home."

As she and Priscilla followed the steward toward the portico, she glanced back at Damalio. He tipped his head to her and smiled. But before her gaze returned to the steward, her faithful guardian was rubbing his lip.

# Chapter 15

## Germanic Hospitality

As they traveled along Lacus Lemmanus, Licinia had seen many villas like this, with substantial houses set back from the road, flanked by the buildings that served the needs of running an estate. The main floors were made of stones set in mortar, the upper stories of timber supports with wattle and daub sections between them, often plastered to make them look more substantial.

The portico before her had a stone wall that reached waist high before the row of large wooden columns that supported the tile roof began. Behind the narrow portico, a wall with a few windows at waist height supported the roof for the single-story front of the house. The front half turned at the ends to include two wings that closed off on each end of the portico. The back was two-story, making a clerestory that ran the length of the building. Its row of small windows would light the interior.

The roof was solid; no openings would let rain and light into an atrium or peristyle. Glass was not part of the windows at home, but here snow fell often and blew in the wind. A roof with no openings and glazed windows would be welcome when the weather turned cold.

It was already colder than she'd ever experienced, and it was only fall. That thought sent a shudder through her, but she drew her cloak closer and marched on behind Sextus's steward who didn't act like one.

They stepped onto the portico by the right wing. Antistes opened one of a pair of doors carved with interweaving vines and stepped into the house ahead of her. A long corridor stretched to her left. To the right was a room with a mosaic floor of hunting scenes and some chairs facing a hearth. A geometric mosaic ran the length of the corridor.

"It's quite lovely."

Antistes tipped his head but said nothing.

Ahead was a large open space, clearly intended to serve as a public room like the atrium at home. A row of four massive columns aligned with the wall of the rooms that opened onto the corridor. They supported the clerestory wall above them. Deeper into the great room, another row of columns supported heavy wooden beams that bore the weight of the rooms above them. To the right, a stairway led up to a balcony that ran along the row of rooms and let the light from the clerestory windows into the public room below.

Several doors carved to match the entrance overlooked the great hall. Where the wall of the public room extended to the roof, the balcony turned into a hallway.

Antistes took a step toward the stairs and glanced back over his shoulder. "Your chamber is above."

With Primula right behind, Licinia followed him up.

The first room was the largest, and the details of the carving bespoke the importance of the one who slept there.

Antistes's hand rested on the doorframe. "This is the steward's chamber." His hand extended toward the room two doors down. "And that will be yours."

Licinia raised an eyebrow. The spacious room at the head of the stairs most certainly was not built to be a steward's chamber. It was meant for the *dominus*, not his top-ranked servant.

And the room of the dominus was usually separated from the room of the domina by a small chamber where her lady's maid and sometimes the manservant of the master slept.

An unfortunate choice lay before her. She could tell Antistes to remove himself from the master's chamber, but that would embarrass him in front of all those he commanded and make a true enemy from a man who was already unfriendly. Or she could have the door to his chamber boarded up from her side so no one could use it. The second was the wiser choice...at least for now.

He continued down the balcony past the door to the servant's room and pushed open the domina's door.

"The room hasn't been used for some time." He cleared his throat. "There hasn't been a domina here since I became steward, and that was before the previous Sextus Crassus bought the estate."

The scurrying footsteps of a mouse greeted her. "It would appear not, but it's nothing that some cleaning won't solve."

She strolled across the room to look out the window. "It has a lovely view of the mountains. I'm sure I'll find it quite pleasant once it's clean. The winter snows will make the mountains spectacular, and the spring flowers should make that meadow seem like a garden."

She glanced over her shoulder in time to see his jaw twitch. But his unhappiness over her planning to stay was not going to diminish what pleasures she could find where Sextus had sent her. Antistes would accept her in time.

She drew her finger along the dust-coated dressing table and raised it for him to see. "It needs a very thorough cleaning, but at least the worst of the dust can be removed this afternoon before I sleep here tonight."

A tight-lipped frown accompanied a single nod of his head. He stepped onto the balcony. "Olga!"

Licinia startled. Had the outer door been open, the whole farmyard would have heard his bellow.

A skinny blond girl in her late teens scurried out of the corridor and stared up at him. Licinia didn't understand a single word of the exchange between them. Damalio better find that tutor immediately.

The girl turned and hurried back into the corridor.

"Olga will remove some dust and bring sheets. Tomorrow you can tell her exactly what you want done."

"Does she speak Latin or Greek?"

The corner of his mouth turned up. "No, but I'm sure you'll figure out how to tell her what a domina needs."

The door opened below them. Fidus and Robustus entered, one on each end of her heaviest trunk.

"Your men are bringing your things. I'll leave you to direct them where to put them. I have work to finish." With a sideways tip of his head, Antistes headed down the stairs. As he passed her men, he pointed up at her.

They hadn't reached the top of the stairs when Damalio and Sollus entered with a second trunk. She stepped back into the room and waited for them.

As soon as Damalio set down his end of the trunk, she motioned for him to follow her into the servant's chamber.

She pointed at the door. "That leads into the room where Antistes sleeps, and he's made it abundantly clear he considers that the steward's chamber."

Damalio's eyebrows shot up under his hair that had grown too long during the trip. Then they plunged down, accompanied by a deep frown.

She cleared her throat to silence the chuckle. "I quite agree, but I don't want to order him out and make an enemy. There's an easy fix."

"What do you want me to do?"

"For tonight, push the heaviest trunk against the door. I don't want him surprising Primula in the middle of the night. Tomorrow, you can find some boards and nail the door shut from my side."

His eyebrows still dipped. "And the door to the balcony?"

"I'll ask him for the key."

"Push the other trunk against it as well. He might have two keys."

"You'll sleep in one of the smaller guestrooms down the hall. If the steward thinks it's appropriate for him to sleep in the dominus's chamber, he can raise no objection to my understeward sleeping like a guest. I want you within earshot in case there's a problem I can't handle alone."

"A wise choice, domina. Anything else?"

"Before you tour the estate with him tomorrow, I want the four of you to inspect it unescorted."

He nodded.

Her gaze locked on Damalio's eyes. "And I want you to join us for dinner. I need a man I can trust to observe one I don't."

"As you wish. But first I'll take the men where there are no ears to talk about what we'll be looking for. If you'll excuse us..."

Her nod sent the four men she trusted completely out of the room. She drew a breath between her teeth and blew it out between pursed lips. *God, please let Antistes be more trustworthy than I fear.*

German words came from behind her, and she turned to find Olga with a broom and some rags.

She drew her finger across the dusty dressing table. After showing her dirty fingers to Olga, she rubbed thumb and fingers together to brush it off. "Dust."

The Latin word drew a blank stare.

Primula took a rag from Olga and made one swipe across the grimy surface. "Dust"

Olga's head bobbed, and she stepped forward to begin the task.

Licinia strolled to the window and contemplated the tallest mountain.

The grandest bridge across the wildest river began with a good foundation, carefully placed stone by stone. Bridging the differences between her and the strangers she must now lead should be no different.

When Damalio returned, he had the leather pouch containing Sextus's letter and the money they hadn't spent during their trip. She pulled a chain with the three trunk keys from beneath her tunic and handed it to him.

"Keep however much money you think appropriate. Lock the rest and the pouch in one of my trunks, and show Primula where it is."

She headed downstairs and settled into one of the padded couches in the great hall to wait for them. When they joined her, she motioned them to pull up two chairs, and they talked as they waited for Antistes to call them to dinner.

At least she and Primula talked. Damalio sat in silence, arms crossed, watching the mountains through the several small windows arranged close together to provide a good view.

After an hour, there was still no sign of Antistes.

She raised her eyebrows at Damalio. "Where can he possibly be? You must be as hungry as I am. Perhaps we'll just start without him."

She rose, and they strolled down the corridor to find the kitchen at the far end. Inside, an old woman was stirring a pot of stew.

Damalio tapped on the door frame. The cook jumped and spun.

"Is dinner almost ready?"

He smiled at her, but panic still filled her eyes.

"Is it almost ready to eat?"

The cook stared at him and kept shaking her head. He made hand motions for eating and pointed to the dining room that was a few feet down the corridor.

The shaking turned to nodding, and she flicked her hands to head them toward the dining room.

"Antistes?" Damalio's eyes and voice asked the question without Latin words.

She shook her head again and waved toward the room.

When they entered the dining room, three dining couches were stacked along the back wall. In the middle of the room was a table with six chairs around it. Primula opened the cabinet on the back wall to reveal some stained napkins but no sheets for the couches that could be removed for cleaning.

Licinia rested her hand on the back of a chair. "This is still better than stools around a campfire." She seated herself at the head of the table. "Do join me."

For several minutes, they waited.

"I'll go see if it's almost ready." Damalio had just pushed back his chair when the cook entered with a pot of stew. She set it on the table and left.

Olga trailed behind her with two bowls and two spoons.

Licinia raised two fingers, then a third before pointing at Primula. "Bring a third set."

Olga's brow furrowed; then she shrugged.

Licinia picked up a spoon. "Bring a third spoon." She waved the spoon. "And bowl." She tapped the bowl.

Olga's head tipped.

"One, two, three." Licinia held up another finger as she added each number. Then she touched a bowl. "One bowl." She touched the other. "Two bowls." She held up three fingers. "Three bowls." Then she tapped a bowl.

Olga's smile appeared as her head bobbed up and down. She disappeared into the corridor and returned with another bowl and spoon.

Primula rose to get them, then she showed Olga how to serve the stew to each of them. The girl's eyes were riveted on Primula. Then her nods began again, and she repeated each Latin word as Primula pointed to something.

Licinia held up the spoon. She pointed to herself and then to the spoon before naming it in Latin. Then she pointed to Olga before holding up the spoon.

When Olga replied with the Germanic word, smiles spread among them all. One more time with Latin names brought the German names in response. As Licinia repeated each Germanic word, Olga nodded.

Licinia marked the end of the language lessons with a nod, a smile, and "That will be all." After a flick of Licinia's hand, a happy-looking Olga left them to eat.

One bite of the stew, and Licinia wrinkled her nose. It barely had more flavor than breakfast porridge, and she could count the vegetable pieces in her serving on one hand. She wouldn't even serve such pitiful food to her slaves.

Damalio stirred his bowl. "If this is what he serves his mistress, what is he feeding the slaves?"

Her mouth curved down. "From the look of Olga, I'd say not enough. When you're looking around tomorrow, make that one of the questions."

He scooped the last runny spoonful from his bowl before he rose. "I want to check on the men to see if they got fed. If not, I'll have Sollus make something." A slow smile appeared. "After this dinner, I might do that anyway. If you'll excuse me..."

A tip of her head, and he left the room.

She rested her hands on her still-hungry stomach. She had half a mind to join the men herself.

*Evening of Day 24*

After dinner, Licinia and Primula wrapped themselves in their woolen cloaks and entered the vegetable garden through a door by the kitchen. All had been harvested and dried for winter use, and the withered remains of dead plants were still scattered atop the rectangular beds.

Her mouth turned down. When was the gardener going to turn the soil so what was left behind could become nourishment for what would grow in the spring?

Perhaps things were done differently where winter was harsher, but she would ask Damalio's opinion before he spoke with Antistes about her men.

She glanced toward the barren crags to the east. As the sun set the western sky on fire, it was turning the early snows soft pink.

Licinia pointed, and Primula's eyes followed her own. "Sunset in the west marks the end of the day, but the pink on the mountain is the color of sunrise clouds. God is reminding us when something ends, He also gives us a new beginning."

Primula's smile warmed. "I think it will be the beginning of something wonderful."

Licinia pulled her cloak closer and stopped a sigh before Primula could hear. "I'll be praying that you're right."

Chapter 16



## NOT AS IT SHOULD BE

*The Octodurus estate, Day 25*

After a breakfast of too-old bread, cheese of questionable age, and hard-boiled eggs that appeared only after she insisted the cook send someone out to check under the hens, Licinia was ready to inspect the house and grounds.

She was ready, but where was Antistes? No one had remained in the room while she ate, or she'd send them to find him. With no master in residence for so many years, perhaps the current kitchen workers had never been taught what was expected when serving their domina.

Her lips tightened. Or perhaps Antistes was planning to hasten her departure with poor accommodations. One corner of her mouth turned up. She'd spent three weeks with food fit for a legionary on campaign and found it satisfying. She'd slept on a cot with the tent flapping in the wind, and she'd awakened as refreshed as she had on the pillow-soft mattress in her old room. He'd be sorely disappointed if he thought her a pampered noblewoman who couldn't bear to live without the elegance of life in Rome.

When Primula entered, Licinia swung her legs off the couch. "How was breakfast?"

Her maid's eyebrows lowered. "I hope it wasn't what's normally served. The porridge was runny, and there was barely enough for each to have a small bowl. They could have added some herbs to give it a good flavor, but it was just barley boiled in water. Too much water and not enough barley."

Licinia stood and ran her hands down the front of her stola to smooth a few of the wrinkles. "Damalio is making a private tour of the farm now. Since Antistes hasn't deigned to appear to guide me through the house, we'll conduct a surprise inspection without his aid."

Primula smoothed the wrinkles in back . "I think he won't like us doing that."

"If he's done as good a job as he claims, he has nothing to worry about."

"And if he hasn't?"

"Then he'll have to do better."

Primula fell in behind her as Licinia entered the corridor. "Olga."

Broom in hand, the girl turned.

"Bring Lepus to me."

"Lepus?" Olga leaned the broom against the wall and disappeared into the kitchen.

Licinia strolled down the corridor to the great hall and settled onto a couch with a view of the mountains to wait.

"Domina."

She turned in her chair to find Lepus standing in the doorway. His name meant rabbit, and that fit him. His gray eyes flitted from her to the window to the floor, and even though he stood fairly straight, Licinia's slightest movement might trigger a jump and a dash for the outer door.

She smiled to reduce his fear, and he relaxed some.

"Lepus, where did you learn Latin?" She spoke each word slowly.

"First master...owns taberna. Learn from soldiers."

"Do any of the other slaves know as much Latin as you do?"

"No, mistress."

"Domina, not just mistress."

His brow furrowed, then relaxed. "Domina."

"I want everyone on the estate to learn enough Latin to understand what Damalio and I say to you. Can you help with that?

Lepus's eyes darted toward the steward's office before returning to Licinia. "Steward Antistes...he wants me to do it?"

"He will want you to do what I decide you should do." She tipped her head back to look down her nose. "I am your domina now."

He shifted his feet. "I can try, if it's all right with him."

"It will be. Think about how you would teach it while also doing the regular work Antistes has given you. He should be pleased when you do both at once."

"Should be, but..."

Licinia lowered her eyebrows.

That brought a quick nod from her newly created tutor. "Yes, domina."

"You will come with me now to interpret what I say to the others and then tell me what they answer."

He opened his mouth and glanced at the closed door of Antistes's office. Then his mouth shut. "Yes, domina."

Licinia stepped toward the kitchen, Primula two steps behind her and Lepus trailing behind Primula.

First the kitchen, then the house and grounds, then the entire estate. She would inspect it all, and if things were not what they should be, they would have to change.

Licinia ended her self-guided tour in the library off the great hall. Antistes had failed to appear, and each time she had Lepus ask a slave if they had seen him, the answer was no.

As she stood by the window, gazing at the distant peaks, her jaw clenched. Perhaps she should be glad he had chosen to act as if she wasn't there. She had seen things he wouldn't have shown her.

The house slaves worked slowly, and what they did wasn't done as well as it should be. But how could they be expected to do their best when they weren't cared for properly?

Their food was poor quality, and there wasn't enough of it. Their clothes were only suitable for summer weather. When she asked Lepus when the new clothes for winter would be ready, he looked at her as if he didn't understand the question.

She leaned against the window frame. Some cattle grazed in the field between her and the foothills. God had provided all the cows needed, but the men who herded them were now her responsibility. Neither Father nor Sextus would ever allow such neglect of the slaves who worked at the estates in Italia. She would not tolerate it here.

Antistes was well dressed and well fed. He was probably taking what should provide for the workers for himself. Damalio would be able to tell when he examined the estate accounts.

She turned away from the majestic view and focused on the room she would make her own office. It was no more than eight feet wide and about as deep. Whoever owned the estate before Father bought it had lined the wall opposite the window with cubicles for scrolls.

A powdery film covered the desk, and she started to write her name in it. After the L and the I, she paused. Licinia had been left in Rome. She was still Calvia here, so she changed the I to a V and wrote the rest of her new name to the left and right before sweeping the dust away with her palm.

One chair for the dominus faced the window; two chairs for guests sat across the desk from it. She patted the cushion of one, and a cloud of dust billowed around her hand.

A man cleared his throat behind her, and she turned to find Damalio.

"I'm going to make this my own office. It's filthy now, but Olga can take care of that. I brought some favorite scrolls from home, but I won't unpack them until I have a clean place for them."

Damalio drew a finger across the bottom of one cubicle, and his nose twitched. "Fidus made shipping crates and plain furniture at the Crassus estate. His first task here can be making a cabinet with cubicles for your scrolls and codices and whatever else you might not want Antistes poking into. I can get a lock made in Octodurus. But it might be wiser to keep that in your room for now. I'd suggest keeping anything you value locked in your trunk with Master Sextus's letter."

Her eyebrow rose. "You doubt Antistes's honesty?"

He drew a deep breath. "Maybe. The way this estate is run...it's nothing like Master Sextus's estate where I oversaw shipping. The slave quarters are built well enough, but there's no provision for anything but sleeping on the stone floor. There aren't enough blankets for each person to have one, and the smallest and weakest suffer the cold. The men and women are housed apart, but no provision is made for those who would like a slave union to raise a family."

"Before it gets any colder, I want warm clothes and good blankets for everyone and straw mattresses. What else is wrong?"

"After you sent Lepus to me, I asked him where all the children were. He said Antistes sells any children quickly rather than letting their parents raise them and train them to work the estate. The one exception is his own son by one of the slave women before your father bought the estate. Primus is barely twenty, but he's been made overseer. He doesn't know how to encourage work without threatening harsh punishment, and he enjoys delivering on that threat."

"He cleared his throat. "There's something that's common on many estates, but it's not allowed by your brother. A dark-haired man came from town and headed toward the women's lodging. When I asked where he was going, he answered in decent Latin."

Damalio opened his mouth, then turned his gaze from her to the window, closing his mouth without speaking.

She stopped the smile his reluctance triggered. "Say what you're thinking. I'm not some delicate maiden you have to protect from facts a domina needs to know."

"The steward and his son take their pleasure with the women, and Antistes lets some men from Octodurus do the same for a price. I told the man that the estate was not a brothel, and he could tell others who came for that purpose not to come again."

Licinia swept dust from the desktop as her jaw clamped.

She glared at Damalio, but he must know it wasn't directed at him. "Send someone to summon Antistes and return right away."

"Yes, domina." One quick dip of his head, and her guardian left to fetch the man who would not like what she had to say.

But Sextus had made her domina, and what a steward who didn't deserve the position thought didn't matter.

When Antistes entered the library a quarter hour later, he wore a patronizing air. "Canis said you wanted me. I have matters to attend to, but if this won't take long..."

"I am your domina. Other matters can wait when I send for you." She arched an eyebrow. "Next time, come more promptly. I've begun looking into matters here, and what I find is not as it should be. Things are going to change."

Antistes stiffened, and his superior smile vanished.

"The first change will be in how the slaves are treated. When you treat people well, they work well for you. I will expect you to treat our workers here like Sextus treats the workers on his Italian estates."

Antistes's eye widened. "But expenses will rise. Master Crassus expects good profits from this estate. It's my duty to deliver those."

"Sextus gets good profits from his estates in Italia without mistreating his slaves. What works there will work just as well here. I will be including a private letter to him with each monthly dispatch you send. I will explain the extra expense, and he will be content with what that means for his profits."

Defiance lurked behind his eyes, even though his expression was compliant. "As you wish...domina."

"Damalio was understeward at Sextus's largest estate south of Rome. He knows what Sextus expects, and he'll help you make the necessary changes. The first change: this estate is not a brothel, and the women will not be treated like prostitutes." She arched her eyebrows. "Am I understood?"

His eyes veiled. "Yes, domina."

"This afternoon, the two of you can go over the estate accounts and discuss changes. First thing tomorrow morning, I want to inspect the accounts myself, and then you can give me a tour of everything."

"Yes, domina."

She softened her stern expression and offered a reserved smile. "Being so far from Rome and with neither Sextus nor his father coming here often, I realize you had no way to know his standards for treatment of Crassus slaves are higher than many. But I'm certain you can make the needed changes and become the kind of steward Sextus wants."

His jaw clenched, but his response was a single nod.

"You may go now. Damalio will find you after lunch."

After a stiff bow, Antistes turned and strode from the room.

Damalio rubbed his lower lip. "You have an enemy now. He'll need to be watched."

"I don't care. The slaves on Sextus's estates are people, and they will be treated that way as long as I have control."

Approval shone in his eyes. "Yes, domina. There are a few more things I want to check before I meet with Antistes. If you'll excuse me…"

One tip of her head, and Damalio left.

She rubbed her forehead. Domina. Father had called her domina of his household, but that had been a simple task. All had run smoothly there without her doing much. But now she was domina in fact, not just in name.

She could make a difference in the lives of people who were suffering, and if that meant having an enemy, it was worth it.

# Chapter 17

## The Fate of a Human Soul

*Morning of Day 27*

Outside Licinia's bedchamber window, the mountains still blocked the sun, even though it had risen to the east of them almost an hour before. But the towering peaks couldn't keep it from painting the clouds above them with warm shades of pink.

They couldn't stop the color, but they blocked the warmth. She drew a woolen shawl closer around her shoulders before picking up the gold pen that had once been Father's.

What to say in the first of what would be monthly letters to her brother? Each would be just one more sheet included in the dispatch of estate reports Antistes sent. While pretending to be Sextus's freedman, she could never include the expressions of affection they had so often shared over dinner at their father's house. This first would be quite formal, but when Sextus wrote back, she'd be able to tell how open she could be in future letters.

She spread a small sheet of papyrus on the writing desk, dipped pen in ink, and made the first stroke.

> Sextus Licinius Gratus to Sextus Licinius Crassus, my noble patron, greetings. If you are well, then I am glad. I write to tell you the entire party has completed the task you assigned. Your choice to place Damalio in charge of arrangements has proven exceedingly wise. The rest of the men have also performed their tasks well.

Steward Antistes has been accommodating since our arrival. He will be able to use the special skills of my party to benefit the estate. I will let you know how that goes in future dispatches.

I hope all will continue to be well with you. May the most powerful god guard your safety.

As Licinia sealed the letter with wax, the first tear slipped down her cheek. A dozen more followed.

She'd always hoped to convince Father and Sextus that following Jesus was the only wise choice a man could make. It was too late for Father, but she'd thought she would still have many years to work on Sextus.

Now that chance was gone. It was likely she would never see him again, laugh with him again, share her deepest thoughts and inmost longings with him again. He didn't know anyone else who followed Jesus. No one would tell him about the forgiveness and peace that brought. She'd prolonged her own life by leaving, but what would that mean for the eternal fate of her brother's soul?

*The Brutus estate, Day 28*

As he'd done too many times, Brutus trudged out to the grove and sat by Camilla's grave. The sun was setting and catching the clouds on fire. Before this evening, he'd watched the days die in silence as his heart and mind battled a relentless adversary. During the day, keeping busy was a shield that held the loneliness at bay, but the quiet of a house where her laughter no longer echoed disarmed him. The stillness of their bedchamber was a dagger in his side. Silence was the enemy, but would words with no one to answer be friend or foe?

"I don't know if you can hear me, but in case you can, I want to tell you some things."

He plucked a blade of grass. "I'm trying to keep my promise not to grieve too deeply, and I'm failing."

He split one end of the blade and tore it in half. "Marcus is growing well. Vera is doing her best to make him feel safe and loved. I am, too, and every time I look into our son's eyes, I see you."

He tossed the pieces over his shoulder and plucked another blade.

"I did what you asked and buried you like a Christian. I waited to tell your parents you were dead until afterwards so they wouldn't demand you have a Roman funeral. They're still angry with me, but what you wanted matters more to me than anything they can say or do."

He split the second blade. "I lied to them and said I gave you a proper burial. They think they'll see you on the Plain of Asphodel. But a Christian burial, like you wanted...could that ever be proper?"

He placed his hand on the ground above her body. "By putting you here without Roman rites, did I condemn your soul to walk the earth forever? Are you still this side of the River Styx, forced to wait for all time because I didn't bury you properly? I put the coin for Charon with you. Did he take you across?"

Brutus buried his face in his hands. Camilla was the closest to perfect of anyone he'd ever known. She should have gone to the Plain of Asphodel, but she'd blasphemed the gods. Was she in Tartarus being tortured now? Did she have to return to the Roman gods for that blasphemy to be atoned for? Nothing else in her life would have put her in that place of utter darkness and pain. He'd always been told no one had to stay there forever, but was her sin so great it would keep her in Tartarus longer than he could bear to think of her suffering?

With the sky flames dying overhead, he rubbed his mouth. The Roman gods weren't real, so why should denying them trap anyone in Tartarus? Was the whole story of the afterlife he'd been taught as a child even true? When a man died, did he simply cease to be? When her breathing stopped, was she gone forever?

He dropped on his back and stared at the darkening sky, watching for the first star to appear. So many times, he'd lain there with her head on his shoulder, and they counted the stars together as the points of light revealed themselves, one by one.

A puff of wind stirred the leaves. Then it stilled, as Camilla had done as her final breath escaped. And with her dying sigh, she left him...alone.

What was the truth about the fate of a human soul? Did any choice he made even matter? Could any man know this side of death, before it would be too late to change anything?

# Chapter 18

DISTURBING QUESTIONS

*The Baths of Trajan, January, AD 123*

Brutus descended the steps into the steaming pool in the *caldarium* and settled onto the submerged bench. As the hot water wrapped his torso in its wet embrace, he closed his eyes and rested his head against the sidewall.

It had been a day of uncomfortable conversations, and the worst had been offering his condolences to Lucius Drusus Fidelis on the death of his son Marcus.

It was almost three months since Camilla died, long enough for many to think him mostly past his grief. At least they'd stopped speaking of it. He disliked the customary words of condolence from his myriad acquaintances. He hated the genuine condolences from his friends. They knew or at least suspected the loneliness that plagued him most days and every night. Their words only focused the dull ache back into a sharp pain.

The flicker of pain in Drusus's eyes as Brutus spoke of the nobility of death in service to Roma...he knew what kind of agony could lie behind that subtle sign of well-concealed grief.

He'd trained so many young men for war that the word of their deaths in battle saddened but no longer shocked him. But when word spread that Marcus Drusus had died in Judaea, a rumor that his own brother had killed him spread with it. While Marcus had never been one of his favorites, Lucius and their younger brother Tertius were. If any truth was behind that rumor, Brutus would gladly wager Lucius had been forced to do it and now struggled with grief of his own.

Killing a brother—that would have been Brutus's worst nightmare if he hadn't been an only child. Losing a son rent the heart of any good father and even most bad ones.

If his own baby boy grew up like Lucius, Camilla would be proud of the father Brutus had become.

Brutus's mouth turned down. He'd been a fool to postpone adopting an heir. If he'd persuaded Drusus to let him adopt Lucius or Tertius, she might not have died trying to give him one.

"Master." Africanus's near-whisper popped Brutus's eyes open. "Licinius Crassus is coming out of the *laconicum.*"

Brutus twisted on the bench to see the entrance to the sweat room. As Crassus took the towel the slave offered him, Brutus climbed out of the hot pool.

With Crassus's eyes closed as he toweled his hair, Brutus claimed his own towel unseen.

"Salve, Crassus."

Crassus startled at Brutus's voice beside him. His head swiveled toward Brutus, and the rest of his body followed before he wiped the sweat from his chest.

Then the social smile of a politician lifted the corners of his mouth. "Salve, Antonius Brutus." The pause between greeting and name was so short one might have thought them friends instead of acquaintances who'd shared only one conversation.

That conversation had confirmed Brutus's suspicion that Crassus's sister was responsible for Camilla's death. He greeted the senator's smile with his usual smiling frown.

Crassus tossed his towel in a basket as Brutus rubbed his own chest dry. He'd had plenty of time to plan the sharp words he'd speak to the Christian, and he was eager to plunge them into her and twist them like a dagger before she corrupted another.

"It's been some weeks since we last spoke. Is your sister still enjoying her time away from Roma?"

The corners of Crassus's smile tightened. "When the sea is closed, no one expects to hear from travelers."

"Do you expect her to return when the sea opens? I would still like to speak with her."

Crassus's shoulders tensed. "I expect to hear from her when she chooses to tell me her plans. She's no foolish young girl; I trust she's spending her time wisely and well."

Brutus kept the furrow from his brow. An odd answer from a man known for taking good care of all in his *familia* and any who were his clients.

"I look forward to hearing of her return. I still need to ask her something about my wife."

Crassus's smile stiffened but didn't dim. He stretched his hand toward the slave and received another towel. Fresh sweat had appeared on his face. His eyes scanned the room before returning to Brutus.

"Word of her return will spread quickly." He dropped the second towel in the basket. "It's been a pleasure, but a senator I must speak with is leaving. If you'll excuse me..."

Brutus scarcely had time to nod before Crassus strode toward three senators talking by the exit. As he watched their conversation, it was clearly about nothing of great importance.

Brutus heard Africanus behind him, but he kept his eyes on Crassus. "Your thoughts?"

"He wanted to escape your questions. Licinius Crassus takes care of those under his authority. Family, slaves, freedmen, clients...he keeps track of them all. He would know where his sister is."

"Exactly. He's hidden her, but I'll find her. And when I do..."

Africanus cleared his throat.

"I know. Search, not hunt. No matter what I want, I won't do more than talk."

As he slipped once more into the hot water, Brutus silently rehearsed the words he'd one day speak to the woman who'd cost him everything.

*The Octodurus estate, late January*

Licinia's gaze swept the mantle of fresh-fallen snow on the fields and foothills. She adjusted the long sleeves of her winter tunic as Primula wrapped the silver chain around Licinia's chest and waist. The sun peeked over the mountain, making the snow crystals sparkle like chips of mica scattered on white sand.

"It's so beautiful as long as I don't have to stay out in it too long." The view vanished as Primula dropped a heavy woolen stola over Licinia's head before belting it at the waist. "I'm glad Damalio was able to get proper winter clothes and boots for all our people before the storms started. With the rain and the snow and the mud after the snow melts, it would have been miserable working outside."

Primula draped the first quarter of the blue wool palla across her mistress's back before wrapping the rest across Licinia's front and tossing the remaining length over her left shoulder. She finished with a brass shoulder pin that held the wrap in place.

"Blankets and mattresses, too, mistress." She shuddered. "To think they used to sleep on the floor before you came."

"Sextus would be appalled to know how his slaves have been treated here." She sighed. "I miss him so much, but at least my banishment from Rome brought good for everyone here." She turned from the window. "Perhaps he'll visit some time."

Primula adjusted the palla's folds. "Damalio says it only takes two weeks to take a ship to Genua and then ride across the pass." Her gaze fixed on the mountains, now buried under deep snow. "But that would have to be in summer."

Licinia leaned against the window frame. "We should go to the top of the pass sometime. I've never been where no trees can grow. I'd love to watch the eagles soar."

She pulled the drape across the window to keep the heat in. "I'm glad Damalio chose Sollus to come with us. Two months with him in charge of the kitchens, and it doesn't look like a famine around here anymore."

She led Primula downstairs and into the dining room.

Bread and cheese awaited them on the table. As Licinia settled into her chair, Olga entered with two steaming bowls of porridge on a tray. But the bright morning smile that had become her usual way to greet her domina was missing.

The girl kept her eyes focused on the bowls as she set the tray on the table. She placed one bowl before Licinia as Primula served herself. When she picked up the tray and stepped back, her eyes stayed downcast.

"Olga."

The girl dropped her chin to her chest, but her eyes rolled up once for a fleeting view of Licinia.

"What's wrong, Olga?"

Another quick glance and the girl swallowed hard.

"Tell me what has happened." Licinia kept her voice soft and her Latin words slow. No need to frighten Olga more than she already was.

Quick footsteps in the hall brought a grim-faced Damalio into the room. "Domina, there was a problem last night. It needs a resolution this morning." His hand squeezed the back of his neck. "And there's no easy choice that will solve it."

Licinia's heartrate ramped up as she watched his lips tighten as his shoulders squared. "What's the problem?"

"Primus came home from Octodurus late and almost too drunk to ride." He rubbed his lip. "One of the women his father used to rent to men from Octodurus refused to let him lie with her. Fidus heard her struggling and dragged Primus out of the women's lodging. Then Primus pulled a dagger and was about to stab him when Robustus grabbed him from behind and took the dagger away."

Anger surged within her. "Has Primus forced himself on any of the women since you put an end to his father letting men come from town?"

Matching anger burned in Damalio's eyes. Damalio drew a breath as if to speak, but paused until his eyes cooled. "None of the women want to talk about it. I think they're afraid of what he'll do as overseer."

Olga had slipped back against the wall and was sidling toward the door.

"Olga." Licinia used her domina tone. "What do you know about this?"

"I...do not... understand question." But the twitch of her mouth said otherwise.

"Get Lepus now, and you come back with him."

One quick tip of her head, and Olga scurried from the room.

Licinia pressed her cheeks with her palms. "I'm learning more Germanic every day, but this needs words our tutor hasn't taught me."

Words she hoped she wouldn't need to use again.

Licinia paced, glancing out the window each time she passed it. Why did it have to be Primus? Anyone else, and she could have simply sold him as an example to the others. But Primus was Antistes's son. She couldn't allow what Primus had done to go unpunished, but what she did to Primus could turn Antistes's restrained resentment into open hostility.

*God, please give me wisdom and courage as I deal with this.*

"You want me, domina?" Lepus's voice pulled her eyes from the mountaintop. He kept shifting his weight from foot to foot. Olga stood behind him, her back pressed against the wall.

"Yes. I want to hear what you know about Primus and how the women are treated. Then I want you to translate for me."

Lepus swallowed as his eyes bounced between Licinia and Damalio, whose frown and crossed arms left no doubt someone was in trouble.

"He treats them… mostly good." His eyes focused on the floor before the last two words.

Licinia looked at Damalio and raised her eyebrows.

"Lepus." Damalio's quiet tone raised Lepus's gaze from the floor. "Before Domina came, he used the women for pleasure. He was supposed to stop. Did he? Or was what he tried last night something that happens often?"

Lepus's eyes flitted to Licinia before returning to Damalio. "He mostly stopped."

"Ask Olga the same questions."

Lepus translated to Germanic, Olga shook her head to the first question, and, after a long pause, nodded to the second.

Damalio's jaw clenched. "Ask her which of the women."

"Ursula and Padma." Olga didn't wait for the translation.

"Is that all?" Silence followed Licinia's question. "Has he bothered you?"

"No, domina, and I don't know others for certain. I sleep in the kitchen."

"You may go back to the kitchen." Licinia's permission sent Olga scurrying from the room.

A huge sigh escaped Licinia as she faced Damalio. "Take Lepus and talk to those two. Ask for any others. When you return with what you learn, I'll decide what to do."

"Yes, domina." With a curl of his fingers to summon Lepus, he strode from the room.

Licinia placed her palms on her cheeks, closed her eyes, and shook her head. She opened them to see Primula's worried face. Clothing, bedding, better food—those had been easy fixes to improve the lives of the workers. But solving this would make enemies.

*God, please guide me to know and do what's right. Then protect us from whatever that brings.*

# Chapter 19



Like a light gray blanket, the snow clouds had been drawn across the sky from west to east until the last patch of blue was gone. An occasional snowflake drifted down, and Licinia tried to count them as she waited for Damalio.

She turned when his footsteps announced his return. "What did you learn?"

"I spoke with Ursula and Padma. They started out afraid to tell me anything, but when they learned you truly wanted to know..." He cleared his throat. "Every time Primus goes to Octodurus and comes home drunk, he expects one of them to lie with him. They're both young and the prettiest two in the barracks, so he's confined his attentions to them. Antistes hasn't done anything with any of the women since we came, and he no longer lets men come from the town."

Licinia closed her eyes and rubbed her forehead. "That's a relief. At least I won't have to reprimand a steward, but I must have him deal with his son. Please send someone to fetch him then come right back."

"Yes, domina." He left the room.

Primula came to Licinia's side. "Anything I can do, mistress?"

"Pray." Licinia closed her eyes. *God, please show me the right way to handle this. Please give me the words I need.*

Her eyes popped open when Primula cleared her throat. Damalio stood against the wall. Tromping feet advanced down the hallway, and Antistes, wrapped in an aura of impatience, entered the room.

"I understand you need me, domina." His smile declared his own sense of importance.

"I sent for you because there is a problem with the overseer." Antistes's smile stiffened. "The use of our women for personal pleasure... that ended the day I came. That should have been perfectly clear to every man on the estate. Primus has no excuse for forcing himself on two of the women. No one will use our women that way. Not your former customers, not him as overseer, not even you as steward."

"I heard what happened last night, and it doesn't amount to anything." His voice was too patronizing. "I am sorry Primus drew a knife on one of your slaves, but he was attacking Primus. Primus was too drunk to know who it was. As for that weaver, she's never complained before, and young men have needs."

Licinia raised her hand to stop his words as she glared at him. "No. Young men have desires, and they can control them. If Primus can't, then he has no place on this estate. I would sell him if he weren't your son. Since he is, I'm only going to demote him to herdsman so he can't threaten the women as overseer."

Antistes bristled. "But the estate needs an overseer. One as good as Primus will be impossible to find."

"Damalio was understeward at one of Sextus's largest estates. He can replace Primus as overseer."

If eyes could throw real daggers, she'd be dead. Then the hot fury in Antistes's eyes cooled into an icy glare. His silence hung heavy in the room.

"As domina, I bear responsibility for the wellbeing of this estate, including its people. As steward, you bear responsibility for not teaching your son properly and not monitoring his actions as overseer after such use of the women was halted."

Antistes jaw clamped. He should have said "yes, domina," but she let that omission pass.

"I know he is your son by one of the women who belonged to this estate before Sextus's father bought it. By law, Primus is only one of Sextus's slaves, no different from the rest. When Sextus made me domina, he gave me authority to sell any I deem a problem. You will tell Primus I have decided to give him a chance to change rather than sell him immediately. You will tell him I expect nothing like this to ever happen again, or I will sell him."

A deep breath, and Antistes's jaw relaxed. But his eyes stayed glacial.

"You may go speak with him now and send him to join the herdsmen. Then you or Damalio, if you prefer, will inform the others about their new overseer."

"Yes, domina." Stone-faced, he spun and strode from the room.

Damalio rubbed his jaw as he watched Antistes leave, then turned a grim face toward Licinia.

"Was I too harsh with him?" She clasped her hands to stop the slight tremble.

He blew a slow breath out between pursed lips. "You have the right to do what you did..."

"But what? Tell me what you're thinking."

"You forced a proud man into a corner and overrode his authority without giving him a chance to act. He hates you for it. And you forced him to shame his son. Whether he will do anything...I don't know."

"But you think he might."

His tightened lips and single nod were answer enough.

"But I couldn't let what had happened pass without acting."

"No, you couldn't. But doing the right thing can earn undying enmity from those who don't think they did wrong."

"I made you his target, too. I'm sorry."

Damalio shrugged. "Two can watch for an attack better than one, and six can see more than two. I'll tell the men to be alert. Time cools most anger, even for men who don't follow our Lord."

She bit her lip. Sextus had sent her here for her safety. Had she just defeated his purpose?

Shoulders squared, she raised her chin. "For the sake of all our people, I know I did the right thing. We'll just have to pray that God continues to protect us from our enemies, both back in Rome and here."

*The Sabinus villa, February*

A single clap of Quintus Sabinus's hands brought his bath slaves to attention. "Leave us."

The last one closed the door behind him.

The scent of fresh-cut pine drifted across the heated tub in the private bath chamber. The tub walls were scalloped to allow up to a dozen men to drape their arms comfortably on them. Sabinus had persuaded numerous senators to support him while soaking there, but this afternoon, only Manius relaxed with him, enjoying the heat and the finest

Falernian wine before he must attend a banquet at the villa of Consul Articuleius Paetinus.

He swirled the amber liquid in his golden goblet. "When we get something to pressure Sextus Crassus, he'll become my source of Brutus's special vintage for honorable men." His lip curled at the word honorable. "That shouldn't be too long."

Manius adjusted the towel that padded the tub's rim, then climbed in to join him. "Your gift to Crassus has already found something useful?"

"Not yet, but he will. He's now trusted with a few routine matters beyond taking notes during the salutation."

Manius stretched his arms along the edge. "What has he learned?"

"Crassus has an interesting mixture of visitors. Everything from senators and ex-consuls to wealthy foreign merchants and recent freedmen." He took a sip. "An unusually high number of freedmen. It seems Crassus often frees men when they reach thirty and sets them up in business. If the business is legal for a senator, he might be a partner. If not, he makes no demands that they share profits with him as a 'gift' to avoid the restrictions."

Disdain showed in Manius's frown. "Surely he could figure out how to do it. Lucius Drusus Fidelis had that brilliant old man run his illegal activities by providing the start-up money as a gift and having the profits returned to him as gifts of land."

Sabinus sneered. "Drusus lost that option when his wife divorced him and fled with their daughter. The old man went with her after passing Fidelis's own ventures back to him as a gift to turn into land or gold. He'll never find another man he can trust like that one." He tipped his head and drained the last of the Falernian. "Drusus is another one who will never buy Brutus's wine without help."

"More wine?" Manius left a trail of wet footprints from the tub to the table where the wine pitcher waited. He filled both goblets before slipping back into the hot water.

Sabinus took the offered goblet. "He doesn't want his freedmen to come more than once a week unless there's a particular reason they need to speak with him. But when they do come, he knows about more than their business. Wives, children's names and ages, useless information like that."

Manius's brow furrowed. "Perhaps it pays off in loyalty. Licinius Certus was going to spy for me after I bought his debt, but somehow Crassus heard he was in trouble and gave him what he needed to pay with coin instead of information. I lost my source, so it's good you provided a better one."

"I had the slave renamed Custos before he was given to Crassus. Guardian, watchman…a suitable name for one entrusted with knowing the private affairs of a man." Sabinus chuckled. "But it can also mean spy."

Sabinus set his unfinished wine on the edge of the tub and rose. "As with any planting, time will tell how great the harvest will be. I have high hopes for this one." He climbed from the tub and scooped up a thick towel. "Time to prepare for the banquet." He grinned at Manius. "Who knows what information I'll harvest after Paetinus's guests drink too much?"

"Will he serve Brutus's vintage?"

Sabinus's snort made the corner of Manius's mouth curve. "Not likely."

# Chapter 20

## A Dangerous Pair



*The Crassus estate near Octodurus, early March*

Antistes's bimonthly report lay on Licinia's desk, ready to send to Rome. As soon as she penned her own letter to Sextus, Damalio would wrap and seal the packet and take it to the private courier service in Octodurus. He stood by the window, watching the mules grazing in the nearest field as he waited.

Eight days on horseback to Arelate, another week on a coastal ship to Portus and up the Tiber to Rome. Double that before any reply from Sextus could reach her. So much could happen in a month. A letter was a pathetic substitute for chatting face-to-face over dinner, sharing thoughts and laughing with her brother.

Elbow on the desk, she rested her cheek on her palm and gazed out the window. Clouds shrouded the mountain peaks, but the sun shone in a clear sky over the estate. Was Sextus looking up at a blue sky, too? Or was a cool rain falling from gray clouds in the city she used to call home?

Would Rome ever be her home again? Would she ever get to hold Camilla's son and see the joy in her dear friend's eyes as they watched little Marcus grow? Would they ever get to pray together again, giving thanks for all God's blessings and asking Him to touch and change the hearts of Brutus and Sextus?

A sigh drained Licinia's lungs. At least she still had Primula as her sister in Christ, and Damalio was a brother she could rely on for wise counsel and thoughtful action guided by the Spirit.

She shifted her gaze from the mountain heights to the papyrus before her and dipped the silver-tipped pen in the bottle of ink. Calvia Lucilla would write as Sextus Gratus, but beneath either alias, she was still Licinia.

> Sextus Licinius Gratus to Sextus Licinius Crassus, my noble patron, greetings. If you are well, then I am glad. I have much to tell you about changes in the state of affairs since I arrived.
>
> Damalio is now overseer, and the estate is following the practices of your estates in Italia. With better clothes and improved lodging, the workers are healthier and perform their tasks with greater diligence.
>
> We plan to add family quarters in the summer. There are some new slave unions, and some babies will be born by fall. When the babies come, the women will need a change of tasks so they can care for them. Damalio has found a market for the woven goods they will be making.
>
> The snow storms are finished here in Octodurus, although storms still whiten the foothills. I have been told it might frost for two more months. Some of the crops cannot be safely planted until then. It is certainly easier to farm in Italia.
>
> The mountain tops never lose their snow. The pass opens by June, but the way from Arelate is already clear. If you come to inspect the estate, which I hope you will do soon, you will be pleased with the changes Damalio has overseen. You chose well in sending him here.
>
> I hope all is well with all those for whom you care. I think of you often. May the most divine guard your safety.

She folded the letter and lit the sealing-wax candle. Three drops of wax fell across the flap, and she pressed one of Sextus's own signet rings into it. He'd given it to her because she couldn't risk using her own seal, and there had been no time to make one for Sextus Gratus.

There was more she'd like to tell her brother, but he'd warned her to be careful. What she could say and what she shouldn't say—some wisdom was needed in choosing both. Would Sextus wonder why she made no mention of his steward or why Damalio had replaced the steward's son as overseer?

Damalio was delivering the packet to the courier, but would Antistes find some way to see what she had written before it left Octodurus? He was working well with Damalio, even if his hostility toward her sometimes showed in his eyes. Over time, that should fade.

She rubbed her lip as the wax hardened. If Sextus asked, she'd have to explain, but she hoped he wouldn't ask. She had four men loyal to her against only God knew how many friends of Antistes. And with Primus's friends included, that number was even greater. If they decided to act against her, Antistes and Primus would be a dangerous pair.

Four men and God. More than enough for anything a German steward might try.

"Damalio." A smile curved her lips as he came to the desk. God had protected them so far. She had no reason to think that would change.

*The Baths of Trajan, late March*

Brutus touched the end of the cold-water pool two body-lengths ahead of Africanus and stood. His fingers swept the water off his eyelids as Africanus rose from the water beside him.

"You have to hold back when we spar." He grinned at his friend. "But in the water…"

Africanus's mouth twitched as he shrugged. "Perhaps you're part dolphin, master."

Brutus led them up the steps to collect their towels. He dried face and hair, then chest as he scanned the other bathers.

"Sextus Crassus is here. The sea is open, and it's been long enough his sister should be back."

Africanus raised one eyebrow.

"I know. Search, not hunt." Brutus tossed his towel onto the damp pile.

He sauntered along the edge of the pool until he reached his quarry. "Salve, Licinius Crassus. Fortuna has smiled upon us today that we should meet like this."

Crassus's social smile didn't quite warm his eyes. "Salve, Brutus. Fortuna often smiles, but why today?"

"Young Quintus Paetinus and three more noble sons have gone to their first tribune postings, so I have openings for new students. Your oldest son, is he not almost ready to begin his training? Most start when they're fifteen, but some start a little younger."

He offered Crassus his signature smiling frown. "I would be proud to claim I'd helped prepare the sons of Sextus Licinius Crassus for their service to Roma."

Crassus's social smile relaxed into a natural one. "I intend to begin my son's training as soon as he comes of age for it. He's almost fifteen now, and I can think of no one better to have influence over my boy than you."

Just behind Crassus, Manius Sabinus stopped midstride and pivoted on his heel to come stand beside Crassus.

"Salve, Brutus. My son has just turned fifteen. I've been considering where he should train, but if you're taking new students, I need look no further."

Brutus mouth shifted more towards a smile. The prospect of a man like Manius Sabinus wanting his son under Brutus's influence was incongruous at best and laughable at worst. "The training I provide goes beyond skill with weapons. My goal is to help young men grow in honor and devotion to Roma."

Sabinus blinked as his smile stiffened. Then his displeasure disappeared behind the mask of a politician. "That's exactly the kind of training I want for my son. Our family has served Rome for generations."

"Then send your boy to the Ludus Bruti any morning. I'm usually there. He and I can talk before the decision is made on whether what I offer is right for him."

Satisfaction overspread Sabinus's face.

Crassus took a step back, as if preparing to leave, but before he could excuse himself, Brutus had questions that needed answers.

"Now the sea is open, has your sister returned or said when she might?"

The change was subtle, but Sabinus's eyes first widened, then narrowed as Crassus donned his politician's mask.

"The last time I heard from her, she didn't name a return date."

Brutus kept his smile friendly. "When we talked in December, you mentioned her interest in Ephesus. Has she shared her impressions of that city yet? I've considered visiting it myself for some time. There are good ludi there and in Pergamum that supply the Ephesian games. I might add some men with eastern training to my *familia gladiatorii*. I might stop at Corinth for the same. Has she shared her impressions of Corinth or any other Greek city?"

"The things women write about in their letters aren't what most men would care about." Crassus's wry smile seemed forced. "What a woman might notice about a gladiator isn't what you would look for, anyway. Licinia enjoys the races, but she doesn't share my enthusiasm for the games. A noblewoman of her intelligence and decorum wouldn't write about gladiators even if she did."

Crassus's eyes didn't match his fake smile. He made a point of looking past Brutus at a cluster of senators by the tepidarium door. "I see someone I need to speak with is leaving. We'll speak more later about my son's training. Now if you'll excuse me..."

Sabinus's eyes followed Crassus as he strode toward the senators whose conversation had become more animated. Then his gaze flipped back to Brutus. "My son will probably stop in to speak with you within the week."

"I look forward to that. I must go as well. So if you'll excuse me..." He stepped back. "Vale, Sabinus."

"Vale, Brutus." Sabinus's smile was warm on the surface, but his gaze was focused on Crassus before Brutus could take a second step.

Brutus led Africanus through the tepidarium to the dressing rooms beyond.

When they were out of earshot, Africanus cleared his throat.

Brutus glanced at him. "What?"

"With his father's and grandfather's reputations, are you really planning to train Sabinus's son?"

Brutus scanned the men around him before answering. "That depends on whether I think the boy has been too corrupted already. If not, then I'll take him on. We can show him what honor looks like and maybe get him to value it. His cousin Titianus does." He rubbed his lip. "I regret that I didn't watch Marcus Drusus to see whether he was more like his brother or his father. If I had, maybe I could have changed his direction before it was too late."

Africanus drew a thumb along his jaw. "I watched both men as you asked Crassus about his sister. Before he answered, his eyes flicked toward Sabinus. He seemed to think Sabinus was too interested in the answers."

Africanus's brow furrowed. "Sabinus reminds me of a jackal. He watches for weakness. If he sees any, he's ready to pounce."

"I see the same thing." One corner of Brutus's mouth turned up. "You've never met Manius's father. Crocodile and jackal...they make a dangerous pair."

# Chapter 21

No Longer a Problem?



*The Crassus estate near Octodurus, late March*

Licinia stood by her loom in the great hall, working the shuttle through the warp yarns. With a comb, she tapped the yarn trailing from the shuttle up against the growing cloth. There was room for blanket-sized looms by the windows, and both the light and the view were good there. Primula hummed as she worked the adjacent loom.

After parking the shuttle on the shelf on the top crossbar, Licinia stepped back to examine her work. "I never gave any thought to how people made the different color yarns I used in Rome. These dark and light blues, the pink, the two shades of green...everything but the red —Alba told me they all come from the woad plant." Her mouth curved. "Four months ago, I would have thought it ironic that a woman who was an expert with dyes was named 'white.' But everything isn't Latin, and naming her 'elf' in Germanic makes perfect sense. That little smile she gets whenever I praise her work reminds me of one of the nymphs in the mural in Father's library."

The click of hobnails announced Antistes's arrival before he stepped into the great hall. Licinia's brow furrowed, but she relaxed it before he could see. It was an odd time for him to be dropping in.

"Antistes." She graced him with her social smile. "What brings you here mid-morning?"

He flipped one side of his cloak behind his shoulder. "Something I'm sure you'll approve of. Ursula is with child, and Primus wants to take her as his wife."

One quick glance at Primula...her own surprise was mirrored in her maid's raised eyebrows. Ursula was the reason Primus had been demoted from overseer to herdsman.

She kept her smile in place. "And what does Ursula want?"

His nostrils flared before he stopped the sneer. "What she thinks is not important."

Licinia raised one eyebrow. "Yes, it is, and I would not be surprised if she is less than eager. Primus trying to force himself on her when she hadn't welcomed his advances is why he's a herdsman instead of overseer now."

His jaw twitched as his eyes chilled.

She lifted her chin. "The girl will decide since it wasn't her choice to have a baby coming. She hasn't been expecting long, so there is no hurry for making this decision. If Primus can persuade her...without any force or threat... that he's a man she'd want as her husband, then I'll have no objection to the union."

Antistes straightened. He was more than half a foot taller, but his height didn't intimidate as much as he thought. "The child is my grandchild, and I have a voice in this matter."

That drew Licinia's deliberate snort. "The poor girl was the plaything of however many men you let use her. You can't know it's Primus's child. You gave her no choice in who would be her baby's father, but she will have a choice over whether she wants your son as a husband to help raise her child."

A slight backward tilt of her head, and she projected her superior rank. "You are steward here, but her baby is one of Sextus's slaves regardless of who fathered it. The child remains Sextus's property unless he decides to sell Ursula or her child to you. Until he does, I will make the final decision as domina, considering what is best for all. You may tell your son that he must gain her approval of him if he is to have her as his wife."

As he stared at her, Antistes stretched his jaw to relax it. "Yes, domina. If you'll excuse me..."

She tipped her head. "Of course."

Head high, he spun and strode from the room.

Primula blew out a slow breath. "The venom in his eyes when he looks at you, mistress. It's not always there, and it doesn't last long when it is. But it's definitely there today."

Licinia squeezed the back of her neck. "Damalio has remarked on how working as a herdsman has improved Primus's attitude. He's become a reliable worker who gets along well with the others. Perhaps

Ursula will decide she wants the union, too, and this will no longer be a problem. Then Antistes won't feel he needs to be challenging my authority."

Primula sucked air between her teeth.

"At least not over this." With a weak smile and a shrug, Licinia turned back to the loom.

*The Flavian Amphitheater, Rome, late March*

Throngs of men surged around Sabinus and Manius as they approached the Flavian Amphitheater. With ten of Sabinus's slaves encircling them, they strolled within the moving human fence that kept the rabble away. The lunchtime executions were over, and the serious contests between the professionals were about to begin.

"Septimus is starting to train at Antonius Brutus's ludus." One corner of Manius's mouth lifted. "He came home from his first training session yesterday nearly bursting with excitement because he met Africanus."

Sabinus's glanced at his son. "Brutus's Nubian bodyguard?"

"His undefeated Class 2 who fought as *murmillo* and *secutor*. Brutus retired him from combat a few years ago. Now Brutus rents him out as a problem solver and uses him as a trainer and his personal sparring partner."

"Why did my grandson find that so exciting?"

"The best of the oldest students get to train with him. The speed of thrust and parry astounded Septimus. I remember watching him fight six or seven years ago, and he was impressive. He's still mentioned in any discussion of which gladiators have been the best of all time." A wry smile lit his eyes. "Septimus plans to be among those who get good enough to spar with Brutus's best before his first tribune posting."

Sabinus chuckled. "The young think power is something physical, but we know better. Power comes from acquiring information about your enemy's vulnerable points and knowing when and how to use that knowledge."

Manius's eyes scanned the crowd just past the bodyguards. "Has your man made any progress on finding the missing sister or some other useful weakness?"

"Nothing definite, but Custos has noticed something odd. Horse couriers carry letters all winter, so there should have been some correspondence from Crassus's sister. But there's been nothing since Custos started working there. Even now, with the sea open for easy delivery of letters, nothing has come."

"Has Crassus written to her?"

"Not that he's seen, but he doesn't see everything his master sends out. A small number of letters still go through Crassus's secretary."

Manius's brow furrowed. "So perhaps she didn't travel east, like he's led people to believe. At the baths, Brutus asked her opinion of Ephesus and Corinth and when she would return. Crassus said she'd hadn't told him a date and that Brutus wouldn't be interested in what a woman would write. He didn't actually say she'd been to either city."

"Perhaps she hasn't. Crassus has hidden her somewhere. She's either not writing to him because she's somewhere nearby and he sees her, or she's writing under an alias. Custos expects to be trusted to file correspondence in the estate archives soon. Then he'll have a chance to see who began corresponding since last November. Where those letters come from will be where we'll find the sister or at least pick up her trail."

As they were funneled toward the amphitheater by the growing crowd, Sabinus raised a hand in greeting to a pair of senators converging on the same entrance. His guards stepped apart to allow them to enter his circle of protection.

Soon Crassus would no longer pose a problem, He'd be among those who sought to join Sabinus's circle, whether that noble Roman wanted to or not.

# Chapter 22

SEEKING THE WEAK SPOT

*The Ludus Bruti, early April*

Brutus backed away from Africanus. With the back of his hand, he wiped some sweat from his forehead. As he raised his gladius and prepared to re-engage, a movement along the wall to his left caught his attention.

An eager-eyed Septimus Sabinus, fully dressed after his beginner's lesson with Pugnus, stood beneath the overhanging balcony. The giggles and whispers of the young women who leaned on the railing above him were easy to ignore. They'd only come to watch Brutus's men spar. The rapt attention of a young man Brutus hoped to guide toward honor was not to be wasted.

"Septimus, I want to speak with you after this."

The youth nodded, and Brutus refocused on Africanus. Shield ready and sword raised, he stepped forward. The thud of sword on wooden shield and the clang of metal on metal echoed across the sand while he and his best fighter traded thrusts and strikes.

When sweat beaded his forehead once more, he stepped back. "Enough for today."

Africanus saluted with his sword before heading toward the armor room. A slave scurried over to take Brutus's shield, but he kept the sword. He snatched a towel from the bench before joining Septimus by the wall.

"Enjoy the show?"

Septimus's eyes were on Brutus's gladius as he nodded. Brutus offered it, and the youth took the sword as if it were a precious work of art.

"You were amazing. I want to fight like that."

"When you've practiced with my men for a few years, you probably will. It's not just how you handle the sword. It's how you watch your opponent that makes the difference in battle between a good swordsman and a dead one. They'll teach you both."

Septimus ran his thumb along the unsharpened edge of Brutus's blade. "My father is just like your best gladiators. He's always looking for an opponent's weak spot, even when it's not obvious. Like Sextus Crassus's sister."

The corner of Brutus's mouth turned down. "The arena is not a good example for how to live life. Every contest on the sand has a winner and loser, and it doesn't matter what you do as long as you win. But men of honor help each other and look for the path that is a win for all when that's possible. If you have to do dishonorable things to win, it's better to lose."

Brutus pointed toward Africanus. "He could kill me any time he wanted, but instead he helps me get better by holding himself back to fight just a little better than I do. The honorable man understands the power he holds and controls how he uses it."

Septimus's gaze lifted from the sword to Brutus's face. "I told Father I get to watch you two fight. He says Africanus holds back because he's your slave, and he knows that he'd be punished if he hurt you, even accidentally."

"That's not why. It's respect, not fear." Brutus's mouth curved up at this first of what should be many teachable moments. "Respect and friendship."

The boy's eyebrows shot up. "Friendship with a slave?"

Brutus glanced at Africanus, who toweled his hair as he stood watching a new student spar with Pugnus.

"The worth of a man isn't defined by his family, his wealth, or his power. It's his honor, and Africanus has more honor than many who rule the Empire."

He rested his hand on Septimus's shoulder. "Your cousin Titianus trained with me. He never fought well enough to spar with Africanus. But he's a man of unquestionable honor, and I take more pride in claiming him as my student than in most of the young men whose skill with the gladius let them fight my best man." He squeezed the shoulder before dropping his hand. "I hope I can say the same of you before you go to your first tribune posting."

Septimus nodded. "But I still want to be able to fight with Africanus."

The boy's eagerness triggered Brutus's smiling frown. "I watched you yesterday. It will take hard work, but I think you can get there."

Septimus's grin pulled Brutus's own mouth toward another smile. One final swipe with the towel, and he tossed it into the basket. "Train hard, and we'll see. Take my gladius to the armorer. Ask him to show you how to care for your own sword properly before you leave."

A wave of his hand dismissed Septimus. Making short thrusts with the finely balanced weapon, the boy disappeared into the room where weapons and armor were stored.

"Africanus."

His friend uncrossed his arms and turned from watching Rufus train a young Claudian. Brutus tipped his head toward the doorway by the armor room. Africanus followed him down the hall and into his office.

"Close the door."

Brutus settled into his chair and pointed at the guest chair. Before sitting, Africanus turned the chair sideways so he could stretch out his legs. From the deep side-drawer, Brutus withdrew two gold-lined silver goblets. They were followed by a flagon made of cream-colored clay that held his special vintage that few were allowed to buy. After filling each goblet halfway, Brutus raised his. "Another good match."

He leaned back in his chair, both hands wrapped around the goblet and resting on his stomach. "Septimus sees more than many his age."

He took a sip and let it linger on his tongue.

Africanus swirled his wine. "What makes you think so?"

"We spoke of power and how the honorable man controls how much he uses." He took a sip. "He likened his father to a gladiator, always watching for the weak spot of his opponent." One more sip. "Like Sextus Crassus's sister."

Africanus's spine straightened, and he drew his legs back against the chair. "Weak in what way?"

"He didn't say, but I already know the answer." His nostrils flared. "It's her faith in the Christian god. It's why Crassus sent her away from Roma. I wonder how soon Manius will discover that." The prospect drew Brutus's smile.

"I hope not soon." Africanus's eyebrows lowered. "Mistress Camilla would be grieved by her death. Licinia Crassa won't live long after that discovery."

Brutus's lips tightened. "I hear what you're not saying. I told you

I'd keep it a search to know who she was, not a hunt to kill her. I have no intention of telling Sabinus anything we've learned. Our evidence is only circumstantial, but Christians usually confess when asked. What we know could start someone asking."

Hatred for the woman who had corrupted his beloved would always burn hot within him. Knowing what Licinia Crassa was gave him power to destroy her, but an honorable man didn't use his power simply to please himself. He hadn't promised Camilla in so many words that he wouldn't hurt her friend, but it was the broader spirit of his promise, not the limited words, that he would keep, even if he didn't want to.

*The Circus Maximus, mid April*

Surrounded by a circle of bodyguards, Sabinus had walked half the length of the Circus Maximus with his son and grandson when Septimus pointed at a pair of young noblemen.

"Grandfather, may I watch the races with Gaius and Lucius today?"

Sabinus waved him off. "That's fine. Don't bet too much."

Septimus's grin drew Sabinus's smile. "I won't. As you say, never bet high if it isn't a sure thing, and even then, be careful."

The guards parted, and Septimus hurried toward the doorway through which his friends had just disappeared.

Manius's brow furrowed. "Why did you do that? He's missing an opportunity to spend time with one of the leaders of Rome just to be with his friends."

"The boy's still more colt than stallion, and an impression of immaturity is easier to prevent than to erase. There will be plenty of time to introduce him to our colleagues when his intelligence won't be overshadowed by his impulsiveness."

They walked past their usual entrance that led to the best senatorial seating beside the track.

"Septimus has never watched from the sponsor's box above the starting gates, but there will be other opportunities." He grinned at his son. "One of the advantages of doing a favor for an ex-consul or a future one. Annius Verus has served twice and likely will again." Sabinus's mouth twitched as he suppressed a grin. "I have Hadrian's ear, but Verus has both his ears."

Manius's head bowed slightly, and Sabinus smiled at his son's appreciation.

"I knew Paetinus is indebted to you, but I was unaware Verus has become a special friend."

"I'm always adding to my circle of reciprocal friendships. Even ex-consuls, maybe especially ex-consuls, need friends able to get things done that they don't want to do themselves." He rested a hand on Manius's shoulder. "Or to learn the answer to a question it would be unwise to ask themselves."

With the smallest tip of his head, Manius directed Sabinus's gaze to three senators approaching them. Sextus Crassus walked in the middle.

"One question I'd like answered is how to maneuver Sextus Crassus into a position of...obligation."

"That shouldn't be long." Sabinus's lips tightened as he watched his son's political rival, then relaxed into a smile. "Our man is now trusted with sorting the correspondence that comes in. He's caught the scent of something worth following."

He paused, watching the eagerness grow in Manius's eyes.

"What is it?"

"There's still been nothing from Crassus's sister. Custos sees virtually everything Crassus sends out, and he hasn't written to her, either. Our man sees who comes to the salutation, and none seem to be reporting on the sister. She must be using an alias, and his next step is to figure out what that is."

Manius fingered his lip. "When we were talking with Antonius Brutus about training our sons, Brutus asked whether Crassus's sister was back. Crassus said she wasn't, but that question bothered him. He avoided any real answer when Brutus asked what his sister thought about Ephesus and Corinth and excused himself as quickly as he could."

Sabinus's mouth curved. "It's nearly impossible for a scrupulously honest man to lie when he needs to without giving himself away."

"But when you think about it, Brutus's question seems odd." Manius squeezed the back of his neck. "Why would an equestrian gladiator owner be so eager to speak with Crassus's sister? He's been heard to say he has no intention of ever remarrying, and she's expected to marry a senator now that her father's dead."

"There's some connection." Sabinus's gaze locked on Crassus as his party turned. "The first week Custos was in place, Crassus sent a blanket to Brutus for his new son." Sabinus pinched his lip as his gaze followed Crassus through the circus entrance. "A gift from one honorable man to another upon the birth of his heir —I saw nothing suspicious in that." The pinch turned into rubbing. "Maybe his sister made it, but why would she want to give Brutus anything?"

"Perhaps she knew his dead wife, and she really gave it to the baby."

"Perhaps." Sabinus tossed the thought away with a shrug. Why women did what they did often made no sense, and one giving a baby gift to another was hardly something he could use against Crassus. The two immediate questions were where Licinia Crassa was now and why her brother had sent her there. His spy would soon answer the first, and the answer to the second would give them the power over Crassus that Manius wanted.

They reached the end of the circus and knocked on the door to the stable yard where the racers awaited their turn on the track. A slave belonging to Verus opened the door for them to pass, then closed and bolted it to keep the eager masses out. Sabinus headed for the stairs to the boxes over the gates.

"A moment, Father. Rogatus drove for the Greens last time, and his surprise win filled my purse nicely. I want to speak with him."

Sabinus crossed his arms and nodded his permission. Manius strode to a stall where the charioteer stood with one of the stallions that would be drawing his chariot.

"Salve, Rogatus."

"Salve,..." Rogatus raised his eyebrows.

"Manius Flavius Sabinus. I saw your last win. It was stunning. May Fortuna smile as you race as hard and win today."

"I always race hard and go for the win. Finishing second never satisfies. There's no glory in second place." Rogatus's grin dripped confidence. "You'll be a wealthier man if you bet on me today."

One corner of Sabinus's mouth turned up. Rogatus was wrong. There could be plenty of satisfaction from coming in second if your enemy came in third.

# *Chapter 23*

## Too Content with Less

*The Octodurus estate, mid April*

Antistes's mule waded through rivulets of cold water at the lower edge of the pasture. Snow melt always turned the lowest part of the field boggy, but he was meeting Primus to share a lunch by the cluster of boulders where the ground was dry and the stones held the sun's heat. The ewes assigned to Primus's care had their noses buried in the lush spring grasses and scarcely glanced at him as he rode through the flock to join his son.

His mouth curved down. They used to share dinner every night in the main house. That woman's decision to demote his son had robbed him of that.

A wave greeted Antistes as Primus, staff in hand, pushed away from the boulder he'd been leaning against and approached.

"It's good to see you, Father." He waved the staff toward the rocks as he gripped the mule's halter. "Nothing soft to sit on, but I'll take warm over soft any day."

Antistes didn't fight the frown as he swung his leg over the animal's neck and slid off. "You shouldn't have to stay out here in nasty weather. If Calvia Lucilla hadn't taken offense at what's normal at most estates, you wouldn't have to."

Primus flung one side of his cloak behind his shoulder. "At least she ordered good winter clothes for all of us. What Damalio bought for everyone in Octodurus is as warm as anything I wore as overseer. The weavers will be able to make plenty of what we need for next year."

"Perhaps she and her men will be gone before then, and you'll be overseer again."

Primus shrugged. "Being a herdsman isn't as bad as you think. It isn't hard, and I work with better men than I realized when I was overseer. The nights at the men's lodge when I'm not on duty with the flock are more enjoyable than getting drunk in town." One corner of his mouth lifted into a wry smile. "I tried to kill Fidus that night, but he never holds a grudge. He's a good friend now."

Antistes's brow furrowed. His son should not be so content with less than what he had, with so much less than what he'd given him.

"When I was overseer, I thought I knew what I was doing." Tightened lips accompanied one shake of Primus's head. "But I didn't. I thought fear worked best, but Damalio doesn't use fear. He looks for what each of us do well and lets us do it at least some. He praises people who go beyond what they must do to simply finish a job to what it takes to do a job really well."

Primus's chin lifted. "A lynx had already taken five lambs and was trying to get a ewe that was about to deliver. I chased it off. Then I tracked it and killed it with my bow. Damalio brought fruit pastries to our dining hall that night. Enough for everyone because he said it was a celebration of my bravery."

His eyes warmed. "Ursula was impressed." What had been a smile headed toward a grin. "She stops for a few words when I eat there. I expect she'll want to be my wife before our child is born."

Antistes forced a smile of his own. "I'm glad to hear it. Why the domina insisted Ursula have any say is beyond understanding, but at least the girl has enough sense to see how lucky she is that you want her. Any woman should want you."

Primus's chuckle raised Antistes's eyebrows. "Probably so. Damalio told me he's going to give me more responsibility this summer. I like knowing I earned that myself." His eyes turned serious. "You can be proud of me again."

Antistes rested his hand on his son's shoulder and squeezed. "I never stopped being proud of you. I need to get back, so let's eat."

His son's broad smile did nothing to soothe Antistes's well-concealed irritation as he opened the sack containing their lunch. His son spoke too admiringly of the man who should never have replaced him as overseer. That he was getting back some of what had been stripped from him—that wasn't something Primus should be grateful for. It was his by right as Antistes's son, and no letter from Sextus Crassus giving some woman authority over the estate made that any less true.

Antistes shrugged off his cloak and dropped it on a chair as he approached the triclinium door. Calvia's voice was followed by a soft response from her maid. The maid served Calvia at meals, but that was no excuse for her sitting to her mistress's left and conversing like a friend.

His first view of Calvia seated in his rightful place at the head of the table drew a smile that concealed the banked coals of resentment. He walked toward his seat at the foot. Foot, head—the table was turned so they would look the same to a visitor, but the real power over the estate should be at his end of the table, not hers.

Calvia turned from her maid and smiled. "You're later than usual. Has it been a good day for the estate?"

"It has, domina." That title grated every time he used it.

Footsteps behind him were followed by Damalio walking past to take the chair at her right hand.

Antistes didn't look at her as he pulled out his chair and sat. She didn't repeat her question, but had she asked him or her favorite she'd made overseer?

Damalio should be dining with the rest of the slaves. He shouldn't be sitting beside her in the place an honored guest or good friend might take. Primus had done the same when he was overseer, but it was because he was Antistes's son. No other overseer would have.

Olga entered with a steaming pork stew and ladled a portion into his bowl. He lifted a spoonful and blew on it, waiting to place it in his mouth until Calvia picked up her spoon.

She spoke to Damalio as if he were an equal whose opinion she valued, even if he did always answer with 'domina.' She had him sleeping just down the hall from her, as if he were a guest instead of her slave.

He took a sip of the estate's last vintage. It had been a good year for wine. A good year for him until she came.

What was the real relationship between her and her man? Damalio was handsome and well-muscled. When she first put him down the hall, Antistes thought he must have served her in bed, but he'd watched for anything he could use against her by reporting it to Sextus Crassus, and there was no sign of physical attraction in either direction.

Maybe it was only respect. As much as he hated to, he had to admit Damalio knew how to get slaves to work hard without resenting what he was demanding, and what he did to improve the treatment of the slaves had improved their health and productivity.

Mutual respect wasn't something he could use to unseat Calvia Lusclla from her position as domina and return things to what they'd been before she arrived. But he was a patient man, and something he could use would surface. No one could stay above reproach forever. What would get Crassus to withdraw her domina power?

Why did she even have it when she wasn't related to him? Without that understanding, opposing her might just get him replaced by Damalio, as his son had been.

Maybe she was Crassus's mistress, and he wanted her out of Rome so his wife wouldn't find out. If she got involved with another man, that might do it. Or if he could make Crassus suspicious even if she didn't. Short of getting her killed somehow, there was no obvious solution.

Over the rim of his goblet, he watched Damalio. Her favorite's usual response to what Calvia was saying was a quick tip of his head. Then he glanced at Antistes. Their eyes met, and Damalio's lips straightened. His mistress spoke again, and he turned back to her with a nod and smile.

Antistes took a sip and swirled the wine in his mouth. With the man who seemed to notice everything watching over her, how could he cause her death without getting caught?

*The Sabinus villa, mid April*

Sabinus strolled from the triclinium to his library with Manius beside him. A quiet dinner with his favorite son and a few games of tabula were less exciting than a banquet among rivals and allies, but much more satisfying.

He took two gold goblets and a cream-colored flagon from a cabinet.

"You acquired some of Brutus's private vintage?" Manius's eyebrow rose. "Which of his supposed men of honor gave it to you?"

Sabinus's only answer was a grin as he poured the amber liquid first into Manius's goblet and then his own. He lifted it in a silent toast and took a sip.

Manius swirled his goblet. "I thought Brutus's special vintage was red."

A slight shrug accompanied Sabinus's smile. "He has both red and white."

One sip, and Manius's eyebrows dipped. "This is just like your best Falernian."

Sabinus chuckled. "You have a well-trained palate. That's what it is. But our man in the Crassus townhouse brought me a discarded flagon. As long as the wine I put in it is excellent, who could say it isn't really Brutus's vintage for the honorable?"

He returned his son's silent toast and settled into his chair. "Our spy will soon bring us something more valuable than a flagon. He's now trusted with filing Crassus's correspondence, so he has unfettered access to Crassus's business archives."

"Has he learned anything useful yet?" Manius began placing the game pieces on the board.

"Crassus has several estates north and south of Rome, one in Hispania Tarraconensis, and one in Alpes Poeninae. The one in Hispania is on the coast near Valentia. The Poenina estate is just across the Pasa Alpis Poenina near Octodurus. Each estate sends Crassus a report every month.

"Custos filed the most recent in the archives, but when he was summoned to get them, Crassus slipped one sheet that bore a separate wax seal into his desk. Our man is going to try to find out which estate that came from and whether earlier ones are in the archives."

"Excellent." Manius placed the final piece and pushed the board toward Sabinus. "Knowing which estate...that might tell us where the sister is."

Sabinus fingered a rondel, rolling it over and over between his fingers "Exactly, and once we find her, it won't take long to know why he's hidden her there."

Sabinus leaned back in his chair. "Make the first move, son. You won last time, and winners deserve to go first."

He steepled his fingers. In every contest, there were winners and losers, and if Crassus thought he could keep his honor and still win against a Sabinus, he was a fool.

# Chapter 24

## A Secret Worth Hiding?

*The Ludus Bruti*

Brutus leaned against the wall under the balcony, watching his gladiators train a dozen young men. Sons of consuls, senators, and a few equestrians —the future leaders of Roma. They would be better men after training under him.

Septimus Sabinus turned, and his face lit when his gaze settled on Brutus. Gladius in hand, he trotted over.

"Are you going to the Circus tomorrow?"

Brutus met him with a smiling frown. "I was considering it."

"Don't bet on the blues if you do."

"Something going on with that faction?"

"Their lead charioteer was at a party at our house. He likes his wine unwatered, and after a few goblets, Father was asking about the team he'd be using, which horses by name. He said he wasn't sure. His best stallion had just come back from the stud farm. He'd been off his feed and tired too quickly during training. They hadn't decided yet whether he would be in harness for that race."

"That's not good."

"Not if you support the blues. I like the greens." Septimus shrugged. "After he left, Father told me it would be easy to do something to a stallion when it was servicing mares. He mentioned a few things someone could give a horse that might do that. Then he said he wouldn't be betting on the blues this time. He only bets when he can be sure of the result."

Brutus's mouth shifted toward a frown. "The winner of a race is never a sure bet."

Septimus grinned. "But my father says the loser might be if the right person wants another team to win."

"What your father told you...those things are not worth remembering. It's wrong to deliberately harm another man's horse. It's better to lose with honor than to win by cheating."

Septimus head tilted. His brow furrowed; then it relaxed as he nodded his agreement.

"We'll be sitting in the sponsor's box tomorrow. If I ask Father, I'm sure you could join us."

Brutus kept his face passive. Sitting in the sponsor's box with Manius Sabinus could be misinterpreted as approval of the man. That was the furthest thing from the truth, and he wouldn't tarnish his own reputation by association if he could help it.

"Thank you for the offer, but I usually sit with friends."

Disappointment dimmed Septimus's smile. Brutus slapped the boy's arm. "You did well with Pugnus today. It won't be long before you move up to Fortis."

Satisfaction replaced disappointment. "Soon Fortis and someday Africanus."

"Perhaps. I hope you learn to fight well enough to face him, but it's honor, not swordsmanship that will make me proudest of you." He waved the boy toward Pugnus. "A few more rounds today will get you closer to your goal."

As Septimus resumed a fighting stance, Brutus headed down the hallway to his office. His smiling frown shifted toward a smile. A lot more sparring would get Septimus closer to his goal, but it was more conversations like this that would get him to Brutus's.

*A vineyard east of Rome, late April*

The spring sunshine felt warm on Sabinus's back as he and Manius rode uphill toward their newest vineyard. At the vineyard's edge, Manius dismounted and handed him the reins. As his son walked along the first row, he lifted the leaves aside for a better view of the flowers.

The farther Manius walked, the deeper his frown grew. "I let Catullinus give me this land to clear his debt. He showed me production reports that he said were from the last three years, but the number of flower clusters I'm seeing...these vines won't yield what he claimed."

"Did he cheat you?"

"I'm not sure. I'll have to ask my steward whether my other vineyards are having the same problem. It's been drier than normal."

Sabinus's stallion fidgeted, and he leaned over to pat its neck. "If he did, he can be shown the wisdom of giving you something more to correct that mistake."

"He doesn't seem stupid or reckless. Only a fool would expect to cheat either of us and not regret it. Some years simply yield less profit than others."

"Speaking of which, our spy reported something curious."

Manius raised his eyebrows. "Something useful?"

"Something suggestive. He was reading some older reports as he filed the latest ones. In the January report from Crassus's Poenina estate, the steward apologized for the extra expenditures for housing and clothing the slaves and claimed they were ordered by the new domina, Calvia Lucilla. Custos said he thought the steward might harbor some resentment."

Manius took his reins from Sabinus and mounted. "Domina? Why would a Calvia Lucilla be domina of any Crassus estate?"

"That's the right question. Perhaps she's a mistress he's been hiding. His wife is Octavia Laena, and she's not a woman who would tolerate infidelity if she knew about it. Her family is important enough to crush his political ambitions if she wanted revenge."

A satisfied smile curved Sabinus's mouth. "And if this Calvia is what I suspect, we have what we need to ensure his cooperation. I'll have one of my agents check into her as soon as we return to Rome."

Manius swung his horse toward the villa and nudged it into a fast walk. "Catullinus invited us to stay for dinner. I told him we needed to be back in Rome, but I said we would stop for a drink before riding back."

Sabinus fell in beside his son. As they moved to a trot and then a canter, he let his smile grow. Placing Custos in their enemy's house had been a wise move. Sextus Crassus, the man of unquestioned honor, had a secret worth hiding after all.

*The Octodurus estate, late April*

Licinia sat at her desk and steepled her fingers. What should she tell Sextus this month? The questions she'd like to ask about his boys, about Camilla and her baby...these were not something freedman Gratus could put in writing.

She swept her palm over the papyrus sheet before picking up the gold-tipped pen that had been Father's. Damalio stood by the window, leaning against the frame as his gaze swept the pastures and vineyards that formed a tapestry of different greens. As soon as she finished, he would take her letter and Antistes's report to the courier in Octodurus.

> Sextus Licinius Gratus to Sextus Licinius Crassus, my noble patron, greetings. If you are well, then I am glad.
>
> Were you to visit, which I sincerely hope you will, you would be pleased with the changes we have made since I arrived. Damalio has proven an able overseer, and your people are both happier and more productive. I asked Antistes what the output from the weavers was last year, and I'm pleased to report the numbers this winter are higher by one fifth. There will be enough for our own people and some left over to sell.
>
> Now spring is fully here, it is time to start building some family lodging. We will start with six couples and add more as needed.

Pen poised over the ink bottle, she turned her gaze on Damalio. "By next spring, how many babies do you think we'll have here?"

"If all goes well, I expect four will have come with a few more on the way." He turned from the window as he spoke. Then his gaze locked on something behind her as his smile froze.

"The drawing of the cottages for the slave families and the cost estimate for building them—they were left on my desk."

Antistes's voice startled her, and she pivoted in her chair to find him not two feet from her, holding out a papyrus sheet.

His gaze was riveted on her letter. A letter from Sextus Gratus, not Calvia Lucilla.

Trying not to look hurried, she took the sheet and placed it atop her unfinished letter. Then she offered Antistes her most gracious smile.

"Thank you. Sextus is always interested in the welfare of his workers. He'll be pleased to receive the details of our plans."

His mouth twitched. "What gives pleasure to the master...that I'm always glad to provide, domina." With a tip of his head, the steward spun on his heel and left the room.

Damalio crossed his arms, and his mouth curved into a frown.

"Do you think he saw anything?" She nibbled her lip.

"He was looking at the sheet long enough to see the greeting, maybe more, before you covered it."

"Will that be a problem?"

He drew air between his teeth. "For him to know you write with an alias? If we were closer to Rome, I'd say it was. But I doubt he knows anyone you know in Rome, so who would care if he told them?" He shrugged, and his mouth relaxed into a slight smile.

She pulled her letter from beneath Antistes's drawing. "Quite so." A slow flexing of her shoulders, and the tension drained away. "Just a few more sentences and some sealing wax, and you can take everything."

"Yes, domina." Damalio turned back to the window.

Licinia dipped her pen in the inkwell. If her faithful guardian wasn't going to worry about what Antistes just learned, neither would she.

# Chapter 25

## THE PERFECT PLACE FOR SEPTIMUS

*Manius Sabinus's townhouse, early May*

Sabinus strolled into the stableyard, and the slave preparing the horses for Manius, him, his manservant, and his bodyguards began to work faster.

Manius strode through the door connecting peristyle and stable. "I'm sorry I've kept you waiting, Father. I just got home. After you left the banquet, the entertainment turned wilder. I spent the night."

"As I hoped you would."

Sabinus had excused himself early, leaving Manius to watch what happened in the wee hours of the party. He wasn't so young anymore, and before the long ride to Tibur to inspect the progress on Hadrian's new villa, the extra sleep was welcome.

He smiled at his favorite son. "The new senator from Hispania... will he align with us?"

The corners of Manius's mouth lifted. "I believe so. It was an evening well spent."

Sabinus held out his arms, and the manservant unwrapped his toga. His slave folded it, slipped it into its tote bag, and secured the tote to his saddle. He did the same for Manius.

"Anything else, master?"

Sabinus shook his head and mounted his gray stallion. The young animal fidgeted and tossed its head while he waited for Manius to mount, but that was exactly the kind of horse Sabinus preferred. His thin hair and lined face made him look like an elder statesman, but he would ride an animal with a spirit to match his own as long as he was able.

"Go." A single word was sufficient to start the first pair of bodyguards through the gate. He and Manius fell in behind them, followed by his slave and two more guards.

Sabinus glanced at the sky—mostly blue with a few scattered clouds. "It should be a pleasant day to inspect the progress on Hadrian's new villa. He appreciates my private reports on what the builders are doing. The old villa has been in Vibia Sabina's family for many years, and she was fond of it. Incorporating it into the new buildings instead of tearing it down reconciled her to the changes. When all is finished, it will be fit for an emperor of Rome."

"If we're only touring a construction site, why bring togas?" Manius's hand flicked away a fly that kept circling.

Sabinus leaned forward and patted the stallion's neck. "We'll ride on to Tibur, visit a couple of ex-consuls, maybe a senator or two. I'm sure one of them will invite us to spend the night." He flashed his son a smile. "A man must always be prepared to dress for a banquet."

Manius returned the smile. "I always like crossing the bridge over the falls. The roar of the river, the rainbows in the spray, such uncontrollable power. Power beyond what even Hadrian can aspire to, no matter how strong his legions are." His smile broadened to a grin. "But power, even if limited, still satisfies."

They rode a few blocks in silence.

"Too many people on the streets today." Manius's nostrils twitched. "And too many need to visit the baths." He tipped his chin at the men riding ahead of them. "Where did you buy the four Germans?"

"Puteoli. I prefer guards who have no circle of acquaintance in Rome. That makes them harder to bribe."

"Circus, games, baths—Brutus always has his Nubian with him. He doesn't need more than that. Septimus keeps telling me about watching Brutus spar with his best trainer. He claims it's like watching two gladiators fight from only ten feet away." The fly landed on his shoulder. One slap, and his fingers flicked the carcass off. "Septimus wants me to come watch him spar. Brutus told him he's ready to move up to a second-level trainer."

"Your boy is making good progress, and Brutus's ludus is the perfect place for him to form some useful friendships. So many sons from the best senatorial families train there."

A wry smile tugged at the corner of Sabinus's mouth. "I expect Sextus Crassus's oldest to be among them. Speaking of whom, I've had one of my agents trying to discover what he can about Calvia Lucilla. What he's learned is odd."

Manius's eyebrows asked the question as they rose.

Septimus glanced over his shoulder. The guards rode some distance ahead, and his manservant was far enough behind. But he lowered his voice anyway.

"There's a senator's wife who owes me some favors for keeping one of her secrets. She can't find anyone who's ever met a Calvia Lucilla." His brow furrowed. "One of Crassus's trusted clients is Calvius Lucillus, but he has no living daughters. His sons are thirty and twenty now. His wife lost some between those two, a daughter and a son. My man found a record of the daughter's birth in the archives, but not of her death."

The corners of his mouth turned down. "I'm wondering whether Lucillus knows there's a woman using his daughter's name at a Crassus estate."

"Hmm." Manius's smile came slow, then broadened. "I'll see what I can learn when we get back to Rome."

Sabinus leaned over to slap his son's arm. "We both will."

They passed through the city wall at the Porta Esquilina. The traffic on the Via Tiburtina thinned past the fortress of the Praetorian Guard, and the two tall Germans leading the party kicked their horses into a trot. It was almost twenty miles to the villa, but half a day in the saddle was still a pleasure when his best son rode beside him.

*The Ludus Bruti, early May*

Brutus escorted Sextus Crassus's son down the hallway from his office to the edge of the arena. "Give your father my greetings."

"I will. Vale, Antonius Brutus." The boy flashed a smile and headed up the stairs that led to the balcony and out to the street.

Brutus was moving toward the armor room when a sweaty Septimus Sabinus stepped back from Pugnus and trotted to his side.

"Was that Licinius Crassus?"

"It was."

"Is he going to be training here?"

Brutus's mouth curved down. "Why do you ask?"

"My grandfather said I should become friends with him, and I wasn't sure where I could do that."

The frown deepened. "Why is your grandfather telling you whom to choose as a friend?"

"There are several Grandfather wants me to spend a lot of time with. He says they'd be good companions for the games and the circus." A shrug was followed by a grin. "And for private parties. Grandfather likes to know what the sons and grandsons of his friends are like. He says the more you know about a man's family and friends, the easier it is to work with him."

"Who are some of the others?"

Septimus rattled off a list of names, and they were all sons of political opponents of Sabinus. All were young men who would be future leaders of Roma, and most would probably train at his ludus.

"Did he say why those?" Brutus kept his growing suspicion out of his voice.

"No, but Father and Grandfather like to know everything about anyone important. They say knowing the private affairs of a man makes it easier to reach an agreement that gets him to help you. That it leads to mutual understanding...but I'm not sure why Grandfather laughed when he said that."

"Do you think trying to make a man your friend just so you can use him is honorable?" Brutus crossed his arms as his eyebrows dipped.

Septimus rubbed his lip. "Probably not."

One corner of Brutus's mouth rose. "Solid friendship is built on looking out for each other. On being there for your friend even when things go badly for him." He glanced at Africanus, who was sparring with one of his former students who was home on leave from his tribune posting. "Especially when things turn bad. You can trust a friend to back you up when trouble comes and to tell you the truth even when you don't want to hear it."

Septimus kicked the sand. "I don't have any friends like that."

"Not yet, but as you grow into manhood, I expect you'll find one. But you might not find him among the young men your grandfather wants you to cultivate. A loyal friend can come from an unexpected place."

A smile tugged at Brutus's mouth as Africanus slapped his opponent's arm when they finished sparring.

Septimus's brow furrowed. "You said Africanus doesn't fight his best with you out of friendship."

"Friendship and respect."

"Is he that kind of friend? He's only your slave. Father doesn't trust any of ours."

"He's earned my complete trust over the past ten years. He always tells me the truth, and he would never betray me."

"Father says no one can be trusted completely."

"Not many can, but there are some."

"But how can I find one?"

"Be that kind of man yourself, and one will be drawn to you." He slapped the boy's arm. "But don't be in too big a hurry to trust someone completely. Trust that goes both ways takes time."

Brutus rested his hand on Septimus's shoulder and squeezed. "Pugnus is waiting. Show me some of what you've learned."

After flashing a grin, Septimus trotted back to a stern-faced Pugnus and assumed a fighting stance.

Brutus leaned against the wall under the balcony and crossed his arms. Africanus snatched a towel from the bench and strolled over to join him.

As Africanus toweled off, Brutus's smile grew. "We made the right choice taking on Septimus. His grandfather is trying to make him into a snake like his father is, but the right question is enough to get the boy to think for himself. He usually finds the right answer."

Africanus flipped the towel over his shoulder and joined Brutus against the wall. "You'll have two dangerous enemies if you turn the boy into an honorable man."

Brutus shrugged. "I'm only doing what his father said he wanted—helping his son grow in honor and devotion to Roma."

Africanus raised an eyebrow. "When you're in a room with a snake, you'd better pay attention when it starts to coil, whether you think it plans to strike you or not."

"I don't have to worry. I have you to look out for me." Brutus slapped his friend's arm. "Get dressed. I'd like to get to the baths while Crassus and Manius Sabinus are still there. I've seen an eagle take a snake in the Alpes. That's no contest, but it's not so certain who will win when it's two senators of Roma."

# Chapter 26

## A Father's Care



*The Crassus Estate, first week of May*

Licinia sat at the head of the table, eating her last spoonful of breakfast porridge with Primula beside her. At the foot of the table, Antistes finished his meal and wadded up his napkin before dropping it by his bowl. Although his short remarks and brooding silences gave neither of them pleasure, he insisted on joining her for morning and evening meals.

Damalio entered the room, a satisfied smile lighting his eyes. "Good morning, domina."

"It is." She waved her hand at the chair beside her. "Join us if you haven't already eaten. You look pleased this morning."

He settled into the chair and took a roll. "I believe you will be, too. Primus tells me Ursula has agreed to become his wife, and he asked me to seek your approval."

Antistes squared his shoulders. "She'd be a fool not to."

Licinia glanced at Antistes, then returned her attention to Damalio. "What does Ursula say about it?"

"I haven't asked her, but she doesn't avoid him like she used to."

Her brow furrowed. "I want to speak with the girl before I give my permission."

Damalio took another roll from the basket and rose. "I'll get her."

Antistes leaned back in his chair. Arms crossed, he showed no sign of following Damalio out the door.

Licinia wiped her mouth and folded her own napkin. "You may leave. I want privacy with Ursula."

"Primus is my son, and it might be my grandson the girl bears. I have a right to stay."

"No, you do not." She tipped her head back enough to look down her nose at him. "If you'd taught your son how to treat the women properly, that might be so. But I want Ursula to feel she can speak freely, and that won't happen with you here."

He gave her a dagger-eyed look, unsuccessfully masked with a frigid smile. "As you wish, domina." Chin high, he pushed the chair back and strode from the room.

Licinia sucked air between her teeth as Primula rose to clear the dishes. "Damalio says it's unwise to deliberately get him mad, but I'm sure he'd agree Ursula won't feel safe sharing her real thoughts if Antistes is listening."

Damalio returned with Ursula trying to hide behind him. Her eyes widened as her gaze swept the room. Serviceable and far from elegant by Roman standards, but the upholstered chairs and Greek vases on white limestone stands dazzled the girl who'd slept on a stone floor until five months ago.

Licinia offered a smile. "Come here, Ursula. You have nothing to fear. I simply have a question for you."

Damalio stepped aside and waved the girl forward.

"Thank you for bringing her, but I'd like to speak with her alone."

"Yes, domina." With a quick smile to reassure the girl, he took a step back before he turned and left the room.

Ursula still hung back, eyes fixed on the mosaic floor.

"Come closer. I won't bite." Palm up, Licinia reached toward the girl and motioned her forward.

"Yes, domina." Ursula came within five feet, then stopped.

"Damalio tells me Primus thinks you want to marry him. Is that true?"

The girl's eyes met hers for a moment, then her gaze retuned to the black and white tiles. "Yes, domina."

Her lips said yes, but Ursula stood rigid as a soldier on guard duty. Had she spoken her agreement because she meant it or because she was afraid to do otherwise? Licinia had reduced Primus to herdsman, but if she ever left, Antistes would make him overseer again.

"I know you had some problems with him before. Are you afraid to refuse him because of what he might do if he were overseer again?"

Ursula raised her head, eyes wide like a startled deer. "No, domina. He's different now."

"Different?" Licinia raised one eyebrow. "How?"

"He used to like us to be afraid of him." She dropped her gaze to Licinia's feet, then raised them to her face. "And we were. But he's not like that now."

A shy smile curved her mouth. "Gebhard...he led the herdsmen when I was a little girl. He's old now and slow sometimes. Primus...he watches how Gebhard is doing and helps him."

Her gaze shifted to the window and the mountains beyond. "Primus...he carves wood, mostly animals. Alfbern...he's seen 9 years, and he watches after we eat. Primus asked if he wanted to learn." Her eyes warmed. "Primus shows him how, praises what he does, even when it's not so good. Shows him how to do it better, like a father would." Her smile grew. "Like my baby will need."

She bit her lip to subdue the smile. "Primus says my name means little bear. He carved a bear cub. He gave it to me when he asked me to marry him last night."

"He does sound like a different man. A much better man." Licinia broadened her smile, and Ursula's shyness melted under its warmth.

"When he or his friends from town came for me, they did what they wanted. I had no choice." Ursula rested a hand on her bulging belly. "I can't know if it's his child, but he tells me I can't know it isn't. He says he doesn't care if we ever know, anyway."

Licinia glanced at Primula, whose smile was almost as big as Ursula's. One quick nod from her maid confirmed her own decision.

"If Primus has become the kind of man you describe, I gladly give my blessing to this union."

"Thank you, domina."

Ursula's breath caught. She looked at her hand, still resting on her belly, before turning glowing eyes on Licinia. "My baby...it moved!"

"Perhaps your baby heard that you and Primus will be making a home for the three of you."

"I hope so, domina."

"Next Sunday morning during your half-day rest, we'll have a special ceremony for you and Primus to declare before all of us that you are a family now. I will tell Sollus to prepare a wedding feast for the midday meal to celebrate your union and the baby who is coming."

"Thank you, domina." The girl was beaming.

Licinia's own smile broadened to match Ursula's. "You may return to your weaving. If you see Damalio, you may tell him what we decided and ask him to come to me."

"Yes, domina." A quick dip of her head, and Ursula almost danced out the door.

Licinia's smile dimmed. As a senator's daughter, Roman law would only let her marry a man who'd been born free, and custom dictated that man must be from the noble orders. As Calvia, she wore the stola of a married woman, but she would never find a Christian nobleman to marry. Never have the chance to feel her own baby move within her.

Memories of Camilla swirled in her mind. How they laughed together the first time Camilla's son kicked. How Camilla had guided Licinia's hand onto her stomach to feel it.

How big was little Marcus now? Did he have his mother's eyes and smile?

And even though she rejoiced at Ursula's happiness, she couldn't completely quench the flicker of envy for the joys she would never know.

*Brutus's villa near Roma, 14th of May*

It was late afternoon when Brutus, with Africanus and Rufus behind him, rode into the stableyard at his villa near Roma. Brutus swung his leg over his stallion's neck and slipped off.

"Extra oats for him. We rode hard."

Stabularius dipped his head after taking the reins. "Yes, master."

Brutus stretched and flexed his shoulders. Africanus reined in beside him, and Brutus rested his hand on the horse's neck.

"A good trip." A slap on its shoulder before lowering his hand, then he looked up at his friend. "With another heavy crop for the Capena and Ocriculum vintages and those new boats that can handle the Tibur's current, I expect profits well above other wines coming by wagon to Rome."

Africanus slipped from his horse, but Rufus remained mounted.

"Rufus, you can go." The disappointment that flitted across Rufus's face shifted Brutus's mouth toward a smile. "But the food here is better than at the ludus, so you can choose whether you leave before or after dinner."

"After, master." With a big grin, Rufus reined his horse toward an empty stall.

Brutus tipped his head toward the portico door. "My office." With Africanus beside him, they walked through the peristyle garden and settled into the chairs on each side of the desk.

"All seems well at the local estates, so we can leave for Lousonna next week." Brutus picked up a stylus and drummed it on a wax tablet. "I'll be taking Marcus with me."

Africanus drew a slow breath through his teeth, triggering Brutus's frown.

"I gather you still don't approve."

"Travel always has some risk, even more so for a baby." Tightened lips accompanied a single shake of Africanus's head. "I think it's unwise to take him on a long journey while he's so young."

Brutus leaned back in his chair as he crossed his arms. "There is no way I'm leaving Camilla's baby where I can't protect him." He leaned forward to rest his arms on the desk. "I don't want to have her boy near Roma during the summer months when so many die of fever. We'll stay at Lousonna until at least the beginning of October. That will get us back to Italia near the end of fever season but while the sea is open. We can go to the Liternum estate until late November, when it should be safe to come back here."

Africanus's lowered eyebrows shouted his disapproval of the plan more than any words could.

Brutus shrugged. "The trip won't be difficult. I'd rather cross the pass, but we'll stay on a coastal ship as far as Arelate. We'll buy a raeda there and go upriver to Vienna, then cut across to Genava. It's only a few miles up the lake from there. I rode that route with Father when I was Septimus's age, and it's good roads all the way from the coast."

"But Marcus is about to be crawling everywhere. Babies are harder to care for when they start moving on their own."

Brutus's hand swept that warning aside. "We'll get something installed to block the door opening at his level. Then he can crawl around the carriage as much as he wants. Vera and Nutrixia will be watching him the whole time."

He pointed at Africanus. "You traveled with me often when yours were babies. Your wife managed to care for them all by herself when you did. If Dorcas could handle three small children without any help, surely two women can handle one baby."

He glanced out the door toward the stairs that led to Camilla's empty room. "Summer by the lake will be better for Marcus than staying near Roma where he might take a fever and die."

Africanus's mouth opened, then closed without a word. But his eyebrows remained lowered.

Brutus leaned across the desk and slapped his arm. "I appreciate your concern, but I do know what's best for my son, at least in this matter. It will be a good trip and a good time at the lake. We'll be laughing at all your worries when we return to Roma in the fall."

*The Crassus townhouse, Rome, 14th of May*

Custos folded the sheets and placed them under the pillow on one end of the couch in Vicarius's room. With arms crossed, he watched the dozing secretary.

Vicarius was lucky. The assistant he'd replaced had been run over and crushed by a chariot in an 'accident' that wasn't one. The galloping drunk who'd swerved to hit Vicarius as he crossed the street had only broken the secretary's collarbone.

With a groan, Vicarius rose and rubbed his face with his left hand. The physician had placed his right arm in a sling with strings that tied around his back to keep it from moving and shifting the broken bone.

Custos picked up a fresh tunic. "Left arm through the hole, other arm inside—that should protect well enough."

"Hmph." Vicarius's frown deepened as Custos dropped the tunic over his head. "Organizing the salutation for the next two months without my toga—disgraceful for a man who is now a citizen. But with this collarbone and my right arm in a sling, I need my left hand free."

Custos fastened the belt and adjusted the tunic's folds under it so left and right sides matched. "Did Master Crassus's father free your father or you?"

"I was freed by the elder Crassus within a week of my thirtieth birthday. But the young master would have done the same. Father and son both prefer to free a worthy slave early rather than in a will after they're dead."

Vicarius slipped his feet into his sandals, and Custos knelt to wrap the laces around his ankles and tie them. "That's more generous than most. I don't know of anyone my last master freed early."

As Custos rose, Vicarius's frown flipped to a smile. "You've done a fine job here. I won't be surprised if you're freed while still a young man. Master Sextus usually waits until thirty so he can bestow citizenship with the manumission."

Custos smiled at the good man whose trust he'd been sent to betray. "I'll try my best to be worthy of that."

The older man pointed at the desk covered with tidy piles of wax tablets and stacks of papyrus. "After the salutation, Master Sextus will want to look at the monthly estate reports. First stack of tablets, second stack from the left of papyrus."

"I'll carry everything for you." Custos balanced the tablets on his hip and scooped up the papyrus. All had been opened and flattened... except one. It bore an inscription "for Sextus Crassus only" and was sealed with wax imprinted with Crassus's own seal.

Vicarius's hand reached past him to grasp the scroll. "I'll take that one."

Custos's pulse sped up. He'd been warned of Sabinus's displeasure that he'd found no chink in Crassus's honor after so many months. At last, this might be something.

"Is that from one of the overseers? Will I be filing it with one of the estate reports?"

"No. It's from Gratus. Master Sextus will attend to it himself."

As he followed Vicarius toward the tablinum where Sextus Crassus awaited his clients, colleagues, and friends, Custos fought a smile. Why would anyone be using Crassus's own seal on a private letter? Who was this Gratus, and which estate had included his letter with its report?

The last assistant had been killed so he could be slipped into the house as the replacement. Another could just as easily replace him. Sabinus was a dangerous man to disappoint, and Custos's time to deliver what he wanted could be running out. But with Gratus's letter, that was about to change.

# Chapter 27

## LEAVING FOR LOUSONNA

*The Ludus Bruti, Ides of May*

Brutus closed the wax tablet and handed it to Felix, lanista of the ludus in Roma. "I've sent letters to my lanistae in Florentia and Luca telling them to consult you as needed. Cellarius will be gathering the reports from the estates and the shipping office in Ostia. If anything needs my special attention before I return in the fall, he'll contact me by horse courier. If a problem arises here, he'll help in whatever way he can."

Felix took the tablet. "If a training slot opens, do you want me to fill it?"

"You can. I'll make a list of those who've asked for the next one, but they might have started elsewhere. Just go down the list until you find one."

He leaned back in his chair. "I'm taking Rufus, so you'll need to spread his students among the other trainers."

"Anything else, master?"

"No."

Felix had almost reached the door when Brutus straightened. "Wait. Is Septimus Sabinus training today?"

"He's with Pugnus now."

"Don't let him leave before I speak with him."

Brutus pulled a tablet from the drawer. Twelve men had asked him to train their boys; he would list them in order of their service to Roma. While he wrote, Africanus's deep voice echoed in the hallway as he spoke with Felix about Pugnus or Fortis checking on his wife and children daily.

That caused a flicker of regret. Many times, he'd taken Africanus from his family for one to three months. But this time it would be six. A long time for a father not to see his sons. Perhaps next time, since he'd be taking Marcus, he would have Africanus bring his family as well. Two raedas could travel just as easily as one, and Vera could learn about mothering a growing boy from Dorcas.

His friend entered the office and settled into the chair across from him.

"If she wants, Dorcas can take your children and stay at the villa. Felix can arrange it."

"I'll tell her tonight."

Fast footsteps in the hallway were followed by Septimus stepping into the room. "You sent for me?"

Africanus rose and pointed at his chair before moving to the wall. Septimus came to the desk but remained standing.

"I did. I'm leaving tomorrow for my estate in Germania. I expect to return in the fall." The boy's smile dimmed. "I'm taking Africanus and Rufus. Felix tells me you'll be moving up to Fortis next week. If you work hard with him this summer, you might be ready to train with Rufus when we return."

"Rufus?" The boy's big smile returned. "I'll work however hard it takes to be ready."

"Good. I've been pleased with how much you've improved in the short time you've been here." He rose and walked around his desk. With a curl of his fingers, he summoned Africanus from where he leaned against the wall. After resting his hand on Africanus's shoulder, he fixed serious eyes on the boy. "It's a fine goal to become good enough with a sword to spar with Africanus. It's an even better goal to become a man of honor like him."

Septimus's happy eyes turned serious as well, and the boy nodded.

Brutus's smiling frown shifted into a warm smile. "Always ask yourself what a man of honor would do when faced with a difficult choice."

"I will."

Brutus slapped the boy's arm. "Go back to Pugnus. I need to finish something before I leave, but I'll watch you a while before I go."

Africanus crossed his arms and listened until the retreating footsteps faded to silence. "It's hard to grow up in a snake pit without becoming a snake, but I think Septimus might."

"I'm counting on it." Brutus grinned at his friend. "And it will be your fault as much as mine. So, if the crocodile and jackal are unhappy about it, you'd better do a good job of protecting me."

His joke didn't draw the smile Brutus expected.

"I always do the best I can." Africanus's eyes cooled. "I hope that will be enough."

"It will be. Spend the rest of today and tomorrow with your family. I asked Galbius to arrange passage for seven leaving day after tomorrow. We'll spend tomorrow night at his house."

"Seven?"

"Vera and Nutrixia for Marcus, Burdonarius to drive the raeda, and the three of us." He rubbed his neck. "You're right...only six. A babe in arms doesn't pay for passage."

"I'd charge for one if I was the captain." Africanus's nose twitched. "A babe in napkins...the extra washing, the smell." One corner of his mouth lifted. "Maybe I'd charge double."

"It's not as bad as you claim. Vera will manage it without any problem." Brutus waved his hand toward the door. "Go. Enjoy your time with Dorcas, and I'll see you in Ostia tomorrow night."

Brutus settled into his desk chair after Africanus left and poured himself some of his best vintage. He leaned back and took a sip.

It would be good to get away from Roma for a while. Away from the villa, where every room held memories of Camilla talking, laughing, smiling at him, her eyes warm with love. Away from the grove where he'd spent so many nights with her head on his chest as they counted the stars. Away from the grave where his beloved lay.

And maybe, where the snow-capped mountains reflected in the lake he had never shared with her, he could get away from the pain of feeling so alone.

*Port of Genua, May 21*

The corbita still rose and fell on the waves as it sat in the harbor in Genua, waiting for the rowboats to pull it to a pier. For Brutus, the quiet slaps of the waves against the ship's hull were a soothing sound. But today they were accompanied by the sound of Vera vomiting.

Yet again, he was holding Marcus as Vera's already-empty stomach kept her at the railing on the far side of the ship.

The retching sounds stopped, and Vera's tunic rustled behind him. He turned.

"I'm sorry, master." Vera still looked greenish as she held out her arms.

"I'll keep him for a while. You can lie down until we're ready to unload."

"Thank you, master." Gratitude flooded her face. With one hand on the railing to steady herself, she headed for the cabin.

Galbius had booked two rooms: one for him and Africanus, one for the women and Marcus. Rufus and Burdonarius slept on deck with the crew and a handful of other passengers.

The women's room had been used less than he expected. Both Vera and the wet nurse had spent much of the last four days at the rail. Except when Marcus was being fed, Brutus and Africanus had passed him back and forth between them. An older woman who'd boarded the ship at Luna chuckled whenever she looked at Africanus, the un-defeated Class 2 whose frown could make grown men tremble, holding a sleeping baby.

When Africanus reached for Marcus, Brutus shook his head. "I'll keep him a while longer."

Africanus returned his hands to the railing. "Seasick for four days, and nothing helped. That's worse than when I took Aulus Secundus and Marcus Drusus to Luna four years ago. A ginger root mostly solved Marcus's problem, and Aulus is a natural-born sailor."

Brutus blew out a breath. "We're only halfway to Arelate. I'm not going to spend another four days as nursemaid like this. We'll buy a raeda in Genua and go over the pass. That will shorten the trip as well. It should only take one more day to drive over the pass from Genua than it takes to go up the Rhone from Arelate. With four days less at sea, we'll even arrive in Lousonna three days sooner."

Africanus drew air between his teeth. "Half a week quicker might sound good, but taking a baby over the pass...I don't think it's a good idea."

"But I do." Brutus's lips tightened. "All military roads are built for supply wagons. We've never crossed the pass when we haven't seen carriages. Even with the carriage, it should only take us a day to reach the summit from Augusta Praetoria. Quintus Paetinus is tribune there. He wrote last month about missing his bouts with you. He can autho-rize a night in the *mansio* at the summit."

Marcus reached for Brutus's nose. Brutus intercepted the tiny hand and blew on its palm, drawing a giggle. "From there, a hard day's drive will get us to Octodurus. We can let the mules rest for half a day and still get to Aemilianus's estate at Penne Locus before evening. I'll send Rufus ahead to let him know we'll be arriving late in the day so he'll be ready to receive us."

"It would be better to take the Via Julia Augusta along the coast to Forum Julii, then cross-country to Arelate instead." Africanus squeezed the back of his neck. "I have a bad feeling about crossing the pass with your boy."

"Based on what?" Brutus's hand swept the warning aside. "We both know the gods aren't real. Omens and oracles and prophesies are only ways to manipulate people. Going by land to Arelate would add an extra week to our journey. I'm not willing to do that. Over the pass will be fine."

Africanus's mouth straightened. "As you wish, master. We've bought good horses in Genua before. The horse trader can tell us where to buy a sturdy carriage and mules strong enough to pull it over the mountains. I'll tell the other men there's been a change of plans."

Brutus's nod sent Africanus toward the ship's stern, where Rufus and Burdonarius lounged with their backs against the gunwale. But as Africanus walked away, Brutus still saw the disapproval in his friend's eyes.

## *Chapter 28*

### The Accident

*Pasa Alpis Poenina road near Octodurus, Kalends of June*

The sun rose early in June, and Brutus was glad. That meant many hours of sunlight for the drive from the summit to Octodurus. The road up from Augusta Praetoria was easy enough for a well-conditioned horse and for men accustomed to riding one. Africanus had bought three fine mounts in Genua and two sturdy mules. But Brutus had underestimated what that climb could mean for a mule team pulling a raeda carrying three adults and several small trunks.

A night in the mansio at the top of the pass had rested their mules enough to continue, but they had labored more pulling the raeda up from Augusta Praetoria than he'd expected. Other carriages had passed them often, so the problem wasn't the road. But his animals had come from the coast. They'd been pulling a heavy load for eight days by the time they reached the foothills, and they weren't used to the thin air of an Alpine pass.

The descent had been easier. Roman roads usually ran straight, but the wagons that accompanied a marching legion were too heavy for the steep grade that would require. Many shorter stretches with lesser slopes ran across the face of the mountain and connected with short, sharp curves. What never slowed a horse required caution with the raeda.

But now they followed an easy grade straight across the side of a steep hill. The road was mostly flanked by leafy trees that arched across it, creating a green tunnel. But there were open stretches where the hill dropped steeply beside them, offering sweeping vistas of ter-

145

raced vineyards, valley fields and pastures, and the mountains beyond. A milepost at the side of the road proclaimed them within four miles of Octodurus. One more hour, and they'd arrive at the reputable inn where he always stayed.

Marcus's fussy cry in the raeda behind him was quickly silenced. Hunger or a wet bottom...Brutus knew the sound as well as any nursery slave now. He wouldn't miss it when they reached the estate.

With eyebrows dipping, Africanus rode beside him.

Brutus leaned over and nudged his shoulder. "Cheer up. Two more days, and Vera can take him beyond our hearing when he fusses."

"That's not what's wrong. It's...a feeling. I sense danger."

"Danger?" Brutus's hand swept the view before them. "A good road in a peaceful province. The only hard part was crossing the pass, and that's behind us now. It couldn't have been a smoother journey, even if we'd gone the way you wanted."

"I agree, but...there's something." Africanus's lips tightened. "I can't tell what, but it's there."

Brutus cocked his head. "I know you sense danger others miss. It's why you always come with me." He shrugged. "But this time...it's nothing a few nights rest in our own beds at the estate won't ease."

"Perhaps." A slight shake of Africanus's head contradicted his word. "I'm going to check with Rufus."

Brutus nodded his approval, and Africanus wheeled his horse to join Rufus where he trailed some distance behind the raeda.

They entered another tunnel of trees. Patterns of light and shadow danced on the road ahead as a breeze rustled the leaves. Ahead, the tunnel opened to a sky with fluffy clouds scattered like the sheep on the hillsides.

The sunshine made Brutus squint as he rode clear of the trees. To his right, a steep slope led from the road edge to a grassy stream far below. A skylark flew up from the meadow, making tighter and tighter circles until it hovered fifty feet away and burst into song.

It drew his smile. A plain brown bird with a magnificent song. Camilla had loved them. A reminder, she said, to never judge only by what you see. You must listen with your heart.

He turned his eyes from the hovering bird. How could a man listen with his heart when the best part of it had been ripped out of him?

Crack!

The sound turned him in his saddle and drew his eyes to a towering beech. From near its top, a dead branch began its descent, first dropping straight, then bouncing off branches and boughs as it fell.

And when it cleared the last bough, it struck the rump of the left-hand mule.

A fear-filled bray, and the animal lunged against the harness. Its teammate startled and joined it as the first broke into a run.

Brutus's heart leaped to his throat as Vera and Nutrixia shrieked while Burdonarius hauled back on the reins, to no avail. He spun his horse and maneuvered to grab the reins or halter as the terrified mule passed.

But just as he reached for the reins, his stallion lunged ahead, into the path of the mule.

The impact knocked his mount off its feet. As the animal toppled sideways and rolled on his leg, Brutus heard the snap as the bone broke. Then he felt the pain.

But that was nothing compared to the heart-wrenching horror of watching the mules lunge over the edge of the road, dragging the raeda with them. It tilted at a crazy angle, almost straightened, then tipped too far again as it disappeared from view. A man's yell, a horrendous crash, and then...

Rufus and Africanus thundered past him, and their horses jumped the low curb in pursuit.

Waves of pain washed over him as he lay beside the rock retaining wall on the uphill side of the road. He rolled to his stomach, where he could get on his hands and one knee. The rocks gave good enough handholds. With his good leg and the arm strength born of years of sparring, he managed to rise. With one leg still able to bear his weight, he hopped toward what he didn't want to see, dragging the useless one.

The women had stopped screaming, and the silence ripped into him. Were they quiet because they were dead? Was Marcus crushed and lifeless in the splintered wreckage?

He clamped his jaw, not against the screaming pain in his leg, but against the rising panic that he'd killed Camilla's son. His selfish impatience, his stupid stubbornness when Africanus urged caution—those had brought them over the pass.

When he reached the edge of the road, the sight before him triggered a swirling mix of relief and fear.

The carriage lay on its side, the pole wrenched free of the yoke. Only some leather straps still tied it to the mules and kept it from tumbling downslope to the stream below. Rufus and Burdonarius gripped each end of the yoke, joining the straining mules in holding the carriage in place. Africanus lifted Nutrixia through the window and set her beside him.

But where was Marcus? Brutus froze. He swallowed hard, and then a high-pitched wail reached his ears.

Marcus lived! But was he badly hurt?

The nursemaid was waving her arms and pointing at the window. Africanus gripped her upper arms, and she stood still. A few quick nods, and she stepped back. He climbed atop the carriage, lowered himself through the window, and disappeared.

Brutus glanced at his leg and cursed the broken bone that was keeping him from running to help.

A small trunk was pitched through the window. Then another. The carriage shifted, pulling the mules and his men a few steps down the slope.

The snap as one of the straps broke sounded too much like a whip. With one anchor gone, the carriage twisted, but the other straps still held.

Then Vera's head and shoulders appeared. She climbed out the window onto the carriage sidewall, and Nutrixia helped her down.

Lungs that were ready to burst from holding his breath released an explosive sigh when Africanus appeared and handed a bawling Marcus to Nutrixia. As the two women climbed the slope with his son, a deep breath turned into a deeper sigh.

Africanus was halfway out the window when the next strap broke. He hoisted his seat onto the sidewall and was pulling his legs out when the third strap snapped.

He had just jumped to the ground when the carriage broke free, smashing the yoke pole into him as it hurtled downhill to shatter on the rocks beside the stream.

Africanus tumbled and rolled several feet. He lay sprawled where he stopped, his hand clutching his left side. As Burdonarius led the mules back to the road, Rufus ran to him.

Brutus's gaze darted between Marcus and Africanus, desperate to know whether either had been badly hurt.

"You need to sit, master." Burdonarius's voice pulled him back from the precipice of panic to the reality of pain. "Lean on me."

Brutus wrapped his arm across his shorter driver's shoulders and welcomed the arm around his chest that kept him standing.

"Vera! How is Marcus?"

She was limping as she reached him, but she took Marcus from Nutrixia and cradled him. The baby's cries stilled. "He's fine, master. He was only frightened." Her eyes shifted from Marcus's face to his leg and widened. "You need to sit, master." She tipped her head toward a boulder beside the road. "Take him over there."

With his driver as a crutch, Brutus hopped where she pointed, and with Nutrixia's help as well, he sat with his back against the sun-warmed stone.

"Go see if Rufus needs help with Africanus, then tend to the horses."

A dip of his head, and Burdonarius did as ordered.

Brutus patted the ground beside him. "Sit, and give me Marcus."

Vera settled beside him, and he held out his arms. After pinning his son to his chest, he closed his eyes. A grimace of pain squeezed his eyes shut, but he opened them quickly to find a smile on Marcus's lips. A broken leg would heal, but if his boy had died... He'd barely survived losing Camilla. The poets claimed a broken heart could kill a man. If he'd lost their son, he would have proven them right.

Africanus reached the road, supported by Rufus. With stumbling steps, he came to the boulder, and Rufus helped him sit. Eyes closed and a hand clutching his left side, he drew a breath and held it. His teeth clenched until he released it.

"Rufus."

"Yes, master?" His gladiator looked as worried as Brutus felt.

"It's not far to Octodurus. Borrow a wagon from the first estate you pass and get back as quickly as you can. We need the gladiator physician as soon as possible."

Rufus trotted to where the driver had tied the horses and galloped away.

Africanus opened his eyes. "Is Marcus hurt?"

"He's fine. And we will be, too, after the physician finishes with us. My leg's broken. Your ribs are. But broken bones heal."

The corner of Africanus's mouth twitched. "I know broken ribs. It's more than that."

"Maybe not." Brutus's jaw clenched, but not from the pain in his leg. "We'll see what the physician says."

Africanus's gaze settled on the baby with his small arms stretched across Brutus's chest. Marcus reached toward him, two tiny teeth showing as he grinned. Africanus grimaced as he reached over where five small fingers could wrap around his large one. He shook the wee hand before lowering his arm.

"Your son is safe. That's what matters." Africanus's eyes squeezed shut, then opened. "And he'll grow into a fine man with you to show him how."

"As you're showing your sons."

Africanus closed his eyes.

Brutus held Marcus with one arm and rested his hand on his friend's thigh. "As you'll keep showing them. And I'll keep learning from you."

Africanus nodded once, but his eyes didn't open. "We've both seen enough death to know when it's coming." His eyes squeezed tight before he opened them to gaze at the mountains. "I'd hoped to show my boys the Alpes someday. At least once, every man should ride where the eagles soar."

"We'll bring our sons here together. You can't give up."

"And a slave must obey his master." Africanus's weak smile forced Brutus to fake one, too.

"So must a friend. I'm not ready to lose my closest one."

"Dorcas and my children..." Africanus's breath caught.

"I'll care for them."

"Your respect and friendship...that has been better than freedom."

"You'll always have them...and today I give you freedom as well."

"I was born a free man." One corner of Africanus's mouth lifted as he turned his head to meet Brutus's gaze. "It's good to die one."

"But not yet." Brutus slapped his friend's leg, and Africanus's wince made him wish he hadn't. "Rufus will be back soon. Hold on, friend."

A half-smile, a nod, and Africanus closed his eyes. "I'll try."

Brutus watched his friend's chest rise and fall, hoping it would continue while dreading it would stop. And the dagger that had sliced open his heart as he held Camilla for the last time pierced his chest once more.

# Chapter 29

## Gifts of Love and Friendship

*The Crassus estate*

Licinia stood with arms crossed, mirroring Antistes's stance. Why must her brother's steward try to turn everything into a contest of wills? If not a contest, at least a discussion in which he spoke the final words.

"We can build separate huts or a single building divided into several apartments. Since Primus and Ursula will be among the first moving into the couple's housing, perhaps we should ask their opinion." Licinia's suggestion flipped Antistes's frown into a smile.

The steward relaxed, his arms dropping to his sides. "He'll finish his turn watching the flocks before dinner. We can ask him then."

Damalio pointed at the courtyard wall between the kitchen of the main house and the women's quarters. "We can open a gate there. If we choose the single building, it can form part of the wall for a small courtyard to keep the little children safe."

The hoofbeats of a galloping horse spun all three toward the courtyard gate. A brawny, red-haired man reined in on the other side of the vegetable beds. He slipped from his lathered horse and trotted toward them, stepping over each row of cabbages. A dagger hung at his side, and one hand gripped a sword to keep its scabbard from bouncing as he approached. Damalio stepped forward, placing himself between Licinia and the armed man.

"Why are you here?" Antistes moved beside Damalio as the man slowed, then stopped.

"An accident a mile up the road. My master's leg is broken, his other bodyguard hurt. I need to borrow a wagon to take them to the physician in Octodurus."

Antistes's gaze raked the man from head to boots and back again. "Not from this estate."

Licinia slipped past the protection of her two men. "Of course we'll help. Lepus!"

Lepus rose from the garden bed he was tending. "Yes, domina?"

"Get a wagon hitched, and put a mattress and pillows in the back to soften the ride."

Like the rabbit he was named for, his eye's widened, and he froze.

"Fidus is mending a harness. He'll take care of it." Damalio's calm words launched Lepus toward the stable. "Are there only the two injured men?"

"No. The master's baby is with them with his day nurse and wet nurse and their driver. It's the raeda that went off the road."

"Will the wagon and my raeda be all you need?" Licinia's words made the stranger's shoulders relax, but they didn't erase all worry from his face.

"Yes, but we need to hurry." The stranger's hand squeezed the back of his neck. "Africanus is hurt bad."

Damalio stepped up beside her. "Then I'll take the raeda. Fidus is alone in the stable today."

"Bring them here as quickly as you can." Licinia's smile failed to calm the stranger's anxious eyes. "We'll be ready for them."

"Can you help harness a team?" The redhead nodded. "Then come with me." Damalio strode toward the stable, the anxious bodyguard matching stride for stride.

Licinia turned to Antistes, whose tightened lips betrayed his irritation with her contradicting him. "We'll decide about the new buildings later."

"Yes, domina." He turned and walked away.

As Licinia hurried toward the main house, a sigh drained her lungs. People were in desperate need of help. Help that was easy for them to give, and Antistes had refused to help them.

*Thank you, God, for having me in the courtyard at the right time. Be with the injured men, and bring them all safely here.*

Her eyes rose to the mountains, still capped with snow. She still missed Sextus and Camilla every day, but coming to Octodurus had done more than protect her. It had given her the chance to help others, and even though she regretted leaving those she loved in Rome, she gave thanks for this place that had almost become home.

*On the Pasa Alpis Poenina road*

As long as Brutus didn't move, the pain in his leg stayed closer to ache than agony. He'd broken his arm in a fall from a horse when he was seven. The break between his knee and the midpoint of his thigh hurt worse than that, but he was no longer a boy. What had pulled howls and tears from him then only made him clench his teeth and hold his breath until the latest surge of pain passed.

He glanced at Vera, her back against the rock on one side while Africanus rested on the other. Nutrixia had fed Marcus, and now his son dozed in Vera's arms. Eyes closed, his mouth made tiny sucking motions as he dreamed. Brutus started to smile, then his mouth drooped. If Marcus had died, it would have been the end of him, too.

He turned his eyes away and stared down the road toward Octodurus. It had been too long since Rufus galloped off to find help. Was he almost back? Would he come too late?

It had pained him to watch Africanus's jaw muscles tighten so often it was as if they never relaxed. Unremitting pain…not a good sign. But he'd give anything to see his friend's jaw clench again. Africanus was unconscious now, and Brutus knew what that could mean.

Rufus cantered into view, and Brutus's eyebrows plunged. No wagon? Rufus reined in and slipped from his horse. He got down on one knee at Brutus's feet.

"Help is right behind me, master. A wagon for you and Africanus and a raeda for the rest." Rufus's eyes shifted to Africanus. "How is he?"

Brutus shook his head, and worry shifted to sadness in Rufus's eyes.

At the jingle of harness, Rufus rose. The wagon kept going, but the raeda stopped.

A tall German climbed down and came to stand at Brutus's feet. "There's a place just ahead where Fidus can turn the wagon. As soon as he's back, we'll load you both, and he'll take you to the estate. I'll bring the rest of your people."

Brutus glanced at his unconscious friend. "He needs a physician right away. How much longer to go straight to Octodurus?"

The German's brow furrowed, then straightened. "Your man can ride to Octodurus and bring someone back to the estate faster than you could get the wagon to town. I'd recommend that."

"Do you need Rufus's help to load us?"

The German's gaze swept Burdonarius. "I think he and I will need to do it. Your driver can turn my raeda around while we do."

Brutus snapped his fingers and pointed at the raeda. Burdonarius hurried to it and climbed aboard. The reins snapped, and the raeda disappeared up the road.

Hoofbeats announced the return of the wagon before it passed the boulder and stopped.

"Load Africanus first, then me." Brutus shifted, and that was a mistake. With breath held until the surging pain subsided, he stared at the clouds overhead. Africanus wasn't going to feel them load him, but he was.

Rufus moved to Africanus's side and lifted him to a standing position. With Rufus holding Africanus's shoulders and the German holding his feet, they carried him to the wagon. The wagon driver stepped into the bed and supported him while Rufus climbed in and took his shoulders again. After settling him in the right side of the wagon, the men returned for Brutus.

"Where is it broken?" The German rubbed his jaw.

Brutus pointed.

The German pulled off his long-sleeved shirt and folded it to make a fat strip of cloth. He pointed to the ground by Brutus's good leg, and Rufus knelt.

"Support below and above the break while I wrap it."

Lighting bolts of pain shot up his leg as Rufus gently lifted it from the ground. The German made a few wraps around the break and knotted the sleeves together. His mouth curved into a wry smile. "Not quite what I'd like, but better than nothing to hold it while we move you."

"I can carry him alone." Rufus picked Brutus up as if he were a boy, and took him to the wagon.

The German climbed in to guide Brutus into place beside Africanus, then hopped out. "Your man can go now. Robustus can help me get you both into the villa."

Brutus loosened the purse from his belt and tossed it to Rufus. "In case you need to pay the physician to come. Take both fresh horses."

A quick nod, and Rufus mounted Brutus's stallion. Holding the reins of Africanus's mount, he kicked the horse to a fast trot as he rode past the wagon and disappeared from Brutus's view.

With eyes that radiated calm, the German stood beside him. "As soon as I load the rest of your party, we'll go. It's less than a mile."

Brutus eyed the stranger with his aura of competence and his own driver, who sat on the driver's seat of the borrowed raeda. His driver who hadn't been able to control the bolting mules. "Have you driven much?"

"I drove that raeda over 300 milia last fall." A slow smile appeared. "I'll be very careful with your son. We'll be right behind you all the way."

Vera stood by the raeda, holding Marcus close. When she shifted her gaze from the baby to him and smiled, he relaxed. Burdonarius climbed down and helped the women in, but Brutus didn't want his man's hands on the reins. His mouth twitched. Burdonarius was a good driver, but for his own peace of mind, he needed the German to drive today.

The wagon driver had already tied Brutus's mules to the back of the raeda. Now he was leading Rufus's horse to the wagon.

"Burdonarius."

His driver hurried over but kept his eyes downcast.

"Ride Rufus's horse."

"Yes, master." Relief washed across his driver's face as Brutus's mouth shifted from frown toward the slightest smile. Maybe no one could have stopped the bolting mules. He'd broken his own leg trying.

The German rested his hand on the sidewall. "I'll send some men back with pack mules to gather what they can from the wreckage." He returned to the raeda and climbed aboard. "Go, Fidus."

A snap of the reins, and Fidus started the mules off at a walk. An answering snap, and the raeda fell in behind them.

Brutus watched Africanus's slow breathing. He'd give anything to hear his friend's voice again, but would he?

"Fidus." The man turned to look at him. "Pick up the pace. My friend's in urgent need of the physician." The driver's eyes shifted to Africanus. His eyebrows rose, and he nodded. With a flick of the reins and a clucking sound, he took the mules to a fast trot.

Brutus closed his eyes. His closest friend was dying, and nothing could stop it. A man in his business was an expert on what it takes to kill a man. Heavy internal bleeding was unavoidably fatal.

He turned his eyes on the mountains and fought the waves of emotion that threatened to capsize him like a ship caught in a December storm.

First Camilla, now Africanus. How much loss could one man bear?

His eyes returned to the raeda behind them. Camilla died giving him Marcus. Africanus was dying from saving him. Gifts born of love and friendship that he never wanted and wished he'd never received.

Then Marcus began to cry, only to be silenced when Vera started singing to him. And though that baby had cost him everyone, the fierce love of a father still burned in his heart.

# Chapter 30

## If Only She'd Stayed

*The Crassus estate*

As Licinia walked the corridor from the kitchen to the great hall, she ran through her mental list of their visitors and what they would need. A man with a broken leg, one injured bodyguard and one healthy one, a baby and two women who cared for it, and a driver.

She'd told Sollus there would be extra people to feed, both at her table and in the slave dining hall. The old cook knew where the rocking crib that Primus had used was stored. One room upstairs for the baby and nurses, one for the injured bodyguard until he healed, and the room to the right of the main entrance for the master with a broken leg.

She would never wish harm on anyone, but it would be nice to have someone new for conversation for the six weeks or so it would take a broken leg to heal.

She heard the jingle of harness and hoofbeats through the open window and stepped out onto the portico to greet the new arrivals.

The wagon moved past, and the raeda stopped in front of her. She hadn't taken three steps when the first nurse stepped out. Their eyes met, and both froze.

What was Camilla's maid doing as a baby's nurse in this province?

Vera's eyes widened like a rabbit trapped by a pack of dogs. Why was the girl frightened to see her? What had made Camilla sell her or give her to another?

She opened her mouth to ask when the second nurse stepped from the carriage holding a sleeping baby. With a strange pair of ears listening, Licinia left the question unspoken. There would be time to find out later.

A rustle behind her pulled her gaze to the villa door. "Olga."

"Yes, domina?"

"Take these women and the baby upstairs to the room you prepared for them." She spoke in Germanic. "After you get them settled, find Primula and send her to them."

Olga nodded and swept her hand toward the door. "Come. Follow. Please."

Her passable Latin drew Licinia's smile.

She offered Vera a slight smile as she walked by. "We'll speak later."

Vera gave one quick nod, but the fear didn't fade from her eyes.

Licinia moved on to the wagon, where Damalio stood beside an equestrian with wavy dark hair receding slightly at the corners of his forehead, a closely trimmed beard, and eyes that looked like he bore the weight of the world. Then his jaw clenched, so maybe it was only pain.

"I'm Calvia Lucilla, domina of this estate. Welcome."

He drew a deep breath. "Antonius Brutus. I thank you for your welcome and your assistance." His smile was strained.

Vera's presence was no longer a mystery. Camilla's husband had reassigned her to his son.

She tipped her head and responded with a warm one. "I'm glad I was able to send Damalio to help immediately. I've sent your nurses and the baby to a room where they can rest." Her brow furrowed. "Where is the man who came earlier?"

"He rode into town to get a physician." Damalio's voice came from behind her. "The injuries are serious. Fidus is fetching Robustus to carry them."

"My men will take you inside, and we'll try to make you as comfortable as possible. I hear the local physician is good. He'll be able to help."

Brutus's eyes closed longer than a normal blink before he opened them and looked at the man at his side. "An impossible task, I fear."

One look at the dark, muscled man beside him, and her eyes darted to Damalio. His lips tightened, and he shook his head.

Robustus reached the wagon and leaned on the sidewall.

"We'll take Brutus in first." Robustus nodded, and before Damalio could move to help him, the big man scooped up Brutus like a child.

"Put him in a chair in the great hall for now."

As Robustus disappeared through the doorway with their guest, Licinia covered her mouth and stared at the bodyguard. "What's wrong with him? He looks terrible."

"He was struck by the yoke pole as the raeda toppled down the slope." Damalio squeezed the back of his neck. "He's been unconscious since before we reached them."

"Is he dead yet?"

He pressed his fingers against the bodyguard's neck. "His heart still beats."

"Then take him up to the room next to yours. We'll pray for him."

Robustus returned, and Damalio motioned him into the wagon. "You get his shoulders; I'll get his legs. We're taking him upstairs for prayer."

◆

Brutus's gaze fixed on Africanus as Damalio and the burly slave carried his friend into the house and up the stairs leading off the large room where he'd been deposited.

Calvia entered behind them, but she also ignored him.

"Primula!" Her call down the hall brought a young woman scurrying. "We're needed upstairs."

As they began the climb, the girl who'd escorted Vera and Marcus was descending.

"Keep the Roman company in case he needs something." Calvia's words were Germanic.

Brutus wasn't fluent, but he knew some from his many summers at the Lousonna estate. Calvia's perfect accent declared her a native of the imperial city. It was odd to hear a matron from Roma call him 'the Roman' as if she weren't one herself.

The girl came and stood before him, "I help if you need." Her Latin was clumsy but better than none at all.

His reply was a nod before he closed his eyes. Pain and loss wrapped around him. Then he opened his eyes to watch the stairs. Somewhere overhead were his son, who was safe, and his friend, who was dying. What had started with soaring eagles at the top of the pass had turned into the second worst day of his life.

◆

The heat had flowed from Licinia's palm where it rested on Africanus's forehead up past her elbow. Eyes closed, she tipped her head back and reveled in the healing presence of the Spirit of God.

"We give You thanks for hearing our prayers and healing Africanus. As his body has been healed, let him know You as the one true God Who can heal mind and spirit as well. Use us as Your hands. Give us Your words. Draw him to You, and claim him as Your own. We ask this in the name of our Lord Jesus."

Three amens echoed around her, and she opened her eyes.

Damalio lifted his hand from Africanus's shoulder. "The power of God that passes all understanding..." His smile started slowly and turned into a grin. "I'd like to see Africanus's face when he wakes up."

Robustus chuckled, and Primula's smile revealed her joy.

Licinia straightened. "We've just seen the Great Physician at work, but I sense it would be wise to let the physician from Octodurus deal with the broken leg downstairs."

"I agree, domina." Damalio stroked his jaw. "There's something about Antonius Brutus that makes me think caution is in order. It would be better if he doesn't learn of our faith."

"I agree. The baby's nurse was handmaid to my dearest friend whom I led to our Lord. I need to speak with her before she talks to her master again. Camilla hadn't told him she followed Jesus when we left Rome. He still might not know."

"I'll come back as soon as Robustus and I get Brutus settled in the tablinum. Africanus might sleep for some time, but I want to watch him awhile in case he wakens quickly. He'll want to know where he is."

They left the room, Damalio and Robustus to head downstairs and Licinia with Primula to see Vera.

◆

Footsteps of two large men passed over Brutus's head. They materialized as Damalio and his helper at the head of the stairs.

The calm-eyed Damalio approached. "Master Brutus, we're going to move you into the tablinum where there's a couch. Then you can lie down while we wait for the physician."

"Is Africanus still alive?"

"Yes." The German's mouth started to open, then closed. Brutus's gaze returned to the stairs. Alive now, but he couldn't be much longer.

Damalio turned to the girl. "Fetch a pillow and a sheet to cover the couch. Then find Lepus."

One dip of her head, and she hurried up the stairs. She'd barely disappeared before she was back with the bedding. Damalio took the bundle from her arms, and she went out the open door. Through the door to the room that opened off the hallway, Brutus watched Damalio make the couch into a bed. When he finished, the giant they called Robustus scooped Brutus up and moved him into the reception room.

The chair where a dominus would receive salutations looked unused. Was the owner only away, or was the woman he'd met at the wagon always in charge?

Robustus walked out the door to be replaced by a much smaller man. His eyes darted from Damalio, to the floor, to Brutus, and back to Damalio.

"Yes, overseer?"

Damalio placed his hand on the man's shoulder. "This is Lepus. He knows a fair amount of Latin, so he'll serve you until your own man returns." His hand dropped. "Now, if you'll excuse me…" Without waiting for permission, he turned and headed back up the stairs.

Lepus's eyes followed Damalio. Then he walked to the doorway and leaned against the frame so he could stay in the tablinum but still look up the stairs.

A crushing weariness settled on Brutus, body and mind. Sleep might dull the pain, but then he couldn't send the physician first to Africanus in case something could be done.

His mouth turned down. He couldn't lie to himself. As he'd kept a deathwatch with Camilla in his arms until her final sigh, he'd done the same with Africanus beside the accursed road they never should have taken. When Africanus slipped into oblivion, what they'd shared was over.

"Lepus." Brutus's word snapped him to attention. "I want to take my bodyguard's cremated remains home to place in our family mausoleum. Who do I need to talk with to arrange that?"

"Damalio." Lepus's brow furrowed. "But the mistress told Olga your man will be fine."

"Did you see him?"

"No, but if the mistress says he'll be fine, then he will be."

Brutus's lips tightened. Africanus was near death when they reached the estate. If he wasn't already dead, he soon would be, and no words spoken by a provincial matron could change that.

◆

Licinia rapped twice on the door, and Vera opened it. "It's good to see you, mistress." She glanced over her shoulder to the chair by the window where the nursemaid was feeding the baby. "Can we talk in private?" Her words were whispered.

Licinia swept her hand toward her chamber. "Come."

As soon as the chamber door was shut, Vera covered her cheeks with her palms. "I hoped I'd never see you again, mistress." Her hands dropped. "Did you tell the master who you are?"

Licinia's head pulled back. Never see her again? "Why?"

"If you haven't already, you mustn't. He hates you."

"Hates me? But he's never met me before today."

"He's Mistress Camilla's husband. He's furious that you told Mistress about Jesus. He blames you for her rejecting the Roman gods."

"But she said she'd hide it from him until it wouldn't upset him."

"She did, but she told him at the end."

"The end?"

"No one told you?"

"Told me what? My brother sent me out here two weeks before her baby was due." Licinia pointed to the wall separating her from the baby's room. "That's Marcus, isn't it?"

"It is."

"Where's Camilla?" Tears started pooling in her eyes as she braced for the answer.

Vera wiped at the corner of her eye. "Marcus came early. Mistress died right after he was born. Master blames you for that even more."

Licinia's tears broke free, turning into a torrent as her body shook with silent sobs. Camilla gone, and she hadn't even known. Surely Sextus knew, and he'd hidden it from her. How could he do that when he knew how much Camilla meant to her?

Primula's arm slipped around her, and Licinia buried her face in her sister-in-Christ's shoulder.

When the torrent turned to a trickle, she stepped back. "Sextus wanted me to leave right away so his enemy wouldn't learn I was a Christian. I should never have agreed. I should have insisted I stay until after Camilla delivered. If Primula and I had been there, we would have prayed. Maybe God would have healed her."

Primula touched her hand. "But we can't know that, mistress. Sometimes He heals, but not always, no matter how hard we pray."

Vera's eyes brimmed with tears. "When your blanket came, Master tried to force me to tell him who you were. He threatened to sell me if I didn't. But when I told him I'd promised Mistress I wouldn't and begged him to let me stay, he let me keep my word to her. He told Africanus he always keeps his, and he couldn't make me break mine."

She wiped away an escaping tear. "But he and Africanus found out who all of Mistress's close friends were, and then he figured out you were the only one who didn't worship the Roman gods." She took

Licinia's hand. "I've never seen Master Brutus so filled with hate. He usually controls his temper, but if he learns who you are...I think only Africanus could stop him from hurting you."

More tears trickled down Vera's cheek. "Africanus was like a brother to Master. He helped Master through his grief. Master's heart broke again today with Africanus dying."

"But he isn't dying." Primula took Vera's other hand. "We asked God to heal him, and He has."

Licinia squeezed Vera's hand before releasing it. "He's resting peacefully now. He might need to get his strength back, but he'll be fine."

Vera beamed. "Does Master Brutus know?"

"Damalio and Robustus went down to move him into the tablinum, but I don't know if they told him." She turned to Primula. "Go see if Damalio is back with Africanus and bring him here."

Primula slipped from the room, closing the door behind her.

"I told Brutus I was Calvia Lucilla. Sextus had me use a different name on the ship leaving Rome. Damalio thought it wise to keep using it." She gave a delicate snort. "I thought him overly cautious when he first suggested that. But his caution is usually wisdom as well, so I agreed. No one here except the four men I brought with me, you, and Primula knows who I am."

"I'll keep your secret."

"Thank you. Keeping it protects us all."

One knock, and Damalio entered with Primula. "Is there a problem, domina?"

"Maybe not a problem, but something that requires caution. The man downstairs is the husband of my dearest friend. Camilla had converted and hidden it from him."

Vera tipped her head to look up at Damalio's face as he stood beside her. "Master Brutus might hurt her if he knew who she is." She lowered her gaze, then looked up at him again. "He blames her for Mistress Camilla's death."

His eyebrows rose. "His wife's death?"

"In childbirth. We'd prayed for God to give her a son." Licinia wiped away an escaping teardrop. "Her baby is next door."

Damalio took a deep breath. "That could be a big problem. But if we're all careful, he won't ever know. From our arrival, we've told everyone you're Calvia Lucilla. There's no reason Brutus would suspect otherwise."

"I'm glad you think so." Licinia rubbed her forehead. "But do keep an eye on him anyway."

"I left Lepus watching him, and with his broken leg, he isn't going anywhere for a while." He rubbed the back of his neck. "For at least four weeks he'll be here. His broken leg has to heal enough for him to ride a horse or climb into a carriage."

His eyes softened. "But you might want to hide you've been crying before he sees you."

She felt below her eyes to see how puffy she was.

"It's not bad, mistress." Primula picked up the pitcher and poured some water into the wash basin. She dipped a small towel in the water and wrung it out before handing it to Licinia. "A cool, wet cloth will fix it."

She'd reduced the puffiness and was handing the towel back to Primula when someone knocked. Damalio opened the door.

Nutrixia stood outside. "Vera needs to take Marcus for a while. I need to go."

Marcus held out his arms and leaned toward Vera. She balanced him on her hip and kissed the top of his head.

The nursemaid's eyes were on Damalio, and her appraisal of the tall, handsome German finished with an alluring smile.

His lips tightened as he turned his eyes away. "If that's all, domina, I'll return to Africanus."

Licinia's nod sent him through the doorway, slipping sideways past the nursemaid with as much space between them as his large frame allowed.

The nursemaid's slight shrug spoke her indifference to a man with no interest in her.

"Why don't you take a break and go for a walk as well? It's been a hard day."

"Thank you, domina." Her broad smile proclaimed her approval, and she headed for the stairs.

Vera kissed Marcus's forehead and offered him to Licinia. As she took the precious bundle, a small hand reached toward her. She blew on his palm, and the giggle it triggered was music to her ears.

She glanced at Vera. "Have you noticed he has Camilla's eyes?"

"I agree. So does his father. Master Brutus loves him deeply for his mother's sake. Marcus's death would have crushed him if Africanus hadn't been able to rescue him."

"Sextus should have told me, but at least he delivered the blanket I made for Marcus."

"He did, and your note as well. It made Master think you were still near Rome. He'll never suspect it's you in this distant province."

"Many times, I've wished this was Rome so I could see Camilla and Sextus. Half my reason is gone." Tears welled up in her eyes again, but as with Father, time would blunt the pain of loss.

She looked down at the smiling baby snuggling in her arms. For at least a month, she could watch Camilla's son grow. Perhaps that was why God brought Brutus's man to her for help.

"It was so hard to leave everyone and everything, but the longer I stay, the more this feels like home."

# Chapter 31

WHAT HE COULDN'T KNOW

Brutus lay on his back, keeping his breaths slow and measured. His whole body throbbed, but concentrating on breathing helped him ignore all except the sharpest pain in his thigh. Nothing helped the ache in his heart.

"They're in here." Fidus's voice in the hall opened Brutus's eyes.

Lepus pointed at Brutus, and the gladiator physician from Octodurus led Rufus into the room. He was scrawny-limbed and short. Brutus's own gladiators could easily pick him up and toss him like a ball between them. A squint and a frown proclaimed his irritation at the trip to the estate, but Brutus had never seen a more welcome sight.

"Antonius Brutus, I'm Gaius Silo, physician to the Ludus Octoduri. Your man tells me a horse broke your leg. I've brought what I need to fix that."

"There's a bigger problem upstairs you need to attend first. One of my men was struck in the side by a yoke pole. He's bleeding internally. Lepus will take you to him."

Rufus perked up. If only he could share Rufus's baseless hope that Africanus could be helped. His gladiator knew the signs of coming death as well as he did. Rufus's eyes had mirrored his own before he rode away. It would take an intervention of the gods to change anything, and figments of a man's imagination could do nothing to save a dying man.

Lepus called out as he started up the stairs. "I'm bringing the physician up."

Several stairs creaked under three pairs of feet. Then silence. A few moments later, Lepus's light steps returned him to the room.

"Is he still alive?"

Lepus's eyebrows shot up. "Why, yes. He was sleeping when we went in. Damalio was watching him."

Brutus closed his eyes. Sleeping? Not likely. Unconscious looked like sleeping. So did dead.

A hand on his shoulder jerked him awake. He would have sworn it was impossible with the pain, but he'd dozed off. He awoke to find Rufus's hand on his shoulder and a smile on his bodyguard's face.

Silo stood beside him. "So, a horse rolled on you."

"Yes. A break above the knee. Straightforward to treat, but what about my man upstairs? Were you able to do anything for him?"

"No."

Brutus's next breath ended in a deep sigh. "I was afraid of that."

"I don't know why. He was sleeping deeply when we entered. He woke while I examined him, but he's asleep again. I checked his abdomen. It was as pliable as I expect for a man as fit as he is. No sign of pain when I probed it. No deep bruising to signal internal bleeding. There was nothing for me to do. There's nothing wrong with him."

Brutus's eyebrows dipped. A ludus physician should know better. "Nothing wrong? I own three ludi. I know a fatal injury when I see it. I watched the yoke pole slam into him. I sat beside him as he slipped unconscious. I've seen men die from that kind of injury too many times to think it simply healed itself on its own."

Silo shrugged. "Perhaps your man was faking a greater injury than he had. Maybe he's a better actor than fighter."

"I know when my men are truly hurt, and Africanus would never fake anything."

A patronizing smile accompanied Silo's condescending eyes. "I defer to your better knowledge of your man. All I can tell you is there's nothing seriously wrong with him now."

The physician thought him a fool, and that rankled. Brutus opened his mouth to argue, then closed it. It didn't matter what the physician thought. All that mattered was Africanus would recover, however that came to be.

"Silo." Damalio stood in the doorway. "Do you have everything you need?"

"I need four strong men. The leg needs to be pulled to get the ends of the bone back into proper alignment. I brought the straps to attach above and below the break, and two will pull in each direction until I say stop."

"Lepus, fetch Robustus and Fidus." Damalio moved to the head of the couch. "Now what?"

"I'll attach the straps, and when your men come, we'll align the bone ends."

When he finished, Silo took a thin piece of wood from his satchel. He offered it to Brutus. "Bite on this. It's going to hurt."

It was all Brutus could do not to roll his eyes. As if he hadn't been hurting already? He had a high tolerance for pain, but he was at his limit, even without someone pulling his leg as if they would rip it off. He held out his hand for the wood.

Too soon, Robustus and Fidus joined them. With that pair on one end of him, and Damalio and Rufus on the other, Brutus braced for what was coming.

Silo positioned himself by the break. "Are you ready?

Brutus bit down on the wood. "Do it."

"Pull." At Silo's command, the four men began stretching his leg.

An avalanche of pain engulfed him, and he barely choked back the scream before it escaped. Was this as bad as what Camilla suffered to give him Marcus? Or worse? He squeezed his eyes shut when the room began to swirl and sparkle.

"Done. Your legs look the same length now." Silo patted his shoulder. "Now I only have to wrap it to keep it from shifting apart again."

Maybe it was only by comparison to the torture he'd just endured, but the pain seemed a little less than before they stretched him.

Silo removed the straps and returned them to his satchel. From it, he took one of two spools wrapped with cloth strips. "Today I'll make a three-layer wrap. That will loosen as the swelling goes down over the next three days. Then I'll return to do the six-layer wrap that will immobilize the bone while it heals. Six to eight weeks, and you'll be able to do most of what you usually do."

"You two." He pointed at Rufus and Damalio. "Watch closely so you can adjust the wraps if needed without sending for me."

Brutus watched as well. Silo dipped the first linen in a shallow bowl containing oil and wine. Then starting a little below the break, he wrapped the cloth strip in a spiral up his thigh and as far above the break as it was below. The second strip started past where the first stopped and spiraled down the length of his thigh before Silo reversed the wrapping direction and spiraled up past the break once more. After securing it, he covered everything with a wide linen wrap.

"Your man told me you were on your way to Lousonna. I'd recommend against climbing in and out of a carriage, even with help, for at least four weeks."

"I need to replace my raeda before I'll be going anywhere. Is there a wagonmaker in Octodurus?"

Silo rubbed his chin. "Yes...but I'm not certain he's any good."

"I'll be able to tell." Damalio handed Silo the spool he'd left on the couch. "I can arrange for a new one to be made, and I'll check to make sure it's built properly for a long journey."

"I accept your offer." Brutus's smile came easily now that his leg was set and he knew Africanus was all right.

"Mistress Calvia wants you to remain with us for as long as needed. The women can stay upstairs, and I already have a place prepared in the men's lodge for Burdonarius and Rufus. Where did you want Africanus to stay?"

After almost losing him, there was only one possible answer. "Put a bed for him in here. He'll help me as needed when he's fully recovered himself. If there are tasks for a man familiar with horses and mules, feel free to put Burdonarius on them. Rufus has trained only for fighting, but if he wants to help with something, he can."

The prospect of doing something other than waiting around broadened Rufus's smile.

A knock on the open door drew Brutus's attention to the young German standing there.

"Primus." Damalio raised a hand in greeting before turning back to Brutus. "He's taking some men to gather what survived your wreck."

Rufus untied a purse from his belt and offered it to Brutus.

Brutus waved it away. "Pay Silo and then go with Primus. Or do you need to go with Silo to bring back my horse?"

"No, master. He rode his own." He set the purse on the couch and followed Primus.

Silo snapped his satchel shut. "And I'm going to ride him home now. Dinner and my guests await me."

"I appreciate you coming despite the inconvenience." Brutus summoned a smile. "No physician knows his trade better than a ludus man. I look forward to healing with no lasting problems."

Silo's smile looked genuine. "Your man already paid me for this visit. I'll be back in three days. Vale, Brutus."

"Vale, and thank you." Brutus kept the smile on until Silo left the room.

"I have some things that need my attention." Damalio took a step back from the couch. "Lepus will stay with you until Rufus returns. Now, if you'll excuse me..." After Brutus's nod, he left.

And that opened the door to getting an explanation of what was unexplainable. "Lepus."

"Yes, Master Brutus?"

"How did your mistress know Africanus would be fine? He was dying when they took him upstairs. Did your mistress do something to him?"

Lepus glanced at the door through which Damalio had gone. "I wasn't in the room, and it's not my place to tell you anyway without the mistress's permission."

"Hmph." Lepus jumped at the sound. He was well named. "Is she a sorceress? Since it's not your place to answer, is she too dangerous to ask myself?"

He dropped his gaze to the floor before returning it to Brutus. "I'm sorry, Master Brutus, but we don't discuss the mistress with strangers."

A boy of about eleven walked by the door. "Sorex."

The boy entered, and Lepus turned to Brutus. "I need to finish some work in the garden just outside. Sorex will come get me if you need any help."

Brutus waved toward the door. "Go."

As Lepus walked past the boy, he leaned close. "You're not to answer any questions about the mistress or her people."

"I won't."

Germanic words whispered between them. It was a good thing he knew more than Latin.

Brutus closed his eyes. He was tired past exhaustion, and it was time to sleep. But he couldn't help wondering. What was it about Calvia Lucilla that no one wanted him to know?

Holding Marcus in her arms was everything Licinia had dreamed it would be. He fingered her face and giggled when she blew on his hand, his two tiny teeth showing as he smiled. Eyes like Camilla's followed her finger when she pointed out something to him, and he listened with rapt attention to her words, even if not one made sense.

When she felt the moisture on her hand, she handed him back to Vera.

"I'm being a neglectful hostess. I should check on Brutus."

"I should see if Master wants to see his son. If I give him to Nutrixia to change, may I join you?"

"We'll wait for you." She stood with Primula while Vera disappeared into her room and returned without Marcus.

The usual three stairs creaked as they descended. By the doorway of the tablinum, Sorex held a finger to his lips. "He's sleeping, domina." A whispered warning that her own eyes confirmed.

Licinia lifted her hand, signaling the others to wait while she approached Brutus's bed. His hair mussed, his mouth relaxed—he looked at peace. Like Sextus's boys while they dozed on the dining couches when one of Father's family dinners had run too late.

In the wagon, his eyes had been dulled by too much pain, and the sadness as he looked at his bodyguard beside him had tugged at her heart. Damalio or the physician would have told him Africanus was alive and recovering. Perhaps that helped him sleep like a youth with none of the cares of a grown man.

She left his bedside and signaled the others to follow her outside.

"I think all will be well with Brutus now."

Vera looked over her shoulder at the tablinum window. "I'm glad Master Brutus wasn't hurt worse. He's a good man, and he loves Marcus dearly. Mistress Camilla would be proud of the father he's become."

"Sextus has always been good with his boys, too. Not all Roman fathers are."

"Master didn't start that way. He didn't even look at Marcus for the first week after Mistress died. It was Africanus who got him to come see his son. His face was so hard. I was afraid to hand Marcus to him. Then Marcus reached up. Master gave him his thumb, and I saw the father Mistress thought he'd be."

"Camilla wanted so badly to give him a son. We were so sure she would. So sure they would raise him together." Licinia plucked at her stola. "If only Sextus hadn't insisted I leave before the birth. Maybe God would have answered our prayers with a safe delivery." A small shake of Primula's head pulled her back from blaming herself. "I'm glad Rufus came to us for help. I'm sure God brought you all here. Only He could have healed Africanus."

Vera's eyes lifted to the window of Africanus's room. "He's like a brother to Master Brutus. Losing him so soon after the mistress's death might be more than he could bear."

Their stroll had brought them to the courtyard gate. It stood open, and the pasture beyond held the newest lambs and their mothers.

Vera leaned against the gatepost. "Mistress told me all about Jesus, about how he paid for the sins separating us from God. She called him the lamb that God himself provided as the final perfect sacrifice. She told me how she confessed and told him she believed he took her sins away. That she would follow and worship only him."

The persistent bleating of a lamb was followed by silence as it found its mother's milk and began to drink.

"After you prayed with her, she said she knew she'd give Master a son because your god had healed her. She wanted me to believe like her, to be her sister in Christ like you and Primula."

Her sandal traced a circle in the dirt. "I was almost ready to join you until Mistress died in childbirth. She said your god had helped her carry a baby to birth for the first time, but I saw him abandon her and let her die after Marcus was born." She drew a line across it. "I couldn't understand how Mistress Camilla could still be joyful and giving thanks to that god, even when she knew she was dying."

One lamb feeding gave three others the same idea, and their corner of the field turned quiet.

"New life and joy—she said they were gifts from the Christian god. And even though she wanted to see her son grow up, she said she wasn't afraid to die. Eternal life was his gift, too."

With a sweep of her sandal, she erased the drawing before raising her eyes to Licinia. "But if he was the loving god Mistress claimed, why did he give her the son she'd wanted for so long and then let her die?"

Licinia met her gaze. "I don't know why God says 'yes' to some of our prayers and 'no' to others. But I trust that He gives us what's best, even when I don't understand. Those 'nos' can hurt so much when I first hear them. But with time, the pain fades. Only then can I see why. But not always and sometimes only partly." A lamb bleated and chased the ewe that was walking away. "I don't understand why Camilla died, but I can see God's hand in taking me from Rome and bringing me here."

A smile curved Vera's lips. "The answer was 'yes' for Africanus. Your prayers pulled him back from what he and the master thought was certain death." The smile faded. "They've both seen enough death to know."

"Not our prayers. It was the healing power of the Holy Spirit that saved him. We only asked Him to heal."

Vera closed her eyes, and when they reopened, they lit with bright determination. "It convinced me Mistress was right. Your god has real power over life and death. He's everything Mistress claimed. I've decided I want to follow Him, too."

Licinia opened her arms, and Vera stepped into her delighted hug. "Camilla would be rejoicing if she were here." Licinia beamed at a grinning Primula. "Nothing gives more joy than having a new sister. That makes seven believers here."

"Seven?" Vera tipped her head. "Who?"

"Damalio, Sollus, Fidus, and Robustus came with me from Rome. They're all brothers. But the others here don't know we follow Jesus. Damalio thought it unwise to tell anyone yet. Especially our steward, Antistes. He's still angry about some of the changes I had to make."

"Mistress only had you two. It was hard for her to hide what she loved most from the master. She almost told him several times, but he always said something that stopped her."

"Was she afraid of what he'd do to her?"

"Oh, no. Master would never do anything that might hurt Mistress. He loved her so much her death almost killed him."

Vera glanced at the house. "But Master Brutus mustn't find out I follow Jesus like Mistress did. He doesn't believe in any gods, and he told me I was never to tell Marcus anything about the god his mother loved. If the master knew, he'd think I couldn't keep from telling Marcus and sell me." She bit her lip. "I couldn't bear leaving Marcus. I love him as much as his father does."

Nutrixia walked onto the portico with Marcus. "Vera, he wants you."

Licinia took Vera's hand and squeezed. "Come to my room after Nutrixia is in bed. Primula and I will pray with you as you confess your sins to our Father and receive the Holy Spirit. Brutus will never know."

"Vera!" Impatience coated the nursemaid's voice.

"Time for me to take Marcus. She feeds him, but she doesn't love him." Vera's beaming smile dimmed, but her eyes kept their glow as she headed for the house.

"Another sister." Primula's eyes turned heavenward. "I've prayed for this since Mistress Camilla joined us."

Licinia wrapped her arm around Primula's shoulders. "My name, her faith. I wonder what else we'll need to make sure Brutus never knows."

# Chapter 32

SOMETHING PECULIAR

Brutus awoke to pain throbbing in time with his heartbeat. It was focused near the break, but it radiated out into parts of his body that had no reason to hurt so much.

The couch had been turned to put the end against the wall, giving him a view into the hallway. Then a movement to his left drew first his gaze and then his smile.

"How do you feel?" The most welcome sight he'd ever seen was Africanus moving a chair over beside him.

"Better than you look." One corner of Africanus's mouth turned up; then the full smile appeared. "Tired, but otherwise...not bad."

Brutus rested his hand on the linen wrapping his thigh. "Silo seemed to know what he was doing. Rufus and three of the men here stretched my leg to get the bone aligned right. Silo said the legs were the same length afterwards. I hope that means no limp. Four weeks before I should travel. Six to eight, and I can do most of what I usually do."

"That's not so long." Africanus lounged in his chair, legs out-stretched.

"So says the man who doesn't have to wait that long to be well again."

Africanus's crooked smile was accompanied by a shrug.

"Why is that?" Brutus rubbed his lip. "Silo told me you showed no sign of serious injury. He said you were faking."

Africanus spine straightened as his smile flipped to a frown. "We both know that's not true."

"I know. I thought we'd spoken our last words when you passed out by the road. We arrived here with you near death, but when Silo came down, he said you were only sleeping. How is that possible?" His eyes narrowed. "What happened upstairs?"

"I don't know. The last thing I remember was pain like I'd been gutted and leaning against the rock next to you. I woke when Rufus shook my shoulder to find the physician there. The pain was gone. Silo looked me over. He said some things about false alarms and lying slaves, but I dozed off before he finished. I woke later with the overseer watching me, and he brought me to you."

Brutus crossed his arms, which did nothing to help the pain. "Something is peculiar here. When I asked Silo if he'd been able to help you, he said no. I thought he meant you were too far gone. Then he told me you didn't need help. You weren't hurt."

He returned his hand to his thigh, closed his eyes, and took three deep breaths.

"Can I get you something?" Concern softened his friend's voice.

"No. Time will fix this. Until then, I can bear it." His gaze focused on Africanus's serious eyes. "My men who get hurt in the games don't complain. Neither should I."

"I'll be here for whatever you need."

After a nod and a smile at the best friend he'd ever had, Brutus closed his eyes. Dinner would come soon, but sleep would help him hurt less until it did.

A hand on Brutus's shoulder woke him from a fitful sleep. "Dinner is here, master. Are you ready to sit up?"

His nod put Africanus's arm behind his back to raise him to a sitting position.

Calvia Lucilla and her maid stood next to the bed, each holding two pillows. Calvia moved around Africanus to stack the pillows behind him.

"Is that comfortable?"

It wasn't, but nothing would be for some time. "That's good. Thank you."

He stopped his brow from furrowing. Why was the domina of the estate doing the task of a house slave for a stranger when her maid stood beside her?

"I know you're tired, but you'll feel better after a good meal." Her smile felt friendly, not formal. "Sollus is an excellent cook."

A parade of people entered: Damalio with a small table the right height to eat from, Lepus with a rough-hewn chair sturdy enough for Africanus to sit by the table, and Olga with a loaded platter.

A steaming pot of stew filled the room with the aroma of pork and savory herbs. Two each of plates, bowls, spoons, and napkins were placed before him, along with a loaf of bread. The girl ladled large portions into the bowls and placed one within his reach. "Wine...I bring it now?"

A nod from Calvia sent her out the door.

"As soon as Fidus finishes, I'll get a rope bed set up in here. He's threading the ropes now." Damalio pointed to the wall opposite Brutus's couch. "Over there?"

Brutus's nod sent Africanus and the overseer to move two carved chairs to make space.

Calvia watched the men for a few moments before turning to Brutus. "I've had you served here tonight, but you and Africanus are welcome to join us in the triclinium when you're able. Fidus is extending the table so it will seat ten. We can place you at the end so your leg will have enough room. But Damalio thought it wiser to wait until after Silo rewraps it in three days. We don't want to risk hurting you more before he protects the broken place better."

Brutus caught the widening of Africanus's eyes before he masked his surprise. This was a Germanic province, but an invitation for his bodyguard to sit at the table with a noblewoman born in Roma was not what either of them expected.

"We'll leave you to enjoy your dinner, and we'll be back later to see how you're faring."

"I'll look forward to that." It was what he should say, but he meant it.

With a final sincere-looking smile, Calvia led the rest from the room.

He raised his eyebrows at Africanus and got raised eyebrows and a shrug in return.

This was a peculiar household, where people came back from the brink of death and social conventions were ignored. If a man had to be stuck in a strange place for six weeks, at least this one wouldn't be boring.

*Near the Baths of Trajan, Rome, first of June*

Custos had enjoyed his solitary trip to the baths that evening, but now he sat at the back of the taberna Quintus Sabinus's agent had chosen for their meetings.

It had been half a month since Vicarius's accident, and the trust the secretary showed Custos grew daily.

Good thing. He rubbed his mouth with the back of his hand before taking another sip from the cup of cheap wine.

The last time he'd met with Sabinus's agent, Festinus had told him a story about a slave who failed to get Sabinus what he wanted promptly enough. It ended with hints that his time to deliver incriminating evidence had shifted from whatever it took to better be soon...or else.

He still didn't know which estate was the source of the Gratus letters, but he'd finally read one. Written by Sextus Licinius Gratus, one might assume it came from a freedman or freedman's first-born son. But what started as a simple report of building lodging for couples to get new slaves from their unions had drifted into a discussion of how happy the couples were and delight over how soon some of the babies would be born.

Then there was an inquiry about Crassus's sons. Not the insincere kind from a person cultivating a powerful man's favor, but one with an undertone of genuine caring.

The closing was strange as well. May the most powerful god guard your safety. Who ended a letter like that? The proper closing asked all the gods to guard a man. Who knew what the receiver of a letter might be doing and which gods should be invoked to protect him?

If he were a betting man, he'd say it was written by a woman who couldn't quite conceal her softer nature or her fondness for Crassus and those he cared about.

It might have been written by the sister Sabinus was so eager to find, and that information should buy him time to learn more.

Festinus entered and headed toward Custos's table by the back wall. Custos rubbed his mouth again. It was time to betray what was probably the most honorable man he'd ever know.

But what choice did he have? If he didn't betray Crassus, he'd die himself.

Brutus tipped his head back and drained the last of the wine. It wasn't as good as his personal vintage. It wasn't even as good as the wine from his Lousonna estate, which used a cold-tolerant grape variety different from those of his Italian estates. But it was good enough, and even though the plates and bowls were of common clay, the goblets were silver.

A knock on the doorpost caught his attention.

"May we come in, master?" Vera stood with Marcus on her hip.

"Bring him to me." Still propped up by the pillows, he took his son in his arms.

A small hand reached for his face, drawing his smile. Little fingers touched his mouth, and, with lips covering his teeth, he nibbled them. Marcus snatched them away, giggling, only to reach for him again.

After three rounds of touch and nibble, Brutus took his hand. Marcus's fingers wrapped around his thumb before his boy closed his eyes and relaxed in his arms.

"Do you have everything you need for Marcus?"

"Yes, master. Rufus and the others brought the trunks that hadn't broken open and all the loose things that had scattered when the carriage broke apart. They took some pack mules to go down the hill to get everything and a wagon to haul it back here."

When Marcus's eyes opened and he reached toward her, she gave him her hand. "Mistress Calvia said she would get anything else we might need for him." She shook his arm as he held on, getting a grin in response. "The old cook can't stop smiling when she sees him. She wants to make a special porridge and squished carrots for him. It seems Germanic babies start eating more than milk a little younger than they do in Rome." She shook his arm again. "She's sure he's ready for solid food, and I think she's probably right."

"Where are Rufus and Burdonarius?"

"The overseer put them in the men's lodge. When they brought up the things from the raeda, Rufus said Primus told him food was good here and always as much as he wants. Sollus cooks for the main house, but he's also in charge of the workers' kitchen."

Brutus glanced at Africanus to find a raised eyebrow, and one corner of his mouth lifted in response. "I've tasted his cooking, and good is an accurate description. But with the amount Rufus usually eats, I'll offer to pay for what my men are going to cost the estate over the next six weeks."

Movement in the hallway drew his gaze. Calvia, Damalio, and another German approached the door with one man each side of her. The German lengthened his stride, as if he would enter ahead of her, but at the last moment, he slowed so she passed through first.

But while they were still walking toward him, his mouth opened. "Antonius Brutus, I'm Antistes, steward of this estate for Sextus Licinius Crassus." His glance at Calvia was fleeting but contained a challenge. "You are welcome to stay as our guest for as long as you need. Since that will be for some time, is there someone I should notify that you're here?"

"There is." Brutus looked at Calvia, who had introduced herself as domina with no mention of Sextus Crassus owning the estate. She smiled as if unperturbed by the impudence of the steward. "But we can discuss that tomorrow at your convenience." A corner of his mouth lifted. "I'll be here."

A social smile accompanied the proud dip of the steward's head. "Then I bid you good night." The smile turned wooden when he turned to face Calvia. "And you, domina."

She acknowledged him with a subdued smile. He left the room and disappeared up the stairs.

Her smile warmed as she moved closer. "I hope you enjoyed Sollus's stew. We usually eat more Germanic than Roman here. The market in Octodurus is not that of Rome, so we mostly make do with what we grow ourselves."

"As I do at my own estate near Lousonna. Your chef did well."

Marcus stirred, his eyes moving under closed eyelids.

Calvia's eyes lowered from Brutus's face to his son, and her expression softened. "He looks comfortable, but how are you feeling now?"

"As well as can be expected." Her gaze refocused on Brutus's eyes. "Silo knows what he's doing."

"I'm glad to hear it." Her gaze strayed to Marcus again. "It's my pleasure to have you all here while you heal." She glanced at her overseer. "Damalio will start replacing your raeda right away, but rest assured we're in no hurry for you to leave."

Damalio cleared his throat. "Vera has taken charge of the trunks and loose things Primus brought from the wreck. The body of the raeda was broken beyond repair, but he'll take some men back and salvage the two good wheels, some of the wood, and the iron hardware that could be used to build another. That should help keep the cost of the replacement as low as possible."

Brutus raised his hand, and the movement woke Marcus. "Expense isn't an issue. I'll be taking it to Arelate in the fall, so I'm more interested in strength and reliability."

Marcus reached for Brutus's face and got a kiss on his hand before Brutus held it. "You can keep the salvaged wheels and other material. If the carriage maker wants to use the hardware, fine. If not, you can keep that as well."

"We'll use what you don't need." Brutus's offer drew a slow smile from Damalio. "Are there any special requirements I should tell the wagon maker?"

"My needs are simple. It must carry me with my leg stretched out, two women, Marcus, and the trunks you recovered from the wreck. I might sell it in Arelate when I return to Italia, but I might rent it out or store it until I return next spring. So well-built is important but rich-looking is not."

Marcus's eyes drifted shut again, and Brutus summoned Vera with a curl of his fingers. He handed her his drowsy boy. But as she left, Calvia's gaze, which had focused on Marcus during his conversation with her overseer, followed his son from the room.

Odd that she would look at his son as if she were fond of him, but some women doted on babies. Perhaps she was one of them.

Vera disappeared up the stairs, and his hostess's attention returned to him. "It's been a trying day for you." Her smile turned on Africanus, then him. "It's probably time for both my guests to rest. If you need anything just call. Lepus will be sleeping in the great hall tonight in case you want something."

"I will, and thank you for everything."

"It's my pleasure. Sleep well." With a gracious nod, she left the room. But she paused just outside the door until Damalio was beside her. At the foot of the stairs, he stepped back for her to go up ahead of him.

Brutus waited until the stairs had finished creaking and counted to ten. "Get the door."

Africanus scanned the hall and raised one hand at Lepus before shutting the door that was thick enough to muffle any conversation.

"That was unexpected." Brutus flexed his shoulders, and Africanus adjusted the pillows.

Africanus settled into the chair beside the couch and crossed his arms. "A steward often stays in the villa, but for an overseer to do so... that is odd when there's a good men's lodge like this estate has."

Brutus's smiling frown curved his mouth. "Some intriguing relationships here. Your thoughts on our hosts?"

"The domina is a gracious woman who's good to her people, but the steward dislikes her, maybe hates her. She makes it clear she's in charge, and he resents it. I think she sees it, but she seems to ignore his hostility. The overseer watches him closely, like a guard dog watching a wolf. Maybe that's why he sleeps upstairs."

"Nothing more between them? Damalio's a handsome man, and she's alone here a long way from Rome."

"Maybe, but from what I've seen, I'd say no. There's a power struggle here. Rufus stopped in to see how you were. He said the three were outside together when he came. He only asked to borrow a wagon, and the steward spoke first and refused him. Her response—of course they'd help. Without her telling him, Damalio took over as if he was the steward." Africanus rubbed his neck. "She asked nothing about who we were. Only if we needed more than a wagon. She volunteered her raeda and men before Rufus even asked. So eager to help, and the steward was furious when she did after he'd refused."

"I saw the same eagerness in Damalio. I expected to be taken to Octodurus, but he said the physician would see us quicker if he brought us here instead. He asked no questions before he made that decision." Brutus rubbed his chin. "Any of my stewards would at least ask who we were and where we were from, even from someone in senatorial stripes."

"Damalio was there when I woke, but this is the first time the steward has come near either of us." Africanus stretched out his legs. "That one doesn't impress me."

"Why wouldn't he come sooner to inspect strangers who'd be staying for at least a month?"

"That was his domina's decision." Africanus shrugged. "Perhaps it was his way of showing he didn't approve."

"The subtle power struggles in Roma can be entertaining." Brutus's mouth relaxed into a smile. "We're trapped here for longer than I'd like, but these Germans and their domina should keep us from getting bored."

*The Crassus townhouse, Rome, June 2*

Custos cradled the stack of wax tablets in his arms as he headed for Crassus's library. The topmost tablet had been delivered to Vicarius only moments before. An immediate response was required, and the courier now waited in the stableyard for it.

He freed one arm to knock on the door, which stood open.

"Enter." Crassus didn't look up but kept writing on a sheet of papyrus.

Custos placed the stack on a corner of the desk and picked up the one requiring an immediate response.

Crassus glanced at him, then returned his focus to the sheet. "You can go."

A quiet clearing of his throat drew Crassus's attention.

"What is it?"

He offered the tablet. "I beg pardon for disturbing you, master, but the courier who brought this was told to wait for an immediate response. Vicarius told me to ask for it."

Crassus's brows lowered as he read. After sliding the papyrus to one side, he picked up a silver stylus. With the tablet on the desk before him, he rubbed his lip. A deep breath was followed by a deeper sigh before he pressed the stylus into the wax and began to write.

Hands clasped in front of him and head lowered, Custos remained by the desk. His pulse ramped up. The letter, so casually moved aside and left where he could read it upside-down, started "Sextus Licinius Crassus to Sextus Licinius Gratus, greetings."

Crassus might finish writing at any moment, so he scanned the letter as swiftly as he could. It started with the standard sentence about all being well. But then, it turned to family details that no freedman would need. Crassus had just learned Octavia was expecting a child again.

He had both boys starting private instruction with the son of the man who trained him, but the older one would start formal sword training in midsummer. He'd already talked with Brutus about when and with whom the boy should train. Despite what Gratus might think, training at a ludus by gladiators was best for young men to ensure they had the necessary skill with a sword before serving with a legion.

It ended with the standard closing asking the gods to guard Gratus's safety.

His eyes were once more focused on his clasped hands when Crassus closed the tablet and handed it back.

"Take this, too." Crassus flipped the papyrus and addressed it to Damalio, overseer for S. Licinius Crassus, Octodurus. After rolling it, he lit the rod of sealing wax that was his signature dark green. Three drops of wax and his signet ring pressed into them marked it as his own.

He handed the letter to Custos. "Send this by courier to the Octodurus estate."

Custos took the letter. "Yes, master." He took one step back, dipped his head, and left the library.

His mouth turned down when he was past were Crassus might see. Sabinus would want to know what he'd just learned immediately, but how long could he delay telling the agent without drawing Sabinus's wrath down on himself?

The letter he held...who would be hurt after he told Sabinus what it revealed? The sister? Maybe. Crassus? Probably. When his old master went after someone, he never left them alone without first extracting something he wanted, and he didn't care who got hurt in the process.

Vicarius stood on the portico when Custos entered the stableyard. He handed the tablet to the older man, who scanned what Crassus had written. One nod, and he returned it to Custos. The hand-off to the courier sent the man out the gate at a trot.

"Master Crassus wanted this sent right away to the Octodurus estate." He offered the rolled papyrus.

Vicarius waved it away with a smile. "Take it to our regular courier. Then you can go to the baths. You've been a great help this week, and we've finished work for today."

"Thank you." Custos tried to make his smile look natural. "I won't be gone long."

As he passed through the gate himself, tendrils of unease wrapped around him. Would Sabinus's agent see him at the baths and want an update? Vicarius would ask where he'd gone if he didn't look and smell like he'd bathed. But there was a small private bath between the town-house and the Baths of Trajan. That would do for today.

Once a week he met the agent at the taberna. Sabinus could wait until then. There was no reason Festinus would discover he'd kept what he knew to himself for almost a week. But could he delay longer?

He'd been given to Crassus, not simply loaned, so Sabinus didn't own him anymore. But that didn't mean he could protect his new master from his old one without risk. One dead assistant and one broken collarbone were proof of what might happen if Sabinus suspected he'd kept information from him. It might prove fatal if Sabinus thought his spy wasn't going to get the job done and should be replaced.

# *Chapter 34*


## Difference of Opinion

*The Octodurus estate, June 4*

Three days confined to the couch in the tablinum with only a view of the hallway and part of the great hall could have bored Brutus to distraction, but his hostess had done her best to provide entertainment. Calvia had brought in a wooden board engraved for tabula on one side and latrunculi on the other. She'd offered to play if he needed an opponent, but he'd told her Africanus was expert at both.

Odd that she looked disappointed, as if she would have liked to match wits with him. She'd lent him the first scroll of Tacitus's *Germania*, with a promise of bringing the next as soon as he finished it. She'd even offered to read it to him if he found it too tiring to hold for as long as he wished to read.

A gracious woman eager to help—Africanus had pegged her perfectly.

Vera brought Marcus to him each day. After they left his room, she gave Marcus to Calvia, who also played with him for a while in the great hall. She cuddled and tickled and talked to him like he understood her, her eyes laughing most of the time. She gave him back to Vera only when he got drowsy or wet.

Women and babies...the only one he cared about was his own. What made women so fond of the babies of strangers?

But it was now the fourth day since the accident. The swelling was down, and he was more than ready for the new wrapping that would

185

let him get around with the help of his men. His leg still throbbed, whether he moved it or not, but much of the rest of the pain was gone.

Silo had pronounced that odd when he first came. Some returned with a vengeance while the physician stood at his bedside, wrapping his leg with six spiral layers of cloth, changing direction with each layer and explaining to Africanus and Rufus what he was doing.

Silo had frowned the first time Africanus asked why he did something, but he explained it anyway. Perhaps he decided it would mean fewer trips from Octodurus for him if Brutus's man understood what to do and why. Or perhaps the frown Africanus returned as he repeated the question in the icy tone he used as a "persuader" had convinced the physician he didn't want to anger a gladiator he'd once accused of lying. After promising to return in a week to check his healing and redo the wrappings, Silo had gone back to town.

But with the broken bone now stabilized and cushioned by the layers of cloth, he could have Africanus and Rufus help him outside. Fresh air and a change of scenery...it was about time.

After getting him settled in a wicker chair on the portico and lifting his leg onto a footstool, Africanus and Rufus started some relaxed sparring. The first clang of metal on metal brought many faces to the doorways of the buildings surrounding the stableyard. Fearful at first, a few men turned curious and stayed to watch a while. But most looked bored and returned to work right away.

Brutus rested his hand on his right thigh. His admiration for the courage of his wounded men had grown ten-fold in the past four days. They managed to bear pain without groans or complaints, something he struggled with himself. Hour after hour, with full relief only when he slept—but it would get better, and in six or eight weeks he'd be sparring with Africanus again.

Or so he hoped.

His men took a break and went to the well for a drink. It would be good when he could work up a thirst the same way.

The scent of roses announced Calvia's arrival as she came to stand beside him. Her maid followed with a plate of sliced cheese and some fruit for the small table next to his chair.

"It's good to see you out here." Her friendly smile drew one of his own. "My brother always says it's hard for a man to do nothing."

"As pleasant as you've made the tablinum, it's still much better outside."

She was facing him when the men returned and assumed fighting stance. She spun around as the first strike made the swords ring.

"I hate to watch men fight." A shake of her head accompanied the crossing of her arms.

"I want my men prepared for anything, and practice is what does that. I'll be sparring with them when my leg is healed."

"But why on earth would you do that?" Her eyebrows dipped. "Surely you don't have to defend yourself with two bodyguards."

It was the first time he'd seen her confused by anything, and it drew his chuckle. That raised her eyebrows instead.

"It's not a question of have to. I don't expect a woman to understand the satisfaction of a well-trained body and skill in a sport."

Not even Camilla had, even though she understood him better than anyone else.

"Sport?" Calvia's snort was delicate, but not what he expected from a noblewoman. "Fighting isn't sport, but treating it as such—didn't that lead to the great Roman sickness of killing for entertainment?"

"You think you know better than all Roma what's right and wrong?"

"In this, yes." A fire he hadn't seen before lit her eyes.

He accompanied his smiling frown with a shrug. "But people all across the greatest empire the world has ever known disagree with you, as do I."

Her lips tightened. "Then you're all wrong. What G—" Calvia's back arched as a word froze in her throat. Why would her maid have just poked her from behind? And why didn't Calvia reprimand her for it?

His hostess's eyes cooled, and her social smile appeared. "What good does it do for us to discuss this? Neither of us will change our minds."

Brutus relaxed his own smile from amused by her naivete toward simply friendly. "I won't, and I suspect you're as firm in your opinions as I am."

"Quite. I came out to see if you wanted some Tacitus to chase away boredom, but you seem entertained enough without it. Until dinner, then. I'm glad you'll be joining us in the triclinium. Sollus is trying something new."

He tipped his head back to look up at her as she walked past. "I'll look forward to it."

A gracious smile and nod were her answer before she vanished into the house.

He would look forward to dinner, and not just for Sollus's new recipe. Antistes's eyes were those of a wolf, Damalio's were those of a guard dog, and Calvia's were...he hadn't quite figured that out yet.

◆

Licinia crossed the great hall and entered her office. As soon as Primula stepped in behind her, she closed the door. Tipping her head back, she leaned against the solid wood. "That was close."

Eyes wide, Primula nodded.

She secured it with the bolt Damalio had installed. "Thank you for stopping me. Damalio cautioned me about speaking too freely with the decurion. He'd want to scold me if he'd heard what I almost said."

She settled into one chair and pointed at the other for Primula. "Vera told us how upset Brutus was about Camilla becoming a Christian. He hates the woman he holds responsible. He can't possibly know I'm that woman, but his hatred might extend to all Christians. I must be more careful."

"It is better if Master Brutus never suspects he's hated you for months. It's enough to have one enemy here."

"Antistes?"

"Yes. I don't like how he looks at you when you're not watching."

Licinia picked up her stylus and tapped it on the desk. "Neither does Damalio. But with both of you watching out for me, I'm safe enough…as long as I don't do something foolish myself."

She stood and went to the window. Snow still capped the peaks, and it would never melt. It was a land of dangerous beauty, but she preferred it to the gentle charm of Italia. Like Brocchus, she had no desire to leave this land. Except for Sextus, there was nothing left in Rome she missed.

"I'm glad Rufus came to us for help. I wanted to be with Camilla at her son's birth. I'll never have my own children, but it would have been wonderful to be an aunt to hers. Marcus will only be here a month or so, but I see her in his eyes every time I hold him."

She looked over her shoulder at Primula. "I'm glad Brutus kept Vera to care for him. She loves him dearly. Camilla would want that for her son."

"Master Brutus loves him, too."

"I've never seen a man so comfortable with a baby." The remembrance of Marcus snuggling on his father's chest drew her smile. "Sextus loves his children, but he never did much with them until they were older."

She pointed at the folded shawl in one of the cubicles. "Speaking of babies, let's go see how Ursula is doing. It can't be more than two months before her baby comes." Primula draped the shawl around Licinia's shoulders. "Hers will be the first baby in the couple's lodging. The first of many, I hope."

Primula took her own shawl from the shelf. "Primus has turned into a good man."

"I see more of Damalio in him now than I do of Antistes. If we ever have to leave here, I'd feel comfortable making him overseer again. He'd look after our people."

"But we shouldn't have to leave, mistress. It's so far to Rome, and no one here will ever suspect anything."

"True. I questioned whether I really had to leave like we did, but Sextus is wiser in the ways of powerful men than I ever hope to be. If he sees danger, it's probably there." She offered Primula a sad smile. "I miss him so much, but it's safer for me and better for him to have me out of the reach of his enemies."

Primula unbolted and opened the door. Licinia squeezed her maid's hand as she passed through. "God blessed us all by bringing us here."

"He did, indeed, mistress."

On the portico outside, Brutus still watched his men sparring. He raised a hand in greeting as the door clicked shut behind them, but his attention refocused on the clashing swords before she could respond.

But she didn't take it as a sign of unfriendliness. He was merely a man with interests very different from her own.

Camilla would have been happy to see how Brutus treated their son, but what was it about the man that made Camilla love him so much? Perhaps she'd understand before he healed and moved on.

# Chapter 35

## LIONS AND JACKALS

It was dinner time, and Brutus stood on one leg at the triclinium door with Africanus supporting him. Calvia was rearranging the chairs herself while Primula held two pillows. She had pulled an armed chair away from the table, clearing the right end, when Damalio entered and took over. He moved the master's chair to the wall and replaced it with a plain one.

She took a pillow from her maid and greeted him with a smile. "Almost ready. A pillow to soften your seat and a second to support your leg. I think that should do nicely."

"It should, indeed." With Africanus's help, he hopped to the assigned place and sat.

Africanus lifted his leg onto the second pillow. "Comfortable?"

"Yes." It wasn't truly comfortable, but it was comfortable enough. He pointed at the chair to his left, and Africanus settled in beside him.

Calvia sat directly across from Brutus with her maid to her right. Antistes took the second armed chair at the foot, and Damalio's chair was between the steward and the maid. It was the seating arrangement Brutus would have predicted, given what he'd seen of the household so far.

"You are in for a treat tonight." Calvia's smile was directed first at him and then at Africanus. "Dinner will be more like you were accustomed to in Rome. There's nothing in Octodurus like the spice shops on third floor of Trajan's market where your chef would get his seasonings, so Sollus has created some delicious dishes flavored only with local herbs."

She shook out her napkin and placed it in her lap. "But he went to Octodurus for olive oil and salt when Damalio went to the wagon maker this morning. The shop had just received a shipment of several of the spices he used in Rome. Apparently, they get one shipment in the spring and one more in the fall. Expensive compared to prices in Rome, but he bought some of his favorites. He made a special stew to celebrate your first dinner at the table with us."

"I look forward to it." Brutus kept his amusement from showing. He liked good food, but how a chef prepared it had never inspired his curiosity.

But observing people he'd just met did, and Calvia and her men were different enough that he expected good entertainment if he asked the right questions.

"Having the accident so close to this estate was most fortunate for me. I was talking with Sextus Crassus shortly before starting this trip. That I would end up recovering at one of his estates...neither of us expected that." He sipped his wine. "Are you related to Crassus by marriage?"

"Indirectly." She picked up her goblet and swirled it, but was that only to keep from looking at him?

"What's your husband's name? Perhaps I've met him."

She stared at him, more like a startled deer than the woman in charge he was used to.

"Gaius Aelius Valerius." Damalio's answer raised Brutus's eyebrow. Why had her overseer answered for her?

"I don't recall meeting him." Brutus's shifted his gaze from her to her protector. "So, do you belong to Valerius or Crassus?"

Damalio opened his mouth as if to speak, then closed it. One corner of Brutus's mouth curved as her man's eyes veiled.

Dinner was proving more entertaining than he'd expected.

"He's mine. Valerius is no longer with us." She'd stiffened, and unease colored Calvia's voice.

"My condolences." His mouth straightened. "My wife died last fall. Has it been long?"

Calvia's smile was strained. "I'd rather not talk about it."

That he understood. It had taken months before he could speak of Camilla with any except Africanus and Vera without it tearing the scab off the wound and making it bleed again.

"Does Crassus visit here often? Has he brought his wife Octavia?"

Antistes cleared his throat. "I've been in charge for the last ten years. He's only visited once, and that was when young Master Crassus was on his way home from his tribune posting in Germania. His father trusted me to run the estate and make a good profit for him without oversight."

Brutus glanced at Antistes at the start of his speech, but he mostly kept his eyes on Calvia. "Ten years is a long time. So, Calvia." Speaking her name turned her eyes from her goblet to his face. "How long have you been domina here?"

"Since November, but it already feels like home."

"Hmph." Antistes's set his goblet down harder than he should have. "Women are too soft-hearted. That isn't what an estate like this needs."

Calvia's spine straightened. "That's not true. It isn't soft-hearted to treat your workers like people instead of animals. People work harder when they know what they do is appreciated. It's the best way to run an estate."

Brutus lifted his goblet to her. "I agree. I have high expectations for the performance of my men, but when they work hard and do their best, I let them know I'm pleased with their effort."

Antistes bristled. "Coddling slaves leads to a drop in profits."

Calvia's chin rose. "Providing decent food and lodging isn't coddling. We take good care of our horses. Our people deserve better than a horse. Our weavers already produce more and higher quality cloth, and the men work harder and better together than they did."

"Damalio." Brutus directed his frowning smile at her man. "As overseer, what's your opinion?"

"Men always work better when they know what they do is valued."

"Is that what Crassus thinks?"

"Yes. The estate is now being run like the Crassus estates in Italia, and it's still earning a good profit. Master Crassus prefers a good profit with a well-run estate over a higher profit in the short run but treating his slaves poorly. They're not simply disposable property to him."

Brutus gaze shifted between steward and domina. "It's been my experience that two people can share control well only when they agree on how that control should be exercised."

Calvia's social smile appeared. "That's true, and Sextus gave me domina authority because he knew that he and I agree. And now that Antistes knows how Sextus likes his estates run, he's doing a good job trying to meet those expectations."

Her faint praise drew Antistes's icy smile. "Master Crassus can rely on me to do what's best for his estate, whatever that might be."

Brutus was preparing his next question when he glanced at Africanus. His friend's jaw was clamped, and his eyes were fixed on the goblet he was swirling.

The sound of footsteps behind him was followed by Olga and Lepus bringing the next course. As Lepus held the heavily loaded tray, she placed a steaming bowl before each of them.

Calvia closed her eyes and inhaled. "Tell Sollus it smells marvelous, and I expect it will taste even better."

Conversation ended as each picked up a spoon and began eating.

The only one who was sorry the exchange was over was Brutus. These three were as entertaining as the ruling elite to watch.

He took a bite of the stew, and the savory richness exploded across his tongue. Good food and lively conversation. A month with Calvia Lucilla and her men would pass much quicker than he'd feared.

After dinner, Africanus and Damalio helped Brutus back to the couch in the tablinum.

"Is there anything else you want before I leave?" Damalio wore a slight frown. "Lepus will sleep in the great hall in case you need him later."

"Not this evening. Africanus will take care of me." Brutus's smile failed to draw one in response.

Damalio took one step back. "Then I'll bid you good night." A dip of his head, and he left, closing the door behind him.

"I wonder what's bothering him." Brutus flexed his shoulders. Not the best choice. His leg still throbbed in time to his heartbeat, but the rest of him ached some as well. "And why were you so tense at dinner?"

"The conversation was too much like a prelude to battle."

"Calvia and Antistes? She took control of the estate; he wants it back. You didn't find it entertaining? You do when I get two Roman senators sparring with words."

Africanus's lips tightened, just as they had at the table. "The senators you do that to aren't Antistes. Damalio watches him with bodyguard eyes for good reason."

"He resents losing his authority to her, but he's not dangerous." Brutus shrugged.

"The steward reminds me of the lions I watched hunt antelope when I was a boy." His mouth turned down. "Given the opportunity, he would act against her. He's not a lion, but even a jackal can kill if you're already hurt."

"He doesn't strike me as a fool. Calvia must be important to Crassus for some reason, or she wouldn't be domina. Antistes would lose his position if he did something to hurt her."

"A wounded lion will charge, even when that will hasten its death. The steward's pride has been hurt. Too many men stop thinking clearly when that happens. You've seen it among senators. I see it here."

Africanus took all but one pillow from the stack behind him.

"Perhaps." Brutus lowered himself onto his back and closed his eyes. Whatever Antistes might want to do, he was too tired to think about it tonight.

# Chapter 36

## SNAKES AND CROCODILES

*A taberna near the Baths of Trajan, Rome, June 8*

Custos sat at the back table, running his finger around the rim of his cup. The slave girl who circulated the room, filling empty glasses and flirting with the men, kept returning, even though he'd told her one was all he wanted.

His tunic was why. Sextus Crassus took care of his people, and those who worked in his household were dressed better than many freeborn Romans. Well fed, well clothed, well treated...that was what it meant to be part of the *familia Crassi.*

And he was about to betray the man who'd treated him like a person instead of property. He watched the girl but dropped his gaze to the graffiti carved into the table before she caught him.

Festinus was late. If Sabinus's agent didn't come soon, he'd have to leave without revealing where Gratus was. He'd taken too long at the baths, figuring this meeting would be as short as the others.

Vicarius must not ask what made him late. It was bad enough he was betraying his master. He didn't want to lie to the man who'd become like a father to him as well.

A tall, muscular German, obviously gladiator-trained, entered. He scanned the room before sauntering toward his table.

"Are you Custos?" The voice was almost a growl.

"Yes."

The man pulled out a chair and turned it to put his back toward the wall. He crossed his arms, and his mouth turned down as he watched the other patrons. Then his gaze shifted to Custos and stayed.

Silence coiled around them like a snake.

Custos's foot began to bounce beneath the table until he stilled it. He cleared his throat. "Where's Festinus?"

"He's laid up for a while. You'll be meeting me instead."

"What happened to him?"

The silence tightened around Custos until the gladiator's disdainful contemplation ended in a smiling frown. "You don't need to know. What do you have today?"

He did need to know, but did he really want to?

"How do I know you're his replacement?"

"Would I be here if I wasn't?" Cold eyes and an icy smile discouraged any answer.

Custos released the breath he hadn't intended to be holding. The gladiator might be there if he was the one who hurt Festinus, but that was too dangerous to tell the man.

"I've been trusted with a tricky mission, and I won't tell just anyone what I know. What can you tell me that proves we serve the same master?"

The ice melted, only to be replaced by a cruel smile. "Festinus told me you were a smart one. What kind of proof do you want?"

"What's the name I gave him already?"

The man snorted. "You think they'd tell me that?"

"If they didn't, I can't be sure you came from the master. You could be a spy."

The man's low chuckle raised the hair on the back of Custos's neck. "Smart and careful. But maybe a broken collarbone would encourage you to talk. What's good for a secretary is good enough for his assistant."

Custos fought the urge to swallow hard and won. "That will do instead." His hand lifted from the tabletop, but he beat back the urge to rub his lip as well.

The new agent crossed his arms. "Well? What do you have today?"

Custos stomach clenched. If he revealed the estate, what would he set in motion? But if he didn't, what would happen to him? Maybe Gratus was only a freedman who was a good friend, not the sister Sabinus was hunting. It was possible. And if he was only a friend, no harm would come of Sabinus knowing he was in Octodurus.

"A location. Crassus sends his Gratus letters to Damalio, overseer of the Octodurus estate."

It was a simple fact, and Sabinus would have already considered it as one of seven possibilities. So, why did he feel like a filthy traitor for speaking the name?

"Anything else?"

"No, but I'll keep watching."

The agent stood, and stepped close to tower over him. "You do that. I'll be back next week." The cruel smile returned. "And you'd be wise to have more. The master isn't a patient man, and his patience with you has almost run out."

A silent nod was Custos's answer before the agent turned and left.

With elbows on the table, he cradled his head in his hands. He'd been living the name Sabinus had given him. Custos meant guardian, watchman, and sometimes spy. But if Crassus were to rename him, it would have to be Serpens, for he was a snake in the grass who'd just bit his master's heel. Only time would tell what harm the venom would do.

*The Sabinus estate, June 9*

Sabinus led Manius past the orchard to the pasture for his prize mares. Bays and grays and a few blacks grazed while their foals fed or frolicked nearby.

He pointed at a coal-black colt. "Only two months old and already showing the kind of spirit that brings top money. His sire is one of the Crassus racing champions."

"Nice." Manius's smile and nod declared his appreciation. "And how is my newest sister faring?"

"She's small but healthy. When she's old enough to betroth, I'll be able to seal a valuable alliance with her."

"Sextus Crassus could have done the same with his sister if she hadn't disappeared." Manius leaned on the fence rail.

Sabinus waved a fly away from his face. "Custos may have found her for us."

Manius straightened. "Where?"

"At his estate near Octodurus. Since January, Crassus has been getting a monthly letter from Sextus Licinius Gratus. Custos thinks that might be a woman. It's taken too long, but he finally found out Crassus replies to Gratus by sending his letters to someone called Damalio. He's the overseer of his Octodurus estate."

"Why not address them to Gratus?" The fly had moved to Manius, and he shooed it away.

"Except for this Damalio, the others at the estate might not know Gratus is there. If he is really a she, then letters can't be addressed directly to Gratus."

"Some interesting possibilities if it is a woman." Manius slapped his shoulder where the fly had landed. He missed. "If Calvia Lucilla is Crassus's mistress, he might write her using the alias. Octavia is not a woman who'd willingly share her husband, at least not if anyone knew. But would a mistress write about estate affairs or care about the children of the woman she'd like to replace? Custos never reported anything that suggested passion between them."

"Whether it's the sister or a mistress, she'll still be useful to us. I've sent one of my most trusted agents with a couple of bodyguards to find out. They should be there in less than two weeks."

"And when they get there?"

"That depends on what they find. I've given complete instructions. Until they return, I'll leave Custos in place. He might still be of use for a while."

One slap to his chest, and the fly's carcass spiraled to the ground.

# Chapter 37



*The Octodurus estate, June 10*

Brutus shifted in his chair on the portico, trying to find the position that hurt the least. It was ten days since the accident, when pain had been a brutal companion that only left when he slept. Now it was an unwelcome visitor that bothered him only when he moved wrong.

He removed one of the pillows Calvia had insisted would make him more comfortable and dropped it beside the chair. There were more wrong ways to move than he'd ever imagined, and pillows weren't much help.

Africanus leaned against a column. "Rufus could go without me. He's visited enough ludi with us to know if someone might be worth buying."

Brutus pointed at the pair of crutches leaning against the chair. "I can get around well enough with those, and if I need more help, Robustus is working at the forge by the stable today. Antistes said there are games in Octodurus in three days, and I want you both to watch the training before then. That can tell us more about whether I want to buy a man than how he performs in a single bout."

"Are you planning to cross the pass going back so you could leave any you buy here until we head home?"

"Since the accident, I favor the easier route through Arelate, but we're only a day and a half from Lousonna. If I could find another one like Otto, that would be worth a three-day trip back here to get him."

Africanus crossed his arms. "Another with equal skill with a gladius? I don't think you'll ever find one."

"Gaius Crassus matched his skill. An impressive man, despite his size."

"Or maybe because of it." Africanus shifted to sit on the half-wall that supported the columns. "Selling Otto for half what he was worth— you gave Crassus a bargain that surprised me."

"A man with loyalty and courage like his deserved one. But how he paid was odd. As a Licinius Crassus, why did he get the extra money he needed from Tiberius Lentulus instead of Sextus Crassus or his father. The elder Crassus was still alive when we fought."

"Maybe a breach in the family over something. Or maybe he'd been in Germania too long to know which relative to ask. Maybe family ties in Germania don't give the right to ask for help like Roman family ties do."

Rufus rode over from the stable, leading Africanus's horse, and Africanus stood. "I'll be back soon. We'll only watch long enough to judge what the ludus has to offer."

With a wave of his hand, Brutus swept that promise away. "Take your time. Enjoy yourselves a while at the baths."

"I'll be back in time for dinner." Africanus jumped and swung his leg across the horse's rump. As he kicked his horse into a trot and led Rufus toward the gate, Brutus raised his hand in farewell.

He rested his head against the back of the chair and closed his eyes. A day of boredom stretched out ahead of him. Lepus was working in the garden, but watching a man weed was sleep-inducing, not entertaining.

Women's voices speaking Germanic came from the direction of the weavers' workshop. He cracked open his eyelids to find Calvia and a very pregnant young woman with smiles on both faces. A quick bow, and the pregnant one disappeared inside. Calvia turned, raised a hand in greeting, and started toward him.

He glanced at the pillow he'd dropped on the floor. She'd be handing it back to him the moment she saw it. She'd probably tell him what he should do with it. What was it about women that they had to mother a man even when he didn't want it?

When she entered the portico, her gaze settled on the pillow, and her lips twitched as she scooped it off the floor. But she clutched it to herself instead of offering it to him.

"How are you feeling today? Are the crutches Fidus made working well for you?"

"They are. It's good to be able to get around on my own again."

"I've never seen someone use two before." She placed the pillow on the empty chair beside him.

"It's what my men use when they hurt a leg. Hobbling with one crutch is slow. Keeping your weight balanced and off the bad leg entirely as you swing the good one forward is much faster. Less painful, too."

"I'll remember that if someone hurts a leg, but I hope it's knowledge I never need." She glanced at the gate. "I saw your men ride out. If you need something before they return, Lepus will find someone to help you. If you know something you'd like now, I'll send it out."

"Africanus won't be back from Octodurus for a few hours."

Boring hours, unless... "There is something I'd like now. Is your offer to play tabula with me still open?"

"Of course. I'll get the board from your room." Her eyes lit with silent laughter. "I'm not your expert friend, but I hope you'll enjoy our game."

She moved the table to the right of his chair where he could reach it without stretching. "I'll be right back."

As she walked past, her mouth twitched like he'd seen when she picked up the pillow. What was so funny?

She'd scarcely disappeared through the door when she returned with the board and the box of game pieces. Without speaking, she moved Africanus's chair to face him across the table and laid out the blue and beige bone rondels.

"As my guest, you should go first."

Africanus was an expert, and he won as often as he lost. He and Brutus were both fiercely competitive. Although Africanus held himself in check while they sparred, it was full-on combat when they played tabula or latrunculi. But Brutus would play a relaxed game today. It was never enjoyable to be defeated, but it might embarrass her if he overwhelmed her with his usual game.

Twenty moves in, he abandoned that strategy. He was the one losing...and losing badly.

He glanced at her as she awaited his next move. Her eyes were on the board, her face serene with a slight smile playing at the corners of her mouth. No wonder she'd laughed when she said she wasn't his expert friend. She was used to opponents of his caliber, and he'd be willing to wager she often beat them.

As she made the last move that sealed his defeat, he raised his eyebrows at her. "I misjudged you. I didn't start with my best game, so I demand a rematch."

"Of course. Anyone can lose a single game. I prefer best two out of three."

"Or first one to win four."

"Will your men be gone that long?"

"Probably. How did you learn to play so well?"

She began placing the pieces back on the board. "I used to play almost every day with my father and often with my brother. My brother said sisters and brothers shouldn't wager with each other on principle." She flashed him a smile. "But I think he just didn't want to lose his allowance to me."

After losing to her four out of seven, Brutus leaned back in his chair and rested his eyes.

"You look tired. Perhaps that's enough for today."

She meant well, but he didn't need a mother. "Tired of tabula, but not tired of my opponent. If you play latrunculi, flip the board and set it up."

"It's been several months, so I might not provide much challenge for you."

There was a playfulness in her eyes that made him doubt that. "I'd offer to take it easy on you, but our first tabula game showed that's a foolish plan."

"I've kept my skill in that playing with Damalio."

"Does he beat you?"

"Occasionally."

He'd wager those were occasions when she chose not to focus.

Ten moves into the first game, and he was planning to challenge her daily until he left. He and Africanus played enough they could often predict each other's moves. She provided novelty in the way she played.

After a hard-fought battle, the game ended in a tie.

"Are you ready to rest now?"

If he were honest, the answer would be he needed to. But he didn't want to. Pinned down with his broken leg, he'd been bored half out of his mind. Who would have thought his hostess would prove so entertaining a companion?

"No. Best two out of three."

As she began setting her rondels and kings back in their starting places, his men rode through the gate.

She looked up at the sound of hoofbeats and set the remaining pieces down. "Now Africanus is back to give you an expert opponent, I have some work to attend to."

"If you're willing, I'd be pleased to continue playing with you. Can't your slaves do whatever it is?"

"Some, but not all, and they have their own work to complete as well. We can play again tomorrow." She rose. "I'll see you at dinner. Sollus tells me he has something delightful to try on us tonight."

Brutus tipped his head back for a better view of her face. "I'll look forward to both."

Africanus dismounted by the portico, and Rufus led his horse toward the stables. One glance at the board, and the corners of his mouth turned up.

Calvia stepped away from the chair, and her upturned hand invited him to sit. "I hope your ride to Octodurus was enjoyable."

"It was." Africanus gaze moved from Calvia to Brutus and back.

"I leave you in expert hands." With a gracious smile directed at both of them, she entered the house.

Brutus's brow furrowed. She asked no questions about why his men had gone to town. Most women were curious even about things that didn't affect them and which were none of their business. Camilla had even suffered from that a little, but she was better than any other woman he'd known.

Africanus settled into the chair. "Would you like anything before we start?"

"A better understanding of Calvia. She intrigues me."

Domina of a Crassus estate when there was no obvious connection. Clearly in charge and seemingly unperturbed by her steward's open hostility. A gifted strategic thinker, at least as far as tabula and latrunculi were concerned. A lover of history who'd brought Tacitus's complete works when she came from Rome.

Africanus crossed his arms. "She's like most women on the surface. No man knows what goes on inside a woman's head. But one thing is clear. She likes your son very much."

"Probably because she has no children of her own. As motherly as she's been toward me, she wouldn't be one to shove the raising of her child off on a slave."

Brutus tapped the board. "Set it up for latrunculi."

As Africanus placed the pieces, Brutus's eyes were drawn to the door through which Calvia had disappeared. It would be interesting to share board games and conversation with a woman as smart as she was. It was already entertaining to watch the wolf, the guard dog, and the domina react to each other at dinner.

It would be four weeks until he could travel, but they wouldn't be boring after all.

# Chapter 38

## More Like a Brother

*June 13*

Sword rang on sword behind her, and Licinia barely heard it as she considered her next move. The morning sparring had become Brutus's favorite time for their daily board games. She didn't blame him. She would be bored to tears if all she had to entertain herself was two men swinging swords at each other.

Hoofbeats joined the rhythm of sword strikes; then silence fell.

"There are two executions scheduled before the gladiators fight. If you want to watch, you're welcome to join me." Antistes's accented Latin drew her eyes from the board as soon as she moved her piece.

Rufus raised his eyebrows, and Africanus shook his head. "We'll wait for the main bouts."

Showing no disappointment, her steward kicked his horse and trotted out the gate.

As Rufus headed for the stable, Africanus entered the house and emerged without his gladius. "It's a short program, so I expect we'll be back midafternoon."

"Enjoy yourselves. No hurry for you to return."

As Licinia watched Africanus stride toward the stables, her nose wrinkled.

Brutus moved his piece and leaned back in his chair. "What's wrong?"

Licinia fingered her blue rondel. "I will never understand the bloodlust of so many Romans. Father and Se—my brother...you couldn't find finer men. Good husbands, fair masters, respected by everyone. But they both loved the games. They said a woman couldn't understand, that it was about honor and courage. Well, women have honor and courage, too, but most of us don't want to watch men being murdered to entertain a crowd. And the poor slaves who have to kill or be killed... it's not right."

Brutus's lips narrowed. "So you say, but all true men of Roma would disagree with you. Your father and brother were right. Honor, courage, excellence...men value *virtus*. Gladiators face death with great courage and superb skill with their weapons that only dedicated training can give."

Shoulders back, spine straight, she met his gaze with certainty equal to his own. "I would gladly die to save another, but it is an utter waste of a life to train to kill simply so others can cheer as they watch someone else being butchered. And the rich men who make money off the slaughter...there's no honor in that."

Brutus's eyes narrowed as his jaw clenched. "You don't know what you're talking about. Have you ever been to the games?"

"No, and I'll never go if I have any choice in the matter."

Their gazes locked, eyebrows lowered, lips tightened.

A baby's babbling came through the door before Vera stepped out with Marcus in her arms. Brutus's lips relaxed into a smile as he reached for his son.

Snuggled against his father's chest, Marcus reached for Brutus's face. Tiny fingers stroked the bearded cheek, and Brutus snagged his hand to place a kiss on his palm. Big fingers tickling the little boy's belly triggered a delighted squeal that brought a smile to Licinia's lips as well.

When Brutus looked at her again, the angry man was gone, and the loving father remained. He lifted Marcus so he could blow on his tummy, and a gale of giggles erupted from the small pink mouth with its two white teeth.

Marcus would have his father's mouth. He already had his mother's eyes. But whose heart would he have?

It was easy to see why Camilla longed to give Brutus a child. It was just as obvious that he treasured her gift.

Licinia rose. "If you'll excuse me, I have some things to attend to, and Marcus clearly wants your undivided attention."

The smile inspired by his son remained as he turned his eyes back on her. "I'll see you at dinner and look forward to our games tomorrow."

"As will I."

She glanced at him as she passed through the doorway. Marcus had grabbed his father's thumb, and Brutus gave it a small shake. She was several steps into the hallway when his voice drifted through the door.

"I'll keep him. You can do whatever you want for a while."

"Yes, master." Vera's relaxed voice was drowned out by Marcus's giggles. Together, they broadened Licinia's smile.

It was easy to see why Camilla had loved this man, even with his Roman values that would keep him from seeking the Truth.

She strolled to the loom by the great-hall window. The blanket was half made, with bands of blue and green that were the muted shades of sky and grass. It seemed like yesterday she was back in Rome, finishing the blanket she would give Camilla for the newest Marcus Brutus.

So many times since she left Rome, she'd imagined that blanket wrapped around Camilla's son as her dear friend cuddled the baby she'd prayed for. What would it have been like to wrap it around him herself and hand him to her sister in Christ?

That was not to be, but she'd seen him wrapped in that woolen expression of her love as his father cradled him. She'd held him and sung to him and seen Camilla's eyes looking back at her. If those who had joined the Lord could see those still on earth, Camilla would be pleased. If only she'd lived to cross the mountains so they could be together again, even for a moment.

"Domina." Damalio's voice turned her from the window. "Are you all right?"

"Yes. I was just thinking about Camilla." Her words were too quiet to reach the man on the portico.

Damalio's silent nod spoke words of condolence that required no ears. "I have the count of new calves and lambs. Master Sextus will be pleased."

When Vera came into the hallway, she raised one hand to her waist and gave a small wave.

With a much larger wave, Licinia called her over. Vera stopped beside Damalio. She was barely chin high on him, and she had to tip her head back to look at his face. When he returned her gaze with a smile, she quickly lowered her eyes.

Licinia's next words were even softer. "I'd like to hear the details later. I want a few moments with Vera while she's off duty."

Damalio smiled down at Vera. "Our newest sister. Welcome to our Lord's familia."

A quick glance at his face and a shy smile accompanied her "Thank you."

"If you'll excuse me, domina…" Licinia's nod sent him out the door.

"We'll talk in my office. No unfriendly ears there." Licinia bolted the office door behind them.

She pointed at a chair as she settled into her own and clasped her hands on the desk. "How are you doing? Any problems since you joined us as a believer? I might be able to fix them, or at least give you some advice on how to deal with them. It can make friends we had before not as friendly."

Vera leaned back in the chair and relaxed. "Not really. Nutrixia doesn't like to talk with me, and she does as little as she can beyond feeding Marcus. That's nothing new.

"But I did get her mad at me. She likes to spend time with men. She was talking too much about wanting time with Primus, and when I pointed out he was married and about to be a father, she told me to be quiet and mind my own business."

"My men all know they aren't to be using the women for their own pleasure, but if she tempts them…" Her lips tightened. "I'll let Damalio know, and he'll keep an eye on her. He'll know what to do if she's a problem."

At Damalio's name, the corners of Vera's mouth lifted. "Everyone says what a nice man he is." The pink that washed Vera's cheeks triggered Licinia's full smile.

"I don't know what I would do without him. He took care of everything as we came from Rome, and he's fixed most of the problems that plagued this estate when we first arrived."

"Steward Antistes doesn't like either of you." Vera's shy smile was replaced by a slight frown.

"No, he doesn't, but if you're going to do things the way that pleases God, you're going to make some people mad at you." She shrugged. "And some would gladly kill you for it. Doing right is never risk-free."

"Master Brutus wanted to kill you when Mistress first died. Africanus helped him get past that."

Licinia picked up a stylus and drummed on the desk. "Theirs is an interesting relationship. Africanus is more like a brother than a slave. At dinner, they speak to each other with their eyes."

"Master Brutus has owned Africanus since before I joined his household six years ago. Master always takes him along when he travels and most places he goes in Rome, too. When Master thought he was dying, he freed him. He's only waiting until the local council meets to record it."

"Will Africanus stay after that?"

"Oh, yes. He's Master's closest friend. When Mistress died, grief was crushing the master. He wanted nothing to do with Marcus until Africanus convinced him Mistress would want him to love his son like she would have. They're closer than most brothers. I saw that same grief on Master's face when it looked like Africanus was dying."

"Then it's a double blessing that Rufus came here for help. God knows what's best for us all."

"He blessed me when we came. Seeing Africanus healed...it finally convinced me Mistress was right to follow Jesus." Her eyes saddened. "It's going to be hard to leave everyone here and be alone in my faith."

"Maybe you won't have to. Would Brutus sell you to me?"

"He kept me for Marcus because he knew I would love him like my own. I don't think I could bear to leave. Master Brutus has forbidden me to ever speak of Mistress's faith to him, but maybe that will change someday. Mistress would want Marcus to believe."

Licinia picked up her father's stylus and rolled it between her fingers, like he and Sextus used to do. "That's something I'll pray for. If he were my son, there would be nothing I'd want more than for him to be saved like us."

Brutus would heal, and Marcus would leave. Already Camilla's son owned more of her heart than she should let him. She loved him for Camilla, and she loved him for himself. She blinked to drive back the tears. Father, Sextus, Camilla, Marcus...why was it so many she loved were taken away too soon? And only one was saved.

Although time blunted the first anguish of loss, some goodbyes would last forever, and the dull ache would remain.

When Africanus rode through the gate, Damalio was talking with Lepus in the garden. A light slap to Lepus's upper arm, and Damalio headed toward the house.

"Damalio." The overseer turned at Africanus's call. "Wait."

After slipping from his horse and handing Rufus the reins, he joined Damalio.

"What can I do for you?" The slight smile Damalio wore when he listened to Calvia at dinner appeared.

"Answer a question."

"If I can."

"You were there when we first came and I was taken upstairs."

"I was." Her overseer's mouth straightened.

Africanus leaned against the column of the portico and crossed his arms. He tipped his head toward the clerestory above them. "What was done to me up in that room? Some special medicine? Sorcery?"

Between blinks, Damalio's eyes shifted from relaxed to cautious. "What do you remember?"

"I got everyone out of the raeda. I was climbing out as the last harness straps were breaking and the raeda started slipping into the ravine. I jumped; the tongue slammed into my side. The last I remember I was with Master Brutus by the boulder."

Africanus straightened and uncrossed his arms. "Then I woke up here, tired but barely even sore. Master Brutus said you carried me upstairs with me near death. Your mistress and her maid went upstairs, too. But when he told Lepus he wanted to take my ashes back to Rome, Lepus said his mistress had said I'd be fine. When the gladiator physician came, he thought I'd been faking.

"I know death and when nothing can save a man. I was dying. Master Brutus thought so, too. He freed me to die as I was born...a free man."

Damalio's smile came slowly. "It's worth almost dying for that."

"Even as his slave, he treated me like I was free." Africanus rubbed his neck. "Calvia speaks to you as if you're free, but you treat her as if you aren't. Are you free?"

"Yes and no." Damalio shrugged.

Africanus's brow furrowed. "Explain."

The smile grew. "Mistress Calvia's brother owns me now, but I've belonged to a man who showed me how to be free even while someone owns me. He'd planned to free me when I turned thirty to make me a citizen, but he had to leave when I was sixteen."

"Leave? He died?"

"Not that I've heard. He only left."

Africanus's eyes narrowed. "What makes a master just leave?"

Damalio's eyes turned wary, then relaxed as the slow smile returned. "When someone wants to kill him."

"Here in Octodurus? There's a garrison to protect Romans. He could have reported the threat."

"Near Rome, and there's no one who can protect you when the garrison sends the men to get you."

Africanus's head drew back. "What had he done?"

"Nothing wrong."

"Rome doesn't usually arrest citizens for doing nothing wrong."

In the arena, Africanus could read any opponent. Most men paused before deciding to defend or attack. Damalio had that same look as he weighed his next words.

"It does when they're Christians. With less than half a day's notice, he left with his wife and two young children. He took one small wagon and left everything else. His paterfamilias gave the estate to his cousin. The cousin sold me to Mistress Calvia's brother three years ago."

"So he never freed you."

"No and yes. He told me the truth, and that set me free."

"You talk in riddles. And you haven't answered my first question. What was done in that room?"

Damalio's mouth opened as if to speak. Then his eyes focused behind Africanus, and he shut it without a word.

Africanus turned to find Brutus coming through the portico doorway with the two crutches keeping his weight off his broken leg. He started toward them.

"If you want an explanation, we can talk later, just the two of us." His voice was almost a whisper. "What I would tell you is not for Brutus's ears."

Africanus's massaged his neck. What could have happened that Brutus shouldn't hear?

When Brutus reached them, Damalio dipped his head. "Can I help you with anything?"

Brutus's mouth curved into his smiling frown. "Not unless you can make my leg mend sooner."

Damalio's slight smile reappeared. "Not today. If you'll excuse me..."

He took a step back before Brutus nodded. Then he turned and strode toward the stable.

Brutus lowered himself into the wicker chair and tipped his head toward the departing Damalio. "There's something about him. I can't say exactly what. Calvia relies on his opinions more than I'd expect. She treats him more like a brother than a slave."

Africanus positioned the padded stool and lifted Brutus's wrapped leg onto it.

As Brutus settled back against the pillows, he blew a breath out. "What were you talking about?"

"Freedom."

Brutus leaned forward and slapped Africanus's arm. "I haven't forgotten what I said. In Roma, I'd already have had a praetor come by the villa to free you. Here, I have to find out when the council meets. I'm getting around well enough now. We can make the manumission official as soon as they do."

Brutus pointed at the chair Calvia had brought out for their board games.

Africanus turned it so he could stretch out his legs. "When you promise something, I consider it done. It can wait until you're walking again."

"I don't want to wait. I'll have Damalio get it scheduled for their next meeting date, and we'll do it then. He'll lend me the estate raeda." His lips tightened, and he rested his hand on the bandage. "I wish I could make you a citizen, but since you're a gladiator, that's not possible."

A corner of Africanus's mouth lifted. "As I told you by the road, your respect and friendship are better than freedom. The arena brought us together; that's worth more than citizenship."

Brutus laced his fingers behind his head and relaxed against the chairback. His gaze rested on the snow-capped peaks as a hawk screamed overhead.

"When your boys are big enough, we'll bring them along," His smile turned sad. "I should have taken Camilla to Lousonna. If I hadn't left her alone, she might not have listened to that Christian."

"Nothing can keep a woman from listening to her friends. It would have made no difference."

"Maybe not." Brutus closed his eyes and rubbed both sides of his nose with his fingertips before his gaze settled once more on the mountains. "So many nights, we shared the stars. I wish I'd brought her with me to watch the eagles soar."

# Chapter 39

RESIGNED TO HIS FATE



*The taberna near the Baths of Trajan, June 15*

Custos's leg bounced under the table. Once more, Sabinus's agent was late meeting him. That was a bad sign. Festinus was always prompt, and he'd hoped the gladiator had been a one-time replacement because his regular contact had been ill.

He'd only taken one sip from his cup of wine when the enforcer entered and strode toward him. Custos's mouth curved into what he hoped looked like a confident smile as he raised his hand in greeting.

The gladiator pulled out a chair and turned it so he faced the door. Then his huge hand wrapped around Custos's cup and lifted it to his lips. He tossed back his head and drank half of it before returning it to the table and wrapping both hands around it. "What do you have today?"

Custos willed his leg to stop moving. "The estate reports come only once a month, so it will be at least two more weeks before something comes from Octodurus again. I watch for something useful all the time, but until then, there probably won't be anything new of interest to the master."

"By then, the master might already know what's going on there. He sent Festinus and two like me to check it out right after we met."

Custos's gut twisted, but he kept the smile in place. "Good. It's likely Gratus is only someone Crassus freed, and if so, it's better to know sooner than later. I'll keep watching for something more useful."

"You do that." The gladiator drained the cup. "If this turns out to be a false lead, the master won't be happy that he has to wait for another."

"I'm doing my best, but it's hard to find any wrongdoing by a man like Crassus."

"That's your problem, not mine." The gladiator stood. "I'll be back next week."

"And I'll be here."

The gladiator's sneer was his only answer before he turned and left the shop.

Custos slumped in the chair. Nothing he did would satisfy Sabinus. His betrayal of Crassus the week before had done nothing to protect him. Sooner or later, he'd be disposed of, and his futile attempt to stop that had only put innocent people in danger.

Six days ago, Festinus had headed north, but it should take two weeks to get there. If he told Master Crassus now, a horse courier could get there in a little less than a week.

Eyes closed, he ran both hands through his hair. He could wait for Sabinus to kill him, or he could tell Master Crassus what he'd done while there was still time to do something about it. He might be a dead man either way, but he'd rather die alone than risk taking another with him.

Shoulders squared, he rose from the table in the dark corner and headed toward the light streaming through the door. Gladiators walked proudly into the arena to face death. He had nothing to be proud of, but was he brave enough to hasten his own death to save another?

*The Crassus townhouse*

Custos entered the townhouse through the stableyard. Vicarius had gone to visit a friend and shouldn't be back yet, but he didn't want to see his mentor before doing what he had to do. Less chance of running into Vicarius in the rear of the house, and he was a man who anticipated risks and avoided what he could.

He pulled a deep breath and released a deeper sigh. But when you were a slave, some traps couldn't be avoided, no matter how careful a man was. And he'd dragged Master Crassus and the woman in Octodurus into this trap with him.

No matter who the woman was, Sabinus would spread rumors that some would be eager to hear. From all he'd seen, Crassus was a man above reproach, and that meant others with flawed characters would be eager to believe something bad about him and to share it with others.

Would Mistress Octavia believe the lie? If she did, what would she do to the master? Theirs was a comfortable partnership, not a love match. She was happy to bear his children, entertain his colleagues, and run his household. But what if she thought he'd betrayed their contract of fidelity?

Crassus mustn't be blind-sided by a false accusation. Lies spread like flames in a field of ripened grain, but it took time to present the truth in a man's defense.

Custos was on borrowed time with Sabinus now. His old master was ruthless in his treatment of senators who might stand against him. That was why he and his son were after Master Crassus. A slave who knew more than they thought he should, who was a liability if he revealed what he'd done...Custos had no doubt of his future. The only uncertainty was how they'd do it.

But even if Sabinus meant to reward him, he couldn't stand himself if he did nothing to stop what he'd put in motion.

Crassus had every right to kill him, and Custos wouldn't blame him if he did. The best he could hope for was being sold, but Crassus might think he knew too much to risk another man owning him. Maybe all he could hope for was a speedy death without too much pain.

He'd been born to one of Sabinus's house slaves. He never knew which one. He'd thought Fortuna favored him when his intelligence and hard work made him assistant to an understeward. That had brought him to the old master's attention and marked him as the man for this task.

But Fortuna had never smiled upon him. What he'd thought were her gifts were a curse instead. They'd tossed him into a high-stakes game he didn't want to play, and now the final die was cast. It had been the moment Sabinus killed the assistant and put Custos in his place. As the die took its final slow tumbles, it was only a question of who struck the death blow and how.

Would this be the last time he walked through the atrium with its marble statues reflecting in the pool and sweet-smelling flowers in pots that lined it? The last time along the row of chairs where clients had waited for their turn to speak with the best man Custos had ever known? The last time past the office where Vicarius had taught him so much and treated him like a son?

He lifted his hand at the master's library door and froze. He closed his eyes, and his jaw clenched. Then he let his fist fall.

One knock, then two more.

"Come in."

He lifted the latch, pushed the door open, and entered. As he bolted the door behind him and turned to face his master, he resigned himself to his fate.

◆

Sextus unrolled another panel of his new scroll of Pliny's *Wars of Germania*, and it drew a sad smile. Licinia loved Tacitus, and she would have delighted in Pliny's work that Tacitus used writing his own histories. Maybe she could return someday, and they could have one of their deep discussions that he missed too often.

Three knocks shifted his gaze to the library door. One knock, then two was Vicarius's pattern. "Come in."

When the door swung open, his secretary's assistant stepped in. "Yes?"

Custos bolted the door and came to stand in front of the desk. He cleared his throat. "There's something I have to tell you, master."

Sextus placed the scroll on the desktop. "What is it?"

Custos's arms hung at his side, and he rubbed his palms on his tunic. "When Vicarius's assistant died and Master Tertullus gave me to you as his replacement, I wasn't his to give."

A strange way to start a conversation. Sextus's brow furrowed. "Why not?"

"I belonged to Quintus Flavius Sabinus. He gave me to Tertullus to pass on to you."

Sextus stiffened. A slave he'd trusted was a gift from his greatest enemy? Worse still, a friend he'd trusted was in the enemy's camp.

Custos bowed his head and stared at the floor. "He ordered the death of your man so he could substitute me." Eyes that had been turned down lifted to meet Sextus's gaze. "As his spy." His head drooped again. "He renamed me before he gave me to you. He laughed when he told me you'd think it meant 'watchman' because you'd never expect Tertullus to plant a spy."

"Why would he do that?" Sextus stood and leaned clenched fists on the desk.

Custos stepped back, his whole body tensed like a deer who'd caught a scent before Sextus let an arrow fly. Then he drew a deep breath, and his shoulders relaxed.

His eyes lifted to meet Sextus's, then lowered. "He didn't say. He only tells slaves what they need to know. He told me to find something that would let him control you, something you'd be afraid to have others know."

Sextus's breaths came too quickly. He forced them to slow down, willing himself to stay calm. He'd sent Licinia to the Octodurus estate just in time. It was barely a week after her departure that he'd received Custos from Tertullus.

He punched the desk before he straightened, and Custos flinched. "What have you told Sabinus?"

"For a long time, nothing he thought useful. His son thought your weak spot was your sister after she disappeared. I was told to figure out where she went and why."

The frown that started when Custos revealed who gave him turned into a scowl. "What did you tell him about her?"

Custos drew a deep breath, and his eyes closed for a slow blink. Then his shoulders squared, and he faced Sextus straight on. "That she never wrote to you, and you didn't seem to write to her. At least I never saw any letters going to Licinia Crassa."

"Did that satisfy him?"

"No. He thought there must be something about her that you were afraid for others to know." He rubbed his lip. "He thought you'd hidden her somewhere, and I was told I'd better discover where that was."

"But since I never received a letter, what did you tell him?"

"That I thought she must be using an alias. And I thought she might write often. I watched for letters from someone who wrote regularly, someone you always answered promptly."

Sextus's stomach knotted. "Did you tell him of any?"

"Gratus wrote at least once a month and with an undertone like he was a woman."

Sextus clamped his jaw until it hurt. He'd been careful, but not careful enough. There hadn't been the slightest reason to suspect a spy. Tertullus owed him a great favor, and Custos had seemed an appropriate way to show appreciation. Vicarius had nothing but praise for the young man since he started, and that had only increased since his broken collarbone made Custos's help essential.

"Anything else?" Anger simmered underneath those two words.

"I told him your steward in Octodurus resented the woman you'd made domina there. Two weeks ago, I told him you sent the letters to Gratus, but I didn't know where."

He shifted his feet. "But last week, the agent I reported to had been replaced by one of Sabinus's enforcers. He said my old master's patience with me was used up. It was time to deliver, or else. So, I told him where Gratus is. I told myself maybe Gratus was only a freedman, like the letters claimed, and there'd be no harm in them knowing."

Custos's hands moved from his sides to in front of him. But instead of clasping his hands, as Sextus had seen so many times, Custos gripped his thumb and squeezed. "But he just told me Sabinus sent an agent and two gladiators to find the woman six days ago. What they'll do...I don't know. Whether or not Calvia Lucilla is your mistress or Gratus is your sister, Sabinus will spin a web of lies to bring you down."

He wiped his hands on his tunic again. "Several times I told Festinus I had nothing to report because there was nothing my old master could use, that you had nothing to hide because you did everything with honor. But Master Sabinus will just make up some lie that people will believe. And he's going to target whoever is at the Octodurus estate."

Another long blink, then Custos squared his shoulders and stared into Sextus's eyes. "He'll stop at nothing to get control over you. He killed your slave, he hurt Vicarius, and he'll kill me when this is over so I can't tell anyone what he did. He'll do it tomorrow if he learns I've told you." He squeezed the back of his neck. "You probably want to kill me yourself. But I can't do this anymore, and I hope by telling you now that you can do something to protect whoever is there. A horse courier might get there ahead of Sabinus's men."

Sextus settled heavily into his chair. Elbows on his desk, he buried his face in his hands. Sending Licinia with Damalio to the distant estate had seemed like the best plan to protect her.

And it should have been.

He lowered his hands and rested his forearms on the table. His gaze settled on Custos and turned icy. His enemy's spy blanched, but he didn't move, except to drop his gaze to the floor. No doubt something he'd learned in the household of a sadist who'd treat any plea for mercy as a request for more pain. For a slave to fail to deliver what Sabinus wanted...that would mean death. Possibly slow and probably agonizing as Sabinus watched.

He would send the horse courier to Damalio immediately, as Custos suggested. Maybe tell him to take her to the estate in Hispania. Would Sabinus's men know where to follow her if she fled? Would they catch up while she was on the way, with only the four men he'd sent with her as protection? Men who were Christians, not bodyguards.

He rubbed his lip. Maybe she should stay in Octodurus, protected by the whole familia of the estate. But once Sabinus found her, could her faith stay secret for long?

His father had said a man of honor was at extreme disadvantage in a fight with a scoundrel. Things he would never do himself were second nature to a rogue. But a rogue's accomplice should have some understanding of how his master thought, of what he might try next. He might know what could lure the hunter away from his prey for good.

"Custos."

The young man he'd trusted with too much raised his head to meet Sextus's gaze. "Yes, master?"

Trusted with too much, but should he trust him with more? Custos believed his confession meant his death, by Sabinus's hand or Sextus's, but he'd come forward while there was still time to protect Licinia. If she were here, she'd be begging him to forgive the man who'd betrayed them and then repented of it.

Perhaps beneath the skin of this traitor was a man who would act honorably, given the chance.

And with no choice that was certain to save her without Custos's help, he would give him that chance.

"If the courier reaches Gratus before Sabinus's agents so they don't find what they're looking for, what then?"

Custos's eyebrows rose at the question, then dipped. He fingered his lower lip. "It depends. Is it your sister or your mistress there?"

Sextus crossed his arms. "I've kept faith with Octavia."

"I beg pardon, master. I should have known." The fingering turned into a squeeze. "Master Sabinus considers many possibilities and plans for them. He will have given his agent instructions that depend on what they find. If she's gone when they get there, maybe they'll send a message back to Rome and stay a while to see if she returns. Or try to track where she went. If they think she was never there, they'll return to Rome and report. If they find any woman there...they will try to learn what she is to you."

With his father's silver stylus, Sextus tapped the desktop. His sweet sister had kept the name she sailed under, but an alias wasn't enough to protect her from these hunters.

"And if they find my sister?"

"They'll try to find out why you sent her there." Custos bowed his head. "I can't say how."

Didn't know or didn't want to say? Custos's grim mouth made Sextus's stomach clench. He knew enough of Sabinus's cruel streak to expect no better from his men. "And then?"

"Once he gets what he thinks can control you, he'll dispose of me and start using it against you. If he doesn't find it, I expect I'll be told to keep looking for something else to set a hook in you."

Sextus leaned back in his chair. "What could get him to stop looking?

"For your sister?"

"Yes."

It was too much to expect Sabinus would stop looking for a way to control him as long as he remained one of those governing the Empire. But if he could draw his enemy's attention away from Licinia...

Hands at his waist, Custos laced his fingers. "I don't know if he will, as long as he thinks she's your weakest point. If you could make him think something else made you more vulnerable, maybe then."

Sextus leaned on the desk and steepled his fingers. "Can you lie convincingly to help me lure him off her trail?"

Custos hung his head. "I lied convincingly to you." Raising his head just enough to look into Sextus eyes, the young man sighed. "I'm sorry for that, master." He straightened. "I'll gladly lie to your enemy, if that's what you want."

"Are you his only spy here?"

"I don't know."

Sextus took a sheet of papyrus from his desk drawer. "Then this conversation stays between you and me." He uncorked the ink bottle. "You will continue helping Vicarius exactly as you have so no one suspects what you told me. You will still meet with Sabinus's agent. We'll decide what you can tell him before each meeting."

"Yes, master."

"You'll take this letter to the courier service as soon as I finish, but tell no one."

A tentative smile accompanied Custos's nod.

Sextus dipped his pen into the ink and began the letter that might save his sister's life.

# Chapter 40



### What's in a Name?

*The Octodurus estate, June 16*

With his head resting on the padded seatback, Brutus relaxed as the changing panorama of fields, forests, and snow-covered peaks moved past the raeda window. Burdonarius had kept the mules at a good pace, and Rufus and Africanus rode beside as bodyguards.

Except for the pillows Calvia had insisted on adding to the seat and the pillowed crate that supported his leg, it was a foretaste of his upcoming trip to the Lousonna estate. The few miles to Octodurus hadn't been bad, but a day and a half trapped in a carriage instead of on horseback would take much of the pleasure from the journey.

Still, it was the best day he'd known since Camilla died. The good friend he'd thought he'd lost as pain racked him by the road was now a free man.

As they pulled through the estate gate, Calvia came from the weavers' building and crossed the courtyard. At the edge of the road to the stable, she turned and waited for them.

Burdonarius reined in to stop the carriage beside her. Her usual smile of greeting appeared as Africanus helped him out. Rufus reached in for the crutches and handed them to him.

Brutus didn't even try to dampen his grin. A crutch under each arm, he rested his hand on his friend's shoulder. "Calvia Lucilla, allow me to introduce Antonius Africanus."

"My warmest congratulations, Antonius Africanus." Licinia's smile was as broad as his own.

Africanus stood taller as his own smile grew. "Thank you."

Brutus moved his crutches and swung his good leg forward. When he was clear of the raeda, Burdonarius snapped the reins, and the mules headed for the place by the stable where the carriage was stored. His men mounted and followed.

Calvia's eyes followed Africanus, and her smile dimmed. "I envy your ability to bestow freedom on someone who's served you so well. I'd free many if I was their owner and have them keep working for me as free men and women."

"With my six estates, I have several hundred. A few would work just as hard if I didn't own them, but many of them..." He shook his head.

"You can't know that. The people here weren't treated well when I came. Antistes treated many like animals, but I changed that. Since I did, they work harder, more like they want to, not just because they have to."

Brutus tightened his lips to stop a skeptical laugh. Farm labor was grueling, and few would do it willingly if they didn't have to. Some of his gladiators loved to fight, but some, like Otto of the Vangiones, would never stay if freed. "Would your husband have agreed?"

"It wasn't something we ever discussed." She wrapped her arms across her chest.

That was enough to declare he wouldn't, but she wasn't bound by what a dead husband thought. "Who owns your men if not you?"

"My brother." She rubbed her arm. "I want to talk with Sollus about making something special for dinner to celebrate Africanus's new freedom." The smile she offered was stiff. "I'll see you then." She stepped back and walked away more quickly than usual.

Alternately swinging the crutches and his good leg forward, Brutus made his way to the portico. Just short of the stone-slab flooring, Africanus joined him.

"I just learned another strange thing about Calvia."

Africanus raised his eyebrows.

"It's neither her nor her husband's family that owns her slaves. It's her brother. Brothers don't usually provide a married woman with slaves."

"Maybe she's here because his father sent her away when he died. She said she didn't want to talk about it. Maybe he even kept the children."

That triggered Brutus's frown. "The way she is with Marcus...I don't think she could be as happy as she seems if he had." He rubbed his jaw. "That first dinner…she looked almost frightened when I asked her husband's name, and it was Damalio who answered. That struck me as odd at the time. Maybe there's a story worth knowing there."

"Maybe. But it might distress her if you knew it." Africanus crossed his arms.

"And you don't think I should do that to someone who's been so good to us." Brutus shrugged. "Perhaps you're right."

He settled into the chair on the portico and Africanus lifted his leg onto the stool. "It's been a good day. I'll free your family when we get back to Roma. I can make Dorcas a citizen now, even if you can't be, and your children will at least be Junian Latins until they grow up. I can get them citizenship then."

Africanus's eyes lit. "They'll have a good future. I thank you for that."

"No thanks are needed. Bring out the board and let's play."

As Africanus entered the house, Brutus laced his fingers behind his head and leaned back in the chair. He couldn't make a gladiator a citizen by freeing him. Could he do it by adopting him? That was something he'd look into when he returned to Rome.

◆

With her request for something special given to Sollus, Licinia returned to the blanket loom in the great hall. Africanus was a free man now, with a new name to go with that freedom. He deserved a celebration, and Sollus could make a simple meal taste like a feast.

She ran the shuttle between the warp threads, then tapped the yarn into place with the comb. Blues and greens and natural off-white—the colors of afternoon clouds and forests and sky fit the freedom she'd felt for months.

When she thought of her life in Rome, so much of it scarcely felt real now. In every way that mattered, she was Calvia Lucilla, busy domina of an Alpine estate, not Licinia Crassa, an idle noblewoman of Rome.

Primula called her mistress. Damalio, Antistes, and all the slaves called her domina. No one had called her Licinia since Sextus told her farewell in Portus.

On the lips of Brutus, Calvia was a comfortable name, one that fit an equestrian woman running an estate. Until she heard him pronounce his friend's new name, she hadn't realized she no longer thought of herself as Licinia Crassa, daughter of the great Sextus Licinius Crassus, sister of the Sextus whose own accomplishments might surpass their father's. Perhaps it was time to fully embrace her new name and identity, just as Africanus was now an Antonius in his own right.

She had become Calvia, and Calvia she would be. Her future was here, not Rome, and that thought brought a smile.

Brutus lay back on the pillow, fingers laced behind his head. Silo had come two days early, stopping by as he returned to Octodurus from treating a broken arm at a neighboring estate.

A satisfied smile curved Brutus's lips. The physician had said he was healing well. Better than well—more like remarkable. It had felt good to have the wrappings removed, his skin oiled and scraped, and six layers of clean wrappings reapplied.

Brutus reached for the table beside the bed and picked up the codex he'd purchased in town. He hadn't expected to find such a fine copy of Ovid's *Amores* in a provincial town, even a capital. Calvia's library was limited to scrolls of Tacitus. Some poetry by the famous poet would be a suitable thank you for all she'd done.

He swung his legs off the bed. Africanus handed him the crutches and received the codex in exchange.

"Calvia planned something special to celebrate your freedom tonight. I'm sure Sollus won't disappoint. I wouldn't mind having him run my own kitchen."

"Maybe she'd sell him to you."

"She'd be a fool to part with him. She'd never find as good a cook to replace him." The corner of his mouth lifted. "I'm not sure she'd sell anyone here. She treats the *familia rustica* more like a family than anyone I've ever seen."

What had seemed so far from his room the first time he ate in the triclinium had become an easy walk. When they entered, all were gathered at the table except them.

Calvia rose. "Welcome, Antonius Africanus, to our celebration of your manumission."

She raised her goblet, and the others, including Antistes, did the same.

Africanus's mouth twitched, and Brutus fought a grin. His friend was used to hero-worship from men as an invincible gladiator. He wasn't comfortable with a fuss being made by friends.

Brutus sat, and Africanus handed him the codex before taking the crutches to lean against the wall.

"While I was in town, I had a chance to pick up something." He held the codex out, and she took it. "A small token to express how much I appreciate your hospitality as I recover."

"It's been our pleasure to have you here, but I thank you. An addition to a library is always welcome." She opened the codex. As she read a poem, her eyes widened, and a flush of pink swept across her cheeks before she closed it.

She looked at the cover where the poet and title were inscribed. "Ovid. I see." She bit her lip. Some women did that often, but it wasn't something he'd seen her do before.

"I thank you for the generous thought..." She held the codex out to him. "But you should take it with you when you leave. I don't read erotic poetry, and it would be wasted here."

It took some effort to keep a straight face, but Brutus managed. He'd been told women loved Ovid, although Camilla had said the same thing.

"Perhaps Damalio would like it."

"Thank you, but no. I don't read such poetry either." Her man's eyes were unreadable.

Brutus was not a fan of poetry in general, erotic or otherwise. He much preferred prose and especially history. Ovid would get no more use in his library than it would in hers.

"Antistes?" Would the steward take it off his hands?

A smug smile curved Antistes's mouth. "I'll take it with pleasure. Ovid is one of Rome's greatest poets. I enjoy all the things that Roman men enjoy. I don't understand men who don't or overly modest women."

Calvia set down her goblet with enough force to make Brutus jump. "Treating women as only something to entertain men, whether in life or in literature, is wrong, and any man of honor would agree with me after thinking about it."

Antistes bristled and opened his mouth, but it closed before words came out.

Brutus raised an eyebrow at Africanus. It was tempting to stir up the argument for some dinnertime entertainment. But Africanus's subtle shake of his head was enough to squash the temptation. Time to change to a subject that would calm Antistes's anger instead of feed it.

"Natural history or philosophy? Is that something you'd like in your library?"

"I always enjoyed my father's volumes of Pliny." Any sign of irritation was gone, and the serene Calvia sat across from him once more.

"Then I'll have Africanus see if he can find some as a more suitable thank you."

Her smile was warm. "I would like that very much."

As he took a sip of wine, he watched Calvia over the goblet's rim. Camilla would have liked her. It was an introduction he would have enjoyed making, if only his beloved were still alive.

# Chapter 41



## KEEPING SECRETS

*June 17*

Calvia had just switched between off-white and green yarns when the main door opened and closed behind her.

"Domina." Olga's excited voice cause her to turn. "The new raeda...it is here."

"I hope they made it suitable for an injured man and a baby." She parked her shuttle, and followed Olga out the door.

Brutus, swinging along on his crutches, was well ahead of her, but it took no time to catch up with him. He turned his smiling frown on her. "It looks well made from here, but I won't judge until I inspect it properly. First appearances can deceive, but I never judge on those."

"Damalio has been watching over the building of it. He has a careful eye for detail, and he would have insisted they redo anything less than good quality."

As they approached, Damalio wrapped the reins around the post by the driver's seat and jumped down. "Ready for your inspection, Master Brutus."

"Did you and Africanus look it over well?"

"We did."

Africanus still sat on his horse, fingering its mane. "It's as well made as the one in Roma. Well worth what you paid. When you're ready to travel, it will serve well."

Brutus moved close enough to look inside. "It should do."

When he withdrew, Calvia slipped by him to look in as well. A well-cushioned seat ran the width of the carriage with a drop-down seat on each side. One would work well for supporting his leg; the other would hold Nutrixia as Vera with Marcus sat beside him. Plenty of room for the trunks as well.

When she withdrew her head, she turned a smile on him. "Even though you have your raeda now, Silo said you shouldn't be traveling until at least four weeks after your injury. You're more than welcome to stay as long as needed for the trip to be safe and easy for you."

He met her smile with one of his own. "I'm content to spend another two weeks with an expert player of my favorite games."

"Good. It's been pure delight to have someone to play latrunculi with again. It was my favorite game to play with Father. I've missed it since he died. I'll miss it when you leave."

She turned her eyes on the snow-covered peaks that flanked the pass. There was a lot she'd miss when he left. The way his smiling frown would appear when something struck him as funny. How it shifted toward a smile when her tease was too close to the truth. The crossing of his arms when he thought he'd made a particularly good move...or when he knew he hadn't and wanted to make her think he had. The twitch of his mouth that always betrayed which it was.

It was almost like having Sextus across the board from her, except Sextus couldn't shake her focus like Brutus sometimes did with a question totally unrelated to the game. And he took perverse delight in doing it.

"Switching between you and Africanus has improved my game."

"Perhaps, if you come to your estate next year, you could bring Marcus and stop for a visit."

The smiling frown she found hard to interpret returned. "If I come over the pass, you can rely on me doing so. I'd much rather spend an evening playing games with you than sleeping at the inn where I usually stay in Octodurus."

"Perhaps you can stay a few nights so I can spend some time with Marcus. Children change so much in a year."

Had she kept the wistfulness from her voice? It was going to hurt too much when she watched Camilla's boy leave. His mother would have loved him beyond measure. She couldn't help loving him herself. She loved watching his father play with him and thinking how happy Camilla would have been to see him loving their son.

Damalio cleared his throat, drawing her gaze. The tiniest shake of his head was all she saw before Brutus's driver walked up and Damalio turned away.

"This is all yours now. You can put it over by the domina's raeda until your master's ready to leave."

Burdonarius dropped to one knee to look under the carriage, and Damalio joined him, pointing at several things of no interest to her but fascinating to the men.

Brutus started back to the portico, and she fell in beside him. Her glance was quick enough he didn't see, and she stopped the sigh before he heard it. The villa would seem empty when Marcus and his father were no longer there.

It was no wonder Camilla had loved him so much.

Any man with six estates and a merchant fleet who chose his bodyguard as his best friend saw the true value of people, not just what society labeled them. She'd never seen a better father or a kinder master. He was as smart as her brother and father, but unlike most men, he could laugh about a woman beating him at a man's game more often than she lost. He treated her as an equal, a rare thing in a world run by men.

Damalio caught up with them. "If you have time now, domina, I need to speak with you."

"Of course. Africanus can provide Brutus with his strategic challenge today."

Brutus's mouth relaxed into a smile as he settled into his chair. "He can, but I may want a game with you later."

Damalio opened the main door, and she led him through the great hall into her office. When he bolted the door, her brow furrowed.

"May I speak freely, domina?"

"You can always do that."

"I see danger." He cleared his throat. "Speaking too freely with Brutus, inviting him to stay here when he's fully healed." His lips tightened. "He's a man who watches everything going on around him. Right now, he's limited in what he can see, but when his leg is healed, that won't be the case. He's more dangerous than Decurion Brocchus."

"I appreciate your warning, but I don't think he's a threat. Camilla always said he was the most honorable man she'd ever met."

His eyebrows lowered. "Brocchus is a man of honor, too, but that doesn't mean it's not dangerous for either of them to know you're a Christian. Mistress Camilla praised her husband's honor, but she never revealed her faith to him."

She opened her mouth to argue, then closed it. He was right. As much as she'd love to have Marcus with her again, as much as she enjoyed Brutus's company, it might put them all in danger. If Camilla had been afraid to tell him she followed Jesus, she shouldn't risk him finding out she did as well.

"Thank you for warning me. I'll be more careful. You can go."

He took a step back before turning and walking from the room.

She rubbed her forehead. The secret her father and brother had kept when she was Licinia—as Calvia, she had to keep it herself.

And keeping secrets always built barriers that kept people out, even when you didn't want them to.

Africanus leaned back in Brutus's wicker chair and lifted his feet onto the stool. The main door opened, and Damalio strode across the portico into the summer sun.

"Damalio." Africanus's quiet word stopped him midstride.

The overseer looked over his shoulder. "Yes?"

"Master Brutus is resting awhile. What were you going to tell me that he shouldn't hear?"

Damalio returned to sit on the wall and leaned against a column. "I can only tell you if you give me your word you won't tell Brutus before you leave."

"You have it." Africanus swung his feet to the floor and leaned forward.

A slow smile curved Damalio's mouth. "We prayed for God to heal you."

Africanus's head drew back. "Prayed? What god do you think listens to such prayers? None of the gods I know are real. Even in fables for children, they don't bring men back from the edge of death. They didn't do it for the men called heroes, and they certainly wouldn't do it for a slave."

"I understand your doubt. I'd been taught the gods always demanded things from us, that they always took before they'd give. I didn't expect any god to care about me when I was Sorex's age. I expected hard labor as a farm slave until I died. But that was before I was sold to Gaius Licinius Crassus. He told me how God loves all the people He's created. How people couldn't help themselves, but He could do what we couldn't. He told His people to pray, to ask for what we need and want."

The slow smile Africanus had seen many times at dinner curved Damalio's mouth. "He delights in giving to us. And when we ask for what He knows is best for us, the answer to those prayers is yes. We asked for your healing, and He healed you."

"Hmph." Africanus leaned back in the chair and rested his hands on its arms. "I wouldn't have thought you'd be a superstitious man."

"I'm not, but I am a man who believes what he's seen with his own eyes." With his hands on the wall beside him, Damalio leaned forward. "Did you expect to die?"

"I knew I was dying." One corner of Africanus's mouth lifted. "I've seen enough death to know when it's coming."

"So how would you explain you returning to health so quickly if God didn't heal you?"

"I can't." Africanus's brow furrowed. "That's why I'm asking what you did."

"I've seen healings, quick and complete, that I can't explain as natural. You're not the first I saw come back from the edge. I was twelve when we were building a new stable. A roof timber fell when they were putting it up. It crushed Taurus's chest. He was coughing up blood, gasping for breath, staring but not like he saw us."

Damalio gazed at the wall past Africanus, but not like he was seeing it. "Then Master Gaius knelt by him, placed his hand on his forehead, and asked his god to heal. He did, and Taurus got up like nothing had happened. That's what we did to you." He shrugged. "We asked God to heal you in Jesus's name, and He did."

"Who is this god?" Africanus had leaned forward without realizing it.

"The only true God, the One who created everything. He's the God of everyone everywhere, but it's the Jews He chose as His special people to tell everyone else about Him. He told them how they could approach Him with blood sacrifices for their sins."

"Sins?" Not a word Africanus had heard before.

"Those are the things we all do that make us unfit for His presence. Then He came as Jesus of Nazareth to pay for all men's sins so we don't need to sacrifice, and He's here with me now as the Spirit."

"Jesus of Nazareth?" Africanus's eyes narrowed. "Isn't that the one Christians say was crucified and rose from the dead?" He drew a deep breath and fingered his lip. Mistress Camilla had died believing in that god, and it had broken his friend's heart.

"Yes. That was the blood sacrifice that paid for all sin for all time. Jesus rose from the dead, proving He could do everything He promised. He gives those of us who believe in Him eternal life."

The door swung open, drawing Damalio's gaze. "I have work wait-ing. We can talk later."

Master Brutus's crutches appeared first, then he came through the door.

Damalio turned his smile on Brutus. "I was just leaving. Until din-ner..." He swung his legs over the wall and slipped off.

Africanus rose from the chair so Brutus could sit. As Damalio strode toward the stable, he watched, rubbing the back of his neck. If the god of the Christians had healed the farm slave and him, why hadn't he healed Mistress Camilla? Surely she'd asked him to.

"Latrunculi or tabula?" Brutus's words turned Africanus's eyes to the board.

"Tabula." Latrunculi required total concentration. An impossible task while Damalio's words still played in his head.

"Set it up." Brutus rested his head on the chairback and closed his eyes.

Africanus started placing the blue and beige rondels in their as-signed places. He knew what to do with them to win a game. But what should he do with what he'd just heard?

# Chapter 42

DISCOVERED!

*June 18*

The clang of steel on steel rang across the courtyard as his men sparred, and Brutus pressed on his thigh. Almost three weeks since the break, and it still throbbed some. But another three to five weeks, and he'd be sparring with Africanus again.

Or maybe Rufus. It would be a while before he'd move with the speed and agility Africanus required. Then again, Africanus held back even when Brutus was fighting his best. Rufus might find it harder to give him a good match without accidentally wounding him.

Africanus climbed the two steps to the portico and slid his gladius into its scabbard. He placed it on the chair beside Brutus and snatched up a towel to wipe the sweat off his face.

"We're going for a short run. Shall I find Calvia for a game while we're gone?"

"No. I'll just watch Lepus and Sorex until you return."

Rufus emerged from the men's lodge without his sword. With a wave of his hand, he invited Africanus to join him as he trotted toward the gate.

A nod and a quick smile, and Africanus jogged away. Through the gate and a turn to the right, then his men headed toward the cattle pasture. They vaulted the fence, and the cows watched the runners pass.

Brutus leaned his head back and closed his eyes. It wasn't the pain; it was the forced inactivity that bothered him most.

When he opened his eyes, three men had ridden into the courtyard, heading for the garden. Three men in tunics, not trousers. Two

233

built like gladiators and the third about his size. They dismounted and swaggered to the garden edge, where Lepus stood to greet them.

"Salve. Do you need something?" Lepus's Latin drew a sneer from the leader.

"Take us to the woman who lives here."

Lepus stiffened and stared, and Sorex moved beside him. "Don't help them."

The taller gladiator slammed his palms into Sorex's chest, knocking him to the ground. Sorex scrambled to his feet and backed away.

Brutus took the gladius from the chair and draped the strap across his chest. He stood and grabbed his crutches from their resting place against the wall. Then he moved to block the entrance to the portico. Placing the right crutch against the column, he balanced on his good leg. With his sword arm free, he rested his hand on the pommel of the sword.

Two specks moved on the hillside past the cattle. His men were jogging back toward the villa. They should reach him soon enough that he wouldn't have to use a sword himself, but he'd rather not look totally defenseless.

His eyebrows lowered. Whatever those three were looking for, they wouldn't be barging in on Calvia. Words could hold them off until his men arrived.

His movement caught their attention, and the three marched toward the portico. They startled when Lepus sprinted past them and vaulted the wall between the columns. He snatched the crutch from its place against the column and held it like a scythe.

That triggered Brutus's smiling frown. Lepus had more courage than he'd expected. The rabbit had come to back him up.

The visitors were still ten feet away when he spoke. "Stop there. Where are you from, and why are you here?"

A sneer like the one he'd shown Lepus twisted the leader's lip. "From an important senator in Rome who has the emperor's ear. You'd better step aside."

As he shifted his grip on the sword, Brutus matched sneer for sneer. "I'll be the judge of whether the man you come from is important enough for me to let you pass."

Africanus and Rufus were halfway back, still jogging. A sprint would be better.

"Quintus Flavius Sabinus."

Brutus shrugged. "Sabinus is of some importance in Roma, but no matter how important he is there, his men can't demand entrance to another man's villa."

The leader's hand settled on his sword. "It gives us the right to talk to the woman who's domina of this estate. It's not your estate, and you have no right to forbid us entry."

"Not my estate? Whose estate do you think this is that you should be allowed to speak to the domina?"

Both gladiators moved their hands to their swords. A quick glance showed Brutus's men were three-quarters of the way back. Today would be a good day for them to race each other home.

With a slight tip of his head, the leader looked down his nose at Brutus. "Sextus Licinius Crassus, and a mere equestrian like you doesn't have the right to tell a senator of Rome that his men can't speak with another senator's sister." The sneer turned into a lecherous grin. "Or his mistress."

Africanus and Rufus entered the gate, and their jog turned into a sprint: Rufus to the men's lodge for his sword and Africanus toward the back entrance to the kitchen.

"Hmph." Brutus's lips curved into a knowing smile. Rufus was coming up behind them fast with gladius and dagger, and Africanus would be armed and at his back in a moment.

The door behind him opened, but Brutus kept his hand on his sword and his eyes locked on the three before him.

"Are you ready for some tickling?"

Brutus froze his face. That should have been Africanus, not Calvia with his son.

The leader craned his neck to look past Brutus, and a cruel smile appeared. "Licinia Crassa? Or is it Calvia Lucilla, and that's Crassus's *spurius* child?"

She gasped, and Brutus glared at the intruders. "No woman here is called Licinia Crassa, and Crassus has no mistress. That is my son, and this woman is with me."

A throat cleared behind Brutus, and the swish of a gladius clearing its scabbard accompanied it. Africanus, wearing his fiercest battle scowl, stepped up beside him. Rufus, sword drawn, lips slightly parted to show clenched teeth, moved in from their left in fighting stance. A yelling Robustus was running from the stable with a pitchfork, and Sorex trotted behind him with a second one.

The taller gladiator froze. "Stop. That's Africanus."

The leader raised his hand, and they came no closer. The tall one shifted to face Rufus while the second turned to confront Robustus.

Unease had replaced arrogance on the leader's face, and Brutus suppressed a smile. No sane man would choose to pit bodyguard gladiators against his men.

Brutus summoned Calvia from behind with a curl of his fingers. When she moved up beside him, he wrapped his arm around her shoulders. She turned rigid as the marble statues by his atrium's pool.

"When I last spoke with Sextus Crassus, he said his sister was touring the eastern Empire, and there is no man in Roma less likely to have a mistress. Go back and tell Sabinus you wasted four weeks chasing a woman who isn't here."

A shiver coursed through Calvia at Sabinus's name, and he slid his hand up, then down her arm. It wasn't his place to do that, but it was the simplest way to show Sabinus's man she was his. The agent's eyebrows dipped, then straightened. Message sent and received, and Brutus let his frown relax.

Calvia didn't pull away from the half-embrace, but he stopped moving his hand. She was too stiff for him to think she wanted his touch. She bent her head to place a kiss on Marcus's forehead. She did that often, but was this time just an excuse to hide her face?

Crassus had danced around every question about his sister's whereabouts. Every answer was vague enough to mislead. His sister in the Eastern Empire? Not then, not now.

The woman beside him was an actress who'd fooled him completely. Licinia Crassa was wrapped in an arm that should have held Camilla.

She had every right to be domina of a Crassus estate because she was a Crassus herself. She looked up at him, a question in her eyes. The eyes of Licinia Crassa, and she lowered them because she saw that he knew.

He snapped his fingers at Sorex. The youth's grip tightened on the pitchfork as he moved it closer to his chest, like a warrior with a battle axe. "Gather their horses."

Brutus's eyes narrowed, and he stared at their leader. "You want to leave now, and you don't want to come back.

"You can tell Sabinus he'll find no mistress of Sextus Crassus in the provinces or in Roma, and he's wasting both time and money looking for one. If he wants Crassus's sister, he should look to the east, not in Germania."

Rufus and Africanus walked behind them as they retreated to their horses. Brutus kept his eyes on them as they vanished through the gate and reappeared as they climbed the slope of the road beyond.

"Watch to make sure they aren't doubling back."

Africanus pointed at the stable. "Sorex. Our horses. Don't take time to saddle them."

His men moved to the gate and watched the riders until Sorex scurried back with their mounts. With the horses at a trot, they followed Sabinus's henchmen over the hill.

# Chapter 43

## What Honor Demands

Brutus turned his gaze back on the woman he'd cursed every day since Camilla died in his arms. The woman he'd just saved when he'd wanted her dead for so long. The woman he'd promised Camilla he wouldn't hunt and wouldn't hurt.

Honor gave him no choice but to protect her from the likes of Sabinus. He owed her a debt for her great generosity toward him and his people. He owed her still more for whatever she'd done that saved his best friend.

Camilla would have wanted him to do exactly what he'd done. But he still wanted to tell this woman she was responsible for Camilla's death. He wanted to make her confess she'd been wrong to get Camilla to deny the Roman gods. He wanted her to beg his forgiveness.

The shock in her eyes when he said she was with him—was that shock because Sabinus's hunters had discovered where she was? Or shock that the husband of the woman who'd died because of her would claim her as his to protect her?

He held his hand out to Lepus. "My crutch. You can go back to your work, but I thank you for coming to back me up."

Lepus's eyes bounced between Brutus and Calvia. "I didn't want Domina hurt. Or you."

"Thank you, Lepus. I appreciate your bravery in protecting me. I'll tell Damalio." Calvia's words triggered Lepus's grin before he headed back to the garden.

That smile on her face, the warmth in her eyes proclaimed the sincerity of her praise. She turned both on Brutus. "You shouldn't have risked hurting your leg like that, but thank you so much for stopping them."

Her thanks were the last thing he wanted.

"Vera!"

Calvia flinched when he bellowed. Marcus whimpered, and her smile vanished.

Why hadn't Vera told him the woman beside him was Licinia? She went everywhere with Camilla. Surely she recognized their hostess the moment they arrived. Recognized her and chose not to tell him he'd found the hated object of his search.

Vera scurried out to stand before him. "Yes, master?"

"Take Marcus."

She held out her arms, and the woman who'd been lying to him since he met her handed over his son.

"Go inside. I'll speak with you shortly."

The blood drained from her face. "Yes, master." The eyes she turned on Calvia spoke a silent cry for help. Or maybe a warning to be careful.

"Calvia...or should I say Licinia?"

She shrank a little as he glared at her. "I'm Calvia here. Sextus thought it necessary to use a different name and pretend I'd been married. Only the five people who came from Rome with me know."

"You knew my Camilla, didn't you." He spat it out as a statement. He had no doubt of the answer.

"She was my dearest friend." Her mouth quivered. "I promised I'd be with her for the birth." Tears welled in her eyes. "But Sextus made me leave before Marcus came. He wouldn't let me wait even one more day, and she wasn't due for two more weeks. But everything had gone so well...I never expected she'd die. I'm so sorry..." One tear escaped.

She should be sorry. It was her fault Camilla tried one more time to give him a son. As much as he loved Marcus, he'd come at too high a price.

"You're a Christian?" No doubt of that, but would she admit it?

She nodded as she swept the tear away. "That's why Sextus sent me away. He didn't want Quintus Sabinus to find out."

It took no imagination to see where that knowledge would lead once Sabinus had it.

"Why did you convince Camilla to become one, too?"

"I didn't. I only prayed for her healing and told her about Jesus. God convinced her to follow Him."

Lies upon lies. No god was real. How could she expect him to believe one made Camilla do anything?

His jaw clamped, and he forced his breathing and heartrate to slow. He'd cursed this woman from the moment his beloved died in his arms. The gods of Rome were mere stories, but the curses he used still invoked their names. He'd longed for her to die, as Camilla had. Yet he was the one who'd protected her from Sabinus's plan to wound her brother by destroying her. How ironic!

She fidgeted under his glare and looked away.

Sabinus wouldn't stop hunting until he found her, but it would be easy to thwart the crocodile. He knew how to do it, but did he want to?

She hung her head and fingered her stola. It announced she was married—just one more lie. But Crassus had made her wear it, and it did help convince Sabinus's men she was his wife.

Was letting them assume that was true the same as speaking the lie himself?

The overwhelming urge to protect her—it had seized him without warning, and he spoke without weighing the consequences. But shielding her once didn't mean he must continue...or did it?

If he chose not to protect her, that wouldn't be breaking his word to Camilla...or would it? He'd accidentally found the one who corrupted his beloved after he'd almost stopped looking for her. He'd promised not to hurt her himself, and he wouldn't. What he once wanted to do to her, Sabinus would do for him.

But Camilla wouldn't want Licinia or whatever name she used to get hurt by anyone, and if he chose to do nothing, she could die. Maybe in a lunchtime execution before his own men fought.

The throbbing pain he'd ignored while he challenged Sabinus's henchmen surged with a vengeance. He needed to sit soon, but he wasn't through with her yet. He wouldn't let weakness control him. He closed his eyes and willed it to stop.

When he opened them, his pain was mirrored in her eyes.

"Please." Calvia's hand moved toward his chair. "You need to get off your leg."

"I haven't finished."

"I won't leave until you've said all you want. But please sit, and I'll help you get comfortable."

A few painful steps, and he collapsed onto the wicker chair. She moved the padded stool to support his leg and sat in the chair she used for games.

That board between them...he'd enjoyed hours of pleasure with her as they played. Hours of getting to know her better than he knew most people. Better than many of his long-time friends, and he liked what he knew. Or so he'd thought.

How could he not have considered the possibility that the matron who was domina of Crassus's estate, no matter what name she used or what clothes she wore, might be Crassus's unmarried sister? But Crassus had made him believe the sister had gone east to Greece or Ephesus, so maybe no one would have suspected.

No one except Sabinus.

"Those men from Quintus Sabinus." Brutus's eyes narrowed. Her mouth, usually so serene with the hint of a smile, straightened. "He sent them looking for Licinia Crassa or for a mistress Sextus Crassus keeps away from Rome. I know the kind of man your brother is, and he wouldn't take a mistress. Sabinus would know that already if he had any honor himself. I only said you were with me, which is true. But if they report my exact words, Sabinus will realize the woman they saw is really you."

His lips tightened. Honor bound a man to do what he knew was right, whether he wanted to or not.

"Sabinus's men will be back, and you can't be here. You'll go with me to my estate, and we'll leave tomorrow."

Shoulders squared, she raised her chin. "I appreciate your concern, but this is my home. These are my people. I'm not leaving."

He crossed his arms. For so smart a woman, she was a fool.

Damalio trotted across the courtyard and into the portico to stand at her shoulder. "Sorex came for me. Is there a problem, domina?" He directed a frown at Brutus.

Brutus gave her no chance to answer. "There most certainly is. Tell her she needs to leave here immediately and go someplace Sabinus won't suspect. Antistes would do nothing to stop Sabinus's men from taking her. His gladiators would have no qualms about killing her slaves. That's only property damage as far as Roman law is concerned. Sollus is no threat to anyone. Any bodyguard could kill Fidus with a single stroke. Robustus's size is no defense against a sword, and you would fare no better. If she doesn't come with me, you and the rest of her men will end up hurt or dead, and she'll be at Sabinus's mercy."

She looked up at Damalio. "What do you think?"

"If Sabinus has found you, it's not safe for you here." He drew a deep breath and released it slowly. "I can take you to the estate in Hispania." He rubbed his jaw. "But he might guess that's where you'd go next."

"But he won't think to look for her at my Lousonna estate." Brutus squeezed his aching thigh. "You can take her there."

Calvia's gaze bounced between him and Damalio. Her man's eyes remained locked on him. Brow furrowed, lips tightened, the guard dog was weighing that option. Whatever he decided, that's what she'd do. But honor was satisfied by making the offer, whether she took it or not.

He should hope for that refusal, but he couldn't quite make himself. Even though Camilla had died because of her, Calvia was a kind, gentle person who probably never meant to hurt anyone. Making her suffer wouldn't bring Camilla back.

If anyone had asked before Sabinus's men came, he would have called her a good friend. But what was she now?

Uncertainty clouded her usually confident eyes, and she turned them on Damalio. "What should I do?"

His sigh was deep. "For now, go to Brutus's estate. We can decide what else to do when we're there."

Her sigh was deeper, and her fingertips wiped the corner of her eye as she turned back to Brutus. "We'll go. But first I want to make Primus overseer again with him understanding he must continue doing what Damalio does. I can't let the estate go back to the way Antistes had it when I came. And we'll be returning as soon as it's safe to make certain it doesn't."

"You'll live at my estate at least until the end of summer. It's only a day and a half by carriage, close enough that you can make unexpected visits to make sure things remain how you want them. You can stay on past my departure for as long as you want, but it would be unwise to move back before the pass closes for winter."

Her guard dog's crossed arms and frown as Brutus gave her orders triggered a smile. "Damalio guards you well, and he will agree with everything I've just told you."

She bit her lip as she turned once more to her man. "Do you?"

"Primus can be trusted to do what he should until you return. Brutus is right that it's safer for you to go where Sabinus won't know to track you. I think you should accept his offer."

She closed her eyes and hung her head. The silence stretched out too long, and Brutus drummed his fingers on his leg.

"Very well. I'll go, and everyone who came with me from Rome will come, too."

Brutus squeezed his leg again. He'd stood too long without both crutches, but he'd do it again if he had to.

Feminine eyes that missed as little as his did focused on his hand.

"Are you sure you're ready for that trip? Silo said four weeks until you should travel, and it's not four weeks yet. Couldn't we wait until then?" Her eyes turned toward the weavers' building. "I'd like to be here when Ursula has her baby."

He snorted. Her life was in danger, and she was worried about a slave's baby and the trip being too hard on him. That was the Calvia he was used to seeing. His mouth turned down. The Licinia that Camilla had loved as well. "I'll be fine. The sooner we leave, the safer you are. Silo's a good physician, and he'll know a good midwife. They can handle the birth."

"But I can—" Damalio cleared his throat, but her hand swept his warning away. "Pray." She smiled at her protector. "He already knows who and what I am. He wants me to go with him anyway."

"Then I'll tell the men and see to packing the wagon." Damalio's eyes spoke a warning to Brutus before turning back to her. "Unless you need my help now."

"No. I'll speak with Primula. We'll take down the looms and have them ready to pack this morning. The rest we'll get ready before evening."

The eyes she turned on Brutus brimmed with tears, but they weren't from gratitude. "I wish I didn't have to go, but for now, it's probably best." She scanned the buildings around the courtyard before turning her eyes back on him with a shaky smile. "Thank you for protecting me."

He tipped his head to acknowledge her thanks. The polite reply would have been "it's my pleasure." But that would be a lie. Pleasure was the last word he'd used to describe why he'd done it. Honor had forced him to act. Only time would tell how much he'd regret it.

# Chapter 44

## For Her Own Safety

*June 19*

From her bedchamber doorway, Calvia watched Robustus and Fidus carry the last of her trunks downstairs. When she returned to the window, she couldn't stop the sigh. How long would it be before she would watch the morning sun rise over the jagged gray peaks she'd grown to love? How long until she would watch the small white spots that were her sheep eating their way across the meadow?

"Are you ready, mistress?" Primula held her folded palla. The casual shawl Calvia had worn on her own estate wouldn't do for traveling.

She closed her eyes, locking away the memory to pull out and savor later. Then she turned. "Almost. Damalio and I need to speak once more with Primus."

"They're waiting in your office."

"Then let's go." Calvia pulled the drapes and led Primula from the room.

When she entered the office, the small trunk holding her scrolls of Tacitus still sat on the desk. It would ride with her, its space in the baggage wagon taken by the larger trunk of dyed yarns for the blanket and whatever she and Primula might need to make for her men.

Damalio and Primus stood on either side of the window, eyes fixed on the land that would soon change overseer. Both turned, Damalio with straight lips and Primus with a nervous smile.

"Primus." He squared his shoulders when she addressed him. "Damalio tells me you are ready to assume his post as overseer while

244

we're gone. That you can be trusted to continue as he would to make sure our people are productive and well cared for."

Pride lit his eyes. "I am, domina. He's taught me well, and I'll do my best to run the estate like you want."

Pride, but not arrogance. She glanced at Damalio, and his slow smile accompanied his single nod.

"Then you will be in charge of the daily running of the estate, as he has been. Antistes will continue as steward for financial and business matters, but I'll expect you to care for my people and keep this an estate Sextus Crassus would be proud to show to anyone. Can you do that?"

"Yes, domina." Primus turned his eyes on Damalio. The nervous smile was replaced by a happy one at his teacher's nod.

"Your baby is coming before month's end. When Ursula's labor is starting or if it looks like there's any problem before then, you are to contact physician Silo immediately and get him or the best midwife in Octodurus to come help."

"Yes, domina." The nervous smile of a soon-to-be father appeared.

"Ursula is young and strong, and the next time I see you, I expect you'll be the proud father of a happy, healthy baby. You can go tell her what I just said."

"Yes, domina." As he left the room, the smile became a grin.

◆

Brutus shifted on Calvia's dining room chair to get more comfortable. A day and half in the raeda, and he'd be at the Lousonna estate. But sharing a raeda with Marcus, Vera, and the wet nurse wasn't his idea of an enjoyable trip. Vera was afraid to look at him since he'd scolded her for hiding Calvia's identity, and Marcus seemed to share her nervousness, fussing more than usual.

Someone hummed in the hallway, and the source of the music entered. Antistes settled into his chair at the foot of the table and took a sip from the goblet Olga had already filled. "No clouds this morning. It should be a good day for your trip."

"It should be." Brutus raised an eyebrow at Africanus. Antistes had worn a satisfied smile, but he turned it off when Calvia entered with her maid and guardian and took her usual place across from Brutus.

"A good trip requires more than good weather." Sadness colored her words.

The rustle behind him announced the arrival of breakfast. Olga carried a tray with six bowls. She set one filled with Sollus's herb-laced porridge before him and wiped at the corner of her eye.

Calvia touched her hand as Olga set another bowl before her. "It's all right. We'll be back."

Olga sniffed and nodded, but as she left the room, she looked back at Calvia. Her mouth quivered before she turned away.

"So." Antistes stirred his porridge. "You're going to Brutus's estate for a while because some men came by yesterday." His spoon stopped circling the bowl. "But they were looking for someone other than you." He loaded the spoon and lifted it to his mouth to blow on it. "I was wondering..." He swallowed the spoonful and returned the spoon to the bowl. "I was wondering why that would make you go with our guest to his estate." The spoon circled the bowl once before he focused calculating eyes on Calvia. "Master Sextus might question that decision."

Damalio glared at Antistes. His mouth opened, but when Calvia raised her hand, he said nothing.

"What I do is between Sextus and me, and it's not your place to question any of my decisions." Her words had an icy coating that Brutus hadn't heard before. "It will only be for a short time. I'll be back no later than November, and I'll be spending the winter here."

Her normal tone had returned. "I expect you and Primus to keep the estate running well during my absence."

Antistes mouth curved down. "I know how to run the estate well, and you can rest assured I will."

"Primus has been told to do his part like Damalio, and I trust him to oversee everything as if I were here."

Brutus took a bite of porridge to keep the smile off his lips.

"My son has always been trustworthy, and I'm sure his work will satisfy you." Behind his wooden smile, Antistes bristled.

As entertaining as these two were, it was time to stop their argument.

"You have my sympathy, Antistes." Brutus lifted his porridge-filled spoon. "Your old cook can manage the breakfasts, but after your domina leaves, you won't be eating as well. Everyone here is going to miss Sollus's cooking, but I'm glad Calvia's chef is coming with her. My own kitchen workers can learn from a master, and I won't have to settle for the merely adequate food I usually get during my summer visits."

Calvia's eyes spoke her thanks for his redirection. "Do you have a good library?"

"My library in Rome is good. The one at Lousonna is not." He glanced at Africanus and got a silent nod in return. "What I do have is a good gameboard, so you won't need to bring the one still in my room this morning."

"I'd forgotten it. But I'll look forward to many enjoyable games on yours."

She gave him her first normal smile since he'd confronted her. It was good to see it again.

Antistes wiped his mouth and wadded up the napkin. He dropped it on the table as he rose. "I'm going to talk with Primus to see if we have questions before you leave."

"You may go do that."

His jaw clenched, but he dipped his head before striding from the room.

"Damalio."

Her man shifted his gaze from the doorway to her. "Yes, domina?"

"Antistes will be sending the monthly report in a week and a half. Perhaps I should have him prepare two copies and send one to me."

Before Damalio could answer, Brutus raised his hand. "That's not a good idea."

Her eyebrows lowered. "Why not?"

Brutus glanced at her man, who was shaking his head. "Damalio could tell you. Antistes wants you gone so he can do what he wants. If you tell him where to send the report, he'll know exactly where to send Sabinus's hunters if they return. Right now, all he knows is my estate is near Lousonna. They would have to find someone to tell them where, and most won't know. The estate doesn't carry my name."

"Oh." She covered her mouth with her fingers. "I should have thought of that."

She'd mastered the strategy of board games, but this was real life. She was no match for a schemer like Sabinus. Damalio was watchful and cautious, but no overseer could foresee everything Sabinus might try.

Brutus rubbed his lip. Damalio couldn't, but maybe he could. "It will take two or three weeks for Sabinus's men to return to Rome. If he decides to send them back here, he'll do it quickly. So they should have come and gone again in six or eight weeks. Late August is soon enough to come check the estate in person."

"So long? I want to know how Ursula and her baby are doing before then."

"You can send Damalio. It's not even a day on horseback, and I'll lend you the horse. Or I can send Rufus."

She rested her elbows on the table and laced her fingers. "Anything else I should or shouldn't do?"

He leaned back in the chair and crossed his arms. "I'll tell you if I think of anything."

Her slight frown relaxed into an ironic smile. "I'm sure you will."

Calvia stood beside her raeda, surveying the courtyard of the estate that had become home. It should be less than four months before she returned, so why was her heart aching as it had on the ship as she watched Sextus's final wave?

Brutus sat by the window of his raeda, watching with eyes that seemed to miss nothing. She'd made certain he had extra pillows, and Vera would keep him as comfortable as possible. To protect her, he'd ignored Silo's advice about traveling. Extra pillows were the least she could do to thank him.

Africanus sat astride Brutus's black stallion because he'd put Fidus on his own bay to ride with Rufus at the rear. Robustus sat alone on the wagon's seat, fingering the reins. Sollus had helped Primula shift the few small trunks inside their raeda before climbing up. Damalio would drive.

All that remained was the final farewells to her workers who'd gathered to see her off. Olga and Ursula were crying, and several other women looked misty-eyed.

"I'll miss you all, but it won't be for long. I expect to celebrate the harvest with you." She waved her hand toward Ursula and the three other women with bulging bellies. "And the birth of your babies. I look forward to holding each of them. Farewell until I return."

Her voice broke, and Damalio stepped up beside her. "You can go back to your work now."

As they filed away, she motioned Primus and Antistes closer.

"Take good care of my people until I come back."

"I'll do my best, domina." Primus wrapped his arm around Ursula, who wiped the corner of her eye and sniffed.

Antistes straightened to his full height. "I've always taken good care of the estate, and I will continue to do so."

Calvia turned to Damalio. "It's time."

He handed her into the raeda and climbed to the driver's bench. A snap of the reins, and he moved her carriage between Brutus's raeda and the wagon.

As the caravan started toward the gate, Calvia leaned out the window. Primus wrapped his arm around Ursula and drew her to his side as they waved. Antistes raised a hand as well, but his lips curved into a self-satisfied smile.

And a flame of triumph lit his eyes.

They hadn't reached the main road before Brutus was wishing he'd bought two raedas instead of one. Calvia had padded the drop-down side seat his leg rested on with twice the pillows he probably needed. Two more served as armrests, which gave Vera and Marcus no more than a third of the seat. With Nutrixia perched on the second side seat and the stacked trunks crowding him, he longed for a horse between his legs with wide-open vistas as he trotted down the road.

Nutrixia finished nursing and handed Marcus back to Vera, which meant even less room on the seat.

"Nutrixia."

"Yes, master?"

"Except when you're feeding Marcus, you can ride up with Burdonarius." He reached out the window and slapped the side of the carriage.

As the raeda slowed and stopped, a self-satisfied smile curved Nutrixia's lips.

"But if I find you're trying to distract him, I'll have Damalio take charge of you."

She started to pout, but when he raised one eyebrow, she stopped. "Yes, master."

Burdonarius climbed down and lifted her up to the driver's seat. She purred a "thank you," and that decided it.

When they reached Lousonna, he'd have his steward sell her. A woman who constantly sought the attention of men was sure to cause rivalries and unhappiness within the familia there. There would be someone else at the estate who could nurse Marcus.

Like Calvia, he cared about his people, and a man who deliberately brought a troublemaker into a smoothly running household was a fool.

He reached for his thigh. For some strange reason, a gentle squeeze made it hurt less.

Except for Antistes, Calvia's people would miss her. But having her and her people would be a pleasant addition at his estate. Sollus's cooking was enough to make any man glad he'd extended her hospitality.

He'd issued the invitation to come with him because honor demanded it. His contempt for Sabinus was a good enough reason to keep her from him, but it went beyond that.

He'd hated the unknown woman whom he'd blamed for taking Camilla from him. But Calvia was nothing like the woman he'd created in his mind. She kept doing things to improve the living conditions of the slaves on her estate, especially the expectant mothers. She was patient with Antistes far beyond what he would tolerate. She'd seen how important Africanus was to him without him speaking a word, and she treated his friend like a welcome guest. She doted on his son, and Marcus loved it.

There was more of Camilla in her than he'd seen in any other woman. Until he discovered who she was, spending time with her had gone past enjoyable to something he'd miss when he left.

Now that he'd taken her under his protection, he was honor bound to see that nothing bad happened to her. He could make her accept that protection until he returned to Roma, but what would happen to her then?

Even if he didn't care, Camilla would. And if he was honest with himself, maybe he cared more than he should.

# Chapter 45

## Two Letters

Alone in the courtyard, Antistes watched the caravan climb the hill and disappear. The woman who'd become the bane of his existence was gone, if only for a few weeks. But perhaps he could make it longer than that.

He strolled to the main house, and when he climbed the portico steps, his gaze fell on the wicker chair. Fortuna had smiled on him when Brutus came with his broken leg. It was still a mystery why Sextus Crassus had made Calvia domina over him, but the best explanation he could find was Crassus was hiding his mistress. And if that were the case, Brutus had just given him the means to be rid of her for good.

He entered his office and closed the door. From a cabinet, he took a flagon of wine and a goblet. After filling the goblet halfway, he returned the wine to the cabinet and settled into his desk chair. A slow smile came as he swirled the golden liquid. A quick sip, and he set the wine aside.

Wax tablet or papyrus? Fast delivery or as if it were not a matter requiring immediate attention? Antistes weighed the options, then took a tablet from the drawer.

It was better to have it appear more casual, as if he wasn't trying to stir up trouble. He could wait until he sent the estate report, but a week and a half might seem too long to a man who cared enough about the woman to put her in charge.

He would write the letter on a tablet and send it right away, but by the regular service that took two weeks. All he needed now was to capture just the right tone.

He picked up a stylus, tapped the tip on the table a few times, and began.

> Antistes to Sextus Licinius Crassus, noble master of this estate, greetings. If you are well, then I am glad. I write to tell you of a major change here.
>
> Calvia Lucilla has taken her men and gone with an equestrian who has been here for three weeks recovering from a broken leg. They spent many hours talking and playing board games, and she is very fond of his baby son. She didn't say when she would return.
>
> She took the overseer Damalio with her and made my son Primus overseer again. Primus had served as overseer before she and her man arrived, so you need not be concerned. The estate will continue to run efficiently and profitably with me and Primus in charge.
>
> I hope all will continue to be well with you. May the gods guard your safety.

The tablet closed with a satisfying clack. He wrapped the leather strips around it, top to bottom and side to side, threading the ends into the seal box. Humming to himself, he lit the sealing-wax candle. A few drops of melted wax filled the box, and he pressed his signet ring into it. He snapped the box lid shut and picked up the goblet.

Then he leaned back in his chair and took a sip. Two weeks, and Sextus Crassus would be thinking his carefully hidden woman had betrayed him. Two more weeks, and he would probably get the letter from Crassus telling him she was not to be domina if she ever returned.

He raised the goblet to his lips and let the fruity liquid flow across his tongue. It was the best of the estate vintages, and it left a pleasing aftertaste when he swallowed. But nothing could satisfy a thirst better than revenge.

*June 20*

Antistes had just checked on the weavers and was crossing the courtyard when a lathered horse cantered through the gate. The rider slowed to a trot and reined in by the portico. He bounded up the steps and with a closed fist, pounded on the door.

"What do you want?"

The man startled and spun when Antistes spoke so close behind him. "Is this the Licinius Crassus estate?"

"It is." Antistes crossed his arms.

"I have a letter for overseer Damalio."

"Who sent it?"

The rider reached into the satchel slung across his chest and withdrew a rolled papyrus. "Licinius Crassus."

Antistes jaw twitched. In the past ten years, no Crassus had ever sent something by horse relay.

He held out his hand. "I'm Antistes, steward of this estate. Damalio reports to me. He's on a special errand and won't be back for several hours. I'll see that he receives it the moment he returns."

The courier paused, scanned him head to foot, then placed the papyrus in his hand. He pulled a leather pouch from the satchel and removed a stylus and wax tablet from it.

After handing Antistes the stylus, he opened the tablet and pointed to an entry. "Sign here that you've received it for him."

A frown grew as Antistes etched his name into the wax and handed the stylus back to the rider.

With stylus and tablet returned to the satchel, the rider hurled himself onto his horse and trotted out the gate.

Antistes scanned the courtyard. No one was there who could have witnessed him taking the letter. Without hurrying, he entered the house. Then he strode into his office and bolted the door.

The sealing wax cracked and fell away in pieces when he broke the seal. He settled into the chair and unrolled the papyrus.

> Sextus Licinius Crassus to Damalio, greetings. If you are well, then I am glad. I write to tell you that three men are coming for Calvia.
>
> You are to take her to the Hispania estate. Leave immediately. The men left Rome June 9 and could arrive any day.
>
> I hope all will continue to be well with you and her. May the gods guard your safety.

He dropped the letter on the desk as if it were on fire. The men had already come, and they'd left without getting what they wanted. Brutus and his bodyguards had seen to that.

But the tone of the letter was not that of a man who'd be jealous of a straying mistress. It implied real danger for her.

Had he included anything in his letter that would anger Crassus when it arrived? He fingered his lip. He'd been careful to write simple facts. He hadn't openly accused her of anything. He'd written just enough to let a man's imagination run toward believing her unfaithful, toward deciding she didn't deserve the power he'd given her. But if she really wasn't his mistress, nothing he'd written should upset Crassus.

He slipped the letter into his desk. No need to send the message on to Damalio. The command to take her away from the estate had already been carried out, even if they were going to Brutus's Lousonna estate instead of the Crassus estate in Hispania. He didn't know exactly where they'd gone, anyway.

He got the flagon from the cabinet and poured himself a drink. Wherever she was, Calvia Lucilla and the men who were hunting her were not his problem. The estate was his to control once more. It was time to celebrate.

# Chapter 46

## No Need to Worry?

*North of Penne Locos, June 20*

Calvia popped the last berry into her mouth for a final explosion of sweetness when she bit into it. They'd spent the night at the villa of one of Brutus's friends just outside Penne Locos. It was much like her own villa, but as tasty as the breakfast of rosemary-laced bread, berries, and cheese had been, she was glad it was almost over.

She'd eaten alone. Primula and her men had been fed with his friend's slaves. When asked, the girl who served her said Brutus had eaten with their host and gone to his private office before she was summoned to breakfast.

She missed him. Had he deliberately avoided eating with her? Would anything be the same now he knew who she was? He said they would use his gameboard, so at least he would spend some time with her, but would they still talk as they played?

When his leg healed, would he spend so much time with the affairs of his estate that he'd have none left for her? If he wasn't busy, would he still seek her out for more than the strategic challenge of latrunculi?

She placed the last slice of cheese on the final piece of bread. It was time to stop thinking about him.

He'd become too important to her. He was a pagan who loved the games and was devoted to Rome, not the kind of man a Christian woman should want to marry. So why did she feel so drawn to him? Was God trying to tell her something, or was it only the longings of her own heart?

As she returned her empty cup to the table, Damalio appeared in the doorway. "Brutus is ready to go. Primula has loaded all you brought in. We can leave as soon as you're ready."

"We can go as soon as I thank our host."

"There's no one to thank. Brutus said he already took care of that before his friend left for the day."

"Then I'm ready."

She followed him to the stableyard. Brutus was visible through his carriage window, head leaning back against one of her pillows, eyes closed.

"I knew he shouldn't be traveling yet. Silo said four weeks. I should have insisted we wait."

The corners of Damalio's eyes crinkled. "We'd still be on the road now, no matter what you said. He thought it too dangerous for you to stay."

"And he's too stubborn to listen to reason once his mind is made up." She reached the carriage, and he helped her in. "Rather like Sextus, the way he hustled me onto the ship in Portus."

"Another wise decision, domina. Good men often think alike."

She settled onto the seat beside Primula. "I suppose they do."

He climbed to the driver seat. The snap of the reins was followed by a lurch, and they began the last leg of the trip to her new safe haven. Safer for her, but Brutus should have stayed where Silo could finish caring for his leg. If he ended up with a permanent limp, it would be her fault.

To the west, Lacus Lemmanus stretched as far as she could see. It was beautiful, but to be traveling its shore once more was the last thing she wanted.

She glanced at Primula, who sat looking out the window as if nothing was amiss.

"Is going with Brutus the right choice?"

Primula's eyes widened. "Damalio thinks so."

"I know he thought it was wise, so it probably is good for me. But I don't want trouble to follow us to Brutus's estate."

"Master Brutus doesn't seem worried about that."

"He doesn't, but he didn't seem worried during the confrontation, either. Why would he put on a sword and challenge those men with his broken leg? He doesn't seem like a fool, but there's no common sense in that. Even I could overpower him."

"But Africanus and Rufus were there, too."

"Not when he first stopped them. I was beside him before Africanus came out and Rufus was still running over from the men's lodging."

She stroked her chin. "One of them recognized Africanus. Called him by name even, and they were all afraid of him. Why would that man have known Brutus's bodyguard, anyway? Vera said he's been with Brutus fifteen years, and the man who knew him would have been a child back then. They seemed scared of Rufus, too."

"Just looking at those two would scare me." Primula faked a shiver.

Calvia chuckled. "If they'd ever watched the morning sparring, they'd have every reason to be terrified. Why men enjoy swords so much is beyond me. Sextus's sons have started training with a sword-master, and he likes to spar with the man, too."

Her smile faded. "I don't know if he had to kill when he served in Germania. He never talked about it if he did."

"Maybe he thought you wouldn't want to know."

"And he'd be right." Her gaze returned to the lake. "I'd hate for any of my men to have to kill someone to defend me. At least by going with Brutus, I've probably made certain they won't."

Kill someone or be killed themselves...it was a choice no one should have to make, and no one should ever force another man to make it.

Just north of Vivisco, the road split, and the caravan went left toward Lousonna. After leaving the lakeshore and climbing a steep hill, they stopped for lunch.

Primula left Mistress Calvia with the men and strolled to a pile of rocks at the edge of the steep slope going down to the lake.

Too many times Mistress had wondered aloud how Ursula was doing, would they send for Silo, would he be able to help if they did. If Ursula died in childbirth...Primula sucked air between her teeth. Too many times Mistress had wondered if Marcus would still have his mother if they'd been there to pray.

Something moved behind her, and she glanced over her shoulder to find Rufus.

He stopped beside her. "You look worried. What's wrong?"

She tipped her head back to look at his face, then quickly lowered her eyes. He was so tall and muscled, and his short-cropped red hair made him stand out in any group of men. Vera had said he was a nice man, but she'd seen how he fought with Africanus. He was a wild man then, slashing and stabbing, and it was a miracle neither of them ended up dead. To have him so close was unnerving, but she forced herself to look at him again.

Then his eyes warmed, and a crooked smile appeared. She silently laughed at her thinking him dangerous.

"I was thinking about Ursula. It's almost time for her baby to come." She turned her gaze back on the lake. "I was remembering the way Mistress Camilla died, how she bled to death. I was wishing Mistress and I could be with Ursula to pray if there's any problem."

She glanced up to find him watching her with his full attention. "Ursula's small, and that can make a first baby hard to deliver. If she doesn't survive the birth, Mistress is going to be blaming herself for letting Brutus convince her that her own safety demanded she leave, just as her brother did in Rome."

"You and she don't have to worry. Silo's as good as I've seen. No one is better than a gladiator physician for dealing with blood that won't stop flowing. Ursula will be fine."

"She's also worried that she's bringing her trouble to Brutus's estate, where his people could be hurt, too."

His chuckle startled her. "She doesn't have to worry about any harm coming to Brutus's people. Not from the likes of those who came to her estate. No one Sabinus could send would be a match for me and Africanus. Or for Master Brutus after his leg is healed."

His shoulders squared. "I've fought and won six times in the Flavian Amphitheater in Rome, as my father did before me. He fought Thracian style."

"When did Brutus buy you out of the arena?"

"He didn't. He bought me for his own school. Master Brutus owns some of the best *familiae gladiatoriorum* in Italia. He has ludi in Roma, Florentia, and Luca, and it's a great honor for him to buy a man to be part of them."

Her breath caught, and his brow furrowed. Did he know how intimidating that made him?

"Does Africanus still fight, too?"

"He used to be one of the best in all Italia, an undefeated Class 2, but Master Brutus stopped putting him on the sand before he bought me." His confident smile turned into a grin. "You don't risk your best friend dying for a few thousand denarii. Africanus trains and solves problems for people who need more than muscle to help them."

By the wagons, Africanus waved. Rufus raised a hand, then turned intense blue eyes back on her.

"Many senatorial sons train at our ludus before their first tribune posting. Your mistress's nephews probably will. I train the better ones when they get good enough, but only the best are skilled enough to spar with Africanus. Master Brutus is as good as the Class 4's, and he and Africanus spar almost every day."

The warmth of his smile was not what she expected from a man so proud of his ability to kill. "You should feel very safe with me protecting you."

"Rufus!" He turned at Africanus's call. "Time to leave."

He swept his hand toward the carriages. "After you. Maybe we can talk more later. We'll be together at the estate for a few months."

"Perhaps we can. I'm being protected in ways you can't imagine, but it's nice to have you on this trip, even if I'm not in any particular danger."

Vera knew Rufus well, and she saw him as a nice man. Beyond what he did for his master, he probably was. But when Mistress learned Brutus made money from the death of other men, what was she going to do?

# Chapter 47

## DEALER IN DEATH

Calvia watched Primula as she returned with Rufus towering over her. Her maid was watching where she stepped, but he was watching her. His eyes and smile both said he liked what he saw.

They were almost to her raeda when he veered away to mount the horse Fidus led over to him. Primula climbed in.

"Ready?" Damalio's voice came from the seat outside.

"We are." Calvia's words were met with a slap of the reins, and they began the final leg of the journey.

Primula turned on the seat to face her. "You'll never guess what Rufus told me."

Calvia squeezed her lips to control her smile. "I saw how he was looking at you. I think I can guess quite well."

"Oh, that. No, that's not what I'm talking about. It's about Master Brutus."

"What about him?"

"Rufus and Africanus aren't just his bodyguards."

"What are they?" Primula's eyes were too serious, her mouth too straight.

"They're real gladiators. Master Brutus owns three schools, including one in Rome, and Rufus fights in the arena for him."

Calvia's hands flew up to cover her mouth, then she stacked them over her heart. "Are you sure?"

"Rufus told me himself that he's fought in the amphitheater in Rome, and Africanus used to. He was a Class 2, whatever that means."

"He was top-ranked. Sextus says those men are almost worshiped by the mobs who go to the games. No wonder they recognized him and were scared."

She rubbed the sides of her nose. "No wonder Brutus got so angry when I told him the men who make money off other men's deaths had no honor."

One hand rested over her heart again. "I wonder if Damalio knows."

"Would he have let you come with Brutus if he did?"

"If he thought that was the best way to protect me...then yes. But I've spent more time with Brutus and Africanus than he has, and I didn't know. So, I doubt he does."

"Will this change anything?"

"If we'd only just left home, I might consider turning back. But we're almost to Brutus's estate. I'll discuss it with Damalio, but I already know what he'll say."

She sighed. "And he'd be right. Coming to an estate Sabinus doesn't know about with a man who isn't in Sextus's circle of friends should put his hunters off our track. It gives us time to decide what to do next."

Calvia turned her gaze out the window again, but the azure hue of the lake and the billowy clouds drifting over it couldn't hold her thoughts.

As they passed each amphitheater on their way from Rome, she'd thought about the greedy men making money off death. Murder was a sin, and forcing others to commit it was an abomination before God.

When they passed through Lousonna, she'd thought it was nice to finally see a town without an amphitheater. But all that meant was men fought and died in the theater instead. Had Brutus sent his men to fight there? How many had Africanus had to kill? Or Rufus? Or all the other men he owned who earned him money from other men's sick fascination with men fighting for their lives?

Camilla never mentioned that part of his business dealings. She'd said their fortune came from his estates and a merchant fleet. As much as he loved watching his men fight, was this only a profitable hobby for him?

Men who owned gladiators and made money off their deaths were doing something terrible, even if they weren't terrible men. But how could a man of honor, like Brutus seemed to be, buy men and send them to die for no good reason? Camilla never said anything about him providing fighters for the games. Surely she knew, and surely she didn't approve. But maybe a wife can't stop her husband from doing what he wants, even the best of them. Especially if they don't follow the Lord.

Camilla had wanted so badly for Brutus to share her faith, but she'd been afraid to tell him what she believed. Now it was obvious why. But she loved him so deeply she was willing to risk anything to give him a son. How could her friend have loved him so much if he didn't have a good heart?

And no matter what shape a man's heart was in, no one was beyond the reach of God to save him.

Brutus shifted his leg on the pillows and let out a slow sigh. Vera startled beside him, and held a drowsy Marcus closer.

"Give him to me."

She did, and then she moved away from him. That triggered a frown, and she pressed herself tighter against the wall.

"Stop that."

Her eyes widened. "Stop what, master?"

"Stop acting like I frighten you. I'm not going to hurt you, and you should already know that."

Marcus reached for his face, and he shook his son's arm, receiving a sleepy smile as his reward. "I know I yelled at you for not telling me who Calvia really was. But I also understand why you did it. You were just keeping your promise to Camilla. I'm not going to punish you for that."

Her whole body relaxed. "Thank you, master."

Marcus's eyes closed, and he went limp as sleep overtook him. Brutus's gaze moved from his son to the trees and fields outside.

Calvia was the woman he'd been hating for months. She was responsible for Camilla thinking it was safe to try again, but she didn't intend to harm anyone.

If he'd only refused Camilla's pleas before he went to Liturnum, she'd still be with him, no matter what Calvia had done. But how could he have denied her what he wanted so badly himself?

Marcus made sucking sounds in his sleep, drawing Brutus gaze and relaxing his frown.

"How did they meet?"

Vera drew a breath and froze.

"I'm not going to get angry at you, no matter what you tell me."

"It was right after Mistress lost the third baby. She tried so hard not to let you see her sadness, but one day at the baths, some of her friends were talking about their children, complaining about what they couldn't do when a baby made them so big and how much the birth hurt. It was a knife into her heart, but she didn't want them to see that. She told them she had to get home to take care of something for you."

Vera's eyes glistened. "She held the tears until she was in the dressing room, and then she couldn't stop them. I opened her palla and held it so people couldn't watch her. But Mistress Calvia came over and asked if she needed help. She said no, but Mistress Calvia invited her to come home with her for lunch. She said she needed to try some new pastries on someone before she had them served to her father's guests.

She wiped the corner of her eye. "Mistress wanted something, anything else to think about, so we went. There was something about her home; it felt peaceful. After the pastries, Mistress Calvia invited her to sit in the garden where she had a loom and talk or not, as she wished. When it was time to go, she invited Mistress back to help make tunics for some widows. So we went many times."

"How long were they friends?"

"Maybe a year and a half."

"Did she start trying to make Camilla a Christian right away?"

"Oh, no." Her eyes widened, and she shook her head. "She wasn't supposed to tell anyone she followed Jesus. Her father had forbidden it. Mistress didn't tell her why she'd been crying for several months, either. Then when Mistress Calvia told her she'd have a new nephew or niece soon, Mistress told her everything about the three babies and how she wanted nothing more than to hold her own baby in her arms. Then she cried and cried and cried until Mistress Calvia said she might be able to help."

"And then she prayed for Camilla?"

"Yes. And after Mistress got pregnant, she wanted to know about the god who had healed her. She swore she'd keep Mistress Calvia's secret, and she had me swear, too."

'But that god didn't heal her. She wouldn't be dead now if he had."

"I've thought that, too." Vera looked out the window and turned quiet.

Marcus stirred and opened his eyes. Then he opened his mouth, and the wail echoed inside the carriage. Brutus handed his son to Vera.

Wet or hungry, it wasn't for him to deal with it. He reached through the window and slapped the outer wall. Burdonarius reined to a stop, and Vera climbed out with Marcus, grabbing the sack of baby things as she went.

Brutus leaned his head back onto the pillows and closed his eyes. One act of kindness had started the train of events that led to death and heartbreak. Camilla had hidden her own agony over losing those babies from him. She'd put on an act, telling him she only wanted a child for him, not her.

Why hadn't he seen that? Why hadn't he let her grieve in his arms, not where a stranger would see and try to help?

When someone was hurting, Calvia couldn't stop herself. She had to try to fix it. Did she ever suspect when she started how much harm that could do?

*The Brutus estate, Lousonna*

As the raeda pulled into the stableyard, Calvia's stomach fluttered. She'd arrived at the Octodurus estate as domina. She knew what that meant, and she'd done what it required.

But here? For now, she was the guest of a man who was protecting her because his dead wife would have wanted him to. What that meant long term remained to be seen.

But she was never one to hide from a challenge. She took a deep breath, and stepped out of the carriage.

Africanus helped Brutus out, and a man in his mid-forties strode toward them.

"Welcome, Master Brutus, Africanus. The message about your accident said you'd be delayed four or five weeks. But it's good to see you earlier."

Brutus balanced on one crutch to slap the man's shoulder. "I've made up for my late arrival by increasing the number of people I've brought with me."

He summoned her with a wave. As she passed by the mules, Damalio jumped down and joined her.

"Bernhard, my steward. And this is Calvia Lucilla and Damalio. Calvia took us in after the accident, but she needs to leave her estate for a while. She'll be staying here until fall. Probably past the time when I return to Roma."

Bernhard's eyes were as welcoming as his smile. "It will be our pleasure to have you here."

Brutus chuckled. "You have no idea how great a pleasure that will be. You're going to be very glad she brought Sollus with her. He's a chef whose cooking would shine in the best houses in Roma, and he does it with what grows here. After Calvia's people get settled, take him to the kitchen to meet those he'll be training to cook like he does."

"Brutus." His smile didn't dim, but it might after her question. "Are you going to let Sollus improve the food for your workers as well?"

"I might, if it won't cost too much."

"The people who work hard for you all day deserve a good meal to look forward to at night."

"Rufus." Brutus raised his eyebrows. "You ate in her slave kitchen. Should I let Sollus direct the one here?"

Rufus patted his stomach and grinned. "Absolutely."

"He can suggest changes for my people's meals. If they seem reasonable, Bernhard, you can adopt them."

Brutus leaned on his crutches to shift his good leg; then the fleeting grimace returned to a smile. "Any more requests before I get off this leg?"

"If I may, I would like to have Damalio quartered near where I'll be with Primula." It was probably safe in his household, but...

"Bernhard, put Calvia in the largest guest chamber, and Damalio next to it. Also, find a place with good light for her two looms. You can show Damalio where that will be, and her men can take care of moving in what she's brought. Africanus and Rufus in their usual rooms, and Vera with Marcus near Calvia."

His smile dimmed. "Since you enjoy my son so much and she prefers protecting you over telling me what she should."

"Please don't punish her for that. She wasn't sure what you'd do to me."

"Maybe her concern was justified."

Calvia's eyes widened, and Damalio stiffened.

"Then, not now. I didn't bring you here for anything but your safety." The smile vanished as his lips tightened. "I promised Camilla I wouldn't hurt you, and this is what she would have wanted."

Calvia opened her mouth, then closed it.

Bernhard's eyes shifted between them until he broke the uncomfortable silence. "If you'll excuse me, master, I'll get everyone settled."

A single nod and a wave of Brutus's hand released him.

As Damalio followed the steward into the villa, he glanced over his shoulder. She waved and received a nod before he disappeared inside.

"Brutus."

He raised his eyebrows.

"Thank you for being so accommodating."

"With Damalio? He seems as much a brother to you as Crassus. I've grown to enjoy your protector's company, and he'll be eating with us and my steward. Rather like the arrangements at your estate, but dinner won't be as lively without Antistes to start some arguments."

"And you won't be able to goad him on to keep them going."

His smiling frown shifted toward a smile. "A man has to entertain himself some way when he can't use his leg."

"I suspect you'd do the same even if you had two good ones."

His chuckle wasn't what she expected. "You're right." He moved his crutches and swung his good leg forward. "Come inside and see where you'll be playing latrunculi until I think it's safe for you to go home."

She fell in beside him. He was a man of contradictions. From wanting her dead to saving her from the man who would kill her—both because of his love for Camilla.

He dealt in death, and she would never understand that. But she'd seen honor and love direct his actions. Camilla had prayed for her beloved to turn to Jesus, believing with all her heart that he would someday. For Camilla's sake and for his, she would pray for that, too.

# Chapter 48

## When a Man Must Choose

When Brutus entered the triclinium, people had been seated around the table like Calvia did, with a pillow on the end chair for his leg. Across from him sat the woman who stirred a confusion of feelings inside him, with her faithful guardian to her right. Africanus and Bernhard completed the company.

Antistes would have made it a livelier dinner. Baiting him always got a response, and part of the fun was the way Calvia's eyes snapped when she responded. He would miss that, but Calvia might not. For certain, Damalio wouldn't.

As the boy mixed water and wine and filled their goblets, Brutus turned his attention to Bernhard. "You're probably wondering why I came earlier than expected."

"I was, but I'm glad you did. We always look forward to your summer visit, and it's a pleasure to see young Marcus with you."

"I couldn't leave him alone in Roma during fever season." He glanced at Calvia, who looked away.

"I'd planned to wait until the wrappings came off my leg, but someone in Roma sent men after Calvia. He wants to hurt her brother using her."

Bernhard drew a loud breath through his nose. "Might they track her here?"

"Unlikely, but possible. Africanus and Rufus can take care of it if they do, and I'll be on both legs in a couple of weeks." He grinned at

Africanus. "You'll need to take it easy on me when we start sparring, but I'll still be able to handle most others."

One corner of Africanus's mouth lifted. "No doubt, but it takes longer to build back muscle than you think. A month or two will have you ready for battle again."

Calvia sipped her wine and looked away again.

"I'll miss joining you and Rufus for the riding and hunting. It's good that I brought some alternate entertainment with me."

Bernhard cocked his head. "What might that be?"

"Someone as good as Africanus at latrunculi."

Bernhard directed a smile at Damalio. "I play well enough, but Master Brutus beats me every time. You must be good if he enjoys your games."

Brutus chuckled. "Not Damalio. It's Calvia."

"I beg pardon for my error. I just assumed..."

"She doesn't look like it, but a strategic mind lurks behind that pretty face."

Her lips twitched, but her eyes proclaimed amusement, not irritation. "My beauty or lack thereof isn't why I beat him. He's used to Africanus. They both think like men. Everything's a battle with them. A woman learns to be more subtle to get what she wants."

The truth of her words was undeniable, and it triggered Brutus's laugh. "Subtlety in the mornings with you. Afternoons with a man who thinks like me. It's enough until I get back on two legs."

Two women entered carrying silver plates. As they placed them before each diner, Brutus inhaled the rich aroma. Pork cubes and leeks and apple slices covered with a sauce. He swiped his finger through the sauce and licked it. Both spicy and sweet and different from any he'd had before.

"Sollus?"

"He made the sauce." Bernhard lifted his goblet to Calvia. "Master Brutus was right. It's already my pleasure that you brought your cook. I'm as pleased as he is to have you both here for a few months."

Brutus lifted his goblet as well. Her gentle smile and nod acknowledged them both. But he watched her over the rim as he took a sip.

Was he pleased to have her there?

He'd considered her a friend until he learned who she was. He'd wished he could introduce her to Camilla until he learned they were friends already. He'd wanted her to suffer like he had, but when that looked certain, he couldn't let it happen.

He'd met many people whom he enjoyed for a while before circumstances parted them. She would have been a good memory after his leg healed and he moved on.

It would never have been his first choice, but he'd taken responsibility for her safety. How long would he have to bear that? Would Sabinus believe what he'd told the ones stalking her? Would he lose interest in hunting her?

If that old crocodile sent men after her again, what would it take to stop him for good?

*June 21*

Brutus had chosen Calvia for his morning opponent, and Africanus wasn't sorry. Playing with Brutus took focus, and he'd spent too much time thinking about Damalio's words.

Too much, and yet not enough.

One more series of thrusts and blocks, and Rufus stepped back. "Enough for today. You almost drew blood with that last one. Did I do something?"

"No. My mind was drifting."

"Warn me if that starts again."

Africanus slid his gladius into its scabbard before scooping up a towel and tossing it to Rufus. With the second, he wiped his face.

"You both look better than last year."

Africanus lowered the towel to reveal Bernhard's friendly smile.

Rufus toweled his hair. "You should have seen Africanus right after the accident. He looked like death when I left him by the road, but he was fine when I brought the physician. Someone must have used sorcery to save him."

"Is Calvia Lucilla a sorceress?" Bernhard stared at the portico as his mouth turned down.

"There was no sorcery. Damalio said they only prayed to their god for my healing."

One corner of Bernhard's mouth lifted. "I've never seen that work."

"I'm proof it worked at least once."

Bernhard shrugged. "Then maybe that's a god worth praying to."

"Master Bernhard." A boy of ten stood with hands clasped. "Damalio has something to show you in the stable."

Bernhard raised a hand in farewell and followed the boy.

Rufus flipped the towel over his shoulder. "I'm hungry. Let's visit Sollus in the kitchen. Maybe I'll get a taste of what you'll get for lunch."

As they carried their swords back to their rooms, Africanus's mind kept churning. Maybe there was a god worth worshiping. He'd put it off long enough. It was time to get Damalio to tell him more.

As everyone left the dining room after lunch, it was time.

"Damalio." Africanus felt his heart rate rise like it had when he stepped from the darkness of the tunnel to the brightness of the sand. He took a deep breath and willed it to slow down. "Let's talk."

"Where?"

Africanus stopped and waited for Brutus and Calvia to pass through the doorway to the portico. They'd been tied when they broke for lunch, and Brutus had challenged her to one more game to decide the day's winner. Before Brutus called him to start playing, he would ask for some answers he wasn't sure he wanted.

Damalio followed Africanus's gaze. "Brutus knows what we were all hiding. Wherever you want is fine."

It was fine with Damalio, but Africanus didn't want Brutus listening. "The garden. There are chairs under the apple tree."

In silence, they covered the distance. Africanus turned one chair to face the other, and they settled in.

"The god you say healed me. Tell me more about him."

It was a dangerous request. A man was responsible for what he knew. What he'd heard so far...it disturbed him, but he still had to know more.

"What I told you already, do you have questions about it?"

"This god of the Jews and now of the Christians...he sounds different. The priests of the Roman gods say you have to make an offering before the gods will listen, that they only help if you give them something worth money." He snorted as he shook his head. "But those gods are just children's stories, and the priests keep the offerings for themselves."

Damalio nodded. His eyes were serious, but his mouth had curved into a slight smile.

"You say your god gives instead of taking. That he loves people."

"He does, like a father but more. Jesus even told us to call Him our father. God wants us to be His children, to give us everything we need and more, but we have to do something first."

"So, he is like the others. Pay first, then maybe receive." Africanus's brow furrowed. "Last time you said all you did was ask him to heal me. Did you give him something before you prayed?"

"Yes and no. Nothing like you're thinking, but we did give him our hearts and minds."

"What are you talking about?"

Damalio leaned forward and rested his arms on his knees. "God told us to love Him with our whole heart, our mind, our soul, and all our strength and to love other people as much as we love ourselves. Anything less than that separates us from Him. The choices we make that don't follow those commands are called sins. But none of us can do that on our own, so none of us are fit to be with Him."

"So, there's no way to do what your god requires."

"On my own, that's right. But I don't have to do it on my own. He'd told His people only blood sacrifice could cover sins so they could approach Him, and only a perfect sacrifice could erase their sins forever. But nothing on earth is perfect, and the blood of an animal can't erase the sins of a man. So God came Himself as Jesus of Nazareth to make it possible. His execution ninety years ago was that perfect sacrifice."

Without realizing, Africanus had leaned forward, mirroring Damalio. He straightened and crossed his arms.

Damalio's eyes bored into him. "Jesus said His death was the price to free me from slavery to sin, the ransom that would set me free."

"Any man could say that, but that wouldn't make it true."

"He proved He could do what He said by rising from the dead."

"Hmph." That was a crazy claim. He'd seen many men die, and they all remained dead.

He left one arm across his stomach and rested the other elbow on it. Then he rubbed his forehead. A crazy claim, but he'd seen so many Christians die for believing it. Sheer insanity if the claim was false, but what if it was true?

"These things he forbids, what you call sin, what are those?"

"Anything I choose that goes against loving God and other people."

"Loving other people?" Africanus's nose wrinkled. "Most people don't deserve love. My family in Nuba, Dorcas, my children...those are all I've ever loved. And some, like Brutus and Rufus, I care about as friends. But most of the rest? I have no special feelings for them. Some I've even hated."

"But the love God calls us to isn't a feeling. It's a decision we make followed by what we do. It's wanting what's best for them, even when that costs us something. It's doing what we can to help when it's needed, even if we'd rather not. It doesn't depend on what they do or how I feel about them."

"I've lived the opposite of that. I've been a gladiator since I was sold at fourteen, more than twenty years. Do you know how many I've killed? I've been proud of it. I enjoyed the fighting. I felt...satisfied as I drove my sword home and walked from the sand with thousands cheering me. How can another man's blood erase that?"

"I don't know how it works, but I know God said it does. Jesus said all we have to do is confess our sins and believe His death paid for them, and it's as if we never did them."

"Even for a man who's done what I have?"

"And worse. If you hadn't killed, you would have died. Two thugs were crucified when Jesus was. As they all hung there, one told Jesus he knew he deserved to die for what he'd done, but he knew Jesus had done nothing wrong. He believed Jesus was more than a man dying next to him, that He would rule a coming kingdom. Jesus told the murderer he would be with Him in Paradise that day."

"How could the thug's words change anything?"

"Jesus said all we have to do is confess our sins and believe He saves us from them, and then we have eternal life with Him starting here on earth and forever after we die."

"Confess and believe? That sounds too simple. How would I even know your god was listening? How would he know if I really believed?"

Damalio looked past him, and his smile, which always started slowly, grew into a grin. Africanus looked over his shoulder, and nothing stood where Damalio was looking. When he turned his gaze back on Damalio, friendly eyes focused on him once more.

"He hears every word, knows every thought. You don't have to fear telling Him anything, because He already knows you better than you know yourself. He'll know if you're trying to hide something, and He simply wants truth between you."

The truth? Africanus squeezed the back of his neck. A god who commanded love would find the truth of his life too ugly to look at. "I don't know what he'd want me to confess."

"Just start, and it will come to you. You couldn't love Him before because you didn't know about Him. But we've all done things to others because we failed to love them. Confess those. Then tell Him you believe Jesus paid for your sins, and ask Him what next."

"How would I know if I've done it right?"

"God will make sure you know." The grin faded, but Damalio's eyes stayed warm. "And then you'll find yourself wanting to love Him and others like He commanded. It will change your life."

Silence stretched out between them as Africanus rubbed his jaw. "I have to think long and hard about what you just said. Choosing to believe it would carry a high cost."

"It can, but choosing not to believe it carries a higher one."

Damalio stood. "I'm helping Fidus make a new style of harness for Bernhard to try. He's waiting for me. We can talk more later."

He took two steps, then turned back. "If I buy you something and tell you which shop it's at and what to do to get it, your failure to pick it up is the only thing that can keep you from enjoying my gift. That's what Jesus did. He told us all we have to do is believe He paid the price, and His gifts of freedom from our sins and eternal life with Him are ours. But you have to decide you want that and make the first move to get it." He took one more step and looked back over his shoulder. "He won't make you take it, but I hope you do."

Africanus leaned back in the chair and crossed his arms as Damalio strode away. He'd been a gladiator his whole life. Even though he'd stopped killing in the arena, he still considered himself one. How could a man like him follow a god who said to love your enemies, to treat them as if they were family or friends?

He was a free man now, but Brutus was still his patron. Brutus hated what following the Christian god had done to Camilla. Would becoming a Christian cost him Brutus's friendship?

But how could he not believe in a god who'd healed him when he was wounded past healing?

Brutus's laugh came from the portico. The man whose hatred for Licinia Crassa had seemed unquenchable now enjoyed spending hours each day with her. Had his hostility to the Christian god faded as his anger toward the Christian woman cooled?

No man valued truth and honor more than Brutus. If the things she and her people believed about Jesus of Nazareth were true, Brutus would accept it, whether he wanted to or not.

Africanus closed his eyes and rubbed his forehead.

How could something that seemed unbelievable be true? But if it was, how could a man not choose to believe it?

# Chapter 49

## If He Would Turn

*Morning of June 22*

Calvia had already helped Brutus get his leg comfortable on the pillowed chair when Africanus entered the triclinium and sank into his usual seat.

Brutus's spoon stopped halfway to his mouth. "You don't look like you slept last night."

"Such nights happen." Africanus swirled his goblet and took a sip. Drooping eyelids accompanied circles beneath his eyes.

It was the first time Calvia had seen him anything but alert. "Are you well?"

"Of course." Irritation iced his words as a scowl appeared.

She straightened. As bodyguard or gladiator, that look would unnerve anyone.

Damalio was stirring his porridge, but his hand stopped. His gaze shifted from the bowl to Africanus's face; then his slow smile grew. Africanus frowned back at him. Damalio's lips tightened as if to stop a smile, and he resumed stirring.

Breakfast remained largely silent, with Africanus brooding, Damalio watching him, and the other two men focused on the food. She glanced at Bernhard, seated at the foot of the table, where Antistes used to be. He ran Brutus's estate with quiet efficiency most of the year, but he was still receptive to Brutus's suggestions. How would she get Antistes to behave like that? More importantly, how could she get him to think like that?

She nibbled at her last piece of cheese. Yesterday morning had been far better than she expected. Brutus had stopped frowning when he looked at her. It was as if they were back at her estate before Sabinus's men came, except they'd exchanged a view of her vegetable garden and the weavers' workshop for a sweeping view of the lake and the mountains beyond.

Everything about his villa was more elegant than her own home. Even his gameboard was inlaid with woods of different colors that made complex geometric patterns surrounding the grids. Her wooden board with the grids for the games and some simple vines carved around them served its purpose, but his was a thing of beauty. His game pieces were polished stone, not slices of bone that had been dyed, and they felt smooth and cool in her hand.

He was once more the Brutus in whose company she found such pleasure. He teased her when his last move put her at a disadvantage, and pretended he'd made a good move when he saw the advantage shift to her. It was almost like before he learned she knew Camilla.

Almost. Several times she'd looked up from the board to find him watching her. No, not watching. Analyzing, like the way he looked at the board as he plotted his next moves.

There was no good reason, but she'd felt her cheeks flush and her ears burn. Then his eyes shifted from analyzing to laughing at her, even though he didn't say a word.

As she finished the cheese, she found herself smiling, and then she felt his eyes on her. When she returned his gaze, he raised one eyebrow. That smiling frown she found so confusing appeared, and once again her ears burned.

When Calvia joined Brutus on the portico for another match of latrunculi, it was already midmorning. It was harder to concentrate with the clash of swords in the background now she knew what they all were. His men weren't just sparring to stay ready to protect him. They were training for brutal battles before thousands, where each bout ended in blood on a sword and a body on the sand. And he made money off it all.

She'd listened for the sound of silence before leaving her loom in his great hall and joining him outside. The sparring was over, and the gladiators had gone for a run.

"Ready for battle?" His voice was cheerful.

He'd already placed the rondels and kings in preparation for their first game. She picked up the blue pyramid that she'd be defending. She won her games with subtle strategy. He and Africanus treated it as war.

"Ready for a game matching wits." That's all it was to her, and she had to admit she loved doing it, especially with him.

He flashed a smile at her. "I trust you got a good night's sleep. I like it when you play your best game. The way Africanus looked at breakfast, I don't think he'd be much challenge."

"Is anything wrong with him?"

"I don't think so. Rufus had a harder time holding his own today. Africanus holds back when he fights both of us, but he didn't this morning. Not entirely."

"On the way here..." Brutus knew all her secrets now. He should know she knew his. "Rufus was talking with Primula. He told her what you are."

"What I am?" His brow furrowed.

"What you all are. That he's a real gladiator, and you put him in fights."

"I thought you knew that." His smiling frown appeared. "How could you not? You were Camilla's best friend."

"She never mentioned it." Could he have known Camilla was too ashamed to tell her?

"Well, that explains a few things. It seemed strange that you'd say things to deliberately insult a guest. But I'm no longer offended by your remarks. You don't have to apologize."

Apologize? She wasn't the one making money off men dying.

"I'm glad you aren't offended, but I have no intention of apologizing, whether you are or not. I meant what I said. The life of each man is infinitely precious to God, and shedding blood to entertain the masses would never be something I could approve."

His eyebrows dipped, and just as quickly relaxed. "I haven't asked for your approval, and I don't need your apology. It's just one more thing about which we can agree to disagree."

But there was a challenge in his eyes before he turned them on the board. "You won last, so I go first."

When he looked up at her again, whatever he was feeling was masked. "Your turn."

She moved her first piece and suppressed a deep sigh. Whatever he might say, a man of honor couldn't keep doing what he did. She would join what must have been Camilla's prayers, that he see the evil in what he was doing and turn.

Turn away from the bloodshed and turn to Jesus before it was too late.

*If he turns to you, Lord, might he then turn to me?*

Lunch had been directed by Sollus, so of course it was delicious. With Marcus sleeping in her arms, Calvia sat under the apple tree while a full stomach and a warm baby filled her with contentment. Damalio leaned against the trunk, arms crossed.

She kissed Marcus's forehead, but he didn't awaken. "I wonder how Ursula is doing. Her baby might have come by now. If I'd left an address for writing to me in Lousonna, I could have known how she and the other three mothers-to-be are faring."

"It's better if Antistes doesn't know where you are."

"He wouldn't have to know exactly where I am. It should be possible to find some business in Lousonna that would be willing to hold any letters for me so they could be picked up when one of Brutus's men goes to town. Even if Antistes isn't trustworthy, Primus might be. Is he?"

"He probably is, but without telling him we don't trust his father, we couldn't count on him not to reveal where you are. They were close before we came. Those habits are hard to break, even when there's good reason. Primus has no reason. He didn't eat with us. He didn't see how his father wanted to challenge you for control of the estate every chance he could."

"I could ask Brutus what he thinks."

"You could, and he'll tell you the same as I am. It was he who stopped you from saying anything before we left."

"You're right, but he did say I could send someone to find out how the estate is faring. You or Rufus could go."

Damalio's mouth twitched. "Rufus wouldn't want to be gone too long."

"You mean from Primula?"

Tightened lips hid his smile. "He likes to talk to her, and she can't always avoid him."

"I agree the attraction isn't entirely mutual. She's trying to discourage him, but gently. He likes to watch her weave when he's not busy with Africanus, but he doesn't talk much, and she talks hardly at all, except for answering his questions. A pagan gladiator isn't what either of us would want, no matter how much other women fawn over them."

Or a pagan gladiator owner. But try as she might, Calvia still found her thoughts straying to the man Camilla had called the finest husband in the Empire. He'd only hated her because he loved Camilla so much. He'd been able to overcome that hatred when honor demanded he protect her.

If he were a Christian...but he wasn't, and he likely never would be. A man like him was not what she should want for herself. But it was hard not to. The gentle smile when he watched Marcus sleep in his arms, the little lines at the corner of his eyes when he grinned at her and when he was trying not to, that ambiguous smiling frown that left her guessing what it really meant—the mere thought of those warmed her. He was so smart, like Father and Sextus, and he was even more fun to discuss history with than Decurion Brocchus had been. And although she knew the heart of a man was what really mattered, it was impossible not to notice his brawny arms and the muscled chest underneath his tunic.

But he wasn't a Christian, and she'd promised herself and God that was the only kind of man she would marry. Which meant she'd probably not marry at all.

"Rufus isn't what Primula wants, but there are two people here who might be just right for each other."

Damalio cocked his head. He was funny when he looked perplexed.

"And here she comes now."

He glanced over his shoulder and straightened. Vera was coming with a blanket-lined basket the perfect size for Marcus.

His ears turned a becoming shade of red under the fringe of blond hair that had grown out since his last haircut.

"She loves young Marcus. She'd never want to leave Brutus while he lets her care for him." He kept his eyes on Calvia, and the red faded.

"I love Marcus, too, but that doesn't mean a woman wouldn't love even more to have a good man and babies of her own." Her smile turned mischievous.

"A wise man doesn't let his heart start wanting what's impossible. Brutus will take her back to Rome with Marcus. We'll be here until fall, and then we return to Octodurus."

"But she's a sister, and God works all things for good for those of us who love Him. We can't know what His plans are until we see them unfold."

"True, domina, but I've found it's better to hold back from wanting what seems unlikely for God to do."

Vera was almost within earshot, and she raised her hand in response to Calvia's wave.

Time to stop their discussion. Damalio was probably right, and it had been a mistake to suggest it.

Laughter came from the portico as Brutus leaned over and slapped Africanus's shoulder. One of them had just won, but she couldn't tell who.

A wise woman shouldn't let her heart start wanting the impossible either, and marrying a pagan man who made money from death was foolish for her to consider.

But there was something about that man that made her wish she could.

*The taberna near the Baths of Trajan, June 22*

With one foot tapping under the table, Custos traced the letters someone had carved into the wine-stained surface. His gaze moved back and forth between someone's idle scrawl and the doorway.

It was too soon for Festinus to have returned, but that might be a good thing. It was harder to hide a lie from a man who knew you than from a stranger.

When the bulky gladiator blocked much of the doorway, Custos stopped his foot, summoned a smile, and raised one hand. Sabinus's enforcer strode to his table. Custos had already turned the chair for him, and it creaked when he lowered his massive frame onto it.

Custos pushed a second cup of wine toward the enforcer before taking a sip from his own. "Any word from Festinus?" He tried to sound friendly, but he got a frown in return.

"You don't need to know."

Did that mean none had come or Sabinus didn't trust either of them enough to tell them?

The enforcer drained half his cup. "What do you have this week?"

"Something that might change where the master looks for Crassus's sister."

That drew a scowl. "So what you said before was bad information?"

"No, I saw the letter myself. I do know where Crassus sends his letters to Gratus. But I don't know who Gratus really is. It could just be some freedman, not the sister, at the Octodurus estate."

"What makes you think it's not the sister?"

"Crassus was complaining to his secretary about her not writing enough. He told Vicarius he scolded her about it. Apparently, he'd written her that he knew the distractions of being in one of the leading cities of the Empire could fill her time, but he would like to hear from her more often than every five or six months."

"So?"

"Octodurus is a provincial capital, but no one would consider it a leading city of the Empire. I don't know that I'd call anything north of the Alpes a leading city. I think of Corinth, Athens, Ephesus, and Antioch. Maybe Alexandria, but I'd guess one of the other four is more likely."

Custos was lifting the cup to his lips when the enforcer's beefy hand cuffed his ear. The wine slopped on the table. He set the cup down and held his hand away from the table as he shook the liquid off. He didn't want to explain a red stain on his tunic.

"Why did you do that?" Gingerly, he touched the sore spot. Would it bruise enough to draw questions?

"It's a reminder. The master expects good information. He isn't going to be happy about sending someone all the way to Octodurus if she isn't there."

"Festinus knows I'm doing all any man can. When the target is as honest as Crassus, it's hard to find anything."

"Hmph." The gladiator stood. "Nothing else?"

"No, but the master should find that plenty. The only thing better might be seeing a real letter between them. You can tell him I'm watching all the time for that."

"You do that, and you'd better get something else soon."

He picked up Custos's cup and drank what hadn't spilled. "Be here next week."

As the enforcer left the room, Custos leaned on the table and held his head.

It was a dangerous game he was playing for Master Crassus now, but at least he'd made a start on undoing the harm he'd done to an innocent woman and an honorable man.

# Chapter 50

## More Than He Expected

*Early June 23*

The villa had been quiet for hours, but sleep eluded Africanus. The moon had risen long ago, and its light cast faint shadows in his chamber. He'd counted each board in the ceiling too many times, so he swung his legs off the bed and went to the window.

It was Damalio's fault. All that talk about a god who could stop death and who cared about him enough to die for the wrong things he'd done had chased sleep away last night. Now Damalio's final words this evening as they parted after dinner rattled around Africanus's head. "Talk to him tonight. He kept you from dying for a reason. You'll know what it is when you tell him you want the gift."

But did he want a gift that might change everything? His life was good. Mostly good, anyway. Did he want to risk what he had for the promise of something better?

Talk to Damalio's god. He rubbed the back of his neck. How did a man talk to something he couldn't see without feeling like a fool?

If that god already knew his thoughts, as Damalio said, he didn't have to speak, but that felt like a coward's way out. Saying the words made anything seem more real.

"God of Damalio, I want to talk to you. Are you here?"

Words spoken to an empty room, but was it? A good bodyguard always sensed when eyes were watching. He felt that now. But not like he felt when someone watched from the woods as they traveled, that feeling that made him rein in, draw his sword, and turn his horse toward the unseen watcher until he sensed eyes were no longer upon him.

It was more like a time so long ago it didn't quite seem real. When he had to tip his head way back to look at his father's face and reach up as far as he could to touch Father's chest. He'd tried to tell Father about the pretty animal sleeping in the tree, the one with yellow fur and black spots. But his words didn't come out like he heard them in his head. Father frowned and pushed him aside before turning his attention back to the words of the tribal elders.

Africanus had gone back to watch the pretty animal. He'd called out to it, and its eyes opened. It stood and stretched and opened its mouth wide. A pink tongue stretched and curled in a mouth framed by pointed yellow teeth. Then amber eyes locked on him. Cold eyes that heated into hungry ones.

Then he felt different eyes watching behind him. Warm, protective eyes. He startled when Grandfather's brother stepped up beside him. With his oval hide shield and his spear with a shaft marked for many lion kills, Great-uncle moved in front of him. When the leopard sprang, he caught the beast on the shield, tossed it on the ground, and drove the spear into its chest.

As the red spread across the animal's yellow fur, Great-uncle knelt to his eye level and rested a wrinkled hand against his cheek.

Whatever was watching now, it felt like Great-uncle's eyes had felt that day.

"Damalio told me you stopped me from dying. I've watched men die for more than twenty years, so I know you did something."

By the cataracts of the Nile on the way to the slave market in Alexandria, he'd realized the gods of his tribe had abandoned him. On the sand in Cyrene, he'd learned it didn't matter what god his opponent worshiped. None of them helped. Every man fell to his skill with a blade and his determination to win.

When Brutus told him no god was real, that was what he already suspected. Their gods hadn't abandoned the men he killed. They'd never been there at all.

The moon shadows disappeared, and the room darkened. A curtain of clouds had blocked the light. But the clouds were broken, and the edges of the one now hiding the moon were still trimmed with moonlight.

So many times, he'd stood by a window and watched the moon slip in and out of cloud cover. Light and darkness—his life had been like that. Love for his family, deep friendship with Brutus, but he knew the darkness of stone-cold ruthlessness when he fought to kill and deep satisfaction when he raised his bloody sword as the crowd screamed his name. What would it feel like to stay in the light?

"He tells me you created all people, that you're the god of everyone, whether we know about you or not. He said you command us to love you above all else.

"If you heard my thoughts as I watched death take the ones who called Jesus their Lord and God, you know I thought they were fools. It never made sense that they chose death over worshiping another god. If no god is real, what did it matter?

"So I've disobeyed your command to love you before tonight, but maybe you won't hold that against me. I couldn't love what I didn't think was real."

The thick curtain had moved, leaving a thin veil of clouds behind. The ghost of a moon shone through. Then the clouds cleared half the moon, and the pale moonlight made shadows again.

"But since you healed me, from now on I will honor you as the only real god. Honor I know I can give you right now. Love you...I'm not sure what that means yet, but maybe Damalio can help me with that."

The moonlight brightened and cast darker shadows; the clouds had passed.

"He also told me you care about people, even love them like a father but more. That you want us with you, but we're not good enough. That we choose to disobey you and do things that make us unworthy. He said we have to treat others like we love them to obey what you command. Enemies as well as friends."

He rubbed his jaw. "If you know everything, then you know I haven't done that. I've killed fifty on the sand. Maybe more. I've lost count." He closed his eyes. He remembered the faces of only a few. Most had worn helmets that hid them, but the men with only tridents and nets... he'd seen life leave their eyes before raising his bloody sword as the crowd cheered.

"He said you made yourself known to the Jews, and you ordered them to offer blood sacrifice to cover up sin so they could approach you. But an animal can't pay for what a man has done. So you came as Jesus to make the perfect blood sacrifice that could pay what they couldn't."

No one had entered through the door or window, but he wasn't alone in the room. Someone was listening, as Damalio had said, and they'd moved closer.

"I know I'm guilty of too much that you forbid, but I want to know the one who kept me from dying. I want to believe you made that possible when Jesus took away my guilt, that he paid for my sins and ransomed me with his blood. So, what should I do next?"

The presence he'd sensed filled the room. Brilliant light shimmered with the colors of the rainbow. He fell to his knees. Words like he'd never heard flooded his mind, and all his doubts vanished like smoke on a breeze as the certainty of God's love filled him.

Then the light faded, and moon-shadows lay across the room once more. How long it had lasted he couldn't say. But it was impossible to doubt that he'd met the God Who was real, the God Who'd kept him from dying, the God Who loved him enough to ransom him with His own blood.

He'd asked for the gift God had paid for, and he'd been given much more than he expected. The presence was no longer in the room listening. The Watcher was inside him, and Africanus knew He would stay.

Sometime tomorrow he'd tell Damalio what happened. Sometime when no one who might tell Brutus was listening.

Telling his friend was his alone to do. It had to be at the right time in the right way.

He'd asked for God's gifts of freedom from sin and eternal life, and he'd received them.

Could he get his closest friend to do the same?

## *Chapter 51*

### A Breach in His Armor

*June 23*

After breakfast, Africanus went to his room to get his gladius. It was time for the morning match with Rufus while Brutus played latrunculi with Calvia. He was coming out when Damalio approached.

"Step into my room."

As soon as Damalio was inside, Africanus bolted the door. He took a deep breath, and Damalio's smile started to build before Africanus could speak the first word.

"I talked with Him last night."

The smile broadened. "I thought so. You looked too rested to have passed the night without it."

"I accepted His gift." Eyes that laughed lit with delight. "You didn't tell me about the light and warmth and..." His hand rested on his chest, and a grin appeared as he shook his head. "And that He'd stay here with me."

"Surprises are good, and God delights in giving them to His children." Damalio's smile finished its growth into a matching grin. "That's the Holy Spirit, and Jesus promised He would come to be with all who follow Him. Since God has adopted you as His son, you're my brother now. You're welcome to join the rest of us when we gather to worship and to enjoy our brotherhood. We meet on Solis."

Africanus crossed his arms. "Who are the rest of you?"

"Everyone who came here with Domina. She has a copy of the writings of Luke. He was a physician who traveled with Apostle Paul.

Luke wrote down what Jesus said and did while He was in Judaea. We gather someplace private, and I read from it." He slapped Africanus's arm. "You'll get to know Him better as you listen. And being with other believers...it doesn't get better than that."

"Tell me when, and I'll join you if Brutus doesn't need me." He rubbed the back of his neck. "Can they be trusted not to tell him what I've done? I haven't told him yet. I'm waiting for the right time." He took a deep breath, and the grin faded. "He'll be asking what's wrong with me if I let too much of how I now feel show. He might not be ready to hear what's right with me instead."

"That's wise. We all have to mask it sometimes. You'll learn when and how. I'll pray for the right time and the right words to come soon." His eyes crinkled. "I asked God to tell me what I should tell you. Ask, and He'll tell you what to say to Brutus when the time is right."

Africanus swung the door open and draped the scabbard strap across his chest. Damalio went right; he went left. The time was right for swords with Rufus. Maybe soon it would be right for words with Brutus.

*The Sabinus villa near Rome, June 24*

When Sabinus rose from the dining couch, the slaves who'd stood like statues by the wall came forward to clear away what was left of dinner. He snapped his fingers at the wine slave.

"Take the Falernian to my office and leave it."

As the boy scurried off, Sabinus stretched and flexed his shoulders.

"Another fine dinner, Father." Manius dropped his napkin on the table as he rose. "Ready to play?"

Sabinus sauntered into the hall, Manius at his side. "Always a good way to end an evening."

He led Manius into his office and settled into his desk chair. While his son filled two goblets at the small table with a pedestal of frolicking nymphs, Sabinus pulled out the chain holding the desk key under his tunic. After unlocking the center drawer, he removed a wax tablet. When Manius offered the wine, Sabinus handed it to his son.

"Festinus sent this by horse relay six days ago. He reached the Crassus estate to find something I didn't anticipate."

Manius handed back the tablet without reading. "What?"

"Marcus Antonius Brutus was there with two of his gladiators and a broken leg. A baby and a woman in a stola of fine linen were there as well. Brutus claimed she was with him."

"Crassus's sister, was she also there?" Manius took a sip.

"When Festinus asked, Brutus said no. When our man asked if the woman was Calvia Lucilla, Brutus said Crassus wouldn't take a mistress. Then he had his men escort Festinus from the villa."

"He has no reason to lie. So, where do we look next?"

"He has no reason to tell the truth, and I don't think he was. He might have closer ties to Crassus than we thought. Remember how Crassus had a blanket delivered for Brutus's new son?"

"I thought you said it was a simple condolence gift."

"I did, but I wouldn't think to give a blanket for that reason. Why would Crassus?"

"Maybe his secretary or steward thought of it?"

"Maybe, or maybe his sister and Brutus's wife were better friends than we've been thinking."

"I suppose it's possible."

"Remember how Brutus made a fool of himself grieving when his wife died? It's been, what, seven months? The baby was probably his. But the woman?"

"Hmmm." Manius swirled his wine before taking another sip. "I heard him say a couple of months ago at the baths that he has no intention of remarrying. That disappointed a couple of my wife's friends. He's richer than many senators, and mourning his wife that way...they thought it romantic."

"So, it seems strange to you as well that he's suddenly got a woman who's at least equestrian with him."

"I guess it does."

"I'd be willing to bet he hasn't remarried. Any woman in a stola there is unlikely to be his wife."

"A mistress, maybe?"

"No. When it came out Barbatus had one, he couldn't buy Brutus's private vintage anymore."

Sabinus tapped the closed tablet with a stylus. "I think the domina at that estate is really the sister pretending to be a married woman, and Brutus lied to protect his wife's friend." He slammed the stylus on the desktop. "I should have warned Festinus to watch for something like that and told him what to do if he found it."

He threw himself back in the chair and crossed his arms. "As soon as Festinus gets here, I'm sending him right back to Octodurus. Brutus and his gladiators should be gone, and we'll get the woman for the leverage we need."

He dropped the tablet back in the drawer and locked it.

Manius moved the board between them. "Tabula or latrunculi?"

"You pick."

As his son set up for the harder game, Sabinus's frown turned into a smile. Three or four more weeks, and Sextus Crassus should be willing to do whatever they told him.

*The Brutus estate near Lousonna, June 25*

As Brutus contemplated his next move, he fought the urge to rub his jaw. Calvia didn't need to see he knew he was losing. Yesterday she'd explained the little things he did that gave away his thoughts. Then she laughed and said his smiling frown was the only thing that sometimes confused her.

But her laughter was musical, and the way her eyes twinkled...Camilla had looked at him just that way when she couldn't resist teasing him. Maybe it was a woman thing they all did, but somehow it took the sting out of any words that went with it.

"You've been here for six days now. I'm glad you were wise enough to accept my invitation." He offered his smiling frown. Confusion was good for her.

"Invitation?" There was that musical chuckle again. "More of a command, but I do thank you for deciding to protect me. Damalio thought it wise to come, and he's never wrong."

"I might have invited you even if you hadn't needed my protection. It's worth having you here to have Sollus directing my kitchen."

She laughed again, and that brought a smile she should have no problem interpreting.

"Bernhard is glad you're staying past my leaving. He'll try to persuade you to leave Sollus when you go."

"He's not for sale at any price, so you can tell him not to try."

He picked up his game piece. There were only two choices for where he could move, and neither held the promise of victory. But if she chose her next move wrong...it could be a tie instead of defeat. He placed the rondel on the one that might lure her into that error.

She made her move and won the game.

"I was hoping you wouldn't see that." He leaned back in his chair.

"Two in a row, and that smile says you're gloating even if your lips don't speak a word."

He'd become expert at watching her lips to read her thoughts. She always admitted it when he was right. Honesty in a woman...it could be hard to find. But even with her fake name, she still had it. Much as Camilla had.

"You're enjoying your victory too much, but I'll get you on the next one."

"Perhaps." She tilted her head as her smile turn teasing. "Perhaps not."

He reached for his drink as she began setting up the next game. "Board games are much like battle. Battle without blood. Victory or defeat without risk of death. But in real life, the best strategies can fail, like your brother sending you to Octodurus. Bringing you here is an extension of that strategy. The first move failed, the second shouldn't. But if it does, a well-placed sword can protect you."

He patted his wrapped leg. "Another two weeks, and I'll be out of this. Then it could be mine as easily as my men's."

Calvia picked up a rondel. But instead of placing it where he expected, she wrapped her fingers around it and froze.

"Is something wrong?"

She glanced at his face, then lowered her eyes. "I don't want to think about someone killing to protect me." Eyes stripped of humor turned on him. "The life of any man is precious, even one who wants to do me harm." Her lips tightened. "I'll never understand why my brother doesn't see that when he goes to the games. Why any man would want to watch another man lose his life. Why some call for death and are disappointed if they don't see it."

Brutus straightened. "It's hard for any woman to understand a man. Camilla came closer than any."

"But she wouldn't have understood that."

He set his goblet down hard, sloshing some wine onto the table. "How would you know?"

Her grip on the rondel tightened. "Because she was my sister in Christ. Jesus taught us to love even our enemies, to pray for them and to do good to them. To forgive what others do to us, no matter how hard that might be."

"Some losses are too great to forgive the one who caused them."

"He forgave the soldiers even as they were crucifying him."

"And I suppose you think I should forgive you? For telling Camilla she could give me a son? For her dying because you led her to believe your god would protect her from what almost killed her that last time? For turning her from the Roman gods?"

"But she said you don't believe in them, either."

His jaw clenched. What he believed didn't make her less guilty.

"I don't. No god is real. Not even yours. But if I'm wrong and what I've always been told about the afterlife it true, you made sure she wouldn't be with me."

"But if you believed my God *is* real, that Jesus died as the full payment for all the things you've done that keep you from Him, then you could be with her. And with Jesus and everyone who's ever believed in Him."

He shoved her words aside with his hand. "I'd wager your brother doesn't believe any of that. Neither did your father. Where did you ever get those ideas?"

"From my Uncle Gaius. He and his wife told me, and they showed me the truth of it all. It was he who taught me about the healing power of prayer, like with Africanus."

"I know Gaius Crassus. I see him at the temple rites. He's not a Christian."

"Different Gaius. Uncle Gaius was almost arrested and sent to the arena. He left just before the soldiers reached his estate. He took Priscilla and their son and daughter north across the Alpes. I wanted to go, too, but Father found out and refused to let me. He said Germania was too dangerous for a girl of twelve, and Uncle Gaius was going to have a hard enough time keeping the four of them from starving."

A different Gaius. Fifteen or so years ago, there had been rumors...

"Gaius Licinius Crassus?"

"Yes."

"You say he went to Germania?"

She placed the rondel where he expected. "I don't know for certain. That was his plan."

"How old was his son?"

"Six when they left."

He made his next play. "Was he unusually small?"

"Small, but who can say what's unusual? Uncle Gaius was short." Her head tilted. "Why?"

Brutus's smiling frown escaped before he thought to stop it. "I think I met him. Your cousin, not your uncle. I bought a big German in Octodurus last summer. Best man with a gladius I'd ever seen until a month later. His friend tracked him to my ludus in Roma and fought me for the right to buy him cheap. A short Roman, barely came to my chin, but he beat me." He nudged the piece he'd just played to center it. "He got the money to free his friend from Tiberius Lentulus."

Young Gaius Crassus a Christian? Brutus's eyes narrowed. "I thought it odd that he went to a former governor of his province instead of another Licinius Crassus. But maybe a Crassus wouldn't give it to him after his father disgraced the family."

"There's no disgrace in following Jesus. There's wisdom and joy and peace in it."

"It cost your uncle everything."

"It cost him nothing worth keeping compared to what it gave him. Camilla would tell you the same if she could."

Her eyes widened as he glared at her. How dare she say that, as if she bore no responsibility? Even if she never expected Camilla to die, it was still her fault.

"But she can't, can she." His breaths came faster. "Believing in your god caused her death. You made her think she could give me a son, and that killed her."

Calvia's voice softened. "She did give you a son. And she had peace and joy before then. She has them now with Jesus."

"Peace and joy." He spat the words at her. He'd had neither peace nor joy since Camilla died. "What's that worth when it costs your life?"

"Everything."

As he stared into Calvia's eyes, it was as if they were Camilla's. His beloved's words while she lay dying in his arms echoed in his mind. How her god gave her love and peace and joy...before he took her from him.

He swung his wrapped leg off the stool and grabbed his crutches. "Enough of this." He rose and left her sitting by the gameboard. But he glanced back as he entered the house.

Were those tears in her eyes?

The first game after lunch had gone to Brutus, and Africanus started setting up for the second. For having just won, his friend was too quiet. No jokes about Sollus's food taking the edge off Africanus's game. No remarks on how Calvia would have played the last few moves.

Brutus rubbed his jaw. "Do you remember the Roman who came from Germania after Otto?"

"The one who bested you with moves only a short man could do?"

Brutus's lips tightened to conceal a smile. "Yes, but he'd trained with a soldier, and the unexpected is what keeps you alive on the battlefield. Calvia just told me he's her cousin."

Africanus placed the next game piece. "He seemed more German than Roman."

"Not surprising, considering what his father did."

Africanus raised a questioning eyebrow.

"His father was the Gaius Crassus who became a Christian. He was about to be arrested, but he ran off to Germania. She said it was the father who persuaded her to become one. She would have gone with them if her own father hadn't stopped her."

Africanus's head drew back. Was this the opening he'd been asking God for? "So the son was a Christian? Maybe that's why he followed his friend to Rome and fought you to free him. They're supposed to love other people as much as themselves."

"Christian or not, he was a true man of honor. But he had a fool for a father, and that foolishness spread from Calvia to Camilla. No one in their right mind would believe what the Christians claim their Jesus did."

Eyebrows dipping, Brutus leaned toward him. "If I ever start to say otherwise, stop me. I never want others to think me a fool."

Africanus opened his mouth, then closed it. Damalio had said God would tell him when to speak and what to say. Which meant He'd also tell him when not to, and he'd just felt God's restraining hand.

"I lost. I go first." Africanus moved his first piece and planned his next move.

Under Brutus's words lay anger, and anger kept a man from thinking clearly. So could pride. Anger and pride together...that was a barrier he didn't know how to breach. But he was living proof that God could pierce any man's armor, and he'd be ready to strike the moment God did.

# Chapter 52

## Where Is the Sister?

*The Sabinus villa, morning of June 29*

With a scroll of the *Satyricon* on the desk before him, Sabinus selected another raisin. Bursting with juice that would shoot across his tongue at first bite, a fresh grape would be better, but even he couldn't make fruit that ripened in September be ready two days before the Kalends of July.

"Excuse me, master."

Sabinus looked up to find his agent standing in the doorway. "Festinus. It's past time you were back. Come in and bolt the door."

His agent approached the desk and stopped, hands clasped before him. "I didn't know speed mattered, master. We rode back instead of catching a ship at Genua. Cheaper and only two days longer. I had us ride longer each day, or it would have been three extra days." One corner of his mouth lifted. "Thrax gets seasick."

"And he'll be seasick again. You're going back to Octodurus immediately."

Festinus's eyebrows rose, and Sabinus chuckled. His best agent usually hid his thoughts better than that.

"What will we do there? As I told you by horse relay, Marcus Brutus was there with a broken leg. Almost healed, though. He had a sword and challenged us before his gladiators came. He didn't say his name, but we knew it was him when Africanus joined him. The only noblewoman we saw was Brutus's woman. They'll likely be gone before we return."

"That woman Brutus claimed as his is probably Crassus's sister. What exactly happened when you saw her?"

"He blocked me from entering the house. I was telling him a mere equestrian had no right to deny you anything when she walked out carrying a baby. I asked her if she was Licinia Crassa or Calvia Lucilla, and Brutus put an arm around her. He said it was his baby and she was with him. No one called Licinia Crassa was there, and Crassus wouldn't take a mistress."

"Why did he say that?"

"I asked if it was Crassus's baby. The woman was wearing a stola, so I thought she was the domina the steward disliked. Why would she be domina of a Crassus estate if she wasn't his mistress?"

Sabinus chuckled. "I can't fault your logic. I've had that thought myself."

He straightened his mouth, and Festinus mirrored him. At times it amused him to play with his slaves that way. But this time he wasn't playing.

"I think Brutus might have closer ties to Crassus than I suspected, and he chose to lie to protect her. He won't expect you to return, and if he's moved on, you'll be able to get her easily. If he's still with her, you'll figure out how to take her away."

Festinus straightened. "I'll get money from your steward, and we'll leave today." He grinned. "But this time I'll take ginger root for Thrax."

Sabinus dismissed him with a wave of his hand. As the door closed behind Festinus, he rubbed his hands. Manius was joining him with Septimus for dinner. His grandson was always commenting on something Brutus had said or done. That sometimes irritated, but knowing he'd outmaneuvered that arrogant equestrian would make it amusing instead.

*The taberna near the Baths of Trajan, late afternoon of June 29*

The surest way to draw an attack from a dog or a bully was to act afraid. But when you really were afraid, it was hard not to show it.

Custos wiped his mouth with the back of his hand. This time he'd bought the white wine, even though the red tasted better. When Vicarius asked about the bruise, Custos had laughed it off with a comment on needing to watch where he was walking better. But if there'd been a wine stain, he would have needed a convincing lie.

The gladiator, who had yet to give his name, stopped to whisper in the slave girl's ear. She twisted away from him, a smile on her lips but fear in her eyes. He understood that feeling.

Custos slid one wine cup toward him as he settled into the chair.

Sabinus's enforcer took the cup and frowned. "White? The red is better here. Get the right one next time."

"I like variety." Custos shrugged and offered a weak smile.

"I don't. What do you have this week?"

"Another conversation with his secretary. A friend had just told him his sister left Corinth a month earlier for Ephesus. Crassus said he'd tell her what he thought of that if she ever bothered to tell him who she was staying with."

Custos raised his eyebrows and shook his head. "I've seldom seen Crassus angry, but that day he used words about his sister's failure to stay in contact that never crossed his lips where I could hear before."

The gladiator chuckled. "So, she's one that needs a man who knows how to make a woman do what she should." He tossed his head back and drank. "I like that kind myself."

Custos nodded. He'd be willing to bet that was true.

"What else?"

"Nothing, but that's already good progress. We know as much as Crassus about where his sister is at the moment. He's mad that she didn't tell him, but I'm not sure he truly cares what city she's in."

"All that matters is what Master Sabinus cares about. He wants information. You'd better get it." He downed the rest of his wine and stood. "Be here next week with more."

Custos raised his cup, as if offering a toast. White had been a better choice. It didn't taste as good, but at least he got to drink it himself this week. "I'll do my best."

A beefy hand grabbed the top of Custos's head and tipped it back to force his eyes to meet the enforcer's glare. "If this is your best, you need to do better." He released Custos with a shake. "Or Sabinus will tell me to do my best on you."

"I understand." He swallowed hard. "I won't let the master down."

"Hmph."

The big man headed for the door, and Custos's shoulders slumped. How many more times did Master Crassus plan on him doing this? He was walking a fallen tree across a chasm, and the branch got narrower with each step. Would he reach the other side before it splintered and snapped and sent him to the rocks below?

*The Sabinus villa, evening of June 29*

"That will do. Leave us."

The manservant who had just wrapped Sabinus in his toga bowed and closed the door behind him.

Manius lounged in the wicker chair. "Anything special I should watch for tonight?"

"Yes. Three will be here who hope to be consuls within the next year. If any seem tense with each other or unusually friendly, signal me. I'll find a reason to join you."

"Your banquets are fertile ground for cultivating gossip, both true and false. It's amusing to start a rumor just to see who'll spread it."

"Even what should be the best sources can mislead."

Manius cocked an eyebrow. "Such as?"

"Our man in Crassus's house. Given what he reported this afternoon, I may have sent Festinus the wrong way."

"I thought either sister or mistress was at the Octodurus estate. What has he found out?"

"Less than he should have, but there are two things. Crassus made a comment about his sister being in a leading city of the Empire. Now he's angry because a friend told him she went to Ephesus a month ago without telling him."

"So she went east instead of north?"

"It's not clear. Festinus learned in Octodurus the estate is run by a young domina. He saw a Roman woman who fit the sister's description at the Octodurus estate. Whether it's the sister or someone else we can use against Crassus... we should know in a little over two weeks. He's on his way back there now."

"But if the sister is in Ephesus...what then?"

"We might need to rethink our approach. I've been disappointed in the spy I placed. He takes too long to gather information, and then he contradicts something he claims he found before."

"Is the problem too little good information or him being incompetent finding it?"

"Or a combination of both. The first can't be fixed. The second can, but it will take longer than I like."

"Are you going to replace him?"

"Not yet. We'd have to wait while the next one worms his way into a place of trust, and Crassus might become suspicious if his secretary's new assistant died in an accident too soon after the last one. If Fortuna smiles on us, the woman in Octodurus will be useful. If not, I'll find someone with a debt to me who has ties in Ephesus and can look for the sister."

"And Custos?"

"I'll leave him in place for now. I seldom discard a tool while it still might be useful. But long term...I need something better."

Sabinus strolled to the door and opened it. "When I hear from Festinus again, I'll decide."

# Chapter 53



UNREASONABLE ATTRACTION

*Brutus's estate, July 1*

Calvia leaned against the portico column, a crutch in one hand, and winced. It was much too soon, and surely it would hurt. She'd tried, but she couldn't talk him out of it.

Brutus had declared at breakfast that it had been four weeks. The bone was healed enough. He was tired of the crutches, and he was going to start walking on the leg.

When she said it might break again, he laughed at her concerns, saying the wrappings would strengthen it enough. She'd appealed to Africanus to tell him how foolish it was. All she'd received was lips tightened to keep from laughing at her and a shrug before he said if it was his leg, he'd be trying it himself.

On the grass off the portico, Brutus handed the second crutch to Rufus, who carried it back to her. Then, with Rufus on one side and Africanus on the other ready to catch him, he squared his shoulders.

She bit her lip. *Oh, God. Please don't let him hurt himself.*

He took the first step...and he was still standing. He looked back over his shoulder, and one corner of his mouth lifted. A full smile followed. Then both sides dipped, and his smiling frown said 'I told you so' before he moved the other foot. Step by halting step, he walked away from her.

The tension drained from her shoulders. She should have known two men who'd seen so many injuries would know how fast a man healed.

It was good he was able to walk again, but did that mean he'd spend less time with her?

Maybe she shouldn't let herself, but she loved his company. He was a pagan owner of gladiators, but underneath that, he was a good man.

There could be no better father. Marcus squealed and reached for Brutus when he came into the room.

He wasn't a Christian, but he still seemed to forgive people. At least some. He'd scolded Vera for not telling him who she was. Then he said he knew she'd promised Camilla to keep that secret, so he wasn't going to punish her.

And even when he blamed someone, like he blamed her for Camilla's choices, he could rise above his anger and be good to them. Like he had been to her when he chose to protect her.

She'd grown fond of him. Perhaps too fond, and it felt like he was fond of her, too. Especially when they talked and teased while they played. And at dinner, sometimes his eyes kept returning to her, like there was no one else in the room.

It was so easy to see why Camilla loved him. She was in danger of loving him herself.

Damalio came out the main door and stood beside her. "Brutus is healing well."

"We've said so many prayers for that, and I'm sure God has heard us. But it isn't his leg that most needs to heal."

Her gaze stayed focused on Brutus's progress. At least thirty steps, and still going. "I do wish he wasn't leaving at summer's end. Vera says he sat by Camilla's grave more nights than not, and every time he did, it was as if he left a piece of himself in the grove with her. She says he's more at peace here."

She drew his crutches closer. "I've tried to tell him that Camilla was joyous over giving him a son, that following Jesus had given her peace, no matter what happened. But he always argues. If he could only see the truth of what she knew, he could be fully at peace. After he leaves, there will be no hope of that. He barely listens to me. He'll never listen to Vera, and he'll keep Marcus from ever hearing the truth."

"There might be more hope than you think." Those words flipped her gaze to Damalio's face. A smile lingered there. "But you must promise not to tell Brutus what I'm about to tell you."

"Of course. What is it?"

His smile broadened. "Africanus has decided to join us."

It was all she could do to keep her mouth from dropping open. "How did a gladiator like him do that? Rufus told Primula he was the best of the best, that no one wanted to fight him because he was certain to win. He said all any could do was hope they fought him well enough he wouldn't kill them outright before they could ask the crowds to spare them in defeat."

"It's hard to deny the reality of God when you know it took a miracle to keep you from dying." He took the crutches from her and leaned them against the column. "He wanted to know about the God who could stop death. I told him how God loves us and what He wants from us before He makes us His children."

"Did you pray with him?"

"No. He said he had to think about it and weigh the cost."

"So how did it happen?" It was good Brutus was still walking away. He might see her beaming smile and ask what it was for.

"Alone in his room a week ago. He confessed his sins and told God he believed Jesus ransomed him, and the Holy Spirit came." He shifted his gaze from her to Brutus and his men. "He wants to be the one to tell Brutus he's become a Christian at the right time and in the right way so Brutus will see he should become one, too. He's not telling everyone until he gets that chance. They're already like brothers. There's no one more likely to lead Brutus to the truth."

"I'll keep his secret. I kept my own faith secret for so many years. I know how hard it can be waiting for just the right time to tell someone you care about." She took one crutch back and leaned on it.

"Like Mistress Camilla?"

"Yes. We'd been friends for a few months, and I hadn't told her about my faith. Father had forbidden it. But when I told her about Sextus's coming child, she told me about the three babies she lost and how much she wanted to give Brutus a son. She started crying, and then she couldn't stop." She gripped the curved padding at the top of Brutus's crutch.

"I felt God nudging me to pray with her. I knew He'd heal her, and then she wanted to know everything. I did what God told me, and that meant disobeying Father. But he never knew. We kept that secret together. She prayed for Father and Sextus; I prayed for Brutus to come to faith."

Her eyes followed Brutus as he turned and started back. He was moving slower with each step, but she wouldn't say anything but congratulations when he reached the portico. Sextus had never liked her "I told you so." Brutus laughed it off in a board game, but it wasn't her place to say anything that might wound his pride. Or was it just confidence?

He laughed at himself easily. He wasn't too proud to listen to Africanus about many things. Would he put aside anger and pride and listen when his friend finally spoke about Jesus?

"I'm going to pray for him to see the truth about God loving him and Jesus dying for him as soon as possible. I sometimes make him angry when I talk about God, but that won't keep me quiet about what I believe. And maybe what I say will help Africanus convince him."

Brutus paused, and his shoulders drooped. They were too far away for her to hear any words. But whatever Africanus said, Brutus shook his head and took another step. He was a stubborn man once he decided on something. Would that keep him from ever turning to God?

If he wouldn't heed Africanus's cautions about his leg, would he hear Africanus's warnings about what denying God would cost him?

*God, let him hear you calling him. Lead him to say yes, and let it be soon.*

One month together, and it was so obvious. He would suit her perfectly as a husband. But his heart was still bound to Camilla, and she couldn't marry a man who refused to believe in her Lord. No matter how much she loved him, she loved Jesus more.

She glanced up at Damalio to find his calm eyes watching her.

"I'm sure you'll pray for him, as will I." His mouth curved into a knowing smile. "I see as well as you do that you would do well together if he shared our faith."

Her ears felt hot. "Is it that obvious that I care for him?"

"Any man with eyes to see and the good sense to set aside past anger would be asking you to marry him already."

"But he mustn't do that yet. I couldn't say yes, even though I want to."

Had he forgiven her enough after losing Camilla that he'd even ask her? If he asked her and she had to say no, would he ever forgive her for wounding his heart a second time?

Damalio's smile broadened. "He's a good man, and you would be good for each other. So I'll be praying for God to claim his heart before he offers it to you."

"What would I do without you? Sextus gave you responsibility for my safety, but he gave me a second brother as well."

"You're my little sister, domina, and I'll always do my best to watch over you."

He'd become as dear to her as Sextus. "You're my big brother and faithful servant, and I love you for both."

She hugged his arm, and smiles lit both faces at the impossibility the world would see in what they'd just said. Only among the children of God did that make any sense.

◆

As Brutus walked back toward the house at a step-pause-step speed, his gaze fixed on the pair in the portico. What he saw triggered a frown.

Calvia stood beside Damalio. Nothing unexpected there. But while she was watching him and no doubt preparing a subtle "I told you so" as each of his pauses became longer, her man was watching her. Then his mouth curved into a knowing smile. He said something, and she blushed more than Brutus had ever seen. She spoke, and her man's eyes warmed as his smile broadened.

Three more exchanges, and she hugged his arm. When they turned their eyes back on him, both looked too happy.

His eyebrows dipped. He would have sworn there was no special affection between them. Friendship, yes, but not the deep feelings of a man toward a woman and the love she returns. A senator's daughter and a slave could never marry, even if he were freed. And Christians were said to do nothing outside marriage.

So, why did that fleeting hug bother him? It wasn't as if he wanted her as a wife himself. A friend, yes, but Camilla still owned his heart. She always would. Yet sometimes in his dreams, Camilla's smile was replaced by Calvia's, and what began as his beloved singing blended with her friend's voice to become a duet of joy.

Camilla had made him promise not to grieve too deeply or too long. He'd broken the first part of that promise every day for months, and the rest of his life hadn't seemed too long. But that was before he heard Calvia singing to Marcus and watched the love in her eyes when she kissed his son. Before all those games stretched his mind to the limit and her many acts of kindness spread balm on his resentment.

Was he letting himself grieve too long? What would Camilla say if she knew how much her friend attracted him? That she brought back the feeling of playful lightness that had filled him when Camilla entered the room?

He turned his eyes away from the woman who'd shredded his heart but somehow was healing it. Then he closed his eyes and summoned the memory of Camilla that both comforted and pained him when he woke to reach for her and she wasn't there. She was walking beside him toward the grove, her fingers laced with his. He raised her hand to kiss it, and she pointed to the first star of evening. Then he spread a blanket on the grass, and they lay with her head on his shoulder as they counted each star when it appeared.

Each time it had been the same, but not this time. She pointed instead at their favorite tree and the woman who held his baby beside it. On tiptoes, she kissed his cheek. Her warm breath caressed his ear as she whispered. "Embrace the future, beloved. Don't cling to the past."

"A problem, master?" Rufus's voice popped his eyes open.

"No. A little tired, but this is easier than I expected. No problem at all."

Rufus's smile declared he believed those words, but the slight lift of Africanus's eyebrow proclaimed them the lie they both knew they were.

*The Crassus townhouse, Rome, July 3*

With the second scroll of Pliny's *Wars of Germania* open before him, Sextus took a sip of Marcus Brutus's special vintage. The red was superb; the white was better, and he kept both in his library to savor while reading.

One knock followed by two more was Vicarius's pattern. "Come in."

Custos entered clutching a wax tablet. "From the Octodurus estate, master."

Sextus rolled the scroll and set it aside. "From Gratus or Damalio?"

His mouth turned down. It would have been wiser for them to write after they left Octodurus, not before. One more letter among the many he received from around the Empire wouldn't be noticed by a spy.

"Neither, master. From steward Antistes. It wasn't marked as private, so Vicarius opened it. It worried him, so he wanted you to see it immediately."

Worried him? Sextus's stomach clenched as he took the tablet and opened it.

A standard greeting followed by "major change." His jaw clenched at the words. But change wasn't always bad. He blew out a deep breath and read on.

"It says my sister left two weeks ago with an equestrian who came there with a broken leg three weeks before that. That's four weeks before you told Sabinus she might be in Octodurus, so this equestrian is probably not working for him."

Who could she have left with? He squeezed the back of his neck. Why had Antistes not mentioned the name of a man who'd been there three weeks? Where could he have taken her? His sister had too much sense to go with a strange man because she liked playing board games with him and was fond of his baby. It had to be someone she knew well enough to trust.

The next paragraph calmed his fear for her safety, at least some. If she took Damalio and the other men, she would probably be safe enough.

"Did you want to reply, master?"

"No. I don't want Sabinus's second spy, if there is one, to report the Octodurus estate has drawn unusual attention from me. There should be more details when the monthly report comes."

He scanned the letter once more before handing it to Custos. "File this with the regular estate correspondence. Then watch to see if someone who shouldn't tries to read it."

Custos stepped back with a single quick nod. "Right away, master."

"Did Vicarius tell you what was in it?"

"No, master. Only that it was from your steward."

"If he asks about my response, tell him I saw nothing disturbing. He won't ask any further."

He flicked his hand toward the door, and Custos left.

Sabinus's henchmen must not have arrived before Damalio escorted her to an unknown destination. He'd rather know exactly where she was and with whom, but until he got a letter from Damalio or his sister, he could only hope by all the gods she was safe.

One corner of his mouth lifted. If she'd still been with him, she would have told him there was only one god who gave real hope, only one god with the power to protect anyone.

Maybe she was right, maybe not, but he'd done what he could to protect her himself. Only time would show if it had been enough.

*Chapter 54*

## Not What He Expected

*Brutus's Lousonna estate, July 3*

Brutus heard her laughter before Damalio came out of the house with Calvia beside him. Damalio was still chuckling when they stepped through the doorway.

"As you wish, domina." Damalio headed toward the stable.

She came to the chair by the gameboard and sat.

"What's so funny?" Brutus picked up his king and fingered it. A smile still played on her lips, but it shouldn't.

"It's a private joke. You wouldn't understand it."

"Perhaps not, but I'm not sure you understand the risk of sharing one."

She raised her eyebrows. "What are you talking about?"

"I saw you hug his arm two days ago. Not wise. A man can easily misinterpret any touch. It's too easy to shift from being a friend to wanting more."

"You're seeing things through Roman eyes, not Christian ones. He knew why I did, and it's not a problem." Her eyes laughed at him.

Her father kept her out of Roman society until he died. Maybe he thought she didn't need to understand the desires of men. But if her father hadn't told her, her brother should have. She was a pretty, charming woman, and any man would feel the attraction.

His eyebrows lowered. "Why not?"

"My cousin got a brother by adoption because my uncle had no sons. Something like that but much more happens when we choose to believe in Jesus. All who believe in Him become children of God. That

305

makes us brothers and sisters in Christ. Damalio serves me because he belongs to Sextus, but he's also my Christian brother, just like Primula serves me, but she's also my sister. Damalio and me…it's like Sextus and me, except for one being a senator and the other a slave. We care about each other, but not the way you're thinking."

"Hmph." Her naivety astounded sometimes, but she'd partly answered a question that nagged at him. "You said you knew what Camilla thought because she was your sister in Christ. But even real brothers and sisters don't think alike. Look at you and Crassus: a loyal son of Roma and a Christian enemy devoted to a dead man instead of the Empire."

"Jesus isn't dead, and being devoted to him doesn't mean I'm an enemy of the Empire. Uncle Gaius never betrayed Rome. Following Christ above all doesn't make me a traitor, either."

With a flick of his hand, he swept her protest away. "I see many brothers who aren't even friends. Sharing a father doesn't require two men to understand or like each other. Africanus knows me better than any relation by blood."

"I've watched you together. You read each other's thoughts, and you talk with only your eyes. You act like brothers who truly care about each other. He'd do anything for you, and I think you'd do the same."

"I trust him as a friend."

"Your best friend. He's a treasure."

That pulled a chuckle from him. "Not the word I'd use, but I'd hate to lose him."

"I'm thankful you didn't."

So was he, and he had her to thank for it. But how had she managed it?

"When we came to your estate, he was near death." He placed the first king on the board and picked up the second. Maybe she'd answer another lingering question. "What did you do to him upstairs? Silo told me Africanus was fine when he examined him, that he'd been faking. I know that's not true."

"Did you ask him?" She tumbled a rondel from finger to finger, eyes gauging him like they did before a killer move.

"Yes. He didn't know. The last thing he remembered before Silo saw him was sitting with me by the road."

"You might ask him again."

Brutus eyebrows dipped. "If he didn't know then, why would he know now?"

That smile that appeared as she sprang a trap he failed to see curved her lips. "Just ask him."

She moved a rondel, and it wasn't the one he expected.

"This whole conversation—you're trying to distract me so you'll win. It almost worked, but..." He moved his king. "You got distracted, too. Focus on the battle. If you don't, your army will be mine."

Her eyes locked on the board, but his gaze kept straying to her face. What did she think Africanus was going to say?

*Afternoon of July 3*

Brutus entered the portico carrying Africanus's sword and wearing his own. He tossed Africanus's scabbard to him. "We can do a little sparring before our first game."

Africanus didn't draw his sword. "I question the wisdom of that. It's too soon to ask that much of your leg."

"It's still wrapped. That will protect it enough."

His friend cocked an eyebrow. "Not the way we spar. Lunging, sidesteps, you moving back when I attack..." A crooked grin punctuated the laughter in his eyes. "Not the best for a leg that's still healing."

"It's mostly healed. I'm hardly limping. It's been well over a month. You always hold back some. You'll just have to hold back more."

"A month and two days. Pugnus fighting like he does the beginners could take you in three strokes. I can't hold back that much."

Brutus chuckled. "Calvia says you watch over me like Damalio watches over her. She's right." One corner of his mouth rose. "And so are you. But I'm ready for more than sitting."

Tightened lips and a slow shake of the head wasn't the answer Brutus wanted. "For the next few days, you can walk to get back muscle. And some slash and thrust at nothing...that should be safe enough. You're healing well, but it doesn't take much to hurt what's only partly healed."

Africanus crossed his arms. "Your unseen attacker approaches." One hand shot out to point. "There."

A satisfying swish as the sword cleared its scabbard—then Brutus fought the invisible enemy and defeated him. When he held his sword aloft in victory, Africanus chuckled.

"Did it look that bad?"

"No, but Calvia came out as you started, and she watched the whole performance."

Brutus rolled his eyes. "Why didn't you tell me?"

"And cheat her out of the show?"

Brutus pointed at the boulder pile overlooking the lake. "Let's sit a while. That should bore her so she'll leave." He rested the flat of the blade on his shoulder and took three steps before Africanus fell in beside him.

It wasn't far to the rocks, but he limped more than he liked by the time they reached them. "You were right. It will take a while to get my leg strength back."

Brutus sat on a boulder, but Africanus rested one foot on the pile and leaned on his thigh.

One quick glance revealed Calvia was still watching them. When he most needed to concentrate during their next game, would she tease him about fighting invisible enemies? If he talked much with Africanus, she'd ask whether he asked what happened upstairs. If he couldn't say yes, her "I-thought-you-wouldn't" eyes would join her "I-challenge-you-to" smile.

Brutus looked up at his friend. "How long did it take to feel normal after you almost died?"

"Less than a week, but I wouldn't expect that for others." His gaze shifted to the mountains across the lake and lingered. Before they returned to Brutus, his eyes warmed. "Felix starts a man back slow, then increases training as he shows he can do it. It can take a few months."

"I didn't expect you to make it." Brutus felt the edge of his blade. "That blow to your ribs, the bleeding it caused inside—it should have killed you." He tipped his head back to look at the man Calvia rightly called his best friend. "I know I asked before, but Calvia said I should ask again. What did they do that healed you?"

Africanus's mouth twitched, then curved. "They prayed for me."

"Prayed for you." Brutus tightened his lips to stop a disbelieving smile, then let it appear. Africanus didn't like being laughed at except when he was joking. But this was clearly a joke.

"Yes. They asked God to heal me, and He did."

It was a joke. Or was it? The tell-tale laugh lines didn't form by his eyes.

"What did they say?"

"I didn't hear them."

"Then how do you know what they did?"

"I asked Damalio. He told me."

"What else did he tell you?" Unease wrapped around Brutus like a serpent. What made him ask that?

Africanus sat on the rock beside him. "Why their prayer worked." He glanced at Brutus then turned his eyes back to the lake. "Why he's a Christian...and why I should become one."

One corner of Brutus's mouth lifted. He could no sooner picture Africanus as a Christian than he could see himself as one. "That was a waste of his time."

"No."

The serpent started to squeeze. Brutus turned his head so he could see Africanus's eyes. "He didn't convince you, did he?"

Africanus twisted to face him. "Yes."

# *Chapter 55*


## What's Proof Enough?

That single word was like a fist rammed into Brutus's stomach. First Camilla, now Africanus? "But why?"

"You think that's strange." Africanus rubbed his jaw. "Maybe it is. It still amazes me. For years, I agreed with what you told me, that no god was real. They were just stories to make us think someone with more power than us controlled what happens. And that is true for the so-called gods of Roma."

He slipped the scabbard strap over his head and set the sword aside. "But just because most gods live only in stories, that doesn't mean there's no God who truly lives.

"By the road, I knew I was dying. We both knew...and then I didn't die. How did that happen? That took power...real power. That doesn't come from something that lives only in our minds. When Damalio said they asked their God to heal me and He did, I had to find out who that God with real power is. How He could heal me. Why He would even want to."

Brutus stared at his friend. Death was a familiar enemy, and past a certain point in the struggle, death always won. But it hadn't this time, and he couldn't explain why. That sent shivers through his core.

He could stop this conversation with a single word, but that wouldn't undo what Damalio had done. It wouldn't answer the question of why Africanus chose to believe him.

He rubbed the old dagger scar on his forearm. Or why Camilla made her choice.

310

What would once more convince Africanus that the Christian god was no more real than the Roman ones? Something built on logic and life as they'd both seen it. The Christian teaching about a crucified man coming back from the dead was logically absurd. But they both had seen Africanus slipping over the edge toward death...and then he didn't die. How could he show Africanus—and himself—that this healing was natural, that no special power was needed to keep him alive?

Real power—Camilla had said the same thing. She claimed she felt the healing that let her conceive as it happened. But she'd conceived three times before, so was there really any healing? But she'd lost those three babies, and the fourth time, she'd carried Marcus to the time of delivery. She'd birthed a perfect boy.

And then she died. If the Christian god had the power to save a dying man who didn't even believe in him, why didn't he save Camilla, who claimed he loved her? Why hadn't he stopped the bleeding? Why had he let her die?

"Maybe we were mistaken about how badly you were hurt. Maybe the rest before Silo came was enough. He's a good physician, and he didn't find anything wrong."

"After they prayed."

Brutus tilted his head. "What?"

"Nothing wrong after they prayed."

"You can't really think some words spoken to an imaginary god did something."

"An imaginary god? No. A real one? Yes."

"You think just asking a god for something gets it? Even if a god was real, you couldn't expect a man like Damalio to have enough influence to stop death taking you."

"Damalio said Robustus, Primula, and Mistress Calvia were there. They all asked, and God healed me."

Brutus had seen the men carry Africanus up, and Calvia had summoned Primula before she joined them. It hadn't taken long before the two men returned to move him into his room. Whatever they did upstairs, it was finished before Damalio reappeared. There was no time for special offerings and complex incantations, so what did that Christian prayer look like?

A quick glance at the portico revealed Calvia in his chair, but she wasn't watching him. Head lying on the backrest, her eyes closed—was she resting, sleeping, or something else?

Praying. His mouth turned down. She had tricked him into this conversation. She almost certainly knew what Africanus was telling him. If these Christians wanted something, didn't they always ask their god for it?

He stared at the mountains across the lake, and the haunting memories of that terrible night pressed in upon him. The healing Camilla thought she'd received—she said that made her want to know the god with real power. Africanus's very words.

But what good had come of that? She'd believed her god loved her, but believing something didn't make it so. She claimed that god gave her peace, joy, no fear of death. He saw all those as she died in his arms. But if that god loved her so much, why did he let her die?

"He did more."

Africanus's quiet words drew him back to the moment. "What?"

What he'd heard already was bad enough. Did he really want to know more?

"God did more than heal me. He paid what I owed for everything I've done."

"What are you talking about?" Brutus turned back toward Africanus to find his friend gazing across the lake, his mouth curved like at their first meeting each morning. Brutus shifted his gaze to the same place. There was nothing special there.

"What's right, what's wrong—the God with real power is the only one who can tell us what those are. He told us what we're supposed to do: love Him with all our heart and mind and strength, and love other people like we love ourselves. And if we don't, we're not fit to be with Him. Anything against those commands is a sin, and every sin puts a barrier between us and God."

"All other people?" Brutus squeezed the back of his neck. "That's an impossible command. The only one I've loved that way was Camilla." He kicked a pebble by his good foot. "And now Marcus."

And Africanus, but he wouldn't say it aloud. Africanus's eyes would roll, and he knew it without the words, anyway.

"Different kind of love. Maybe there's a better word for it. It's not the way I feel. It's a decision about how I'll treat other people. It's wanting what's best for them, even if I don't like them. Even if I don't know them. It's helping someone when they need it, whether I want to or not."

Africanus's gaze shifted from the lake to Brutus's eyes and turned deadly serious. His lips straightened, but it wasn't the battle mask Brutus had seen so many times.

"It's good you freed me. I can fight to defend another person. I can defend myself, but I can't do what I did for you in the arena anymore. Killing for sport is murder, and God says that's wrong."

Brutus's jaw clenched. Hearing Calvia's words from Africanus's mouth—no one could have convinced him that was possible.

His eyebrows plunged. "Since I sent you in to fight, does that make me a murderer, too?"

"Yes."

He'd always told Africanus he wanted him to speak the truth, but that went too far. Too far, but it also gave him a way to rescue his friend from the Christian delusion. One corner of his mouth lifted.

"Then neither of us is fit to be with such a god. So even if he is real, it doesn't change anything for us. He'll have nothing to do with you or me, and that's the same as him not being real."

"No. He loves us enough to do something about it. He told the Jews that only blood sacrifice could cover sins so they could approach Him, and only a perfect sacrifice could erase their sins forever. So God came as Jesus of Nazareth to be the perfect blood sacrifice when He was crucified."

"Who told you that?" Brutus suppressed a smile. No one, god or otherwise, would choose that death. Surely Africanus would see that.

"Damalio, but he was only repeating what Jesus said. He said His death was the ransom to free me from sin."

"Saying something doesn't make it true. I'd never believe that without solid proof, and there's no way a dead man can prove anything."

"No, but He didn't stay dead. Coming back to life proved the truth of His words."

"There's no proof that ever happened. It's been almost a hundred years. Long enough for a lie to become a story believed as truth. Every Christian has been fooled by it."

Africanus's brow furrowed, and that triggered Brutus's full smile. A sure sign his friend was pondering what he'd said, and that could only lead Africanus one way.

"What would be proof enough for you?"

Not the question he expected. The answer...probably nothing, but that wouldn't satisfy Africanus.

"What was proof enough for you?" Brutus suppressed his smile again. Whatever the answer, he'd be able to refute it.

"I had doubts like yours. What sounds too good to be true usually isn't. With what I've done, how could a god who demands love want me? But Damalio said no one has ever been good enough on their own.

Jesus said if we confess what we've done and believe He saves us from those sins, it's as if we never did them."

"But Damalio or anyone else saying something isn't proof. Even if I told you I thought it was true, that wouldn't prove anything." Brutus's sword still lay across his lap, and he traced the engraving near the hilt. "Confess...a man could do that without any god to hear it. Believe... thinking something is so doesn't mean it is."

"But when an answer comes, that's proof."

"An answer?" Brutus's brow furrowed.

"I decided to try it. Aloud, even though Damalio said God knows all our thoughts. He said I'd know if God was listening."

At Africanus's chuckle, Brutus straightened. There was nothing funny about this conversation.

"I asked God if He was there, and I felt someone watching me, not like an enemy but friendly."

"That was probably just Damalio's eyes you were feeling."

"I was alone in my bedchamber."

Brutus opened his mouth, then closed it. No one was better than Africanus at knowing when someone was watching them. With his second-floor room, no one could lurk outside his window and peek in.

"I told God I hadn't loved Him because I didn't know He was real. I promised to honor Him as the only true God. Then I started telling Him about times I hadn't treated people like He wants." One corner of Africanus's mouth lifted. "That took a while. I felt the Watcher draw closer. Then I told Him I believed Jesus paid for everything I'd done and I wanted to know the One Who kept me from dying."

Eyes closed, Africanus tipped his head back. "And then light filled the room, and words I'd never heard before came, and peace and love wrapped around me, and..." He drew a deep breath, and when he re-leased it, the eyes he turned on Brutus were glowing. "I met the God Who saved me from death by the road and also from my sins."

Brutus rubbed the back of his neck and stared at his friend. If he didn't know Africanus almost as well as he knew himself, he'd think him a liar or insane to tell that story.

The glow faded, and Africanus's calm eyes and slight smile reap-peared. "That was proof enough for me."

Brutus slipped his sword into its scabbard and stood. "I can see where it might be." His eyebrows dipped. "When did this happen?"

"Eleven days ago. But there's more. The Watcher is the Holy Spirit, and He's here with me now. He always will be."

"Eleven days? Why didn't you tell me?"

Africanus shrugged. "You didn't ask."

Why on earth would he ask about something that was so far beyond anything he'd ever heard? Brutus opened his mouth, then closed it without a word, and that triggered Africanus's smile.

"So, just as I know you're real while you stand here beside me, I know God is real, too. Now that I've met Him, Damalio and the others are helping me know Him better."

His eyes turned serious. "Do you want to join me when they do?"

"No." Brutus raised both hands. "What you've just said is more than enough to think about."

Africanus's shoulders drooped, then straightened. "When you want to hear more, tell me." His lips tightened, as if suppressing a smile.

Brutus kept his eyes from rolling. For a sensible man like Africanus to be talking about light filling a dark room and hearing strange words and a god being with him...that was more than enough for one day. More than enough for a lifetime.

"Latrunculi now. You can tell me later."

He took a step toward the house and concentrated on not limping. Why had he just opened the door to another conversation? It wasn't what he wanted. But that promise of later broadened Africanus's smile, and it wouldn't hurt to listen if it gave pleasure to his friend. Maybe, after he thought about it, he could find the argument to counter what Africanus had said.

On the portico, Calvia's eyes had opened. That "I told you so" smile played on her lips. They'd been far enough away she shouldn't have heard their words, but she'd challenged him to ask Africanus what he knew.

Would she ask what they talked about, or did she already know what he'd say?

## Chapter 56



From the portico, Calvia watched Brutus fight the air. It was more like a dance, less like a battle than when Rufus and Africanus fought. But as soon as his leg would allow it, Brutus would be fighting like his men. Fighting for sport, not for his life, like Rufus did.

As Brutus walked to the rocks, he favored his leg more with each step. But he limped less with each day. God was answering her prayers for his leg. But what about her prayers for his heart?

He was so like the young stallions at the Crassus estate where Sextus bought Damalio. Taken from the field to a small corral, they paced the rails, nervous about losing their freedom. When the red-haired trainer who was even younger than her entered the corral to saddle and mount them the first time, they watched him, ears up, nostrils flared.

But his soft words in a language she didn't know and his outstretched hand kept them from running before he placed the blanket on their back the first time. Some let it sit there, some tossed it off, but all stayed in place while he spoke and stroked their necks. And no matter how many times he had to replace it, he never lost patience.

When he added the saddle, it was the same thing. But his patience and gentleness always prevailed, and even a horse that had been almost wild would let him ride it before he left the corral. And once that horse accepted him, he'd mount it bareback with no bridle and guide it anywhere with a few words, a hand on its neck, and gentle pressure from his legs.

316

Would Brutus ever hear God's soft words calling and let God guide him through life like that?

When Brutus turned his face up to Africanus and spoke, she closed her eyes. He'd accepted her challenge. It was time to pray for the Spirit to tell Africanus what to say and for Brutus to hear the truth in every word.

When she sensed it was time to open her eyes, the men had almost reached the portico.

She met them at the steps. "You're walking much better than yesterday."

He patted his thigh. "It's not quite ready for sparring."

"Sometimes a walk with a friend and a good conversation are better than anything."

"They can be."

Frustrating man. He wasn't going to satisfy her curiosity without her asking directly, and she wasn't going to give him the satisfaction of her doing that.

A glance at Africanus told her much more. His mouth twitched as he stopped a smile. But Brutus's usual smiling frown had been replaced by straight lips and serious eyes. He hadn't liked their talk as much as Africanus had.

"I finished the blanket, and I don't feel like starting something new this afternoon. Would you mind playing me instead of Africanus?"

◆

That was an offer Brutus wasn't going to refuse. Playing with Africanus could too easily lead back to another conversation about bright lights and peace and joy and an invisible presence that stayed nearby.

"We ended the morning with a tie. It's better to break it."

Then Calvia and Africanus exchanged nods. Maybe he hadn't made the right choice, but it was too late to change it without explanation. Any explanation would just start the conversation he wanted to avoid.

They set up for latrunculi, but it was soon clear he should have chosen tabula. She was beating him easily. His focus slipped each time she opened her mouth. He expected the question about what Africanus said. She never asked it, which made focusing harder. After his second loss, it was clear. He'd have to answer it before she asked.

"I asked Africanus."

"About what?"

Surly she knew what, but he'd humor her. "About what happened that first day upstairs." He picked up a game piece. "He said you prayed."

"We did."

"Did you pray for me?" There was nothing unexpected about his recovery. If she said yes, it was proof their prayers didn't bring special healing.

"We did, but not in the same way." She stacked some pieces she hadn't yet placed on the board. "I've prayed for you since before I met you." Her head tipped. Her mouth opened, and she took a deep breath. "Camilla asked me to, and she prayed for Sextus."

"What did she want your god to do for your brother?" A safer first question than what Camilla asked for him.

"She prayed for his health, for his family, for all to go well for his estates and their people, for good opportunities for him to serve Rome..." She drew a big breath. "And for him to turn to God and follow Jesus like us."

"What did she ask you to pray for?"

"The same plus one more." She bit her lip. "She wanted two things more than anything else in this world: to give you a son and to have you follow Jesus."

His fist clenched around the rondel he was about to place. "Neither of you got all you asked for. We both worship the Roman gods, and we're not going to change."

"But Sextus doesn't believe those gods are real. He goes through the motions of worship because that's what he thinks a good Roman does. It's the same with you."

"It is what a good Roman does."

"But why do you both do that? Pretending to worship something you know doesn't exist is a lie. Sextus doesn't lie about other things. Why is it all right to lie about that?"

"All worship is a lie. No gods are real."

It was good Africanus wasn't beside him. He'd be saying he met God again.

"But I introduced Camilla to the one God who is. She'd tell you if—"

"If she was here?" Anger edged his voice, and Calvia cringed. "But she isn't, and whose fault is that? If your god is real, if he has power to heal, why didn't he heal her? I'm sure she asked him to." His fist hit the edge of the board, jarring the pieces from their places. "He let her die."

"I don't know why." Tears glistened in Calvia's eyes. "I've asked that myself so many times. Why did I have to leave just before she gave birth? Would it have been different if Primula and I had been there to pray with her? God doesn't always heal when we ask, but I've seen Him do it many times. Why not her?"

She wiped one tear away. "But we all die sometime. When isn't up to us, and why might remain a mystery this side of heaven. But even in the uncertainty, I know God's love and peace and joy right now, and eternity with Jesus and all who love Him awaits me." She swept aside another teardrop. "And among those will be Camilla."

She sniffed. "Sextus never told me she died. I spent months thinking about how happy she must be with Marcus and you. Then when you showed up alone with Marcus and Vera told me how Camilla died, I was angry with myself for letting Sextus send me away before the birth. If I'd stayed only two more days, would you still have her? But Primula reminded me God sometimes heals when we ask Him to, but only when He knows it's best. Even when I stood there crying, 'Why, God?'...I still felt His love. And when I'm ready to accept it, He gives me peace with what happened as well."

As the tears trickled down her cheeks, his anger cooled. She had loved Camilla, too.

"She told me that, too, about love and peace and joy, and she wasn't afraid to die." He stared across the lake at the mountains as love and longing and regret surged like the waves in a storm at sea. "I held her at the end. She wanted me to know how wonderful your god was. She said she'd keep praying for me to believe what she did."

He clenched his jaw and stared at the clouds over the mountains. High winds swept them along, changing their shapes as he watched.

Fingertips touched the back of his hand. "She's not really gone. Eternity with Jesus and those who follow Him awaits us on the other side of death. She's still praying for you." She withdrew the touch. "And I still pray for you like I promised her I would."

His eyes turned from the shape-shifting clouds to her face, where a smile contradicted her tear-bathed eyes. "Camilla, you, Africanus... is there anyone else who wants me to accept your god as mine, too?"

"I could name a few others, but I'll let them tell you themselves."

"I asked Africanus what happened and heard more than I wanted to know. He says he met your god in a room filled with light and love and peace." One corner of his mouth lifted. "Sound familiar?"

"Yes."

"Have you seen that yourself?"

"Yes."

"Did Camilla?"

"Yes. Primula and I were there when she confessed her sins and told Jesus she believed He died to pay for them."

He rubbed his jaw. Africanus was alone. Camilla with her friends. Calvia...probably with the father of the short Gaius Crassus he admired. They'd all confessed what they'd done that their god said was wrong, believed Jesus paid for everything, and claimed they met the Christian god. Was there a truth here he could no longer ignore? But what would it mean if he chose to follow what he'd always mocked as the way of fools?

"Hmm." He placed his rondel on the board, and leaned back in his chair. "I'll think about what you and Africanus have said, but that's enough talk about your god for now. Let's play."

As she placed her next piece, his gaze returned to the mountain. Tonight, with Africanus beside him, he would consider those questions and decide.

The sky had still been on fire when Brutus led Africanus into his bedchamber and bolted the door. Now he stood by the window, staring into the dark. The moon had moved from just over the mountains across the lake to high overhead.

Question after question, like the thrust and parry when they sparred, Africanus had answered. Questions about the real god who created everything. How he came to the Jews and told them how he wanted people to know him. How that god had commanded that people should love him more than anything and love others like they loved themselves.

But no one could live a life so perfect that they never built a barrier between themselves and God, so he taught them to cover their sins with the blood of an unblemished animal so they could approach him. Then he came himself as Jesus of Nazareth to be the perfect sacrifice that would not just cover sins, but remove them, if only someone believed in him. How God would forgive all Brutus's sins if he confessed and believed. How each man had to forgive others, too, just as he'd been forgiven.

How believing would make him a son of God and open the door to eternal life.

Brutus stood by the window, watching the familiar clusters of stars. Was the Christian heaven somewhere past those points of light? Was Camilla there now with Jesus?

Africanus cleared his throat, and Brutus turned to find his friend still seated in the chair with legs stretched out and arms crossed. "Was that your last question? If there's more I can't answer, we can wake Damalio. He won't mind."

"I can't think of any. That part about having to forgive because we've been forgiven...it makes sense, but that's not what I'd normally do."

"I'm finding what I thought would be hard gets easier when I ask God to help me. I would have thought anyone who told me God was always right there with them was crazy, but now I know He's really here." Africanus leaned forward and placed his hands on his knees. "You'll know it, too."

As Brutus turned his back on the window, his heart pounded as if he'd fought off a flurry of sword strikes. It was the end of what he'd thought certain and his first step toward the irresistible unknown. "I'm ready." He sat on his bed, elbows on his knees, face in his hands.

The moonlight cast shadows that moved across the floor as he considered his life and confessed his failures to love like God commanded. When there was nothing more to tell, he straightened. "That's what I remember. I'm sure there are more, but since God knows everything I've ever done, I hope He'll know which sins I forgot and include them." He pulled a deep breath and blew it out. "What now?"

Africanus came to the bed and sat beside him. "I took longer, but I probably missed some, too. He'll know." He turned toward Brutus. "Tell Him you believe Jesus died to pay for all your sins, that you know He rose from the dead, and you want to follow Him as Lord."

Brutus took a deep breath and blew it out. "God, I've tried to live a life of honor, but I didn't know what that truly was. I'm sorry for all the things I've done that were not what You want me to do. I'm sorry I've asked what honor required, not what You want, to guide my life. I believe Jesus died to pay for all my sins. I believe He rose from the dead. I want to know You and love You, like You commanded. I want to follow Jesus as my Lord."

The light, the warmth, the peace, the love, and comfort for his aching heart—they all surrounded him as words of praise filled his mind and overflowed.

When he opened his eyes, he found Africanus grinning at him. "Welcome to the brotherhood as a son of God."

As Brutus slapped his best friend's arm, he found himself laughing. Camilla had said she'd keep praying for him to come to Jesus.

He would have sworn that was impossible. He would never doubt the power of prayer again.

Before he joined his beloved for eternity with Jesus, would she know he was coming?

*July 4*

When Calvia entered the triclinium the next morning, Brutus was already there, standing by the window. He turned as she entered, eager to tell her what she probably suspected but would want to hear anyway.

"Did you have a good night?" The lilt in her voice brightened an already shining day.

He came from the window to stand before her. "The best since Camilla died. Actually, the best night ever."

"Why?"

He could tell by her smile she already knew, but he wanted to say it, anyway. "Last night, Camilla's final prayer was answered."

She raised her eyebrows to finish asking the question.

"I decided to believe in Jesus and follow Him as my Lord."

She threw her arms around him and rested her cheek against his chest. "Welcome to the family of God!"

He started to return her embrace but stopped just before his arms made contact. If he touched her, it would be as a man holding a woman, not a brother hugging a sister.

He dropped one arm back to his side.

"I warned you about hugging a man." He placed his finger under her chin and tipped her head back to look at her eyes. "He might get ideas that you don't mean for him to get."

"Oh! I guess I didn't think." She released him and stepped back, revealing cheeks with the prettiest shade of pink. "Nothing could have made Camilla happier, and only hearing those same words from Sextus could please me more."

He knew what his own hug would have meant, but what about hers? Was that only a hug for a brother like Damalio, or might there be some part that was an embrace for a man? And if there was, what did he want to do about it?

When he left Roma, he would have sworn Camilla would own his whole heart until he died. He was certain he could never love another woman after her.

Single-minded, undying faithfulness was a strength, but Camilla had seen the danger it posed as well. Why else would she have made him promise not to grieve too deeply or too long?

Damalio entered the room with Africanus, and Calvia turned to greet them both with warm words and welcoming smiles.

He stroked his jaw as he watched her. She might be the only woman who could help him keep that promise. Only she might understand why he would always love Camilla because she'd loved Camilla herself.

Embrace the future. Don't cling to the past. In essence, that was what Camilla made him promise. She knew it would be impossible for him to do it if he wasn't trying to keep his word.

The breakfast was delivered on serving trays, and the two men sat. Calvia turned to him and held out her hand to invite him to join them. As he took the first step, her joy-filled eyes urged him on.

From kind stranger to good friend to someone he wanted to be with every day—that had taken less than two months. Calvia was a woman it would be easy to love for a lifetime. He might as well admit he'd already started.

But would she ever want to love him, not as a friend or a Christian brother, but as a man?

◆

As Brutus told Damalio about meeting God last night, Calvia's heart sang. Months of prayers for Brutus's salvation would become years of thanksgiving that God had claimed him as His own. Already he spoke of the joy of being right with God and his eagerness to learn more about living a life that pleased Him. Knowing he'd be with Camilla again should dampen his grief until all that remained was precious memories of their time together and anticipation of a future reunion.

And the last barrier to Brutus being the perfect man for her had also fallen. From her perspective, anyway. But what about from his?

He hadn't hugged her back. He'd even warned her about hugging him. When he scolded her for hugging Damalio's arm, he'd said it was too easy to go from being a friend to wanting more.

Did that mean he might be ready to move past friendship, like she was? Or was it merely a reminder from a man who only wanted to protect her as a friend?

She hugged herself and rubbed her arm.

Now that he followed Jesus, he was everything she could ever want in a husband. But would he ever want her, too?

At the end of summer, he'd be returning to Rome, and she'd go home to Octodurus. What a man wanted could change so much in six months. When he came to Lousonna next year, would he come over the pass so he could see her? If he didn't, would he ride a day to come visit? Or would their time together be nothing more than a pleasant memory for him?

God wanted what was best for His children, and she always tried to choose what she thought was His will.

She fingered the stola she'd worn as a disguise. To wear it in truth as Brutus's wife—nothing could be better.

But was it only her desire and not God's will for Brutus to love her as much as she now loved him?

# Chapter 57

## GETTING RID OF A SPY

*The taberna near the Flavian Amphitheater, July 6*

"Is your friend coming again?" The girl eyed the door as she set down one cup of red wine and another of white.

Custos took the white one. "He's coming, but he's not my friend."

"Is he anyone's?" She stopped the shudder as it started, but she needn't have worried he'd see it. He sympathized completely.

"I don't see him enough to say."

She wiped up what was left of a spill from the person before him. "You're lucky."

As she walked away, the gladiator appeared in the doorway. She turned sharply and headed to the far side of the room. One glance over her shoulder, and she sat at the table where two old men were talking. Their eyes widened; then their smiles did as she turned her charm on them.

He'd rather join them, too, but if all went well, today he'd give the enforcer enough to satisfy Sabinus for a couple of months. And if Fortuna would just smile on him again, maybe for longer.

As the brute settled into the chair beside him, Custos pushed over the cup of red. "I remembered."

His contact looked down his nose at Custos's cup of white. "Only one worth drinking? Next week get me two."

Custos nodded. "Two. I'll remember."

One side of the gladiator's mouth curved. "Wise." It straightened. "What do you have this week?"

"A letter from the sister. She's in Ephesus with one of Crassus's friends. Gaius something. She didn't give the whole name. But she wrote she was glad Crassus had told her to get in touch with this Gaius while she was there, so her brother knows who she means."

"You already told me she was in Ephesus. One in four of the Romans is Gaius something, so this doesn't count as something useful."

"But there's more. She said Gaius was more like their father than Crassus ever was. She's never met a finer man, and they've decided to marry. She's looking forward to helping him raise his two sons and to the children she'll have if Fortuna smiles on them. She invited Crassus to visit them sometime, but she doesn't expect it because his service to Rome and the Emperor always take precedence over her. Then the usual farewell asking the gods to guard his safety."

Custos withdrew the wax tablet from the satchel by his feet. "I've seen her signet pattern, and that's what's on the wax in this seal box."

The gladiator snatched it from his hand. With a glare, he opened and read it. "Sabinus will want to see this."

He stood, and Custos rose as well. He'd written the letter as Master Crassus dictated it, and it wouldn't look like a woman's handwriting to a man like Sabinus.

"But I only borrowed it from the correspondence archives. I need to put it back there as soon as I return to the townhouse."

When Custos grasped the tablet, the gladiator drove a fist into his stomach. The explosion of pain bent him over, and he let go as he stumbled back.

"I said Sabinus will want to see this. If he doesn't want to keep it, you can have it back next week. No one will notice it's gone before then."

Arms wrapped across his aching abdomen, he straightened. "But—"

The gladiator wrapped his meaty hand around Custos's throat. "'But' is not a word you use with Sabinus...or me."

Custos nodded, and the hand dropped away.

"Be here next week, and have Gaius's full name."

"I'm not supposed to have seen this letter. Crassus has many friends in Ephesus. How will I learn which is the right Gaius?"

"That's for you to figure out. Use your head."

A hand seized the back of Custos's neck, pushed his head down, and smashed his forehead on the table. He staggered before gripping the back of the chair. When he touched the throbbing place near his hairline, his finger came back with blood.

"Don't fail. You'll regret it."

Custos nodded—big mistake with a thumping headache. But at least the gladiator left.

He slumped in the chair and closed his eyes.

A hand touched his arm. "Are you all right?" The girl's concerned tone drew his gaze to her face.

"I will be. It's nothing."

She offered a sad smile, and her eyes spoke her pity before she moved away.

His hand shook as he picked up his white wine. Good thing Sabinus's enforcer only liked red. One sip, then he cradled it in both hands until they steadied. He finished it slowly, closing his eyes after each swallow. The dark made his head pound less.

But the light streaming through the doorway beckoned, even though it hurt. His task wasn't finished yet, so he stood and gripped the chairback until everything steadied. Time to report what had happened so Master Crassus could plan the next move.

If Festinus found the sister in Octodurus, Sabinus would rage over the lies he was telling now. What torture would the sadist use to make him pay?

He squared his shoulders. Whatever might come, a man had to do what was right. If he had to die for the part he'd played, he'd rather die helping a good man than serving an evil one.

*The Crassus townhouse*

The stableyard gate was closed when Custos reached the townhouse, which forced him to knock on the small door to the left. He'd rinsed the blood from his face at the fountain down the street. His hair was combed forward, but the lump on his forehead peeked out beneath the rough-cut edge. It could draw questions he didn't want to answer.

"It's Custos."

The door swung in with the gatekeeper behind it, and he hurried through, head down. Without pausing for the usual exchange of greetings, he strode into the house.

The library door stood open, but he knocked with the three-beat pattern Vicarius used. Master Crassus glanced up from the scroll on his desk. Then his gaze locked on Custos.

"Come in and bolt the door."

As Custos slid the bolt home, the scraping of chair legs on floor sounded behind him. He turned to find Master Crassus next to him.

As he lifted Custos's hair to expose the purple bump, the master drew air between his teeth. "What happened?"

"I told him what was in the letter you dictated. Then I showed him the tablet with her signet seal. He took it from me, and when I tried to get it back..." Custos shrugged. "I was concerned Sabinus might think my handwriting too masculine to be your sister's, but I couldn't stop him taking it."

Master Crassus rubbed his jaw. "That might be good. It opens a new way for us to make Sabinus believe what we want." He opened the door and leaned out. "Melinda, fetch Vicarius."

A faint "yes, master" was followed by the girl hurrying past the door before he closed it. He returned to his chair and pointed at the one opposite. "Sit."

With hands gripping both arms, Custos lowered himself onto the cushion. What he longed for was his bed and some darkness until this headache passed, but he welcomed the chair. Walking from the taberna had drained him, but standing still was worse.

From a cream-colored flagon, Master Crassus poured white wine into his gold-lined goblet and slid it toward Custos. "You look like you could use this."

"Thank you, master." Custos took a sip and couldn't keep his eyebrows from rising. The famous Brutus vintage was ambrosia. No wonder Sabinus wanted to acquire some by any means he could.

Master Crassus leaned back and watched him drink, a frown hovering on his lips as he tapped on the desk with a stylus.

One knock, then two.

"Enter." Vicarius came two steps into the room. "Close and bolt it; then join us."

As he settled into the chair beside Custos, Vicarius gasped. "What happened to you?"

"He's been helping me with a problem known only to the two of us. Sabinus has infiltrated the household with at least one spy you and I both trusted, and we don't know if there are more."

"Who is the spy?" A warrior scowl darkened Vicarius's eyes.

Palm up, the master's hand pointed to Custos.

Vicarius's gaze bounced from the master to Custos and back. When it finally stopped on Custos, disappointment, then condemnation filled his eyes.

Custos hung his head. Nothing the gladiator had done pained him as much as knowing he betrayed and hurt this man who'd treated him like a son.

Master Crassus leaned across the desk and touched Vicarius's arm. "There's no need to look at him that way. Quintus Sabinus had your assistant killed so he could substitute Custos, but that snake didn't realize an honest man can only be forced to lie for so long. Custos chose to warn me of Sabinus's plans to hurt Licinia, and we've been able to thwart his first attempt. We've been trying to redirect any future attacks. Now, thanks to this young man, Sabinus will be looking for her where she isn't until he grows tired of looking."

He rested his crossed arms on the desk. "But as you can see, it's become too dangerous for him to be playing double agent. It's time to get rid of Custos before Sabinus strikes again. So, from this moment on, Custos is no more, and Fidelis sits before you."

Fidelis? That meant loyal and trustworthy. That Master Crassus would give him such a name...Custos couldn't stop the smile.

He raised his chin and squared his shoulders. "My old master renamed me Custos when he made me a spy, and I lived up to the name. I'll do my best to live up to this one."

The master reached across and slapped his arm. "I'm sure you will, but you can't do it here. If Sabinus realizes you betrayed him or even thinks you might, he will come after you. You can't be here when he does."

Custos's shoulders sagged. "What will you do with me, master?"

"Nothing you should fear. Vicarius, you'll need a new assistant. There are several young men helping my understewards at the estate east of Rome. One of those should be a suitable replacement. When Rome opens to carriages tonight, take Fidelis with you to select the one you want, and he'll take over that man's position. If anyone here asks where Custos went, tell them the master disposed of him with no further explanation."

"He's the best assistant I've had. I hate to lose him, but his safety is more important. When you believe Sabinus is no longer a threat, I'd like to have him back in Rome helping me."

"When a man risks his life to protect someone important to me, that's a man I trust to serve me well. I'll be pleased to have him return."

Vicarius stood. "Thank you, master." His warm smile wrapped around Fidelis and drew one in return.

"Master Crassus?" Fidelis clasped his hands at his waist, and the best man he'd ever known smiled back at him.

"Yes, Fidelis?"

"Thank you...for everything."

"It's my pleasure." With a wave of his hand that dismissed them, the master turned his eyes back on his scroll, and Fidelis followed Vicarius from the room.

As they walked through the peristyle, his friend and mentor placed a hand on Fidelis's shoulder. "I often go to that estate on business with Master Sextus. I'll make sure we get to spend some time together when I do. Write so I'll know how you're doing between visits."

"I will."

Vicarius squeezed and let his hand fall away, but the affection it conveyed still shone in his eyes.

Fidelis's gaze swept over every painting, every sculpture, every mosaic as they passed through the atrium to Vicarius's chamber. He'd thought death was certain as he walked that floor on the way to his confession. But a man of honor gave him a chance to redeem himself, and he'd be forever grateful. A good master, a friend who was like a father to him, and a future with a name he could be proud of...those were more than he ever dreamed he'd have, and he'd make certain Sextus Crassus never regretted what he'd done for the man sent to betray him.

# Chapter 58

## Opportunities Too Good to Miss

*The Octodurus estate, July 8*

When the three men rode through the courtyard gate, Antistes was lounging in the wicker chair in the portico. Two burly men in tunics followed a man who sat his horse like one accustomed to being obeyed.

When they turned toward the house, Antistes rose and left the portico. He glanced at the stable. Magnus was there with Primus, working on a wagon.

The riders didn't look hostile, but he rested his hand on the dagger that always hung from his belt.

"Greetings." The leader dismounted. "I'm seeking Licinia Crassa."

Antistes eyed the bodyguards, who were looking around the courtyard with more than general curiosity. "No woman with that name has been here since I became steward."

"Then I would like to see the domina."

"There's no domina here." By the stable, Primus and Magnus had stopped working and were watching.

The visitor's eyebrow rose. "Isn't Calvia Lucilla the domina here?"

"She did serve as domina for a few months, but she left three weeks ago. I don't expect her to return soon."

"They're the same person. It's important I find her as soon as possible. Where did she go?"

Antistes blanked his face. Calvia was really a Crassus. That certainly explained a lot.

"What do you want with her?"

The visitor's mouth twitched before a fake-friendly smile appeared. "We have an urgent personal message for her from Sextus Licinus Crassus, and anything you can do to help us find her will be appreciated by your master."

Antistes eyes narrowed. Urgent messages from Crassus were delivered by a single rider on a lathered horse, like the last one for Damalio. These three looked too much like the ones Lepus had described. The ones chased off by Brutus's bodyguards.

"Last time Master Crassus sent an urgent message, he used the horse relay. Why did he send you?"

The visitor's smile turned less friendly. "I'm delivering these bodyguards as well as the message."

"It's a long way to Rome. They must have special skills to make it worth bringing them so far. Octodurus has an arena, so there are good bodyguards to hire or buy right here."

The visitor's smile didn't match the calculation in his eyes. "They do. Their owner thought it worth the time and expense to provide her with exactly the right men."

Antistes's smile was more genuine. An opportunity too good to miss was presenting itself. "Then you'll probably want to continue on to where she's gone."

"If at all possible." The visitor's smile broadened.

"It's possible. It's even convenient for you. She left with Marcus Antonius Brutus, and they were supposed to go to his estate near Lousonna. Only a day on horseback. Whether she's actually there, I don't know, but you might find her."

"Thank you for your help." The visitor reined away and signaled his men to follow him.

"It's been my pleasure." The visitor had no idea how true that was.

As they rode out, Primus joined him. "Who were those men?"

"Some men come from Rome looking for Licinia Crassa."

"You told them she wasn't here?"

"Of course. I told them she'd never been here, only Calvia Lucilla. They said they were one and the same, and Master Sextus had sent the bodyguards along with a message, so I told them where to find her."

"You did what?" Primus mouth opened, then snapped shut as his lips tightened. "Brutus took her away so no one would find her. And if Master Sextus thought Domina needed bodyguards, why didn't he just have you hire or buy some in Octodurus?"

Antistes shrugged. "Maybe he didn't think a provincial capital would have something good enough for his sister or mistress, whichever she is."

"The domina isn't anybody's mistress. Damalio and Fidus both think she's the finest woman they've known."

"If she was, she wouldn't have gone off to live with Brutus."

"We couldn't protect her like his men could. Like Lepus said they did." Primus's eyebrows lowered. "How do you know those three even came from Master Sextus? They could be from the same one who sent the first three. They could even be the same ones. You didn't see them."

"They could be, but that's Brutus's problem if they are."

Primus jaw clenched. "You know they are, and you shouldn't have told them where she is. She might get hurt."

"And if she does, then she won't be coming back here to lord it over us."

"I'm ashamed of you, Father. She made this a better place, and everyone can see that...except you. I would never have believed you could betray someone you're supposed to serve."

He turned and strode away.

"Primus!"

His son only raised his hands to shove away his call and kept walking.

Antistes glared at the road where it disappeared over the hill. Calvia Lucilla had taken the estate from him, and now she had driven a wedge between him and his son. If he never saw her again, it would be too soon. But if Fortuna smiled, he'd just sent the three who would make sure he never did.

*Brutus's Lousonna estate, July 9*

"Best three out of five?" Brutus held out his hand, and Calvia dribbled his captured pieces into it.

"You're off your game today." She traced the inlaid spiral of blond wood at the corner of the latrunculi grid. "We could flip this and play tabula."

It was five days since she hugged him as her new brother. Five days since he stopped himself from hugging her back. Five days of pondering whether he was ready to have another woman in his life.

His conclusion? He already did. Her conversation made every meal more than a time for food. Her good-natured teasing added spice to every game. Her love for Marcus was almost as great as his own.

But what if he asked her to become his wife and she turned him down? Would she still feel comfortable staying at his estate so he could protect her?

No wonder his game was off, but switching to tabula wouldn't solve his problem.

"No. I prefer the challenge, even when I lose."

He looked past her toward the lake and frowned. A challenge he would have preferred to avoid was riding toward him.

"Your unwanted visitors have returned. Go inside."

She turned to follow his gaze, and the blood drained from her face. "I'll get help."

At his nod, she entered the house and shut the door.

Brutus moved to stand in the portico entrance, arms crossed. The same three men who'd prompted the move to Lousonna reined in. The leader leaned back, as if to swing a leg over his horse's neck and slide off.

"Don't. You won't be here that long. Speak your business. Then you can leave."

The leader settled back in his saddle. "I have an important message for Licinia Crassa from her brother, and I was told I would find her here."

"Who told you that?" Brutus's frown deepened. "There has never been a woman with that name here."

One corner of the agent's mouth curved. "The steward in Octodurus. Perhaps she hasn't gone by that name in your presence. She has an alias: Calvia Lucilla. She used that name as domina of Sextus Crassus's Octodurus estate, and the steward there said she came here with you."

With a soft creak, the door opened behind him. Calvia appeared at his side and offered his sheathed gladius to him.

Palm up, the stubble-faced agent held out his hand. "And there she is."

Brutus slid the sword out of the scabbard and handed the empty sheath back to Calvia. "Go back inside."

On tiptoes, she whispered in his ear. "I'll be praying."

She went inside, but he didn't hear the door latch. When Sabinus's agent looked past him to the door, he knew she was standing just inside with the door still open.

"Look at me, not her. That woman is my wife and domina of this estate. I thought I made that perfectly clear the last time I saw you."

"So you say, but I've been back to Rome, and Quintus Flavius Sabinus doesn't believe you would remarry yet. So who is she, really?"

"So, you're from Sabinus, not Crassus. I've been told that a man who has no qualms about lying himself often assumes others suffer from the same problem. But a liar shouldn't be applying his or his master's personal standards to more honorable men."

Sabinus's agent swung his leg across his horse's neck, as if to dismount.

"Stay mounted." Brutus coated his words with ice. He fingered the edge of his blade. "I keep my dagger sharp enough to shave with it. A gladius doesn't need that fine an edge to do its work, but I like mine well-honed."

The agent snorted. "Last time I saw you, you could barely stand. You still have that leg wrapped. Trying to threaten me and my men is foolish. Expecting me to obey you is laughable."

"I make no threats I can't fulfill. I have some of the finest fighters in Rome, and I spar with Africanus daily. And right now, two of Rome's finest are behind you."

The bodyguards twisted in their saddles to find Africanus and Rufus behind them, swords drawn. They turned their horses to face his men and drew their swords, but clenched teeth and lowered eyebrows didn't hide their fear. Brutus's other men were gathering, carrying farm tools like pitchforks and scythes. Two were armed with hunting bows.

Brutus called to his gathering army. "Kill them on my order only."

He offered the leader a tight-lipped smile. "This doesn't have to go past talking. You've seen that the woman you're looking for isn't here. You can leave now to go back to your master and tell him."

The agent scanned left and right as more men surrounded his party. With the back of his hand, he rubbed his mouth.

Brutus took one step forward. "I'm feeling patient today, but there are limits to my patience when someone who should know better sends people who threaten me. I could have my men make certain the three of you won't be returning, and they might enjoy doing that. But that wouldn't keep Sabinus from sending others to bother me."

He pointed his sword tip at the leader. "So instead, I'm going to send you back to your master with a message. Marcus Antonius Brutus sends Quintus Flavius Sabinus greetings from Germania, but I want no further visits from any of his men.

"It is not his place to decide if or when I'll remarry. It is no one's business but my own that I've chosen to marry a local woman in Germania. She'll be a fine mother to my son, and she'll give me more children. But if he wants to share that news with others, he has my permission to do so. It might amuse his friends, and if people want to talk about me, I'd rather it be the truth instead of speculation or lies."

He lowered the sword. "I have another message for him to pass on to his grandson Septimus. I expect to be back in Roma in late summer, and I look forward to seeing the progress the boy has made in my absence."

With a sneer, he tipped his head to look down his nose. "Can you remember those messages, or do I need to write them down?"

"I can remember." Resentment smoldered in the agent's eyes before he lowered his gaze.

"Then I wish you a safe trip back to Rome."

Brutus looked past the intruders to the men encircling them. "Let them pass."

Sabinus's agent reined his horse away from the portico and rode past the two walls of men. As they headed down the road away from the villa, the leader kicked his horse into a trot.

Brutus raised his hand. "Thank you for coming to my defense. You can go back to work now."

"Bruno." The youth stopped and turned. "Get on the roof and watch to make sure they don't try to return."

With a big grin and a "yes, master," the boy trotted away to get a ladder.

With his back still to the door, Brutus held his hand out sideways. "My scabbard."

Calvia came from behind and handed it to him. After sheathing the sword and hanging the strap across his chest, he took her chin in his hand. "Next time I tell you to go inside for your safety, you should also shut the door."

"I will. It was probably foolish of me, but I wanted to hear."

"There was nothing worth hearing."

"But there was something shocking." A playful gleam lit her eyes. "That was the first time I ever heard you tell a lie."

"True, and it should be the last. In fact, I want you to do something to correct the error of what I just said."

In business and in life, his father had taught him to see and then seize unexpected opportunities. Had God just given him one?

"I don't see how I can. Words once spoken can't be taken back, and the ones you lied to are gone."

In life and in sport, he'd always thought success came to the decisive and the brave. But it was God's will that really mattered. *God, please let what I want be your plan for us both.*

"It's simple. Become my wife and make it the truth."

Her eyes widened, and her mouth opened. It closed without uttering a sound.

"Before you say no, hear me out. I thought I would never find a woman to take Camilla's place. I was right. She will always be my beloved, but I don't want you to take her place. I want you to take your own place."

He rested his palm on her cheek. "You're already my friend and my sister in Christ. But what I feel for you goes beyond friendship and brotherly love. God has shown me that loving another woman doesn't mean loving Camilla less. Love isn't limited, and together, we can find out how deep a second love can be."

She placed a hand over his heart. "No isn't what I was planning to say. But this is so sudden, and—"

"And I need to get Damalio's approval first?"

She turned her brightest smile on him. "No, I do consult him on important decisions, but I can make up my own mind about you."

"What have you decided?"

"Well...you are reasonably good at latrunculi, and we agree on what should be in a library. You do have a son I love beyond measure. You are rather stubborn, but so am I. So, all things considered, I'm inclined to say yes."

He swept her off her feet and spun full circle and beyond.

"Don't do that. You'll hurt your leg."

He stopped and returned her to her feet. "I'll be the judge of what's wise for me to do, and that includes marrying you."

He drew her against him. She wrapped her arms around him and pressed her cheek against his chest. Then she tipped her head back to look up at him. "You've warned me against hugging a man who might misunderstand what I meant by it. But you should have no trouble interpreting this one. Feel free to let your thoughts go wherever they want."

His lips brushed her forehead. "I will, and you should have no problem interpreting this." From forehead to cheek to lips...

When he finally drew back, her eyes were closed. But they popped open and her mouth curved into that "I've got you now" smile he'd seen so many times as she sprang a trap on the board. But this time, it meant they had each other.

"About Damalio...I know he'll approve of combining our households. He wasn't looking forward to your departure any more than I was because you'd be taking Vera. She would make him the perfect wife, and she'd be getting a truly fine man. Perhaps, as a wedding gift to me, you could buy him from Sextus and set them both free?" With one finger, she traced his lower lip.

"I'm inclined to buy all your men from your brother. Bernhard would be so disappointed to have Sollus leave my kitchen." He trapped her hand and kissed her palm.

"He'll sell them. Except for him making me leave Rome with only one day's notice, he usually agrees to my requests."

"I suspect you'll have the same effect on me, but from what I've seen, I expect those requests will be reasonable."

"For my first request…I know what I want for our marriage celebration. The procession from my house to your house already took place when you brought me here. As for the orange veil and the orange shoes and the belt with the Knot of Hercules you have to figure out how to untie…" She scrunched her nose. "Orange was never one of my favorite colors, so we can forego those. Sextus authorized Damalio as his agent to take care of me, so he can sign the marriage contract, but I don't know how that would work for the dowry."

"Licinia Crassa has a dowry to worry about, but I'm not marrying her. Calvia Lucilla doesn't need one. Bernhard is a citizen, so he can witness the contract."

"So, we'll make our vows before God in the presence of the brothers and sisters, and Sollus can create a banquet for the whole familia."

He kissed her forehead. "When do you want all this?"

"I'd say today, but tomorrow is more practical." She wrapped her arm around his and hugged. "Tomorrow morning immediately after breakfast for the vows. I don't want you to have time to change your mind."

"I never change my mind once I've found what I really want." He fingered a tendril of hair that hung by her ear. "Not just what I want, but what I've prayed about enough to be certain it's what God wants as well."

Her finger traced his jawline. "Since the day you became my brother in Christ, I've been praying for this, too."

She stood on tiptoes to kiss his cheek, but a slight turn of his head brought their lips together and sealed the promise of a future with the woman who'd brought hope and joy to him again.

When their lips finally parted, she snuggled against his chest with a contented sigh. Then she stepped back. "We'll have the banquet in the evening. That will give Sollus time to do something special."

"Are you ready for what's in between?" He knew what awaited them, and the thought of sharing his love with her triggered his biggest grin.

"You mean some games in the morning and you walking with Africanus in the afternoon?"

His eyebrows rose. "I had something different in mind."

The pink started on her cheeks and spread to the tips of her ears. Then her eyes danced as her "I got you now" smile appeared. "I rather hoped you would."

She rested her head against his shoulder and turned eyes filled with love upon his face. "I should warn you. I like to hug, but I'll leave it to your imagination to figure out what each hug means."

"You'll have no doubt what mine mean." He swung her against his chest and encircled her with his arms. As their lips met again, both let their imaginations run free.

# Chapter 59

## Somewhere Safe?

*The Lousonna estate, afternoon of July 10*

With Brutus's arm draped across her shoulder and hers around his waist, Calvia strolled to the rockpile overlooking the lake. Her first day wearing a stola that she truly deserved had been wonderful beyond words. The husband she never expected to have brushed some tiny rocks off a boulder with his hand; then, palm up, he invited her to sit. When he joined her, she slid closer, and his arm wrapped around her once more.

She traced the longest of at least a dozen scars on his forearm.

He laid his hand on hers. "Africanus did that when I first started sparring with him. I got too cocky, and I wasn't paying close enough attention."

"Will you keep sparring?"

"Of course. There are times a man has to defend someone, and it's best to be prepared." He shrugged. "Besides, I enjoy doing something really well that takes dedication and hard work."

Her eyes turned to the lake, and in the distance, Lousonna stretched along its shore. Lousonna, with its theater where music was performed and men bled and died.

He stroked her jaw, and she turned her eyes back to him.

"I can guess what you're thinking, and I've been thinking about what to do. When Africanus was telling me about the sins that separate us from God, he told me we were both murderers: him for killing to entertain others and me for sending my men onto the sand to do it. It made me mad when he first said it, but I see now he was right."

She started to trace another scar, but he took her hand and kissed her palm.

"Did that hurt?"

"No, but I want to tell you some things, and you're distracting me." His lips brushed her forehead.

"I own three ludi and over a hundred fighters. I did provide men for the games, but they also work as bodyguards and trainers for young Romans before they go to the legions. Your nephews are among those who will be learning how to fight well with my men so they can stay alive."

He picked up a pebble from the crevice beside him and tossed it.

"Some I bought were criminals who were condemned to the games. I can't free those. Some were slaves taken in war. Rufus's father was one of those, so he was born into a ludus. Many would have nowhere to go if I simply close my ludi. They're *infames*, and many won't hire such men. But God doesn't want me to be making money off men's deaths just to entertain the crowds, like you told me I did. And rightly so."

His brow furrowed, and he stared at the mountains until she touched his arm. "What are you going to do?"

"I've discussed that with Africanus, and we think we've come up with a middle way. I'm going to free the fighters I can and let each decide if they want to stay on with Felix as their manager. He'll rent them out as bodyguards and oversee the training program. If they want to keep fighting in the arena, he'll help them find a new ludus that will treat them fairly. The ones I can't free, I'll give them the choice of being sold or staying on to work like the free men. I'll do the same with my ludi in Florentia and Luca, with their trainers consulting Felix if they have problems."

"What will Rufus do?"

"I already asked him. He wants to stay as my bodyguard. He's only ever known life in a ludus, but he wants to learn about the vineyards and the livestock and the other things done at the estate." His smiling frown, so dear to her now, appeared. "He finds Primula...intriguing. He's never known a Christian woman before. He has no idea yet how much they can change things."

She flashed him a smile and snuggled closer. "When you return to Rome in the fall, do you have an estate nearby where I can stay so no one will recognize me?"

"I have the one just outside Roma, two with excellent vineyards up the Tiber near Capena, and another near Liternum. The merchant fleet operates out of Puteoli and Ostia. But we'll be staying in Lousonna. I don't want to put you and Marcus at risk, and it should be safer for Christians here.

"Besides, no one would believe I'd merely lost interest in the games if I stay in Italia. I've been too visible in that world for too long. If I stay near Roma, questions we don't want to answer will be asked. In three weeks or so, I'll go back to tell your brother what's happened and to gather what I need to move control of my businesses here."

A loose strand of hair fluttered in the breeze, and he tucked it behind her ear. "As a wedding present, I'll bring you my library. You did say agreeing on what a library should hold helped you decide in my favor."

"I know Africanus has to go with you to get his family, but I'm going to miss you two terribly."

"You'll miss more than that. I'm taking Damalio to show him my holdings and to get his help with setting things up to run in my absence. He'll help me figure out how to move what is needed from Roma to here."

"I hate the thought of you going without me, and I'd love to see Sextus again, but I see the wisdom in Marcus and me staying here." She rested a hand on her belly. "Before you go, can we visit the Octodurus estate? I want to check on Olga and Ursula and the other mothers."

"Of course. I look forward to the conversation with Antistes about him sending those three on to Lousonna."

She raised her eyebrows. "Africanus did tell you about God commanding that we forgive people, didn't he? Even enemies who try to hurt us?"

"Yes, but Antistes doesn't know that we have to forgive, and it will be good for him to worry a little before he does."

"I know which part of Luke's gospel we'll be reading tonight."

He chuckled. "I have much to learn, but God's given me the best teacher."

She stretched to kiss his cheek before resting her head against his shoulder. "And He's blessed me with the right man."

*The Baths of Trajan, Rome, July 15*

At the end of the pool, Sextus rose and wiped the water from his eyes. It was nine days since Sabinus's agent took the letter from Fidelis and two days since he would have gone to the taberna for the next report. Two days since Sabinus's spy failed to show. Two days, and Sabinus would be trying to figure out why by now. But what would he do to get the answer?

Manius had been in the steam room, but he'd only talked with a senator who expected to be consul soon. He was bragging on how much Septimus had improved after training a few months with Brutus's gladiators. But Manius had been telling everyone of importance they needed to send their sons to the Ludus Bruti since his boy started there, so his presence played no role in the next and hopefully final step for getting Sabinus off Licinia's trail.

"Crassus!" From behind him came the nasal voice of the man who'd given him Custos to thank him for his help. Sextus turned and raised a hand in greeting before picking a towel off the stack and drying his hair.

Tertullus walked with all the dignity his praetorship accorded him, followed by his six *lictores* with their bundles of birch rods. "It's good to see you. It's been too long."

Sextus donned his social smile. "It's been many months." He tipped his head toward the lictores. "I trust you are finding satisfaction in serving Rome these days."

"I am, and I want to thank you again for your support that made it possible." Tertullus's mouth twitched before settling into a practiced smile. "I trust the young man I provided is working out well for you."

"He seemed to be doing an excellent job, and I was looking forward to telling you so when we next met. But I caught him stealing. Of all things, it was a letter from my sister, but a man who would steal one thing, no matter how worthless, can't be trusted not to steal something of value." With tightened lips, he shook his head. "Dishonesty is something I will not tolerate, and I disposed of him."

"That surprises me, even shocks me. Like you, I demand honesty, and he'd been commended for it by the understeward who trained him." Tertullus tugged at the shoulder of his tunic. "If you find anything else he stole, put it to my account. Let me make it up to you by providing a replacement."

"Thank you for the generous offer." Sextus's smile turned warm, but only because it concealed silent laughter. "But I've already taken care of it. From now on, I will only fill that position with people born and raised in my familia. Then I can be certain they'll be honest and loyal."

Tertullus mouth drooped, but quickly returned to his political smile. "If you should change your mind, do let me know."

"You'll be among the first." Sextus wiped his chest and arms and tossed the towel into the basket. "I need to meet someone, but we can talk later."

"We will. Salve, Crassus."

"Salve." Sextus turned and headed for the slave who was holding his clothing. Once his back was turned, he had to tighten his lips to keep the grin from escaping. By tomorrow, Sabinus would know why his spy never came. He'd believe the letter was genuine. He'd think neither Sextus nor his sister cared if they ever saw each other again.

Sabinus might decide it was pointless trying to insert another spy. It was unlikely, but he might decide it was too hard to find anything to force Sextus to compromise his honor. But whether he did or not, the gladiator who hurt Fidelis would pay for taking the letter that got their spy caught.

*The Crassus townhouse, Rome, July 16*

As Vicarius stood with the stack of tablets from the estates, Sextus paced in his library.

"So, there's been nothing from Gratus or Damalio, and Antistes didn't mention anything about my sister. How can that be?"

Vicarius replaced the stack on the desk. "You did warn Damalio to take her and leave immediately because someone knew she was there. Maybe he decided there must be a spy here, and he was afraid anything he sent would be intercepted."

"But he must have her well away from Octodurus by now. Surely some message could be sent using another name with the words chosen so I'll know it's from her. We played latrunculi all the time. You can't find a sharper mind for strategic games than hers. And subtle plays on words...there's none better."

"Maybe they're waiting until they get to the estate in Hispania to send a message with the regular reports, like they did before. It takes more than two weeks if they mix sea and land travel. Closer to four if they go by land only. And maybe they stopped for a while at the home of the man Antistes said she left with."

"Perhaps, but why didn't Antistes say anything about who that was? Or where he's from? Or where he was going? What equestrian would she trust enough to go with him, broken leg or not? More to the point, who would Damalio trust enough to let her go with him?"

"I could write Antistes asking for more information. I could tell him to send only a numbered list that didn't reveal the questions. Shall I?"

Sextus rubbed both sides of his nose. If Licinia was standing beside him, she'd tell him she'd ask her god to protect whoever it was he was worried about. But it was only because she wasn't with him and had left where he thought she was that he had to worry at all.

"It's been ten days since we sent Fidelis away. How certain are we that there are no other spies still here?"

"Not certain at all. He was spying as Custos for more than six months, and we only know that because he told us."

"Watch to see if anyone tries to see what came in the Octodurus report. Surely any spy still here will want to look at that first. Maybe store it with something that will show if it's been disturbed." He squeezed the back of his neck. "Better do that for the other reports, too. If they've given up on Octodurus, they'll at least look at the others. We'll wait a week and decide then what to do."

Vicarius stood. "Very well. I'll file these myself and keep watch." He gathered up the tablets and left, closing the door behind him.

Sextus dropped into his chair and picked up a stylus. First he drummed slowly, then fast, then slowly again. Was she somewhere safe, protected by the man he'd entrusted her to? Was she in Sabinus's clutches having who knew what done to her? Or was she already dead and lost to him forever?

# Chapter 60

## A Surprise When He Returns

The Lousonna estate, July 30

Only two months since the accident. Who would have thought so much could happen since then?

Calvia stood by the corral with Brutus as Damalio did a final check of the horses they'd be taking across the pass to Rome.

"They're good enough animals." Brutus wrapped an arm around her waist. "My stallion and Africanus's are better left here. I'll get some good mares and breed them. There should be a market for quality horses in Genava with two roads leading across the Alpes and the main road to the Rhenus starting there."

He shifted his weight to his left leg, and she raised her eyebrows. How would he bear so many hours each day on a horse with his leg barely healed?

"I've been looking forward to the ride, but perhaps it would be better to drive the *cisium*. You want me to take that blanket to Sextus, and I can carry it easier in a small trunk under the seat than on a horse."

"Much easier. That's a good idea."

His wry smile was a much better response than the rolled eyes when she suggested he drive the two-wheeled carriage a week ago.

He kissed her forehead. "It's less fun than a chariot and not as comfortable as a horse, but to make you happy, I'll take it this time. It can easily keep up with the horses, so the trip to Rome will be quick. Coming back is another matter. We'll have a raeda for Africanus's family and a wagon or two."

"For the sake of your leg, I think the cisium is a much better choice.

Riding for hours every day with a barely healed break couldn't be as comfortable as you think. But with Burdonarius riding a horse, you could trade off and ride it a little." Her brow furrowed. "But only for as long as Africanus and Damalio think it wise." She drew a finger down his cheek. "If you let yourself, you'll enjoy the cisium. I think driving a team is fun."

His eyebrows rose. "How would you know?"

"I have many skills you don't know about yet, including handling a team. I had Damalio teach me on the trip out. Maybe I'll get a cisium of my own while you're gone. That would mean only a single day to Octodurus. I can make shorter visits but more often."

"You can go, but by raeda only and with Rufus and another man he picks as your bodyguards. After our last visit, I don't think Antistes is a problem anymore, but there can be robbers even on the best roads."

"That's fine. I really like the team Damalio bought in Arelate. Driving is exciting when they canter."

He opened his mouth to object, and she touched his lips. "But just for you, I'll take a driver and let him sit beside me like Damalio did, and I won't go faster than a trot." She patted his hand where it rested on the rail. "And Marcus can stay here with Vera."

"Damalio, can she handle a team?"

He looked up from inspecting the mule team for the cisium. "As well as Sollus. I taught him, too."

Calvia rested her head against Brutus's shoulder. "I'm only teasing. I'll wait until you return. How long will you be away?"

"Over the pass, it's less than three weeks riding straight to Rome. I need to sidetrack to Luca to deal with the ludus, and it could take a day at Florentia for the same. Two or so days at my Tibur estates, so I should be in Roma in three and a half weeks. A week to settle matters there and three days to visit the Liternum vineyards. I should be leaving for home in five weeks."

"But that's well into September. Will the pass still be open when you reach it?"

"It could be, but I won't risk it. We'll sail to Arelate, then come up the Rhodanus like you did. But Burdonarius and Damalio can both drive four-mule teams, so we'll travel faster."

He took her hand, and they headed toward the house.

The cream-colored sails of a merchant ship drew her gaze to the lake. Today the wind was light and the water calm, but she'd heard the tales of the winter storms. Too many hazards awaited a traveler.

"I know you've made this trip many times, but please promise me you'll be careful."

His eyes laughed at her. She'd only told him that a dozen times already.

"You don't need to worry. Africanus and your guard dog will keep me from doing something I shouldn't. They'll watch over me as well as you would. I have a few Germans who will want to go back to their tribes. They'll be extra guards on the way home. I won't have thirty cavalrymen like you did, but I'll have more than enough. And you'll all be praying for us. Two months, and we'll be together forever."

They passed through the great hall to his office. The trunk containing the blanket sat open on his desk, and Calvia stroked the fleecy fabric. "When you give this to Sextus, do tell him every time he uses it, he should consider himself wrapped in all the hugs and love the best brother in the world deserves."

An eye roll was his first response. "It would be priceless to see the look on your brother's face when I said that, but he'll know it without me speaking those words. There's papyrus and ink in the drawer. You can write it out and put it in the trunk for him."

She lifted the blanket from the trunk and snuggled it against her cheek. "I miss Sextus so much. I wish I could see his face when he gets this."

"Maybe next year you can come with me and stay at the Liternum estate. That's close enough for your brother to visit if Roma can spare him for a few days."

He slipped his arm around her waist and pulled her close. "I'll have you back in my arms before the Kalends of October." He kissed her neck, then whispered, "Maybe we'll give Marcus a little brother or sister someday."

She felt the heat to the tip of her ears. It was too soon to tell him. After Camilla's problems, he'd be worried the whole trip. But she'd told Vera so she could be praying, and Primula knew as soon as she did. She was a week past when her flow should have come, and it always came on time. Would the babe be showing when he returned?

"I'm not sure how I'll be able to do without you for two months. You're taking Africanus, so who can possibly give me a challenge at latrunculi?"

"Is that all you'll miss?"

"I've come to enjoy watching Africanus and Rufus spar." She touched his lips, and he kissed her fingers. "And I love lying with you at night, praying together before we sleep."

"I'll miss that, too. Praying with Damalio and Africanus isn't quite the same."

She pressed her cheek against his chest, and the arms that made her feel like all was right with the world wrapped around her. Except for God, nothing was quite the same since he came, and a silent song of thanksgiving filled her heart, mind, and soul.

# Chapter 61

ANOTHER ONE IN THE FAMILY

*The Crassus townhouse, Roma, August 26*

It was late morning when Brutus and Damalio entered the Crassus townhouse, late enough that any senators or equestrians who might mention seeing him to Manius or Sabinus would have already seen Crassus and left.

Brutus carried the blanket trunk on his shoulder. He'd left his purple-striped tunic at the ludus, opting instead for a plain one that would let him pass as Damalio's slave. Years of sparring had left him looking fit enough for manual service, so no one noble should give him a second glance.

When they were ushered into the atrium, no one still waiting wore purple stripes, as he'd hoped. A man in his forties was sorting documents, but he glanced at them as they walked toward him. The glance turned into a stare.

"Salve, Vicarius." Damalio's self-assured voice drew a couple of glances from those still waiting, but nothing more.

They reached the secretary, whose stare had turned into rapid blinks. "What are you doing back here? Is something wrong?"

"No." Damalio dropped his voice so no one near would hear. "I came through Octodurus on my return from Germania, and I have something for Crassus from Sextus Gratus."

Vicarius's eyes widened. "You'll go in next."

Brutus made his words quiet as well. "Call us after two more go in. Crassus shouldn't look too eager to see us."

The secretary looked at Damalio and got a confirming nod. Then he returned to his sorting.

An empty bench stood halfway between the entrance and Crassus's tablinum. Damalio led them to it, and Brutus set down the trunk. He massaged the place on his neck where the bottom edge had pressed too hard. It would be good to walk back to the ludus without it.

Vicarius escorted two people in, then out of the tablinum. Then he came to stand before them. "Next."

When they entered the tablinum, Crassus was seated at a desk.

Damalio turned to Vicarius. "Bolt the door."

At the click of the bolt, Crassus looked up, and a flash of recognition crossed his face as he stood. "Antonius Brutus?"

"Yes, and I've come bearing a gift and some news I hope you'll like." He set the trunk on the end of the desk. "I have a blanket for you as a thank-you for the one you sent Marcus. They were made by the same woman, and she sends her greetings."

"Licinia?" Crassus's eyes widened. At Brutus's nod, he pulled the chest in front of him.

He opened the lid, lifted out the blanket, and partly unfolded it. "My favorite colors."

"She said the blues and greens remind her of the mountains and sky at your estate. She also said something about love and hugs when you use it." His nose scrunched. "But repeating her exact words could embarrass us both. She wrote it all out in the letter."

Crassus pulled the papyrus sheet from the box, and his smile grew as he read it. "If you see her, you can tell her I'll remember all she wrote each time I use it."

His lips straightened when he looked past Brutus. "Damalio, with you here, who's guarding her?" His eyebrows lowered. "Where is she?" The pitch of his voice had risen. "Is she all right?"

Brutus raised a hand to calm him. "She's at my estate in Lousonna. One of my gladiators and the rest of your men are there to protect her."

"So, you're the equestrian with the broken leg who took her from my estate before Sabinus's men got there." Crassus set the letter on his desk. "I couldn't imagine whom she would trust enough to go with them." His eyes turned to Damalio. "Or more to the point, who would earn Damalio's trust so he'd allow it."

"We left right after they came, and I gave her no choice. Damalio agreed it was wise."

"After?" Crassus's mouth curved into a frown. "My steward wrote when she left with you, but he never mentioned Sabinus's men. I've assumed they arrived at the estate after he sent the letter."

"Interesting. He wasn't at the villa when they came, but he knew they'd come and why I wouldn't let her stay there." One corner of his mouth lifted. "He heartily approved when I took her away."

"I sent a warning by horse relay that they were coming. I assumed that message was why she left."

"No message came while I was there." Brutus patted his thigh. "With a broken leg, I spent most of my day in the portico. I would have seen the rider. No message was sent on to my estate after we left. Antistes probably thought there was no need since I'd already taken her someplace that should have been safe."

Crassus frowned. "But Antistes shouldn't have known the content. It was addressed to Damalio only. You said 'should have been safe'?"

"Your steward told them where I'd taken Calvia Lucilla, which is the name he knows her by. I told them she was my wife and convinced them another visit from a Sabinus agent would be fatal."

"Accept my thanks for protecting her. Will it be safe now for Damalio to take her back to Octodurus or on to my estate in Hispania?"

"Safe? Yes. Will I permit it? No. As I told them, she's my wife, and she'll be staying in Lousonna with me."

◆

Sextus was skilled in the art of shielding his thoughts from view, but he found himself staring at Brutus.

Marcus Brutus was well known for his deep, abiding sense of honor and his fervent loyalty to Rome. If faced with the choice, would he pick Rome over her?

Father had feared she might be unable to hide her faith from a husband. Sextus was certain of it. Could she have chosen a more dangerous man to marry and risk discovering she was a Christian?

The smiling frown he'd so often seen on Brutus at the baths appeared. "Do I detect a lack of enthusiasm for what I just told you?"

"It's surprising. After our father died, she told me she wasn't interested in marrying just any man, and she doubted she'd meet one that met her requirements."

"I didn't satisfy her requirements when we first met, but I do now."

"May I ask what changed?"

Brutus's mouth shifted toward a smile. "Not her requirements. I changed. She got the Christian husband she wanted, and you have one more relative whose faith you'll have to conceal."

Sextus sank into his chair. Elbow on the desk, he rested his chin in his palm and covered his mouth. Then he stared at the last man in the Empire he ever would have thought might become a Christian.

Brutus chuckled. "She'll laugh when I tell her your reaction. But I think you can see why we'll be living in Lousonna. God doesn't approve of making money off death, and too many would wonder why I no longer provide men for the games if I stay in Roma."

"And I'd be among them."

"I'll keep the ludus, but I won't be putting men on the sand anymore. I'll still be providing bodyguards and training for those who want to learn from the best. Your sons will be able to develop the skills they'll need before joining a legion."

"My oldest has started there already."

"While I'm in Germania, my lanista will be managing everything for me. I'll tell him to make sure young Sextus is well trained. Is he enjoying it so far?"

"He's not one to talk much, but he's spoken with enthusiasm about a trainer called Pugnus, and he spends some time with the other students."

"Good. Now for the next important matter. I promised my wife a wedding gift that I can only get from you." Brutus motioned Damalio to his side. "She wants me to buy Damalio and the others who came with her. His service has been extraordinary, and she wants to set him free."

"I'll make that my wedding gift to the two of you. Vicarius."

The secretary came from his place by the door.

"List the sale to Brutus at the regular prices so no one will think anything odd, and get the sales recorded. Damalio can tell you who to include right now."

"We'll take care of that in my office." Vicarius walked to the door, pulled back the bolt, and waited.

"Damalio." He'd started to follow, but he turned back when Sextus spoke.

"Yes, master?"

"I want to commend you for your excellent work taking care of my sister. I hoped that you taking her to Octodurus would keep her safe." Palm up, he pointed to Brutus. "I never expected she'd manage to find a Christian husband there to make her happy."

"He played a role in that." Brutus rested a hand on Damalio's shoulder.

"Guardian and matchmaker...an odd combination."

"He convinced Africanus to become a Christian. Then Africanus convinced me. Or rather I should say God convinced both of us using him."

God convinced them? A class 2 gladiator and a wealthy Roman who fought well enough to be a gladiator himself choosing the one god who would condemn what they did? It was tempting to ask what Brutus meant, but did he really want to know?

"You have a choice before Vicarius prepares the bills of sale. Do you want me to free you or Brutus?"

"You've been a fine master, and I'd be honored to be your freedman. But if I'm living in Germania, it will be easier to render my freedman service to Brutus. I'll be marrying young Marcus's dry nurse as well, so please sell me."

"As you wish." Always reliable, always thinking ahead, always making the better choice. It was why he'd entrusted his sister to this man. It was why he regretted parting with him, but no one deserved a choice more.

Damalio's smile started slow and broadened. "Thank you, master." Then he followed Vicarius from the room

Sextus sat and motioned for Brutus to do the same. "Damalio can return tomorrow to get the certified bills of sale. I'll have another gift for my sister then. I expect she'll enjoy my copy of Pliny's *Wars of Germania* as much as I have. She always loved Father's library, and I moved it all here. I'll fill this trunk with others of her favorites that she used to read aloud to Father and me."

"She'd like nothing better." One corner of Brutus's mouth lifted. "She told me our similarity in what we wanted in a library weighed in my favor when she considered my proposal. I'm taking my entire collection back for her. History, natural history, and philosophy, but not much poetry."

"Poetry is not her favorite." Sextus stroked the blanket. "Every time I got some poetry for her, she'd thank me most graciously and then tell me to give it to Octavia."

"I learned that with the first codex of Ovid I bought her in Octodurus. I ended up giving it to Antistes."

"Speaking of whom, I wonder why he didn't tell me anything about Sabinus's men coming. Or anything about you or why she trusted you enough to go with you. I know my sister, and she's not one to be enthralled by a handsome face or a large fortune." He suppressed a grin. "Or the build of a gladiator."

"I found it amusing to watch the two of them at meals. Your steward didn't want a domina, and he was glad to be rid of her, whatever that took."

Sextus had been stroking the blanket again, and his hand froze mid-stroke. "Should I replace him?"

"No. I already talked with him about sending Sabinus's people to my estate. Antistes has a good imagination, and I asked him what he thought would happen if he ever did anything that might put her at risk again. It didn't hurt having Africanus scowl."

He rubbed his jaw. "He's served you honestly for ten years. He's proud of that, and it's hard to say what he'd do if stripped of his position. He has many friends. The gain might not be worth the risk. His son is now overseer, and he runs the daily affairs like Damalio trained him. It's only a one-day ride, and Damalio can visit to oversee Antistes as needed."

Three knocks on the door, and Vicarius returned with Damalio.

Brutus rose. "We've taken enough of your time today. There are many still waiting, so we'll leave you to complete the salutation."

"How long will you be in Rome?"

"Tomorrow I have to get things in order at the ludus. Then three days to visit my Liternum estate. I'll be back for two or three more days before we sail to Arelate."

"Perhaps we can dine privately before you leave."

"I'd enjoy that. You can arrange it with Damalio when he returns for the bills of sale. He'll know my schedule by then."

Sextus stood. "I'll look forward to hearing more of how my sister is faring. Vale, Brutus, Damalio."

"Until later." Brutus stood. After Vicarius escorted the two men from the tablinum, Sextus sat and stared at the closed door.

Marcus Brutus, of all men, becoming a Christian? Whatever could have convinced a renowned owner of gladiators to embrace a religion that commanded its followers to love their enemies and taught getting angry was the same as murder? Was that something he could ask Brutus?

He certainly didn't know any other Christian men he could talk to about why they'd risk everything to follow Jesus. Or did he? Maybe they were just hiding it, like Licinia had for so many years, and if he watched closely enough, he'd be able to tell.

# Chapter 62

## A Man of Honor

*The Ludus Bruti, August 27*

Brutus leaned back in his chair, arms crossed, as Felix finished the report on what each of his gladiators wanted.

His lanista picked up the tablets listing the men's decisions and stood. "So, nothing much will change except booking into the arena. All but two of the trainers are choosing to stay on, and more than two thirds of the bodyguards. The twenty that still want to fight on the sand...I've started a list of ludi that will suit them. The seven Germans going with you...they all say they can ride, but I don't know how some of them could have learned."

Africanus, who'd been leaning against the wall, pulled out the guest chair and settled into it. "If that's a problem, we'll solve it in Arelate."

"I guess any man can learn something if he really wants to." The corner of Felix's mouth lifted. "Going home...I guess that's worth a few weeks on a horse, even if you hate them. But doing new things can be hard."

Brutus leaned forward to rest his crossed arms on the desk. "You've been handling all but the finances of the ludus for years. Cellarius will stop by weekly to take care of that and to train you. Before you know it, you'll be as good as the understewards at the estates.

"I'm relying on you as my senior lanista. I visited the Luca and Florentia ludi on the way here. Ursus will help Luca with any problems, and he'll contact you if he has any he can't solve. There's always the horse relay if you need to contact me, but I expect you and Cellarius can handle most things without that."

Felix's chin lifted as a smile appeared. "I want to thank you for freeing me. I'll do my best to justify the trust you're placing in me." His gaze moved between Brutus and Africanus. "But I will miss watching the two of you spar."

"We'll be back for a while next summer. We'll give you a show then. When I get back from Liternum in three or four days, we'll finalize the rest of the manumissions. That's all for now."

As Felix turned to leave, Brutus raised his hand. "One more thing. Is Septimus Sabinus here today?"

"He's with Fortis now."

"Send him to me, but tell Fortis he'll be back so stay available."

When Felix disappeared through the doorway, Brutus picked up a stylus and drummed on the blank tablet in front of him. "Now we'll see if Septimus still shows the potential he did last spring."

"Three months with only Sabinus influence..." Africanus's head shake accompanied a frown. "I'd place no bets on it."

The slap of sandals approached in the hallway.

"We shall see."

Septimus's steps were springy as he entered the room. "You're back. I hope it was a good trip."

"Join us." Brutus pointed at the chair beside Africanus. "I broke my leg, and he almost got killed in a carriage accident. But it was still an excellent trip."

Septimus's eyes saucered. "Broken leg? Almost killed? That's a good trip?"

"It is when the woman whose estate we recovered at decides to become my wife. Lousonna is going to be my permanent home. I wanted you to hear it from me."

The boy's smile vanished. "Will Africanus and Rufus stay here?"

"Rufus is back in Germania now, and we'll be returning in a few days. But I wanted to see how you're doing before we leave."

"Fortis says I'm doing well. He thought in a few months I'd be able to fight Rufus, but if he's not coming back..."

"The rest of my trainers will be here, and Felix will pick the right one when you're ready to move up."

"Will Africanus be coming back?" Septimus directed a hopeful smile toward Africanus before focusing again on Brutus.

"You'll have to ask him. He's a free man now."

Septimus eyebrows rose as his eyes turned. "Congratulations. Will you?"

"I'll probably come with Brutus when he visits Rome, but my family is moving to Germania, too."

"I guess good friends should stay together while they can."

Brutus glanced at Africanus and caught the twitch at the corners of his mouth that signaled he was smiling inside.

"How are you doing, other than your fighting? You do know that's more important?"

Septimus nodded. "I'm making some good friends here, like you said I might. And I think I may have found the kind of friend you talked about, the friend you can trust. Kaeso is my tutor's son. We don't try to prove anything to each other, not like my friends at the ludus. He doesn't just see me as a Flavius Sabinus. He sees me as I am, and that's enough. We can speak truth to each other."

"I'm glad to hear it. Truth and honor define a good man."

"I know, and I try to ask myself what a man of honor would do before I do something. You were right that it makes it easier to make the best choice."

"That truth will carry you through life as a man I would be proud to call son. Remember that."

Septimus squared his shoulders, and a beaming smile lit his eyes. "I won't forget."

"Fortis is waiting for you, and I have some things to finish here before I go out of town for three days. But I'll probably see you again before I return to Germania." He stood, and Septimus followed his example. "I'll be looking forward to seeing how much you improve before we return next year."

Brutus waved his hand toward the door, and Septimus left with a raised chin and proud steps.

When he was out of earshot, Brutus got the flask from his cupboard and poured the last of the Liternum vintage into two goblets. He passed one to Africanus.

Africanus swirled the wine before taking a sip. "I questioned the wisdom of taking on Sabinus's grandson. It looks like you were right. Growing up in a snake pit doesn't have to make you a snake." He raised his goblet. "I salute your success in showing him a better way."

"Our success. I couldn't have done it without you." He lifted his goblet to complete the toast. "To Septimus Flavius Sabinus, another man of honor in Roma."

*The Circus Maximus, Rome, August 29*

Too many people pressed around Manius and Septimus as they approached the Circus Maximus. It was easier to reach their seats when Father, with his circle of guards that held back the crowd, was with them.

Thirty feet ahead of them, Consul Metilius Secundus, surrounded by his lictors, walked with Crassus and his oldest son.

"There's Sextus Crassus. I told him how well you've been doing at Brutus's ludus. Is young Sextus training there yet?"

Septimus craned his neck to see the pair. "He is. He's started training with Pugnus at the same time I'm with Fortis."

"So, you see him often?"

"Almost every time I go."

Manius waved a fly away. "He would be good to get to know. Have you talked with him much?"

"Some of us go to the baths or the taberna next door after we train. He comes along sometimes. He's quiet, so he mostly sits and listens. He doesn't handle a sword well. Marcus Faustus was giving him a hard time until I pointed out Marcus only just moved up to Fortis, and he's been at the ludus almost two years. Now Sextus stays near me and Gaius and Lucius when we go somewhere after training."

Manius's mouth curved up at the corners. "Have you been to his house?"

"No. We're not that close."

"I want you to work on getting close to him. Your grandfather and I would like to know more about his family. If you start dining with them, you can help with that."

"How?"

"We'd like to know who joins them for dinner, what they talk about, who they talk about, and what they say."

"That sounds like spying." Septimus's smile dimmed.

"It's not. It's just gathering information that might be useful. It's important to do that to be able to serve Rome well."

"I'd be making a friend just so I could take advantage of the friendship."

Manius rested his hand on Septimus's shoulder and squeezed. Father would be pleased to hear his grandson was developing a sense of how Roman society worked.

"I don't know if he'll become a good friend, but I'm not going to do anything to trick him into it. And if we do become friends, I'm not going to betray that friendship by revealing his family secrets. That's not what a man of honor would do."

"Loyal friendship is a good thing. I won't ask you to betray it."

He waved his hand in front of his face, then slapped his shoulder before sweeping something off. But he swatted an imaginary fly only to hide the true reason for his frown.

Father had his finger on the pulse of Rome. He wanted to know everything about anyone he deemed important. Knowledge was power, and he wielded it with ruthless precision.

But there were things his father didn't need to know, and this was one conversation Father would never hear about.

*The Brutus estate, last night before heading home*

The evening sky had passed through orange to red when Brutus climbed the low hill to the edge of the grove and sat by Camilla's grave. He'd done it so often before the trip. His people at the Roma estate expected it, and he didn't want to give cause for wondering why he didn't do it at least once before he left.

She wasn't really there. But even Calvia wondered whether those who'd gone to Jesus before them knew what was happening on earth. She thought they still prayed for those left behind, but did they know the answers to those prayers?

He sat and rested his hand on the grass that had grown lush since he'd placed her body in a coffin and put it in the ground.

"I don't know if you can hear me, but in case you can, I have some things to tell you. Marcus is growing well. You'd be proud of our son. He has your eyes, and every time he laughs, it's like you're with me again. I'm trying to be the father you thought I could be. I watch Africanus with his boys, and that helps."

He plucked a blade of grass. "The woman who convinced you to become a Christian...I found her after I stopped looking. I was never going to hurt her, but I had to know who she was. Her brother had renamed her Calvia and hidden her near Octodurus. She took us in after a carriage accident. When she prayed for Africanus as he was dying, God healed him. He's a Christian now."

He split the wide end of the blade and tore it in half. "You told me you wanted two things most of all: to give me a son and to have me with you for eternity. You'll have both. Africanus convinced me to follow Jesus, too."

He tossed the pieces over his shoulder and plucked another blade. "I still miss you every day. I will until the moment I die. But I'm keeping my promise not to grieve too deeply or too long. God had other plans for me. Calvia and I have married. Together we'll raise Marcus to know the Lord. Someday, we four will be reunited."

He split the second blade. "I might not come here again. I'm moving to the Lousonna estate. It's safer than Roma for Christians. But I know you're not really here. No matter where I am, I'll know you're waiting for me with the Lord. I'll tell Marcus how we loved the night sky, and each time we watch the stars appear, I'll thank God for you."

The fate of a man's soul. There was a time when he thought it impossible to know, but now he knew better. Eternity with Jesus awaited, and Camilla and Calvia would share it with him.

Brutus sat in silent contentment, watching the points of light appear one by one as the sky darkened, and the stars they'd counted so many times together laughed and sang for joy.

*Finis*

### I'd Love to Hear from You!

If you enjoyed this book, it would be a real gift to me if you would post a review at the retailer you purchased it from. A good review is like a jewel set in gold for an author. Other great places to share reviews are Goodreads and BookBub. If you've read others in the series, it would be great if you post a review of those, too.

I'd also love to hear from you at carol-ashby.com or directly at carolashbyauthor@gmail.com.

**Want to hear about upcoming releases in the Light in the Empire series and free gifts only for newsletter subscribers?**

For free gifts and other special offers, advance notices of upcoming releases, and info about my latest writing adventures, please sign up for my newsletter at https://carol-ashby.com/newsletter/.

# Light *in the* Empire Series



*Honor Bound* is the eighth volume in the Light in the Empire series, which follows the interconnected lives of four Roman families during the reigns of Trajan and Hadrian. Each can be read stand-alone. The nine novels of the series will take you around the Empire, from Germania and Britannia to Thracia, Dacia, and Judaea and, of course, to Rome itself.

## Coming Soon: Please Help Me Choose!
### Who would you like to see in a future story?

I grew to love several of the characters in *Honor Bound* while I was writing. That usually happens, and often the next story for a character takes shape in my head even before I finish. But sometimes that next hero or heroine is chosen because readers tell me who needs to come back as a story lead.

Readers who loved Galen as a teen in *Blind Ambition* wanted to see him as a grown man, so he became the hero in *Faithful.* Since people kept asking what happened to Leander's beloved but long-lost sister in *True Freedom*, it was clear Ariana would need her own story in *Hope Unchained.* I hope the people who asked for Brutus and Africanus to have their own story will be pleased with what happens to them in *Honor Bound.*

But there are many more characters in the books of the series that I would like to spend more time with, and I hope there are some for you, too. Who would you most like to see in a future story? What was it about them that made you want more of them? I'd love to hear what you think. It will guide what I write next.

Some possibilities:
Aulus or Tribune Titianus of *True Freedom*?
Ursus of *Hope Unchained*?
Septimus or Sextus of *Honor Bound*?
Someone else I haven't mentioned? (I can't wait to see who shows up here!)

Please tell me who you'd love to see again as a comment at carol-ashby.com or directly at carolashbyauthor@gmail.com!

I'm planning to write a short story or novella about someone from Sextus's or Calvia's households in *Honor Bound* or Gracchus of *Hope Unchained* to give to newsletter subscribers. Which would you rather have?

Please go to my website, carol-ashby.com, and share your thoughts in the comment box. Sign up for the newsletter, and you'll get the story when I finish it. Looking forward to hearing from you!

# Historical Note

## Christians as Criminals Under Roman Law

While Christians were regarded as a sect of Judaism for the first few years, they were partially tolerated by the state. That soon changed. Nero used the Christians as scapegoats for the fire of AD 64 that burned large areas of Rome, killing many for his own entertainment in his private circus. Trajan expressed his approval of Pliny the Younger's policy in Bithynia and Pontus of giving Christians three chances to recant and sacrifice to Caesar before executing them.

Why was being a follower of Jesus of Nazareth considered a heinous crime by the Roman authorities, condemning them to *damnatio ad bestias*, the feeding of condemned criminals to beasts, in arenas around the Empire? There were several reasons based on Roman law.

1) Treason

Christians were considered guilty of treason (*maiestas*). When it became mandatory to honor images of the emperor with libations and incense, they refused. Jews also refused, but they were allowed to do so by special exception as members of an officially sanctioned religion. When enough Gentiles became Christians and believers broke with following the details of Mosaic Law, Christianity was no longer considered a sect of Judaism. Under the rules of the Twelve Tables, Christians followed a new, foreign, and unauthorized religion (*religio nova, peregrina et illicita*).

2) Sacrilege

The Christians' refusal to worship the state gods was considered a sacrilege that might bring down the wrath of the Roman gods, threatening the Empire with disaster. The state religion was dependent on the rituals being performed correctly, regardless of the personal beliefs of those celebrating. There was a strong element of magic in the rituals, and the slightest mistake could render the ritual ineffective. The refusal of Christians to participate was, therefore, totally unacceptable.

3) Unlawful assembly

Rome did not allow freedom of assembly. During the Republic, any meeting with political overtones had to be presided over by a magistrate. The distaste for unsupervised gatherings continued into the Empire. Guilds (*collegia*) and associations (*sodalicia*), especially secret societies, were suspect for political reasons. From the mid-50s BC on, guilds and associations had to obtain a license from the state and were not permitted to meet more than once a month. Christians gathered in secret and at night, which made their gatherings "unlawful assemblies," throwing them into the same class of crime as riots.

The use of *damnatio ad bestias* for the offense of merely being a Christian was embraced by Nero, but the sentence was not applied at all times and in all parts of the Empire. Other methods of execution were employed where no arena was handy. The enthusiasm with which a particular province persecuted its Christians varied with the individual governor when there was no specific imperial edict in effect. Emperors who decreed Empire-wide persecution included Marcus Aurelius (AD 177), Trajan Decius (AD 249-251) Diocletian (AD 284-305), and Maximian (AD 286-305).

In *Honor Bound,* Licinia's brother Sextus finds himself in a no-win situation. Not a Christian himself, he and their now-dead father had concealed her faith for many years to protect her. As a *praetor* who sits in judgement over people who break Roman law, it's his job to deal with Roman citizens who have become Christians, with penalties ranging from loss of property and exile to execution. If he doesn't want his beloved sister killed, he must send her far away from Rome, hoping she will be safe once she is where his political enemies can't easily find her and expose her faith. But no matter how good that strategy had seemed, God had other plans.

For more on how Roman provincial governors, like Pliny, dealt with their noncitizen Christians and how Emperor Trajan responded, there's an article at the back of *Blind Ambition* and also at my Roman history website:

https://carolashby.com/historical-background-blind-ambition/

For more about life in the Roman Empire at its peak, please go to carolashby.com.

## The Daily Life of Gladiators: Celebrities Yet Social Outcasts in the Roman World

Perhaps the most widely recognized symbol of ancient Rome is the Colosseum, started by the first Flavian emperor, Vespasian, in AD 72 and finished by his son and successor, Titus, in AD 80. During the Imperial era, Romans called it the Flavian Amphitheater after the dynasty that build it. Nothing epitomizes the Roman attitude toward the value of human life better than this marvel of Roman architecture that let up to 85,000 people watch as men fought and died, urged on by the roar of the blood-thirsty crowd. Perhaps as many as four hundred amphitheaters were spread across the Empire, ranging from wooden structures, which might seat one to ten thousand, to stone or concrete marvels that are still in use today for bull fights, concerts, and film festivals in Arles and Nimes in France and Pula in Croatia.

The typical schedule for the Roman games involved more than gladiatorial contests. The morning was filled with animal events, ranging from hunts to *damnatio ad bestias*, the feeding of condemned criminals to beasts. Irenaeus (AD 130-202, Bishop of Lugdunum in Gaul) reported that Ignatius of Antioch was fed to the lions in Rome in AD 107 for the crime of refusing to worship the Roman gods. Condemned criminals or prisoners of war might be forced to fight each other until only one remained to be killed by a gladiator. But the real excitement came in the afternoon, when professional gladiators met in one-on-one combat, fighting until one was dead or so badly injured he was forced to admit defeat.

A loser who fought well enough was often spared to fight again, so the odds of surviving a single fight were about five to one. The typical gladiator fought only two or three times a year. Half died during their first year in the arena, but for those who survived their "rookie year," life after the arena was a real possibility. That life might even be long; a memorial stone in a gladiator cemetery in Ephesus was erected by the family of a retired gladiator who died at age 99.

But how did someone become a gladiator, and what was life like during the 360-plus days of the year when a gladiator wasn't entertaining the masses in mortal combat?

While gladiators were admired for their courage and fighting skills, they were social outcasts. Like a prostitute, a gladiator was an *infamis*, a person of low repute. He couldn't vote or hold public office, and many burial grounds refused to accept a gladiator's remains.

Many became gladiators through no choice of their own. Over half of the fighters in a gladiatorial school (*ludus*) were slaves. Many were taken as prisoners of war and sold into the arena with some fighting skills. Some were slaves who had proven too hard to handle. Some were condemned criminals. These came in two categories: condemned to the sword (*damnatio ad gladium*) and condemned to the games (*damnatio ad ludos*). While those condemned to the sword would be killed during their first appearance in the arena, men condemned to the games could survive as long as they fought well enough and might even hope to be freed someday. If the sponsor hosting the games decided to free a gladiator, he could pay the purchase price to the owner and award a wooden sword to the fighter as the symbol of his freedom.

Some gladiators were free men who were paid a sizable sum of money to sign a contract with a ludus for a fixed period of time, typically four or five years. During the term of the contract, they belonged to the ludus as if they were slaves, swearing the gladiator oath to submit to anything the ludus owner wanted, including having them killed. These voluntary gladiators were called *auctoratii.*

Some auctoratii needed the money to pay debts before they were sold into permanent slavery to pay them. Sometimes former soldiers, especially those who had been dishonorably discharged and were already *infames*, chose to become gladiators if they had no other job prospects. Some were gladiator slaves who had been freed and chose to continue in their profession after receiving their freedom.

While the vast majority of gladiators were men, women gladiators have been pictured in mosaics and listed as special attractions. Whether these were slaves or auctoratii isn't known.

The head trainer of a ludus was the *lanista*, a man who had been a successful gladiator himself. While the lanista was an infamis at the bottom of society, the wealthy Roman who owned the ludus was usually a well-respected member of Roman society. A large ludus might have several hundred fighters, and the money to be made feeding the Roman lust for bloodshed was attractive to many businessmen in the equestrian order. A sponsor of the games hired the gladiators through the schools. For every fighter who died, the sponsor payed a fixed fee based on the ranking of the gladiator, so win or lose, the owner of a ludus made money on every match.

The training regimen for a gladiator was vigorous. Many hours were spent daily practicing with wooden swords weighted to be twice as heavy as real metal ones and shields heavier than those used in combat. Muscles were built up to a level that bones were deformed. Attack and counter-attack were practiced until responses were reflexive and instantaneous. Stamina, strength, and intimate knowledge of how an opponent would fight could make the difference between life and death. Bouts seldom lasted 30 minutes and might be over in a minute, but a longer, fiercer fight might impress the crowd enough that the loser might be spared to fight again. A new gladiator usually trained for a year or more before his first appearance in a professional bout.

The intense training burned many calories, so gladiators were fed large quantities of a mostly vegetarian diet. The gladiator diet differed from the civilian diet in several ways. While wheat bread was a staple for most Romans, gladiators ate mostly barley. Some fruit and vegetables were combined with ample servings of barley porridge (polenta). The goal was to have a layer of fat overlying vulnerable blood vessels and nerves so a shallow cut wouldn't prove disastrous. Fat tissue can bleed impressively, making spectators marvel at the fighter's ability to continue the battle, while not being a crippling injury. To build strong bones, a drink made from the ashes of bones and charred wood was served.

Gladiators and former gladiators worked outside the arena as bodyguards, debt collectors, and enforcers to settle disputes. They also served as sparring partners and personal trainers for men and for women who wanted to fight privately.

Memorial stones in gladiator cemeteries provide ample evidence that many gladiators married and raised families. The stones usually list the names of the relatives erecting the stones and the number of fights, the number of wins, and the age at death. Many died in battle in their twenties or early thirties, but others lived to die a natural death.

The popularity of the games didn't wane until Christianity became the dominant religion. Emperor Constantine replaced sentences that condemned a criminal to die as a gladiator with condemnation to work in the mines, and Emperor Valentinian III banned gladiatorial contests in AD 438.

In *Honor Bound*, Africanus has been a gladiator since he was kidnapped from his home south of Egypt at fourteen. Both he and Rufus, who was born to a father who was himself a gladiator slave, are comfortable in the world of the arenas and proud of their ability to win. Brutus, who has been managing the gladiatorial portion of the family enterprises since his early twenties, sees nothing wrong with men being specially trained to fight for the entertainment of others, even when that means killing an opponent and maybe dying themselves. When confronted with the reality of a god who condemns murder and commands love for both neighbors and enemies, they face the challenge of reconciling their life with the demands of a god whose reality they cannot deny.

For more about life in the Roman Empire at its peak, please go to carolashby.com.

# Discussion Guide

1) Licinia, led to Jesus by older cousins in her youth, lives in a politically prominent Roman household. She's loved and shielded by her father and her brother Sextus, but she's been isolated in her faith after her cousins must flee or be killed. Do you know someone who's been in that position? What did they do to keep their faith strong? If faced with that yourself, what would help you stay strong in your faith?

2) Licinia knows the danger of her faith being revealed, but relieving the suffering of a friend leads to her reveal it. Where does that lead? Would you have made the choice she did?

3) When Sextus learns his enemy is after Licinia and her faith might get her killed, he sends her to their distant estate. But first he renames her Calvia and gives her a fake identity as a married woman. How does she feel about pretending to be someone she isn't? What problems does it cause? What problems does it solve? Have you ever wanted to be someone other than who you are?

4) Marcus Brutus is a man of unquestioned integrity and a devoted husband. When he's devastated by the loss of his beloved Camilla, he's furious with the person he blames for encouraging his wife to try what killed her. He hates the unknown woman who persuaded her to become a Christian, but he promised Camilla he wouldn't hurt her. How does he balance his promise with his desire for vengeance? How is that different from how Christians are supposed to act?

5) Africanus was taken as a slave and trained from age 14 to kill or die. Although it wasn't originally his choice, he's comfortable with being a gladiator. He even finds satisfaction in fighting and is proud of his unparalleled skill in the arena. What leads him to reexamine his life?

6) In a society where class distinctions control so much of life, the noble equestrian Brutus chooses his slave Africanus as his closest

friend, despite gladiators being the lowest rung of the social ladder. Why did he do that?

7) Africanus is sympathetic to Brutus's deepest grief, but he pushes him to return to normal life and to become a good father to baby Marcus instead of blaming his son for his wife's death. Have you known someone who's done the same for a grieving friend?

8) Brutus moves from deep anger with the Licinia of his imagination to friendship and finally love with Calvia. What made that possible?

9) Why did Damalio become a Christian? How did he live his faith while being a slave?

10) Brutus decides to mentor Septimus Sabinus, a young man who's not yet corrupted by the bad influences of his father and grandfather. Why did he decide to do that? If you had the chance, would you do the same?

11) *Honor Bound* is a story of loss and new beginnings, of love and hatred and forgiveness that opens the door to a brighter future blessed by God. What touched you most? What made you think about what your own choices would be?

## WHO WOULD YOU LIKE TO SEE
### IN A FUTURE SHORT STORY OR NOVELLA?

I grew to love several of the characters in *Honor Bound* while I was writing. That usually happens, and often the next story for a character takes shape in my head even before I finish. I knew Ariana would need her own story after introducing her as Leander's beloved but long-lost sister in *True Freedom*. But there are many people in *Honor Bound* that I would like to spend more time with, and I hope there are some for you, too. Who would you most like to see in a future story? What was it about them that made you want more of them? I'd love to hear what you think.

I'm planning to write the story of what happens next to either someone from Sextus's or Calvia's household or Gracchus of *Hope Unchained* to give to newsletter subscribers. Which would you rather have?

Please go to my website, carol-ashby.com, and share your thoughts in the comment box. Sign up for the newsletter, and you'll get the story when I finish it. Looking forward to hearing from you!

# Glossary


*Latin words in italics*

*Assa*: dry-nurse, nurse, nanny

*Auxilia*: large military units of soldiers who were not Roman citizens

*Balneae*: a smaller Roman bath-house

*Bulla*: an amulet worn like a locket given to baby boys nine days after birth.

Charon: boatman who was believed to ferry Roman souls across River Styx to Hades for judgement

*Caldarium*: hot, steamy room with a hot plunge bath at a Roman bath complex

*Caupona*: inn, canteen, tavern; sometimes a place to find prostitutes

*Centurion*: 1st level officer over 80 men; rises through the ranks based on merit

*Cisium*: two-wheeled carriage with forward-facing seat located above the axle

*Corbita*: merchant sailing ship

*Cunaria*: nanny, dry-nurse

*Cursus honorum*: the order of public offices held by men of the senatorial order; a mixture of military and political posts held in sequence: tribune, questor, aedile (optional), praetor, provincial governor, and for the most elite, consul.

*Decurion*: Roman cavalry officer commanding a squad (*turma*) of 30 men

*Denarius*: (plural *denarii*) silver coin worth about one day's living wage

*Doctor*: teacher; in gladiatorial schools, a trainer who assists the *lanista*

*Domina*: female head of a Roman household.

*Dominus*: male head of a Roman household who might not be the *paterfamilias*

*Duplicarius*: second in command to a cavalry decurion.

*Dupondius*: brass coin worth 1/8 *denarius*

Equestrian order: 2nd highest class of Roman citizens; required personal wealth greater than 100,000 *denarii*

*Familia*: the Roman family unit consisting of the paterfamilias, his married and unmarried children regardless of age, and his slaves

*Familia gladiatorii Bruti*: members of one of the gladiatorial schools (*ludi*) of Brutus

*Familia rustica*: the slaves of a rural estate

*Gladius*: short thrusting sword used by the Roman military and some gladiators (*secutors*)

*Hippodrome*: an oval stadium for horse and chariot races

*Ides*: 15th of March, May, July, October; 13th of other months

*Infames*: people of the lowest social class, includes gladiators, prostitutes, and actors

*Kalends*: first day of the month

*Laconicum*: the dry sweating room of the Roman bath complex, adjacent to the caldarium

*Lanista*: the head trainer of a gladiatorial school

*Latrunculi*: military strategy board game involving trapping and removing captured stones

*Lictor*: an officer attending the consul or other magistrate (praetors and above)

*Ludi*: "games," especially public spectacles like gladiatorial contests

*Ludus*: (pural *ludi*) training school for gladiators

*Ludus Bruti*: the gladiator school, including all the trainers, fighters, and slaves belonging to Brutus

*Mansio*: roadside guest quarters for traveling Roman officials

*Mater*: mother

*Milia, milia passuum*: Roman miles. 1 Roman mile (*mille passus*, thousand paces) = 0.92 miles or 1.48 km

*Murmillo*: gladiator type who fights with gladius. large shield, and helmet

*Natatorium*: a swimming pool

*Nones*: 7th of March, May, July, October; 5th of other months

*Nutrix*: wet-nurse, woman who breastfeeds another woman's baby

*Optio*: (plural *optiones*) Roman junior officer ranked below centurion

*Optio statorum*: optio of the military police

*Palla*: rectangular cloth wrap worm by Roman women

*Palus*: wooden stake struck with a sword during gladiatorial practice

*Paterfamilias*: oldest living male of an extended Roman family; the patriarch who owns everything

Plain of Asphodel: pleasant part of Hades where souls of good people were supposed to go

*Plaustrum*: a wagon for carrying goods, often with 4 wheels,

Peregrine: a person who is not a Roman citizen

*Praetor*: Roman magistrate elected each year to serve as judge

*Raeda*: a four-wheeled closed-in carriage

*Retiarius*: gladiator type who fights with net and trident

Rondel: a circular object or shape, used as a game piece for board games

Salutation: daily ritual during which prominent citizens received clients and others seeking favors

*Salve*: Hello, standard Latin greeting

*Saturni*: Saturday

*Satyricon*: a work of fiction by Petronius famous for its erotic passages

*Secutor*: gladiator type who fights with gladius. large shield, and helmet

Senatorial order: highest class of Roman citizens; required personal wealth greater than 250,000 denarii

*Sestertius*: (plural *sesterces*) Roman coin worth 1/4 denarius, also called sesterce

*Solis*: Sunday

*Spurius*: illegitimate, born out of wedlock, *nothus*

*Stadia*: Roman units for distances: 1 mile = 8.7 stadia; 1 km = 5.4 stadia

*Stola*: a long robe worn by married women fastened by clasps at the shoulder and worn over a tunic

*Tabellarius*: courier, usually a slave, hired to carry private mail

*Taberna*: tavern or shop selling prepared food

*Tablinum*: the main office and reception room for the Roman master of the house

*Tabula*: popular Roman board game, often played with betting, similar to backgammon

*Tabularium*: the central official records office of the Roman Empire, located in Rome.

Tartarus: place of darkness and torture where Roman souls were believed to remain until they atoned for sins; could eventually go to the Plain of Asphodel

*Tepidarium*: the warm room at a Roman bath complex with radiant heat from floor and walls

*Thermae*: a Roman bath complex, the "baths"

*Thermopolium*: a shop selling hot foods and drinks

*Triclinium*: formal Roman dining room

*Turma*: a cavalry unit of 30 men commanded by a decurion

*Vale*: Goodbye, standard Latin farewell

*Veneris*: Friday

*Vestibulum*: short hallway between the entrance door and the atrium

*Virtus*: the Roman virtue of manliness that embodies valor, courage, honor, excellence

# Scripture References

In Chapter 41, Damalio shares truths from Scripture with Africanus, who shares them later with Brutus in Chapters 55 and 56. Some key ones are listed here.

And behold, a certain lawyer stood up and tested Him, saying, "Teacher, what shall I do to inherit eternal life?"

He said to him, "What is written in the law? What is your reading *of it?*"

So he answered and said, "'You shall love the LORD your God with all your heart, with all your soul, with all your strength, and with all your mind,' and 'your neighbor as yourself.'"

Luke 10:25-27 (NKJV)

For the life of the flesh *is* in the blood, and I have given it to you upon the altar to make atonement for your souls; for it *is* the blood *that* makes atonement for the soul.

Leviticus 17:11(NKJV)

Because, if you confess with your lips that Jesus is Lord and believe in your heart that God raised him from the dead, you will be saved. For man believes with his heart and so is justified, and he confesses with his lips and so is saved.

Romans 10:9-10 (NKJV)

Then one of the criminals who were hanged blasphemed Him, saying, "If You are the Christ, save Yourself and us."

But the other, answering, rebuked him, saying, "Do you not even fear God, seeing you are under the same condemnation?

"And we indeed justly, for we receive the due reward of our deeds; but this Man has done nothing wrong."

Then he said to Jesus, "Lord, remember me when You come into Your kingdom."

And Jesus said to him, "Assuredly, I say to you, today you will be with Me in Paradise."

Luke 23:39-43 (NKJV)

He was in the world, and the world was made through Him, and the world did not know Him. He came to His own, and His own did not receive Him. But as many as received Him, to them He gave the right to become children of God, to those who believe in His name: who were born, not of blood, nor of the will of the flesh, nor of the will of man, but of God. And the Word became flesh and dwelt among us, and we beheld His glory, the glory as of the only begotten of the Father, full of grace and truth.

John 1:10-14 (NKJV)

# Acknowledgements

Above all, I thank God for this opportunity to tell a story of how He can use those who love Him to help lost souls find peace and joy as children of God. I loved writing how God brought Brutus and Africanus to the point of decision and beyond and how He can heal a broken heart as friendship turns to love. It doesn't get better than writing about lives being transformed by forgiveness and love.

No one can write the best book possible without the help of many others. I want to thank Andrew Budek-Schmeisser for being my critique partner, prayer partner, and good friend. Despite serious health problems, he's always been willing to share his knowledge of good writing, his spiritual insight, and his expertise with horses, combat, and low-tech field medicine. Based on personal experience, he told me Brutus would hear his bone snap and how a break like that feels as it heals. Ouch! Whenever I wanted to try out the latest scene on someone, he was usually online and fast on the feedback. He's helped me with *The Legacy*, *Faithful*, *Second Chances*, *True Freedom*, *Hope Unchained*, and *Honor Bound*, and with many brainstorming sessions about characters for future volumes. None of the books would have been the same without him.

I'm especially thankful for my top alpha beta and treasured friend, Lisa Garcia, who's a wise woman of God and true kindred spirit. She's great at seeing where there's too little or too much to get the story just right. She's also so good at spotting typos that I'll never need a copy editor. Her prayers always help me get the hard parts right.

I also want to thank Sherril Stinnett, my new alpha beta who read the book in sections as I wrote it, helping me make each better even before I wrote the next and spotting some places where a bit more was needed. Her prayers were invaluable, too.

Terry Shoebotham, my local writing buddy and prayer partner, also beta-read part of the manuscript. She's a joy to talk books with.

It wouldn't be possible to write the spiritual sections without my prayer partners. Katie Powner is an award-winning author herself whose debut novel is coming this fall. Thanks also to Mesu Andrews for being my prayer partner for inspiration and meeting deadlines and for being someone with whom I can always share cool archeology reports.

My line editor, Wendy Chorot, has once more blessed me with her skill as an editor and her insights for making the deep spiritual scenes reflect real life. She's a delight to work with as well.

Each time I think Roseanna White couldn't possibly design a better cover than the last one, and each time she proves me wrong. It never ceases to amaze me how she starts with a collection of separate images and combines them to get something that looks like the Romans had color photography. To get the men on the cover right, she took the photos I shot of my son in the two tunics I sewed and transplanted heads and arms and legs to make Africanus and Brutus come alive on the cover. Yet again, she created a design that captures the relationships between the characters in a cover both men and women can love.

I especially want to thank my son, Paul, who posed for Brutus and Africanus to give Roseanna the images she needed. That's his leg that Africanus has resting on the rock. My daughter, Lydia, is inside the woman's tunic and that's her arm as well. I couldn't have better kids when I need help with something.

But my special thanks go to my amazing husband, Jim. He makes every day better with his humor and kindness. It's so easy to write about men who are smart, funny, kind, and patient when you live with one every day.

# About the Author

Carol Ashby has been a professional writer for most of her life, but her articles and books were about lasers and compound semiconductors (the electronics that make cell phones, laser pointers, and LED displays work). She still writes about light, but her Light in the Empire series tells stories of difficult friendships and life-changing decisions in dangerous times, where forgiveness and love open hearts to discover their own faith in Christ. Her fascination with the Roman Empire was born during her first middle-school Latin class. A research career in New Mexico inspires her to get every historical detail right so she can spin stories that make her readers feel like they're living under the Caesars themselves.

Read her articles about many facets of life in the Roman Empire at carolashby.com, or join her at her blog, The Beauty of Truth, at carol-ashby.com.

# LIGHT *in the* EMPIRE SERIES



The Light in the Empire Series follows the interconnected lives of four Roman families during the reigns of Trajan and Hadrian. Join them as they travel the Empire, from Germania and Britannia to Thracia, Dacia, and Judaea and, of course, to Rome itself.

***Forgiven***

*Are some wounds too deep to forgive?*

With a ruthless father who murdered for the family inheritance, Marcus Drusus plans to do the same. In AD 122, Marcus follows his brother Lucius to Judaea and plots to frame a zealot for his older brother's death. But the plan goes awry, and Lucius is rescued by a Messianic Jewish woman. Her oldest brother is a zealot and a Roman soldier killed her twin, but Rachel still persuades her father Joseph to put his love for Jesus above his anger with Rome and hide Lucius until he heals.

Rachel cares for the enemy, and more than broken bones heal as duty turns to love. Lucius embraces Joseph's faith in Jesus, but sharing a faith doesn't heal all wounds. Even before revealed secrets slice open old scars, Joseph wants no Roman son-in-law. With Rachel's zealot brother suspecting he's a Roman officer and his own brother planning to kill him when he returns, can Lucius survive long enough to change Joseph's mind?

### *Blind Ambition*

*Sometimes you have to almost die to discover how you want to live.*

It's AD 114 in the Roman province of Germania Superior, and being a Christian carries a death sentence. Tribune Decimus Lentulus is on the fast track for a stellar political career back in Rome. When he's robbed, blinded, and left for dead, a young German woman who follows the Way finds him. Valeria knows it's his duty to have her and her family killed, but she chooses to obey Jesus's command to love her enemy and takes him home to care for him.

It's not his miraculous recovery that shakes Decimus to his core. It's the way they love him like family and their unconcealed love for Jesus. In spite of himself, he falls in love with the Christian woman Rome wants him to kill. Can Valeria hide her faith to follow him into the circles of Roman power? Or should he abandon his ambition to help rule the Empire and choose to follow a different way?

**The Legacy**

*When Rome has taken everything, what's left for a man to give?*

Betrayed by a ruthless son who'll do anything for power and wealth, Publius Drusus faces death with an unanswered prayer—that his treasured daughter, Claudia, and honorable son, Titus, will someday share his faith. But who will lead them to the truth once he's gone?

Claudia's oldest brother Lucius arranged their father's execution to inherit everything, and now he's forcing her to marry a cruel Roman power broker. If only she could get to Titus—a thousand miles away in Thracia. Then the man who secretly told her father about Jesus arranges for his son Philip to sneak her out of Rome and take her to the brother she can trust.

A childhood accident scarred Philip's face. A woman's rejection scarred his heart. Claudia's gratitude grows into love, but what can Philip do when the first woman who returns his love hates the God he loves even more?

Titus and Claudia hunger for revenge on their brother and the Christians they blame for their father's deadly conversion. When Titus buys Miriam, a secret Christian, to serve his sister, he starts them all down a path of conflicting loyalties and dangerous decisions. His father's final letter commands the forgiveness Titus refuses to give. What will it take to free him from the hatred poisoning his own heart?

Join the people you met in *Second Chances* eight years earlier in this tale of betrayal, hatred, love, and forgiveness, where even bad things can work together for good.

### Faithful

*Is the price of true friendship ever too high?*

In AD 122, Adela, the fiery daughter of a Germanic chieftain, is kidnapped and taken across the Roman frontier to be sold as a slave. When horse-trader Otto wins her while gambling with her kidnappers, he entrusts her to his friend and trading partner, Galen. Then Otto is kidnapped by the same men, and Galen must track them half way across the Empire before his best friend loses a fight to the death in a Roman arena.

Adela joins Galen in the chase, hungry for vengeance. As the perilous journey deepens their friendship, will the kind, faithful man open her eyes to a life she never dreamed she'd want?

A trip to the heart of the Empire poses mortal danger to a man who follows Jesus, especially when he must seek the help of an enemy of the faith for Otto to survive. Tiberius hunted Christians when he governed Germania Superior and banished his own son when he became one.

When Tiberius learns sparing Galen offers a chance at reconciliation, he joins the trio on their journey home. Can his animosity toward the followers of Jesus survive a trip with the Christian man whose courage and faithfulness demand his respect?

Follow the continuing saga of the people you met in *Blind Ambition* from the frontier of Germany to the heart of the Empire.

***Second Chances***

*Must the shadows of the past destroy the hope of the future?*

In AD 122, Cornelia Scipia, proud daughter of one of Rome's noblest families, learns her adulterous husband plans to betroth their daughter to the vicious son of his best friend. Over her dead body! Cornelia divorces him, reclaims her enormous dowry, and kidnaps her own daughter. She plans to start over with Drusilla a thousand miles away. No more husbands for her. But she didn't count on meeting Hector, the widowed Greek captain of the ship carrying her to her new life.

Devastated by the loss of his wife and daughter, Hector's heart begins to heal as he befriends Drusilla. Cornelia's sacrificial love for Drusilla and her courage and humor in the face of the unknown earn his admiration...as a friend. Is he ready for more?

Marriage to the kind, honest sea captain would give Drusilla the father she deserves...and Cornelia the faithful husband she's always longed for. But while her ex-husband hunts them to drag Drusilla back to Rome, secrets in Hector's past and the chasm between their social classes and different faiths erect complicated barriers to any future together. Will God give two lonely hearts a second chance at happiness?

Join the people you met in *The Legacy* eight years later in this tale of hope and a future never imagined until God opens the door.

*True Freedom*

*The chains we cannot see can be the hardest ones to break.*

When Aulus runs up a gambling debt to his father's political enemy, he's desperate to pay it off before his father returns to Rome. His best friend Marcus suggests they fake the kidnapping of Aulus's sister Julia and use the ransom money. But when the man they hired kidnaps her for real, Aulus is catapulted into a desperate search to find her.

Torn from his childhood home by Rome's conquering armies and sold as a farm slave to labor until he dies, Dacius's faith gives him strength to bear what he must and serve without complaining. After a deadly accident makes him one of Julia's litter bearers, he overhears Marcus advising her brother to kidnap her. When Dacius almost dies thwarting the kidnapping, a Christian couple pretend Julia and Dacius are their children to keep her brother from finding them before her father returns.

But pretending to be free again makes returning to slavery more than Dacius can bear, while acting like a common woman opens Julia's eyes to dreams and destinies she never knew existed. With her brother closing in and her father almost home, can she find a way around Roman law and custom to free them both for the future they long for?

Find out what happens to Ariana's brother Diegis twelve years later in this tale of hope and a future never imagined until God opens the door.

### *Hope Unchained*

*Can the deepest loss bring the greatest gain?*

Rome's conquering army took Ariana's family and freedom, but nothing can take her faith in Jesus. When she rescues a tribune's wife from certain death, her reward is freedom and a chance to free her brother and sister. But first she must catch up with the slave caravan before they vanish forever, and tracking them from Dacia to the coast seems impossible for one woman alone.

Discharged from the legion with a hand crippled by a Dacian knife, Donatus faces a future without hope. When the tribune asks him to escort Ariana on her quest, it's the only work he can find. It means four weeks with a Dacian woman and a gladiator bodyguard, but it takes money to eat. A man without options must take what he can get.

But a lot can happen in four weeks. Even battle-hardened men can be touched by love and forgiveness, and it's easier to face an enemy with a sword than to face the truth. When his moment of truth comes, what will Donatus choose, and what will that mean for both of them?

If you read *True Freedom* and wondered what happened to Leander's beloved sister Ariana, you can find out in *Hope Unchained.*

If you enjoyed this book, it would be a real gift to me if you would post a review at the retailer you purchased it from. A good review is like a jewel set in gold for an author. Other great places to share reviews are Goodreads and BookBub. If you've read others in the series, it would be great if you post a review of those, too.

I'd also love to hear from you at carol-ashby.com or directly at carolashbyauthor@gmail.com.

**Want to hear about upcoming releases in the Light in the Empire series and free gifts only for newsletter subscribers?**

For free gifts and other special offers, advance notices of upcoming releases, and info about my latest writing adventures, I hope you'll sign up for my newsletter at carol-ashby.com.

**Who would you like to see in a future story?**
**Help me pick what to write next!**

I grew to love several of the characters in *Honor Bound* while I was writing. That usually happens, and often the next story for a character takes shape in my head even before I finish. But sometimes that next hero or heroine is chosen because readers tell me who needs to come back as a story lead.

Readers who loved Galen as a teen in *Blind Ambition* wanted to see him as a grown man, so he became the hero in *Faithful*. Since people kept asking what happened to Leander's beloved but long-lost sister in *True Freedom*, it was clear Ariana would need her own story in *Hope Unchained*. I hope the people who asked for Brutus and Africanus to have their own story will be pleased with what happens to them in *Honor Bound*.

But there are many more characters in the books of the series that I would like to spend more time with, and I hope there are some for you, too. Who would you most like to see in a future story? What was it about them that made you want more of them? I'd love to hear what you think. It will guide what I write next.

Some possibilities:
Aulus or Tribune Titianus of *True Freedom*?

Ursus of *Hope Unchained*?

Septimus or Sextus of *Honor Bound*?

Someone else I haven't mentioned? (I can't wait to see who shows up here!)

Please tell me who you'd love to see again as a comment at
carol-ashby.com or directly at carolashbyauthor@gmail.com!

I'm planning to write a short story or novella about someone from Sextus's or Calvia's households in *Honor Bound* or Gracchus of *Hope Unchained* to give to newsletter subscribers. Which would you rather have?

Please go to my website, carol-ashby.com, and share your thoughts in the comment box. Sign up for the newsletter, and you'll get the story when I finish it. Looking forward to hearing from you!

9 781946 139214